Terrorist

John Updike

TERRORIST

HAMISH HAMILTON
an imprint of
PENGUIN BOOKS

HAMISH HAMILTON

Published by the Penguin Group
Penguin Books Ltd, 80 Strand, London WC2R ORL, England
Penguin Group (USA) Inc., 375 Hudson Street, New York, New York 10014, USA
Penguin Group (Canada), 90 Eglinton Avenue East, Suite 700, Toronto, Ontario, Canada M4P 2Y3
(a division of Pearson Penguin Canada Inc.)
Penguin Ireland, 25 St Stephen's Green, Dublin 2, Ireland (a division of Penguin Books Ltd)
Penguin Group (Australia), 250 Camberwell Road, Camberwell,
Victoria 3124, Australia (a division of Pearson Australia Group Pty Ltd)
Penguin Books India Pvt Ltd, 11 Community Centre,
Panchsheel Park, New Delhi – 110 017, India
Penguin Group (NZ), cnr Airborne and Rosedale Roads, Albany,
Auckland 1310, New Zealand (a division of Pearson New Zealand Ltd)
Penguin Books (South Africa) (Pty) Ltd, 24 Sturdee Avenue,
Rosebank, Johannesburg 2196, South Africa

Penguin Books Ltd, Registered Offices: 80 Strand, London WC2R ORL, England

www.penguin.com

First published in the United States of America by Alfred A. Knopf 2006
First published in Great Britain by Hamish Hamilton 2006

6

Copyright © John Updike, 2006

The moral right of the author has been asserted

The author thanks Shady Nasser for his invaluable guidance and expertise
concerning Arabic and the Koran, and Emily and Gregory Harvey for,
once again, supplying Philadelphia details, and Paul Bogaards
for his New Jersey expertise. Charlie Chehab's version of the
Revolutionary War in New Jersey owes much to *Washington's Crossing*,
by David Hackett Fischer. English quotations of the Koran have been
taken from translations by J. M. Rodwell in 1861 and N. J. Dawood in 1956

Printed in Great Britain by Clays Ltd, St Ives plc

A CIP catalogue record for this book is available from the British Library

UK EDITION
ISBN-13: 978-0-241-14351-3
ISBN-10: 0-241-14351-9

EXPORT EDITION
ISBN-13: 978-0-241-14355-1
ISBN-10: 0-241-14355-1

And now, O Lord, please take my life from me, for it is better for me to die than to live.

And the Lord said, "Is it right for you to be angry?" —Jonah 4:3–4

Disbelief is more resistant than faith because it is sustained by the senses.

—GABRIEL GARCÍA MÁRQUEZ,
Of Love and Other Demons

TERRORIST

I

*D*EVILS, Ahmad thinks. *These devils seek to take away my God.* All day long, at Central High School, girls sway and sneer and expose their soft bodies and alluring hair. Their bare bellies, adorned with shining navel studs and low-down purple tattoos, ask, *What else is there to see?* Boys strut and saunter along and look dead-eyed, indicating with their edgy killer gestures and careless scornful laughs that this world is all there is—a noisy varnished hall lined with metal lockers and having at its end a blank wall desecrated by graffiti and roller-painted over so often it feels to be coming closer by millimeters.

The teachers, weak Christians and nonobservant Jews, make a show of teaching virtue and righteous self-restraint, but their shifty eyes and hollow voices betray their lack of belief. They are paid to say these things, by the city of New Prospect and the state of New Jersey. They lack true faith; they are not on the Straight Path; they are unclean. Ahmad and the two thousand other students can see them scuttling after school into their cars on the crackling, trash-speckled parking lot like pale crabs or dark ones restored to their shells, and they are men and women like any others, full of lust and fear and infatuation with things that can be bought. Infidels, they think safety lies in accumulation of the things of this world, and in the corrupting diversions of the television set. They are slaves to images, false ones of happiness and affluence. But even true images are sinful imitations of God, who can alone create. Relief at escaping their students unscathed for another day makes the teachers' chatter of farewell in the halls and on the parking lot too loud, like the rising excitement of drunks. The teachers revel when they are away from the school. Some have the pink lids and bad breaths and puffy bodies of those who habitually drink too much. Some get divorces; some live with others unmarried. Their lives away from the school are disorderly and wanton and self-indulgent. They are paid to instill virtue and democratic values by the state government down in Trenton, and that Satanic government farther down, in Washington, but the values they believe in are Godless: biology and chemistry and physics. On the facts and formulas of these their false voices firmly rest, ringing out into the classroom. They say that all comes out of merciless blind atoms, which cause the cold weight of iron, the transparency of glass, the stillness of clay, the agitation of flesh. Electrons pour through copper threads and computer gates and the air itself when stirred to lightning by the interaction of water droplets. Only what we can measure and deduce from measurement is true. The rest is the passing dream that we call our selves.

Ahmad is eighteen. This is early April; again green sneaks, seed by seed, into the drab city's earthy crevices. He looks down from his new height and thinks that to the insects unseen in the grass he would be, if they had a consciousness like his, God. In the year past he has grown three inches, to six feet—more unseen materialist forces, working their will upon him. He will not grow any taller, he thinks, in this life or the next. *If there is a next*, an inner devil murmurs. What evidence beyond the Prophet's blazing and divinely inspired words proves that there is a next? Where would it be hidden? Who would forever stoke Hell's boilers? What infinite source of energy would maintain opulent Eden, feeding its dark-eyed houris, swelling its heavy-hanging fruits, renewing the streams and splashing fountains in which God, as described in the ninth sura of the Qur'an, takes eternal good pleasure? What of the second law of thermodynamics?

The deaths of insects and worms, their bodies so quickly absorbed by earth and weeds and road tar, devilishly strive to tell Ahmad that his own death will be just as small and final. Walking to school, he has noticed a sign, a spiral traced on the pavement in luminous ichor, angelic slime from the body of some low creature, a worm or snail of which only this trace remains. Where was the creature going, its path spiralling inward to no purpose? If it was seeking to remove itself from the hot sidewalk that was roasting it to death as the burning sun beat down, it failed and moved in fatal circles. But no little worm-body was left at the spiral's center.

So where did that body fly to? Perhaps it was snatched up by God and taken straight to Heaven. Ahmad's teacher, Shaikh Rashid, the imam at the mosque upstairs at 2781½ West Main Street, tells him that according to the sacred tradition of the Hadith such things happen: the Messenger, riding the winged white horse Buraq, was guided through the seven heavens by the angel Gabriel to a certain place, where he prayed with Jesus, Moses, and Abraham before returning to Earth, to become the last of the prophets, the ultimate one. His adventures that day are proved by the hoofprint, sharp and clear, that Buraq left on the Rock beneath the sacred Dome in the center of Al-Quds, called Jerusalem by the infidels and Zionists, whose torments in the furnaces of Jahannan are well described in the seventh and eleventh and fiftieth of the suras of the Book of Books.

Shaikh Rashid recites with great beauty of pronunciation the one hundred fourth sura, concerning Hutama, the Crushing Fire:

> *And who shall teach thee what the Crushing Fire is?*
> *It is God's kindled fire,*
> *Which shall mount above the hearts of the damned;*
> *It shall verily rise over them like a vault,*
> *On outstretched columns.*

When Ahmad seeks to extract from the images in the Qur'an's Arabic—the outstretched columns, *fī 'amadin mumaddada*, and the vault high above the hearts of those huddled in terror and straining to see into the towering mist of white heat, *nāru 'l-lāhi 'l-mūqada*—some hint of the Merciful's relenting at some point in time, and calling a halt to Hutama, the imam casts down his eyes, which are an unexpectedly pale gray, as milky and elusive as a kafir woman's, and says that these visionary descriptions by the Prophet are figurative. They are truly about the burning misery of separation from God and the scorching of our remorse for our sins against His commands. But Ahmad does not like Shaikh Rashid's voice when he says this. It reminds him of the unconvincing voices of his teachers at Central High. He hears Satan's undertone in it, a denying voice within an affirming voice. The Prophet meant physical fire when he preached unforgiving fire; Mohammed could not proclaim the fact of eternal fire too often.

Shaikh Rashid is not much older than Ahmad—perhaps ten years, perhaps twenty. He has few wrinkles in the white skin of his face. He is diffident though precise in his movements. In the years by which he is older, the world has weakened him. When the murmuring of the devils gnawing within him tinges the imam's voice, Ahmad feels in his own self a desire to rise up and crush him, as God roasted that poor worm at the center of the spiral. The student's faith exceeds the master's; it frightens Shaikh Rashid to be riding the winged white steed of Islam, its irresistible onrushing. He seeks to soften the Prophet's words, to make them blend with human reason, but they were not meant to blend: they invade our human softness like a sword. Allah is sublime beyond all particulars. There is no God but He, the Living, the Self-Subsistent; He is the light by which the sun looks black. He does not blend with our reason but makes our reason bow low, its forehead scraping the dust and bearing like Cain the mark of that dust. Mohammed was a mortal man but visited Paradise and consorted with the realities there. Our deeds and thoughts were written in the Prophet's consciousness in letters of gold, like the burning words of electrons that a computer creates of pixels as we tap the keyboard.

The halls of the high school smell of perfume and bodily exhalations, of chewing gum and impure cafeteria food, and of cloth—cotton and wool and the synthetic materials of running shoes, warmed by young flesh. Between classes there is a thunder of movement; the noise is stretched thin over a violence beneath, barely restrained. Sometimes in the lull at the end of the school day, when the triumphant, jeering racket of departure has subsided and only the students doing extracurricular activities remain in the great building, Joryleen Grant comes up to Ahmad at his locker. He does track in the spring; she sings in the girls' glee club. As students go at Central High, they are "good." His religion keeps him from drugs and vice, though it also holds him rather aloof from his classmates and the studies on the curriculum. She is short and round and talks well in class, pleasing the teacher. There is an endearing self-confidence in how compactly her cocoa-brown roundnesses fill her clothes, which today are patched and sequinned jeans, worn pale where she sits, and a ribbed magenta shorty top both lower and higher than it should be. Blue plastic barrettes pull her glistening hair back as straight as it will go; the plump edge of her right ear holds along its crimp a row of little silver rings. She sings in assembly programs, songs of Jesus or sexual longing, both topics abhorrent to Ahmad. Yet he is pleased that she notices him, coming up to him now and then like a tongue testing a sensitive tooth.

"Cheer up, Ahmad," she teases him. "Things can't be so bad." She rolls her half-bare shoulder, lifting it as if to shrug, to show she is being playful.

"They're not bad," he says. "I'm not sad," he tells her. His long body tingles under his clothes—white shirt, narrow-legged black jeans—from the shower after track practice.

"You're looking way serious," she tells him. "You should learn to smile more."

"Why? Why should I, Joryleen?"

"People will like you more."

"I don't care about that. I don't want to be liked."

"You care," she tells him. "Everybody cares."

"*You* care," he tells her, sneering down at her from his recently acquired height. The tops of her breasts push up like great blisters in the scoop neck of the indecent top that at its other hem exposes the fat of her belly and the contour of her deep navel. He pictures her smooth body, darker than caramel but paler than chocolate, roasting in that vault of flames and being scorched into blisters; he experiences a shiver of pity, since she is trying to be nice to him, in accordance with an idea she has of herself. "Little Miss Popular," he says scornfully.

This wounds her, and she turns away, her thick books to take home pushing up at her breasts, making the crease between them deep. "Fuck you, Ahmad," she says, still with some gentleness, tentatively, her lower lip of its soft weight hanging loose a little. The saliva at the base of her gums sparks with reflected light from the overhead fluorescent tubes that keep the hall safely bright. To rescue the exchange, though she has turned to end it, Joryleen adds, "You didn't care, you wouldn't pretty yourself up with a clean white shirt every day, like some preacher. How's your mother stand doing all that ironing?"

He doesn't deign to explain that this considered outfit sends out a non-combatant message, avoiding both blue, the color of the Rebels, the African-American gang in Central High, and red, the color always worn, if only in a belt or headband, by the Diabolos, the Hispanic gang. Nor does he tell her that his mother rarely irons, for she is a nurse's aide at the Saint Francis Community Hospital and a spare-time painter who sees her son often for less than one hour in twenty-four. His shirts come back stiffened by cardboard from the cleaners, whose bills he pays out of the money he earns clerking at the Tenth Street Shop-a-Sec two evenings a week, and on weekends and Christian holidays, when most boys his age are roaming the streets looking for mischief. But there is, he knows, vanity in his costume, a preening that offends the purity of the All-Encompassing.

He senses that Joryleen is not just trying to be nice: he arouses curiosity in her. She wants to get close to smell him better, even though she already has a boyfriend, a notorious "bad" one. Women are animals easily led, Ahmad has been warned by Shaikh Rashid, and he can see for himself that the high school and the world beyond it are full of nuzzling—blind animals in a herd bumping against one another, looking for a scent that will comfort them. But the Qur'an says there is no comfort but for those who believe in the unseen Paradise and who observe the injunction to pray five times a day, which the Prophet brought back to Earth after the night journey on Buraq's broad, blazingly white back.

Joryleen persists in still standing there, too near him. Her perfume cloys in his nostrils; the crease between her breasts bothers him. She shifts her heavy books in her arms. Ahmad reads on the edge of the thickest text the ballpointed words JORYLEEN GRANT. Her lips, painted with a luminous metallic pink to make them look thinner, startle him by faltering in embarrassment. "What I was wondering to say to you," she gets out, so haltingly he leans down toward her to hear better, "was whether you might want to come to the church this Sunday to hear me sing a solo in the choir."

He is shocked, repelled. "I am not of your faith," he reminds her solemnly.

Her response is airy, careless. "Oh, I don't take that all that seriously," she says. "I just love to sing."

"Now you *have* made me sad, Joryleen," Ahmad says. "If

you don't take your religion seriously, you shouldn't go." He slams his locker shut with an anger mostly at himself, for having scolded and rejected her when, by offering an invitation, she had made herself vulnerable. His face hot with confusion, he turns back from his slammed locker to examine the damage he has done, and she is gone, the rubbed and sequinned seat of her jeans swishing carefree down the hall. *The world is difficult*, he thinks, *because devils are busy in it, confusing things and making the straight crooked.*

When constructed in the last century, the twentieth by Christian reckoning and the fourteenth after the Prophet's Hegira from Mecca to Medina, the high school on its little rise hung above the city like a castle, a palace of learning for the children of millworkers and of their managers alike, with pillars and ornate cornices and a motto carved in granite, KNOWLEDGE IS FREEDOM. Now the building, rich in scars and crumbling asbestos, its leaded paint hard and shiny and its tall windows caged, sits on the edge of a wide lake of rubble that was once part of a downtown veined with trolley-car tracks. The tracks gleam in old photographs, amid men in straw hats and neckties and boxy automobiles all the color of a hearse. So many movie marquees thrust over the sidewalks then, advertising competing Hollywood hits, that a man could dart from one marquee to another in a rainstorm and hardly get wet. There was even a subterranean public lavatory, labelled in old-fashioned porcelain letters LADIES and GENTLEMEN, entered by two different sets of stairs from the sidewalk of East Main Street at Tilden Avenue. One elderly attendant in each kept the underground toilets and basins clean; the facilities were closed in the 1960s, having become foul-smelling lairs for drug deals, homosexual contacts, acts of prostitution, and occasional muggings.

The city was named New Prospect two centuries ago, for the grand view from the heights above the falls but also for its enthusiastically envisioned future. The river pouring through it, with its picturesque falls and churning rapids, would attract industry, it was thought when the nation was young, and so, eventually, after many false starts and bankruptcies, it did—knitting mills, silk-dyeing plants, leatherworks, factories that produced locomotives and horseless carriages and cables to sustain the great bridges that were spanning the rivers and harbors of the Mid-Atlantic region. As the nineteenth century became the twentieth, there were prolonged and bloody strikes; the economy never recovered the optimism that helped emigrants from Eastern Europe, the Mediterranean, and the Middle East endure fourteen-hour days of strenuous, poisonous, deafening, monotonous labor. The factories drifted south and west, where labor was cheaper and easier to cow, and where iron ore and coke were closer to transport.

Those who occupy the inner city now are brown, by and large, in its many shades. A remnant of fair-skinned but rarely Anglo-Saxon merchants finds some small profit in selling pizzas and chili and brightly packaged junk food and cigarettes and state-lottery tickets downtown, but they are giving way to recently immigrant Indians and Koreans who feel less compelled, as darkness falls, to flee to the still-mixed outskirts of the city and its suburbs. White faces downtown look furtive and dingy. At night, after a few choice ethnic restaurants have discharged their suburban clientele, a police car will stop and question white pedestrians, on the assumption that they are looking for a drug deal or else need to be advised on the dangers of this environment. Ahmad himself is the product of a red-haired American mother, Irish by ancestry, and an Egyptian exchange student whose ancestors had been baked since the time of the Pharaohs in the muddy rice and flax fields of the overflowing Nile. The complexion of the offspring of this mixed marriage could be described as dun, a low-luster shade lighter than beige; that of his surrogate father, Shaikh Rashid, is a waxy white shared with generations of heavily swathed Yemeni warriors.

Where six-story department stores and the closely stacked offices of Jewish and Protestant exploiters once formed a continuous façade of glass, brick, and granite, there are bull-dozed gaps and former display windows covered by plywood crawling with spray-painted graffiti. To Ahmad's eyes, the bulbous letters of the graffiti, their bloated boasts of gang affiliation, assert an importance to which the perpetrators have pathetically little other claim. Sinking into the morass of Godlessness, lost young men proclaim, by means of prop-erty defacement, an identity. Some few new boxes of alu-minum and blue glass have been erected amid the ruins, sops from the lords of Western capitalism—branches of banks headquartered in California or North Carolina, and outposts of the Zionist-dominated federal government, attempting with welfare enrollment and army recruitment to prevent the impoverished from rioting and looting.

And yet the downtown of an afternoon gives a festive, busy impression: East Main Street in the blocks around Tilden is a carnival of idleness, thronged by an onrolling mass of dark citizens in flashy clothes, a Mardi Gras parade of costumes lovingly assembled by those whose lawful domain extends scarcely an inch beyond their skins, and whose paltry assets are all on view. Their joy amounts to defiance. Their cackling, whooping voices are loud with the village fellowship, the luxuriant mutual attention, of those with little to do and nowhere to go.

After the Civil War, a conspicuous gaudiness entered New Prospect with the erection of an elaborate City Hall, a sprawling, turreted aggregation, Moorish in feeling, of rounded arches and rococo ironwork capped by a great tower in mansard style. Its sloped sides are covered in multi-colored fish-scale shingles and contain four white clock faces the size, if they were to be brought down to Earth, of wading pools. The broad copper gutters and downspouts, monuments to the skilled metalworkers of their time, have turned mint-green with age. This civic pile, whose principal bureaucratic operations were long ago relegated to less lofty, more modern, less spectacular, but air-conditioned and easier-to-heat structures behind it, has been recently awarded, after much lobbying, the status of a national architectural treasure. It stands within sight of Central High School, a block to the west, the school's once-generous grounds much nibbled by widened streets and real-estate encroachments permitted by bribed officials.

On the eastern edge of the lake of rubble, where becalmed parking lots alternate with choppy waves of knocked-down brick, a thick-walled ironstone church supports a heavy steeple and advertises, on a cracked signboard, its award-winning gospel choir. The windows of this church, blasphemously assigning God a face, and gesturing hands, sandalled feet, and tinted robes—in short, a human body with all that is unclean and encumbering about it—are blackened by decades of industrial soot and made further indecipherable by their protective grids of wire. Religion's images now attract hatred, as in the wars of the Reformation. The church's decorous glory days of pious white burghers in the hierarchically assigned pews also belong to the past. Now African-American congregants bring their dishevelled, shouting religion, their award-winning choir dissolving their brains in a rhythmical rapture as illusory as (Shaikh Rashid sardonically puts forward the analogy) the shuffling, mumbling trance of Brazilian *candomblé*. It is here that Joryleen sings.

The day after she invited Ahmad to come hear her sing in the choir, her boyfriend, Tylenol Jones, comes up to Ahmad in the hall. His mother, having delivered a ten-pound infant, saw the name in a television commercial for painkiller and liked the sound of it. "Hey, Arab," he says. "Hear you been dissing Joryleen."

Ahmad tries to talk the other's language. "No way, dissing. We talked a little. It was *she* come up to me."

Reaching carefully, Tylenol takes the more slender boy's shoulder in his hand and digs his thumb into that sensitive place below the shoulder ball. "She say you disrespect her religion." His thumb works deeper, into nerves that have been asleep all of Ahmad's life. Tylenol has a square face the color of walnut furniture-stain while it's still sitting up wet on the wood. He is a tackle on the Central High football team and a gymnast on the rings in the winter, so his hands are iron-strong. His thumb is gouging wrinkles into Ahmad's crisp white shirt; the taller boy makes an impatient motion to shrug off the hostile grip.

"Her religion is the wrong one," Ahmad informs Tylenol, "and anyway she said she had no use for it but to sing in that foolish choir." The iron thumb keeps digging, but with a surge of adrenaline Ahmad swats it away, the edge of his hand chopping at the thick branch of muscle.

Tylenol's face darkens and comes closer with a jerk. "Don't you talk to me of foolish—you so foolish nobody give you shit, Arab."

" 'Cept Joryleen," comes the quick response, riding the same adrenaline. Ahmad feels watery inside and suspects his face is shamefully stiff with fear, but there is a holy bliss in confronting even a superior enemy, allowing rage to increase your mass. He dares go on, "And I wouldn't exactly call it shit, what she gave me. It was simple friendliness your type wouldn't understand."

"My type, what is that? My type has no use for your type, that's the truth, you dumb fuck. You weird queer. You faggot."

His face is so close Ahmad smells cheese from the cafeteria macaroni. He gives Tylenol a push on his chest to make some distance. Other Central High students are crowding around, there in the hall, the cheerleader types and computer nerds, the Rastas and Goths, the wallflowers and do-nothings, waiting for something entertaining to happen. Tylenol likes the audience; he announces, "Black Muslims I don't diss, but you not black, you not anything but a poor shithead. You no raghead, you a *shit*head."

Ahmad calculates that a push back from Tylenol that he would accept would be a fair way to ease out of this contention, with the next change-of-class bell about to sound. But Tylenol wants no part of a truce; he gives Ahmad a sneak punch in the stomach that pops all of the air out of him. Ahmad's astonished, gulping expression makes the watching schoolmates laugh, including the chalk-faced Goths, minority whites at Central who pride themselves on showing no emotion, like their nihilistic punk-rock heroes. Plus, there are silvery giggles from several bubbly buxom brown girls, Miss Populars, who Ahmad thinks should be kinder. Some day they will be mothers. Some day soon, the little whores.

He is losing face and has no choice but to wade into those iron hands of Tylenol's and try to make a dent in that shield-like chest and the obtuse walnut-stained mask above it. The bout becomes mostly pushing and squeezing and grunting, since a fistfight lurching into the lockers would make a racket to bring the teachers and security guards. In this minute before the bell rings and everybody has to scatter to classes, Ahmad does not so much blame the other boy—he is just a robot of meat, a body too full of its juices and reflexes to have a brain—as he blames Joryleen. Why did she have to tell her boyfriend the whole private conversation? Why do girls have to *tell* all the time? To make themselves important, like those fat-lettered graffiti for those who spray them on helpless walls. It was she who brought up religion, inviting him so saucily to her church to sit with kinky-haired kafirs, the singe of Hellfire on them like the brown skin on barbecued drumsticks. It gets his devils to murmuring inside him, the way Allah allows so many grotesquely mistaken and corrupt religions to lure millions down to Hell forever when in a single flash of light the All-Powerful could show them the way, the Straight Path. It was as if (Ahmad's devils murmur, as he and Tylenol push and flail at one another while trying not to make noise) the Merciful, the Beneficent, cannot be bothered.

The bell rings, in its little tamper-proof box high on the custard-colored wall. Nearby in the hall a door with its big pane of frosted glass snaps open; Mr. Levy, a guidance counselor, emerges. His coat and pants don't match, like a rum-

pled suit put together blindly. The man stares absent-
mindedly, then warily, at the suspiciously clustered students.
The gathering freezes into instant silence, and Ahmad and
Tylenol back off, putting their enmity on hold. Mr. Levy, a
Jew who has been in this school system practically forever,
looks old and tired, baggy-eyed, his hair thinned raggedly
on the top of his head and a few strands standing up mussed.
His sudden appearance startles Ahmad like a prick of con-
science: he has an appointment with Mr. Levy this week,
to discuss his future after high-school graduation. Ahmad
knows he must have a future, but it seems insubstantial to
him, and repels his interest. *The only guidance*, says the third
sura, *is the guidance of Allah.*

Tylenol and his gang would be laying for him now. After
being dissed to pretty much a standstill, the bully with his
iron thumbs wouldn't be satisfied with anything less than
a black eye or a broken tooth or finger—something that
would show. Ahmad knows it is a sin to be vain of his appearance: self-love is a form of competition with God, and competition is what He cannot abide. But how can the boy not
cherish his ripened manhood, his lengthened limbs, the
upright, dense, and wavy crown of his hair, his flawless dun
skin, paler than his father's but not the freckled, blotchy pink
of his red-haired mother and of those peroxided blondes
who in white-bread America are considered the acme of
beauty? Though he shuns, as unholy and impure, the glances
of lingering interest he receives from the dusky girls around
him in the school, Ahmad does not wish his body marred.
He wishes to keep it as its Maker formed it. Tylenol's enmity
becomes one more reason to leave this hellish castle, where
the boys bully and hurt for sheer pleasure and the infidel
girls wear skintight hiphuggers almost low enough—less

than a finger's breadth, he has estimated—to release into view the topmost fringe of their pubic curls. The very bad girls, the ones already thoroughly fallen, have tattoos where only their boyfriends get to see them, and where the tattoo artist had to poke his needle most gingerly. There is no end of devilish contortions once human beings feel free to compete with God and to create themselves.

He has only two months of his schooling left. Spring is in the air beyond the brick walls, the caged tall windows. The customers at the Shop-a-Sec make their pathetic, poisonous purchases with a new humor, a new palaver. His feet fly across the school's old cinder track as if each stride is individually cushioned. When he paused on the sidewalk to puzzle over the spiral trail of the roasted and vanished worm, all around him new green shoots, garlic and dandelions and clover, brightened the winter-weary patches of grass, and birds explored in rapid, excited arcs the invisible medium that sustained them.

Jack Levy wakes, now that he is sixty-three, between three and four in the morning, with the taste of dread in his mouth, dry from his breath being dragged through it while he dreamed. His dreams are sinister, soaked through with the misery of the world. He reads the dying, ad-starved local daily, the *New Prospect Perspective*, and the *New York Times* or *Post* when these are left lying around in the faculty room, and, as if this is not enough of Bush and Iraq and domestic murders in Queens and East Orange—murders even of children aged two or four or six, so young that struggling and crying out against their murderers, their parents, would seem to them blasphemy, as Isaac's resisting Abraham would have been blasphemy—Levy in the evening, between the hours of six and seven, while his corpulent wife, moving pieces of their dinner from the refrigerator to the microwave, keeps crossing in front of the little screen of the kitchen television set, turns on the metro round-up and the network talking heads; he watches until the commercials, all of which he has repeatedly seen before, so exasperate him that he clicks the imbecilic device off. On top of the news, Jack has personal misery, misery that he "owns," as people say now—the heaviness of the day to come, the day that will dawn through all this dark. As he lies there awake, fear and loathing squirm inside him like the components of a bad restaurant meal—twice as much food as you want, the way they serve it now. Dread slams shut the door back into sleep, an awareness, deepening each day, that all that is left on Earth for his body to do is to ready itself for death. He has done his courting and mating; he has fathered a child; he has worked to feed that child, little sensitive Mark with his shy cloudy eyes and slippery lower lip, and to furnish him with all the tawdry junk the culture of the time insisted he possess, to blend in with his peers. Now Jack Levy's sole remaining task is to die and thus contribute a little space, a little breathing room, to this overburdened planet. The task hangs in the air just above his insomniac face like a cobweb with a motionless spider in the center.

His wife, Beth, a whale of a woman giving off too much heat through her blubber, breathes audibly beside him, her tireless little rasp of a snore extending into unconsciousness her daily monologue, her output of prattle. When, in a repressed fury, he nudges her with a knee or elbow or gently cups in his hand a buttock bared by her risen nightgown, she docilely falls silent, and then he fears that he has woken her,

One

breaking the unspoken vow taken between any two people who have agreed, however long ago, to sleep together. He wants only to jog her up to the level of sleep where her breath will stop vibrating in her nose. It was like tuning the violin he used to play, in his boyhood. Another Heifetz, another Isaac Stern: is that what his parents had hoped for? He disappointed them—a segment of misery where his own and the world's coincided. His parents grieved. He had defiantly told them he was quitting lessons. The life in books and on the streets meant more to him. He was eleven, maybe twelve to take such a stand, and never picked up the violin again, though sometimes, hearing on the car radio a snatch of Beethoven or a Mozart concerto or Dvořák's Gypsy music that he had once practiced in a student arrangement, Jack is surprised to feel the fingering trying to live again in his left hand, twitching on the steering wheel like a dying fish.

Why beat himself up? He has done all right, more than all right: prize student at Central High, class of '59, before it felt so much like a prison and you could still study and take pride in the praise of the teachers; diligent commuter to CCNY before sharing a SoHo apartment with two guys and a girl who kept shifting her affections around; after graduation, two years of draft-era Army, before Vietnam heated up, basic training at Fort Dix, file clerk at Fort Meade, Maryland, south enough of the Mason-Dixon Line to be full of anti-Semitic Southerners, then the second year at Fort Bliss in El Paso, in so-called human resources, matching men to assignments, the start of his giving guidance to teen-agers; afterwards to Rutgers for a master's on the cut-back GI Bill; since then, teaching high-school history and social science thirty years before becoming full-time guidance counselor these last six. The bare facts of his career make him feel

: 21 :

trapped, in a curriculum vitae as tight as a coffin. The room's black air has become hard to breathe, and he stealthily turns from lying on his side to lying on his back, like a stiff laid out at a Catholic viewing.

How noisy bedsheets can be!—crashing waves, next to your ear. He doesn't want to wake Beth. Close to suffocated, he can't cope with her too. For a moment, like the first sip of a drink before the ice cubes turn the whisky watery, the new position eases the problem. On his back, he has the calm of a dead man but with no casket lid inches from his nose. The world is quiet—the commuter traffic not yet started up, the night prowlers with their broken mufflers having at last crawled into bed. He hears a lone truck shifting gears at the blinking stoplight one street over and, two rooms away, a restless fit of soft-pawed galloping from Carmela, the Levys' desexed, declawed cat. Declawed, she can't be let outdoors, for fear the cats with claws will kill her. In her indoors captivity, sleeping away much of the day under the sofa, she hallucinates at night, imagining in the stilled house the feral adventures, the battles and escapes, that she can never have, for her own good. So desolate is the sensory surround of these pre-dawn hours, and so alone does Jack Levy appear to himself, that the furtive uproar of a deluded, neutered cat soothes him almost enough for his mind, excused from sentry duty, to slip back into sleep.

But, sustained in wakefulness by a nagging bladder, he instead lies exposed, as to a sickening blast of radioactivity, to an awareness of his life as a needless blot—a botch, a prolonged blunder—imposed upon the otherwise immaculate surface of this ungodly hour. In the world's dark forest he had missed the right path. But was there any right path? Or was being alive in itself the mistake? In the stripped-down history that he used to purvey to students who had trouble believing that the world didn't begin with their births and the proliferation of computer games, even the greatest men came to nothing, to a grave, their visions unfulfilled— Charlemagne, Charles V, Napoleon, the unspeakable but considerably successful and still, at least in the Arab world, admired Adolf Hitler. History is a machine perpetually grinding mankind to dust. Jack Levy's guidance counseling replays in his head as a cacophony of miscommunication. He sees himself as a pathetic elderly figure on a shore, shouting out to a flotilla of the young as they slide into the fatal morass of the world—its dwindling resources, its disappearing freedoms, its merciless advertisements geared to a preposterous popular culture of eternal music and beer and impossibly thin and fit young females.

Or had most young females, even Beth, once been as thin as those in the beer and Coke commercials? No doubt she had, but he could hardly remember—like trying to see the television screen as she waddles back and forth assembling dinner. They had met in his year and a half at Rutgers. She had been a Pennsylvania girl, from the East Mount Airy section of northwest Philadelphia, studying library science. He had been drawn to her lightness, her bubbly laugh, her sly quickness at making everything, even their courtship, a joke. *What sort of baby boys do you think we would make? Will they be born half circumcised?* She was German-American, Elizabeth Fogel, with a more uptight, less lovable older sister, Hermione. He was a Jew. But not a proud Jew, wrapped in the ancient covenant. His grandfather had shed all religion in the New World, putting his faith in a revolutionized society, a world where the powerful could no longer rule through superstition, where food on the table, decent housing and shelter, replaced the untrustworthy promises of an unseen God.

Not that the Jewish God had ever been big on promises— a shattered glass at your wedding, a quick burial in a shroud when you die, no saints, no afterlife, just a lifetime of drudging loyalty to the tyrant who asked Abraham to make a burnt offering of his only son. Poor Isaac, the trusting shmuck, having been nearly killed by his own father was as an old blind man tricked out of his blessing by his son Jacob and his own wife, Rebekah, brought to him veiled from Paddan-aram. More lately, over in the old country, if you observed all the rules—and for the Orthodox it was a long list of rules— you got a yellow star and a one-way ticket to the gas ovens. No, thanks: Jack Levy took a stiff-necked pleasure in being one of Judaism's stiff-necked naysayers. He had encouraged the world to make "Jack" of "Jacob" and had argued against his son's circumcision, though a slick Wasp doctor at the hospital talked Beth into it, for "purely hygienic" reasons, claiming that studies showed it would lower the risk of venereal disease for Mark and of cervical cancer for Mark's partners. A week-old infant, his prick just a little fat button on the seamed pincushion of his balls, and they were improving his sex life and coming to the rescue of female infants as yet unborn.

Beth was a Lutheran, a hearty Christer denomination keen on faith versus works and beer versus wine, and he figured she would mitigate his dogged Jewish virtue, the oldest lost cause still active in the Western world. Even his grandfather's socialist faith had gone sour and musty with the way Communism had worked out in practice. Jack had seen his and Beth's marrying, on the second floor of New Prospect's ridiculous City Hall, with only her sister and his parents in attendance, as a brave mismatch, a little loving mud in history's eye, like a lot else that was happening in 1968. But after thirty-six years together in northern New Jersey, the two of them with their different faiths and ethnicities have been ground down to a lackluster sameness. They have become a couple that shops together at ShopRite and Best Buy on weekends, and whose idea of a jolly time is two tables of bridge with three other couples from the high school or the Clifton Public Library, where Beth works four days a week. Some Friday or Saturday nights they try to cheer themselves up with a meal out, alternating the Chinese and Italian restaurants where they are frequent diners and the maître d' with a resigned smile leads them to a corner table where Beth can squeeze in; never a booth. Or else they drive to some seedy cineplex that has sticky floors and charges seven dollars for a medium popcorn, if they can find a movie that isn't too violent or sexy or too blatantly aimed at the mid-teen male demographic. Their courtship and young marriage coincided with the collapse of the studio system and the release of dazzling subversive visions—*Midnight Cowboy, Easy Rider, Bob and Carol and Ted and Alice, The Wild Bunch, A Clockwork Orange, Dirty Harry, Carnal Knowledge, Last Tango in Paris*, the first *Godfather, The Last Picture Show, American Graffiti*—not to mention late Bergman and French and Italian films still full of angst and edge and national personality. These had been good movies, which kept a hip couple on its mental toes. There had still been a sense in the air, left over from '68, that the world could be reimagined by young people. In sentimental memory of those shared revelations when they were both new to married sharing, Jack's hand even now in the movies sneaks across and takes hers from her lap and holds it, delicately puffy and hot, in his own while their faces are being bathed in the explosions of some latter-day, dumbed-down thriller, the coldly calibrated shocks of its adolescent script mocking their old age.

Insomniac, despairing, Jack thinks of seeking Beth's hand under the covers but in trying to find it amid the mounds of her slumbering flesh he might disturb her and awaken her needy, tireless, still-girlish voice. With a stealth almost criminal, he slides his feet upward on the bottom sheet and eases the blankets aside and escapes the marital bed. Stepping beyond the bedside rug, he feels on his bare feet an April chill. The thermostat is still on night mode. He stands at a window curtained in sun-yellowed lace and contemplates his neighborhood by the gray light of its mercury-vapor street lamps. The orange of the Gulf sign at the all-night gas station two blocks away is the only emphatic touch of color in the pre-dawn vista. Here and there in the neighborhood a wan low-voltage night light warms the window of a child's room or a stair landing. In the semi-darkness, under a polished dome of darkness weakened by the climbing rot of city glow, the foreshortened angles of roof lines, shingles, and sidings recede to infinity.

Housing, Jack Levy thinks. Houses have compressed into housing, squeezed closer together by rising land costs and subdivision. Where within his memory back and side yards had once included flowering trees and vegetable gardens, clotheslines and swing sets, now a few scruffy bushes fight for carbon dioxide and damp soil between concrete walks and asphalt parking spaces stolen from what had been generous margins of grass. The needs of the automobile have proved decisive. The locust trees planted along the curbs, the wild ailanthus taken rapid root along the fences and house walls, the few horse-chestnut trees surviving from the era of ice wagons and coal trucks—all these trees, their buds and small new leaves showing as a silvery fur of fresh growth in the lamplight, stand in danger of being uprooted by the next push of street-widening. Already, the simple outlines of 'thirties semi-detached and 'fifties colonial-style ranch houses are loaded with added dormers, superimposed sundecks, rickety outside staircases to give legal access to studio apartments carved from what were once considered spare rooms. Affordable housing units are dwindling in size like pieces of paper repeatedly folded. Discarded divorcées and obsolete craftsmen in outsourced industries and hardworking people of color, grabbing for the next rung in the climb out of the inner slums, move into the neighborhood and can't afford to leave. Smart young couples fix up rundown semis and make their mark by painting their porches and gable trim and window frames outlandish colors— Easter lilac, acid green—and the splash on the block feels like an insult to the older residents, a flare of contempt, an unsightly toying. Corner grocery stores have one by one dropped away, leaving the field to franchises whose standardized logos and decors are cheerfully garish, as are the gargantuan full-color images of their fattening fast food. As Jack Levy sees it, America is paved solid with fat and tar, a coast-to-coast tarbaby where we're all stuck. Even our vaunted freedom is nothing much to be proud of, with the Commies out of the running; it just makes it easier for terrorists to move about, renting airplanes and vans and setting up Web sites. Religious fanatics and computer geeks: the combination seems strange to his old-fashioned sense of the reason-versus-faith divide. Those creeps who flew the planes into the World Trade Center had good technical educations. The ringleader had a German degree in city planning; he should have redesigned New Prospect.

A more positive and energetic person than himself, Jack

believes, would be using these hours before his wife awakes and the *Perspective* hits the porch and the star-pricked sky above the rooftops quickens to a dirty gray. He could go downstairs and look for one of the books he has read the first thirty pages of, or make some coffee, or watch the early-morning TV news teams kid and jabber the frogs out of their throats. But he prefers to stand here and soak his empty head, too tired to dream, in the sublunar sights of the neighborhood.

A striped cat—or is it a small raccoon?—skitters across the empty street, disappearing under a parked car. Jack can't tell the make. Cars all look alike now, not like the big fins and grinning chrome grilles when he was a kid, even mock portholes on the Buick Riviera and the bullet nose on the Studebaker, the great long Caddies of the 'fifties—now, *that* was aerodynamic. In the name of aerodynamics and fuel economy, all the cars now are slightly fat and squat and neutral in color to hide road dirt, Mercedes down to Honda. It makes a big parking lot a nightmare, you could never find your own if it weren't for the little keyfob that flashes the lights from a distance or as a last resort blasts the horn.

A crow with something pale and long in its beak lazily flaps up from having poked a hole in a green garbage bag put out last night for collection today. A man in a suit hurries off a porch down the block and gets into a car, a chunky, gas-guzzling SUV, and roars off, never mind waking the neighbors. An early flight out of Newark, Jack guesses. He stands there staring through the chilly windowpanes thinking, *Life.* This is life, living in housing, gulping down grease, shaving in the morning, taking a shower so you won't disgust the other guys at the conference table with your pheromones. It took Jack Levy a lifetime to realize that people stink. When he was younger, he never smelled in his own nostrils, he never noticed that stale aroma he gives off now, just in moving quietly through the day, not even sweating.

Well, he is still alive, seeing what he sees. He supposes this is a good thing, but it is an effort. Who was that Greek, in that book by Camus they all were crazy about back at CCNY? Or maybe it was at Rutgers, among the master's candidates. Sisyphus. The rock uphill. Down it must roll. He stands there no longer seeing but pressing with his consciousness back against the certainty that all this will some day cease for him. The screen in his head will go totally blank, and yet it will all go on without him, dawn breaking and cars starting up and wild creatures continuing to feed in a terrain poisoned by Man. Carmela has silently padded up the stairs and rubs against his bare ankles, purring loudly, thinking of being fed early. This too is life, life touching life.

Jack's eyes feel sandy and heavy. He thinks he should never have gotten out of bed; at his wife's great warm side he might have stolen another hour of sleep. Now he must carry his fatigue through a long and tightly scheduled day, people at him every minute. He hears the bed creak as Beth stirs and relieves the mattress of her weight. The door to the bathroom opens and shuts, its latch clicking and then letting go in that infuriating way it has. In his younger days he would have had a go at fixing it, but with Mark settled in New Mexico and coming home once a year if that, there's no great need for privacy. Beth's ablutions cause water to murmur and tremble in pipes throughout the house.

A man's voice, very rapid and overlaid on music, tumbles from the bedside table; his wife's first act upon awaking is to turn the damn thing on and then walk away. She keeps reaching out electronically to an environment wherein they are physically more and more isolated, an aging couple with their only child flown the coop, their daily occupations surrounding them both with heedless youth. Beth at the library had been compelled to learn computer basics, how to search for information and print it out and pass it on to kids too dumb or lazy to paw around in books, where there still *were* books on the subject. Jack has tried to ignore the whole revolution, stubbornly keeping a few scribbled notes on his counseling sessions, the way he has done it for years, and neglecting to "keyboard" his conclusions into Central High's computerized data bank on its two thousand students. For this failure, or refusal, he is chronically rebuked by his fellow counselors, especially by, in a counseling staff that has tripled in thirty years, Connie Kim, a petite Korean-American specializing in troubled, truant girls of color, and Wesley Ray James, an equally prim and efficient black man whose athletic skills of not long ago—he is still whippet-thin—give him a ready mode of relation to boys. Jack always promises to spend an hour or two and do the updating, and yet weeks go by without his finding the time. There is something about confidentiality that makes him resist feeding the gist of private sessions into an electronic network that blankets the whole school, accessible to all.

Beth is more in touch with things, more willing to bend and change. She had gone along with their City Hall marriage even though, blushing, she had admitted to him that it would break her parents' hearts not to have the wedding in their church. She had not said what it would do to her own heart, and he had replied, "Let's keep it simple. No hocus-pocus." Religion meant nothing to him, and as they merged into a married entity it meant less and less to her. Now he wonders if he had deprived her of something, however grotesque, and if her constant chatter and her overeating weren't compensatory. Being married to a stiff-necked Jew couldn't be easy.

Emerging from the bathroom with her body wrapped in square yards of bathrobe, she sees him standing silent and motionless at the window of the upstairs hall and cries out, frightened, "Jack! What's wrong?"

A certain uxorious sadism in him protects his gloom, only half hiding it from her. He wants Beth to feel his state of mind is her fault, though his reason tells him it is not. "Nothing new," he says. "I woke up too early again. And couldn't go back to sleep."

"That's a sign of depression, they were saying on television the other day. Oprah had a woman on who's written a book. Maybe you should see a—I don't know, the word 'psychiatrist' frightens everybody who isn't rich, the woman was saying—you should see some kind of specialist if you're so miserable."

"A *Weltschmerz* specialist." Jack turns and smiles at her. Though she too is over sixty—sixty-one to his sixty-three— her face is wrinkle-free; what in a lean woman would be deep creases are on her round face lightly etched, smoothed to a girlish delicacy by the fat keeping her skin taut. "No thanks, honey," he says. "I dish out wisdom all day, I have no tolerance for absorbing it myself. Too many antibodies."

He has found over the years that, fended off by him on one topic, she will, rather than lose his attention entirely, quickly resort to another. "Speaking of antibodies, Herm was saying on the phone yesterday—this is in strict confidence, Jack, even I shouldn't know, promise you won't tell anybody—"

"I promise."

"—she tells me these things because she has to vent and
I'm out of the loop that's down there—she said that her boss
is about to elevate the terror-threat level for this area from
yellow to orange. I thought it might be on the radio, but it
wasn't. What do you think it means?"

Hermione's boss is the Secretary of Homeland Security,
a born-again right-wing stooge with some Kraut name like
Haffenreffer, down in Washington. "It means they want us
to feel they're not just sitting on our tax dollars. They want
us to feel they have a handle on this thing. But they don't."

"Is that what you're worrying about, when you worry?"

"No, dear. It's the last thing on my mind, to be honest.
Bring 'em on. I was thinking, looking out the window, this
whole neighborhood could do with a good bomb."

"Oh, Jack, you shouldn't even joke about it, those poor
young men up there on the top stories, calling their wives on
cell phones to tell them they loved them."

"I know, I know. I shouldn't even joke."

"Markie keeps saying we should move out to be closer to
him in Albuquerque."

"He says it, honey, but he doesn't mean it. Us moving
closer is the last thing he wants." Fearing that his enunciat-
ing this truth might have hurt the boy's mother, he jokes, "I
don't know why that is. We never beat him or locked him in
a closet."

"They would never bomb the desert," Beth goes on, arguing as if they are a few debating points away from going to
Albuquerque.

"That's right: *they*, as you call them, *love* the desert."

She takes enough offense at his sarcasm to get off his case,
he observes with mingled relief and regret. She manages an
old-fashioned haughty toss of her head and says, "It must be

wonderful, to be so unconcerned about what worries everybody else," and turns back to the bedroom to make the bed
and, on the same scale of pillowy exertion, to get herself
dressed for her day at the library.

What have I done, he asks himself, *to deserve such fidelity,
such wifely trust?* He is disappointed, slightly, that she hadn't
disputed his rude claim that their son, a thriving ophthal-
mologist with three dear sun-kissed, dutifully bespectacled
children and a bottle-blonde, pure Jewish, superficially
friendly but basically standoffish wife from Short Hills,
doesn't want his parents nearby. He and Beth have their
myths between them, and one is that Mark loves them as
much as they—helplessly, their nest holding only one egg—
love him. In fact, Jack Levy wouldn't mind calling it quits
around here; after a lifetime of an old-time industrial burg
dying on its feet and turning into a Third World jungle, a
shift to the Sun Belt might do him good. Beth, too. Last
winter had been a brute in the Middle Atlantic region, and
there are still, in the constant shadow between some of the
neighborhood's close-packed houses, little humps of snow
black with dirt.

At Central High, his guidance counselor's room is one of
the smallest—a former long supply closet whose gray metal
storage shelves remain, supporting a scattering of college
catalogues, telephone directories, handbooks of psychology,
and stacked back issues of a no-frills, *Nation*-sized weekly
titled *Metro Job Market*, tracking the region's employment
needs and its institutions of technical education. When the
palatial building was erected eighty years ago, no separate
space set aside for guidance was thought necessary: guidance

was everywhere, loving parents innermost and a moralistic popular culture outermost, with lots of advice between. A child was fed more guidance than he could easily digest. Now, routinely, Jack Levy interviews children who seem to have no flesh-and-blood parents—whose instructions from the world are entirely imparted by electronic ghosts signalling across a crowded room, or rapping through black foam earplugs, or encoded in the intricate programming of action figures twitching their spasmodic way through the explosion-producing algorithms of a video game. Students present themselves to their counselor like a succession of CDs whose shimmering surface gives no clue to their contents without the equipment to play them.

This senior, the fifth thirty-minute interview of the weary long morning, is a tall, lean, dun-colored boy in black jeans and a strikingly clean white shirt. The whiteness of the shirt assaults Jack Levy's eyes, his head a bit tender from his early awakening. The folder holding the boy's student records is labeled on the outside **Mulloy (Ashmawy), Ahmad.**

"Your name is interesting," Levy tells the young man. There is something Levy likes about the kid—an unblinking gravity, a wary courtesy in the set of his soft, rather full lips and the careful cut and combing of his hair, a wiry crest that seeks to rise straight up from his brow. "Who's Ashmawy?" the counselor asks.

"Sir, shall I explain?"

"Please do."

The boy speaks with a pained stateliness; he is imitating, Levy feels, some adult he knows, a smooth and formal talker. "I am the product of a white American mother and an Egyptian exchange student; they met while both studied at the New Prospect campus of the State University of New Jersey. My mother, who has since become a nurse's aide, at the time was seeking credits toward an art degree. She paints and designs jewelry in her spare time, with some success, though not enough to support us. *He*—" The boy hesitates, as if he has encountered an obstacle in his throat.

"Your father," Levy prompts.

"Exactly. He had hoped, my mother has explained to me, to absorb lessons in American enterprise and marketing techniques. It was not as easy as he had been told it would be. His name was—*is;* I very much feel he is still alive— Omar Ashmawy, and hers is Teresa Mulloy. She is Irish-American. They married well before I was born. I am legitimate."

"Fine. I didn't doubt it. Not that it matters. It's not the baby who's not legitimate, if you follow me."

"I do, sir. Thank you. My father well knew that marrying an American citizen, however trashy and immoral she was, would gain him American citizenship, and so it did, but not American know-how, nor the network of acquaintance that leads to American prosperity. Having despaired of ever earning more than a menial living by the time I was three, he decamped. Is that the correct word? I encountered it in an autobiographical memoir by the great American writer Henry Miller, which Miss Mackenzie assigned us in Advanced English."

"She did? My goodness, Ahmad; times change. You used to find Miller only under the counter. You know the expression 'under the counter'?"

"Of course. I am not a foreigner. I have never been abroad."

"You asked about 'decamp.' It's an old-fashioned word, but most Americans know what it means. To break up a military camp is the original sense."

"Mr. Miller used it, I believe, of a wife who left him."

"Yes. Small wonder. That she decamped, I mean. Miller would not have been an easy husband." Those lubricated three-ways with the wife in *Sexus*. Was the English department assigning *Sexus*? Is nothing to be held in reserve, for adulthood?

The young man takes a surprising tangent from his counselor's awkward remarks. "My mother tells me that I cannot remember my father," he says, "and yet I do."

"Well, you were three. Developmentally speaking, you could have a few memories." This is not Jack Levy's intended direction for the interview.

"A warm, dark shadow," Ahmad says, leaning forward, with a jerk, in his earnestness. "Very white, square teeth. A small, neat mustache. I get my own personal neatness from him, I am sure. Among my memories is a sweet smell, perhaps aftershave lotion, though with a hint of some spice in it, perhaps a Middle Eastern dish he had just consumed. He was dark, darker than I, but elegantly thin-featured. He parted his hair very near the middle."

This intent digression makes Levy uneasy. The boy is using it to hide something—what? Jack points out, deflatingly, "Perhaps you have confused a photograph with a memory."

"I have only one or two photographs. My mother may have some she has hidden from me. When I was small and innocent, she refused to answer my many questions about my father. I think his desertion left her very angry. I would like, some day, to find him. Not to press any claim, or to impose any guilt, but simply to talk with him, as two Muslim men would talk."

"Uh, Mr.—? How do you like to be called? Mulloy or—" he looks again at the cover of his folder—"Ashmawy?"

"My mother attached her name to me, on my Social Security and driver's license, and her apartment is where I can be reached. But when I am out of school and independent I will become Ahmad Ashmawy."

Levy keeps his eyes down on the folder. "And how do you plan to support this independence? Your marks were good, Mr. Mulloy, in chemistry and English and so on, but I see you switched last year to the voke track. Who advised you to do that?"

The young man lowers his own eyes—solemn black lamps, long-lashed—and rubs as if at a gnat by his ear. "My teacher," he says.

"Which teacher? A course switch like that should have been checked with me. We could have talked, you and I, even if we aren't two Muslim men."

"My teacher is not here. He is at the mosque. Shaikh Rashid, the imam. We study together the sacred Qur'an."

Levy tries to suppress his distaste, saying, "Yes. Do I know where the mosque is? I fear I don't, except for the huge one on Tilden Avenue that the Black Muslims put up in the ruins after the 'sixties riots. Is that the one you mean?" He is sounding bristly, and doesn't want to. It wasn't this boy who had woken him up at four o'clock, or who had fouled his brain with thoughts of death, or had made Beth oppressively fat.

"West Main Street, sir, about six blocks south of Linden Boulevard."

"Reagan Boulevard. They renamed it last year," Levy says, making a disapproving mouth.

The boy doesn't pick up on it. Politics for these teen-agers is an obscurer department of celebrity heaven. Polls show they think Kennedy was the next-best President after Lincoln, because he had celebrity quality, and anyway they don't know any of the others, not even Ford and Carter, just Clinton and the Bushes, if they can tell the Bushes apart. Young Mulloy—Levy had a mental block with the other name— says, "It is on a street of stores, above a beauty shop and a place where they give you cash. It is not easy to find, the first time."

"And the imam of this hard-to-find place told you to switch to the voke track."

Again the boy hesitates, protecting what it is he is protecting, and then says, staring boldly from those great black eyes, in which the irises are hard to distinguish from the pupils, "He said the college track exposed me to corrupting influences—bad philosophy and bad literature. Western culture is Godless."

Jack Levy leans back in his squeaking old-fashioned wooden swivel chair and sighs, "Would that it were." Fearing trouble with the school board and newspapers if they got wind of his saying this to a student, he backtracks: "That slipped out. Some of these evangelical Christians get my goat, blaming Darwin for the sloppy job God did, creating the universe."

But the boy is not listening, pursuing his own point. "And because it has no God, it is obsessed with sex and luxury goods. Look at television, Mr. Levy, how it's always using sex to sell you things you don't need. Look at the history the school teaches, pure colonialist. Look how Christianity committed genocide on the Native Americans and undermined Asia and Africa and now is coming after Islam, with everything in Washington run by the Jews to keep themselves in Palestine."

"*Whew*," Jack says, wondering if the boy recognizes that

he is talking to a Jew. "That's quite a bill of particulars, to get you off the college track." As Ahmad widens his eyes, staring into so much injustice, Jack notices that his irises are not plain black but with a greenish tinge in their brown, a pinch of the Mulloy in him. "Did the imam ever suggest," he asks, letting the chair's recoil lean him confidentially across the desk, "that a bright boy like you, in a diverse and tolerant society like this one, needs to confront a variety of viewpoints?"

"No," Ahmad says with surprising abruptness, his soft lips bunching in a pout of defiance. "Shaikh Rashid did not suggest that, sir. He feels that such a relativistic approach trivializes religion, implying that it doesn't much matter. You believe this, I believe that, we all get along—that's the American way."

"Right. And he doesn't like the American way?"

"He hates it."

Jack Levy, still sitting forward, braces his elbows on his desktop and his chin thoughtfully on his intertwined fingers. "And you, Mr. Mulloy? You hate it?"

The boy shyly casts his eyes down again. "I of course do not hate all Americans. But the American way is the way of infidels. It is headed for a terrible doom."

He does not say, *America wants to take away my God.* He protects his God from this weary, unkempt, disbelieving old Jew, and guards as well his suspicion that Shaikh Rashid is so furiously absolute in his doctrines because God has secretly fled from behind his pale Yemeni eyes, the elusive gray-blue of a kafir woman's. Ahmad in his fatherless years with his blithely faithless mother has grown accustomed to being God's sole custodian, the one to whom God is an invisible but palpable companion. God is ever with him. As it says in the ninth sura, *Ye have no patron or helper save God.* God is another person close beside him, a Siamese twin attached in every part, inside and out, and to whom he can turn at every moment in prayer. God is his happiness. This old Jewish devil, beneath his cunning, worldly-wise, mock-fatherly manner, wishes to disrupt that primal union and take the All-Merciful and Life-Giving One from him.

Jack Levy sighs again and thinks ahead to the next appointment—another needy, surly, misguided teen-ager about to float away into the morass of the world. "Well, perhaps I shouldn't say this, Ahmad, but in view of your grades and SATs, and your way-above-average poise and seriousness, I think your—what's that word?—imam helped you to waste your high-school years. I wish you had stayed on the college track."

Ahmad comes to Shaikh Rashid's defense. "Sir, there are no resources for any college expenses. My mother fancies herself an artist; she stopped her own education at the level of nurse's aide, rather than invest two more years in her own education when I was a pre-school child. "

Levy ruffles his thinning, already mussed hair. "O.K., sure. These are tight times, what with heightened security and Bush's wars soaking up what used to be a surplus. But, let's face it, there's still a lot of scholarship money out there for smart, responsible kids of color. We could have gotten you some, I'm sure of it. Not Princeton, maybe, and maybe not Rutgers, but a place like Bloomfield or Seton Hall, Fairleigh Dickinson or Kean, can be excellent. Still, for now, that's pretty much water over the dam. Sorry I wasn't on to your case earlier. Get your high-school diploma, and see how you feel about college in a year or two. You know where to find me, I'd do what I could. What, may I ask, had you planned to do after graduation? If you have no job prospects, think about the Army. It's not everybody's sweetheart any more, but it still offers a pretty good deal—teaches you some skills, and helps with an education afterwards. It helped me. If you have any Arabic, they'd love you."

Ahmad's expression stiffens. "The Army would send me to fight my brothers."

"Or to fight *for* your brothers, it could be. Not all Iraqis are insurgents, you know. Most aren't. They just want to get on with business. Civilization started there. They had an up-and-coming little country, until Saddam."

The boy's eyebrows, thick and broad as a man's though the hairs are finer, knit into a scowl. Ahmad stands up to leave, but Levy isn't quite ready to let him go. "I asked," he insists, "do you have any job lined up?"

The answer comes reluctantly: "My teacher thinks I should drive a truck."

"Drive a *truck*? What kind of truck? There are trucks and trucks. You're only eighteen; I happen to know you can't get a license for a tractor rig or tank truck or even a school bus for three more years. The exam for the license, a CDL— that's commercial driver's license—is tough. Until you're twenty-one you can't drive out of state. You can't carry hazardous materials."

"I can't?"

"Not as I remember. I've had young men before you who were interested; a lot got scared off, by the technical side of it and all the regulations. You have to join the Teamsters. There's a lot of hurdles, in trucking. A lot of thugs, too."

Ahmad shrugs; Levy sees that he has exhausted the young man's quota of coöperation and courtesy. The boy has clammed up. O.K., so will Jack Levy. He's been in Jersey longer than this pretentious kid. As he hopes, the less experienced male cracks and breaks the silence.

Ahmad feels impelled to justify himself to this unhappy Jew. The scent of unhappiness rolls off Mr. Levy as sometimes it does off of Ahmad's mother, after one boyfriend has let her down and before the next has shown up, and no painting of hers has sold for months. "My teacher knows people who might need a driver. I would have somebody to show me the ropes," he explains. "It's good pay," he adds.

"And long hours," the guidance counselor says, slapping this student's folder shut, having scribbled on the topmost page "lc" and "nc," his abbreviations for "lost cause" and "no career." "Tell me this, Mulloy. Your faith—it's important to you."

"Yes."

The boy is protecting something; Jack can smell it.

"God—Allah—is very real to you."

Ahmad says, slowly, as if betranced or reciting something memorized, "He is in me, and at my side."

"Good. Good. Glad to hear it. Keep it up. I was exposed to religion a little, my mother would light the Passover candles, but I had this father who was a scoffer, so I followed his example and didn't keep it up. I never had it to lose, really. Dust to dust's my sense of it all. Sorry."

The boy blinks and nods, a bit frightened by such a confession. His eyes seem round black lamps above the stark white shirt; they burn into Levy's memory and return at times like afterimages of the sun at sunset, or the flash from a camera when you obligingly pose, trying to look natural, and it goes off unexpectedly soon.

Levy pursues it: "How old were you when you . . . when you found your faith?"

"Age eleven, sir."

"Funny—that's the age when I announced I was giving up the violin. Defied my parents. Asserted myself. The hell with everybody." The boy still stares, refusing the bond. "O.K.," Levy concedes. "I want to think about you a little more. I may want to see you again, give you some relevant material, before you graduate." He stands and on an impulse shakes the tall, slender, fragile-seeming youth's hand, which he doesn't do with every boy at the end of a session, and would never do with a girl these days—the merest touch risks a complaint. Some of these little hot twats fantasize. Ahmad's clasped hand is so limp and damp Jack is startled: still a shy kid, not yet a man. "Or, if not," the counselor concludes, "you have a great life, my friend."

On Sunday morning, while most Americans are still in bed, though a few are struggling out to an early mass or a scheduled golf match in the dew, the Secretary for Homeland Security upgrades the so-called terror-threat level from yellow, meaning merely "elevated," to orange, meaning "high." That's the bad news. The good news is that the higher level applies only to specific areas of Washington, New York, and northern New Jersey; the rest of the nation remains on yellow.

The Secretary tells the nation, in his all-but-sublimated Pennsylvania accent, that recent intelligence reports, in what he terms "alarmingly close and harmonious detail," indicated an attack upon sensitive targets in those specific Eastern metropolitan areas, which "the enemies of freedom have been studying with the most sophisticated tools of reconnaissance." Financial centers, sports arenas, bridges, tunnels, subways—nothing is safe. "You may expect to see," he tells the lens of the television camera, which is like a gun-colored, lens-covered porthole on whose other side presses an ocean of trusting, anxious citizens, "special buffer zones to secure the perimeters of buildings from unauthorized cars and trucks; restrictions to affected underground parking; security personnel using identification badges and digital photos to keep track of people entering and exiting buildings; increased law-enforcement presence; and robust screening of vehicles, packages, and deliveries."

He cherishes and emphasizes the phrase "robust screening." It conjures up an image of strapping men in green or gray-blue jumpsuits tearing apart vehicles and packages, venting in their vigor the Secretary's daily frustration at the difficulty of his task. His task is to protect in spite of itself a nation of nearly three hundred million anarchic souls, their millions of daily irrational impulses and self-indulgent actions flitting out of sight just around the edge of feasible surveillability. This mob's collective gaps and irregularities form a perfect rough surface whereupon the enemy can grow one of his tenacious, wide-spreading plots. Destruction, the Secretary has often thought, is so much easier than construction, and disruption than social order, that the upholders of a society must always lag behind those who would destroy it, just as (he had been a football player for Lehigh in his youth) a fleet-footed receiver can always gain a step on the defending cornerback. "And God bless America," he publicly concludes.

The red light above the little porthole goes off. He is off the air. He abruptly shrinks in size; now his words will be heard by only the handful of TV technicians and loyal staffers around him, here in this cramped media facility sunk a hundred bombproof feet beneath Pennsylvania Avenue. Other Cabinet-level officials get marble-and-limestone federal buildings so long that each has its own horizon, whereas he must function huddling in a small windowless office in the basement of the White House. With a Herculean sigh of

One

weariness, the Secretary turns from the camera. He is a large man, with a slab of muscle across his back that gives the tailors of his dark-blue suits extra trouble. In his massive head his mouth looks truculently small. His haircut, on that same head, also looks small, like a hat belonging to someone else but jammed on anyway. His Pennsylvania accent is not a broad, syllable-swallowing growl like Lee Iacocca's or a piercing honk like Arnold Palmer's; of a generation younger than they, he speaks a neutral, media-friendly English, which only in its tense solemnity and certain vowel shadings betrays its source in a Commonwealth renowned for seriousness, for earnest effort and stoic submission, for Quakers and coal miners, for Amish farmers and God-fearing Presbyterian steel magnates.

"Whajja think?" he asks an assistant, a slender pink-eyed fellow-Pennsylvanian, sixty-four but virginal, Hermione Fogel.

Hermione's transparent skin and fluttering, embarrassed demeanor express an instinctive underling's yearning for personal invisibility. In the spirit of cumbersome fun with which the Secretary expressed his affection and trust, he brought her with him from Harrisburg and gave her an informal title: Undersecretary for Women's Purses. The problem was real enough: women's purses were sinkholes of confusion and sedimented treasure in whose depths any number of compact terrorist-weapons—retractable box-cutters, exploding sarin pellets, lipstick-shaped stun guns— could be secreted. It was Hermione who had helped develop the search protocols for this crucial area of darkness, including the simple wooden stick with which security guards at entrances could probe the depths and not give offense with the rummaging touch of their naked hands.

The majority of security personnel were recruited from

the minorities, and many women, especially older women, recoiled from the intrusion of black or brown fingers into their purses. The dozing giant of American racism, lulled by decades of official liberal singsong, stirred anew as African-Americans and Hispanics, who (it was often complained) "can't even speak English properly," acquired the authority to frisk, to question, to delay, to grant or deny admission and the permission to fly. In a land of multiplying security gates, the gatekeepers multiply also. To the well-paid professionals who travelled the airways and frequented the newly fortified government buildings, it appears that a dusky underclass has been given tyrannical power. Comfortable lives that even a decade ago moved fluidly through circuits of privilege and assumed access now encounter sticking-points at what seem every step, while maddeningly deliberate guards ponder driver's licenses and boarding passes. Where once a confident manner, a correct suit and tie, and a business card measuring two by three and a half inches had opened doors, the switch is no longer tripped, the door remains closed. How can the fluid, hydraulically responsive workings of capitalism, let alone the commerce of intellectual exchange and the social life of extended families, function through such obdurate thicknesses of precaution? The enemy has achieved his goal: business and recreation in the West are gummed up, exorbitantly so.

"I thought it went very well, as usual," Hermione Fogel responds, to a question the Secretary has all but forgotten. He is preoccupied: the clashing claims of privacy and security, convenience and safety, are his daily diet, and yet his compensation in terms of public admiration is nearly nil and in terms of financial compensation distinctly modest, with children approaching the age of college education and a wife who must keep up her end in the endless social rounds of Republican Washington. Except for a black, single woman, a polyglot academic and accomplished pianist in charge of long-range global strategy, the Secretary's colleagues in the administration were born rich and have made additional fortunes in the private sector during their eight-year holiday from public service under Clinton. In those fat years the Secretary had been grinding his way upward through low-paying government posts in the Keystone State. Now all the Clintonians, including the Clintons themselves, are getting pig-rich with their tell-all memoirs, while the Secretary, loyal and stolid, is wedded to tight-mouthed secrecy, now and ever after.

Not that he knows anything his Arabists don't tell him; the world they monitor, of electronic chatter crackling with poetic euphemism and pathetic braggadocio, is as alien and repellent to the Secretary as any underworld of sleepless geeks, even those of Caucasian blood and Christian upbringing. *When the heaven splits asunder in the east and reddens like a rose or stained leather*—the insertion into this clause from the Koran the non-Koranic "in the east" may or may not, coupled with various rambling and extravagant "confessions" of captured operatives, justify the elevation of the level of police and military watchfulness accorded certain Eastern financial institutions of the spectacular, skyscraping sort attractive to the enemy's superstitious mentality. The enemy is obsessed with holy sites, and as convinced as the old Communist archenemies had been that capitalism has a headquarters, a head that may be cut off, leaving flocks of the faithful to be gratefully herded into an ascetic and dogmatic tyranny.

The enemy cannot believe that democracy and consumerism are fevers in the blood of Everyman, an outgrowth of each individual's instinctive optimism and desire for freedom. Even for a stout churchgoer like the Secretary, a will-of-God fatalism and a heavy bet on the next world have been left behind in the Dark Ages. Those who still hold to the bet have one thing going for them: they are eager to die. *The unbelievers love this fleeting life too well:* that was another verse that kept coming up in the Internet chatter.

"I'll be knocked for this," the Secretary gloomily confides to his so-called undersecretary. "If nothing happens, I'm a scaremonger. If it does, I'm a lazy leech on the public payroll who allowed the death of thousands."

"No one would say such things," Hermione reassures him, her sallow spinster skin reddening with sympathetic feeling. "Everyone, even the Democrats, knows you are doing an impossible job that nevertheless must be done, for the sake of our national survival."

"That about says it, I guess," the object of her admiration admits, his mouth pinched even smaller by a conscious wryness. The elevator smoothly returns them, with two armed security guards (one male, one female) and a trio of gray-suited staffers, to the level of the White House basement. Outside, church bells are ringing in sunshine blended of Virginia and Maryland rays. The Secretary muses aloud, "Those people out there . . . Why do they want to do these horrible things? Why do they hate us? What's to hate?"

"They hate the light," Hermione tells him loyally. "Like cockroaches. Like bats. *The light shone in darkness,*" she quotes, knowing that Pennsylvania piety is a way to his heart, *"and the darkness comprehended it not."*

II

THE SOOT-STAINED ironstone church beside the lake of rubble is filled inside with pastel cotton dresses and sharp-shouldered polyester suits. Ahmad's eyes are dazzled, and find no balm in the stained-glass windows, depicting men in parodies of Middle Eastern dress enacting incidents in their supposed Lord's progress through his brief and inglorious life. To worship a God known to have died—the very idea affects Ahmad like an elusive stench, a stoppage in the plumbing, a dead rodent in the walls. Yet the congregants, a few of whom are even paler than he in his crisp white shirt, bask in the clean-scrubbed happiness of their Sunday-morning assembly. The receding rows of seated and sexually mixed people, and the stagy confused area at the front with its built-in knobbed furniture and high, grimy triple window showing a pigeon about to alight on the head of a white-bearded man, and the giddy murmur of greetings and the crackle of heavy rumps shifting on the wooden pews, all seem to Ahmad more like a movie theatre before the movie starts than a holy mosque, with its thick muffling rugs and empty tiled mihrab and the liquid chants, *lā ilāha illā Allah*, emitted by men fragrant of their menial Friday labors and, in their rhythmic unison of obeisance, crammed together as closely as the segments of a worm. The mosque was a domain of men; here, women in their spring shimmer, their expansive soft flesh, dominate.

He had hoped by arriving just as the ten-o'clock bells were ringing to slip into the back unnoticed, but he is tenaciously greeted by a plump descendant of slaves in a peach-colored suit with wide lapels and a sprig of lily-of-the-valley pinned to one of them. The black man hands Ahmad a folded sheet of tinted paper and leads him forward, up the center aisle, to the front pews. The church is nearly full, and none but the front pews, apparently the less desirable, are empty. Accustomed to worshippers squatting and kneeling on a floor, emphasizing God's height above them, Ahmad feels, even seated, dizzily, blasphemously tall. The Christian attitude of lazily sitting erect as at an entertainment suggests that God is an entertainer who, when He ceases to entertain, can be removed from the stage, and another act brought on.

Ahmad thinks he will have the pew to himself, as a sop to his strangeness and his sensed trepidation at being here, but another usher officiously herds down the carpeted aisle a large black family bobbing and bristling with the cornrowed, beribboned heads of little females. Ahmad is pushed to the pew's far end, and in acknowledgment of his displacement the patriarch of the brood reaches over the laps of several small daughters to offer Ahmad his broad brown hand and a smile of welcome in which a gold tooth gleams. The mother of this brood, too far away to reach the stranger, gaily follows suit with a distant wave and nod. The little girls glance up, showing moon crescents of eye white. All this kafir friendliness—Ahmad doesn't know how to repel it, or what further inroads the service will impose. Already he hates Joryleen for luring him into such a sticky trap. He holds his breath as if to fend off contamination and stares straight ahead, where the curious carvings on what he takes to be the Christian equivalent of the *minbar* slowly sort themselves out as winged angels; he identifies the one of them blowing a long horn as Gabriel, and the crowded occasion therefore as the same Judgment Day the thought of which prompted Mohammed to gusts of his most rapturous poetry. What a mistake, Ahmad thinks, it is to attempt depiction, in images whose very grain betrays them as mere wood, of the inimitable work of God the Creator, *al-Khāliq*. The imagery of words, the Prophet knew, alone grips the soul with its own spiritual substance. *Verily, were men and Djinn assembled to produce the like of this Qur'an, they could not produce its like, though the one should help the other.*

The service at last begins. There is an expectant silence and then a swooping, bouncy thunder whose toylike timbre Ahmad recognizes, from assemblies at Central High, as that of an electric organ, poor cousin of the real pipe organ that he spies gathering dust beyond the Christian *minbar*. All stand to sing. Ahmad is brought to his feet as if by chains tying him to the others. A blue-robed mass, a choir, floods down the central aisle and fills the spaces behind a low rail beyond which, it seems, the congregation dare not pass. The sung words, distorted by the rhythm and languid accents of these *zanj*, concern, as best he can understand, a hill far away, and an old rugged cross. From within his resolute silence he spots Joryleen in the choir, a mass of mostly

women, massive women among whom Joryleen looks girl-
ishly young and relatively slim. She in turn spots Ahmad, in
his pew up front; her smile disappoints him by being tentative, darting, nervous. She, too, knows he should not be here.

Up, down, everyone in his row but he and the smallest girl
go onto their knees and return to sitting. There are group
recitations and responses he cannot follow, though the
father with the gold tooth shows him the page in the front
of the hymnal. We believe this and that, the Lord is thanked
for that and this. Then a long prayer is offered by the Christian imam, a stern-faced, coffee-colored man with wireless
glasses and a flashing tall bald head. His gravelly voice is
electrically amplified so that it booms from the back of the
church as well as the front; while he, his eyes tight-shut
behind his spectacles, burrows more deeply into the darkness that his mind's eye sees as he prays, voices from the congregation, here and there, shout out agreement—"Thass
right!" "Say it, Reverend!" "Praise the Lord!" Arising like
sweat on the skin, a murmur of assent continues when, in the
wake of the second hymn, concerning the joys of walking
with Jesus, the preacher ascends into the high *minbar* deco-
rated with carved angels. In ever more rolling tones, moving
his head in and out of the amplifying system's range so that
his voice shrinks and swells like that of a man calling from
the topmost mast of a storm-tossed ship, he tells of Moses,
who led the chosen people out of slavery and yet was himself
denied admission to the Promised Land.

"Why was that?" he asks. "Moses had served the Lord as
spokesman in and out of Egypt. Spokesman: our President
down there in Washington has a spokesman, our company
heads in their lofty offices in Manhattan and Houston, they
have spokesmen, spokes*women* in some cases, being spokes-
persons comes more naturally to them, doesn't it, brothers?"

There were guffaws and titters, inviting a digression: "Mercy, our beloved sisters do know how to *speak*. God didn't give Eve our strength of arm and shoulder, but he gave her double our strength of tongue. I hear laughing, but that's no joke, it's simple evolution, like they want to teach our innocent children in all the public schools. But seriously: nobody trusts himself to speak for himself any more. Too many *risks*. Too many lawyers watching and writing down what you say. Now, if I had a spokesperson right now I would be home watching a TV chat show with Mr. William Moyers or Mr. Theodore Koppel and having a second helping, a second slice or two or three, of that delicious, syrup-saturated French toast my dear Tilly makes for me some mornings after she's bought herself a new dress, a new dress or some fancy alligator purse she feels the teeniest bit guilty about."

Above the chuckles that greet this revelation, the preacher goes on, "That way, I would be saving my voice. That way, I wouldn't have to wonder out loud with all of you listening why God held Moses back from entering the Promised Land. If I only had a spokesperson."

To Ahmad it seems as if suddenly, in the midst of this expectant and heated crowd of dark-skinned *kuffār*, the preacher is musing to himself, having forgotten why he is here, why all of them are here, while mockingly loud radios can be heard from cars swishing past on the street outside. But the man's eyes fly open behind his glasses and with a thump he pounces on the big gold-edged Bible in the *minbar* lectern, saying, "Here's the reason; God gives it in Deuteronomy, chapter thirty-two, verse fifty-one: 'Because ye trespassed against me among the children of Israel at the waters of Meribah-Kadesh, in the wilderness of Zin, because ye sanctified me not in the midst of the children of Israel.' "

The preacher, in his blue big-sleeved robe with a shirt and

red necktie peeking out at the top, surveys the congregation with eyes widened in amazement and seems to Ahmad to focus especially upon *him*, perhaps because his is not a familiar face. "What does that mean?" he asks softly. " 'Trespassed against me'? 'Sanctified me not'? What did those poor long-suffering Israelites do wrong at those waters of Meribah-Kadesh, in that wilderness of Zin? Raise your hand, anybody who knows." Nobody does, taken off guard, and the preacher hurries on, consulting his big Bible again, tugging a thickness of its gilded edges over to a place he had marked. "It's all in here, my friends. Everything you need to know is right spang in here. The Good Book tells how a scouting party went out from the people Moses was leading all that way out of Egypt, they went into the Negev and north to the Jordan and came back and said, according to the thirteenth chapter of Numbers, that the land they had explored 'floweth with milk and honey,' but 'nevertheless the people be strong that dwell in the land, and the cities are walled, and very great,' and furthermore—*furthermore*, they reported—'the children of Anak' are there, and they are *giants* next to which 'we were in our own sight as grasshoppers, and so we were in their sight.' They knew it, and we knew it, brothers and sisters—next to them we were just little old *grasshoppers*, grasshoppers that live in the weeds for a few quick days, in the hay of a meadow before it is cut, in the outfield of the baseball field where nobody ever hits the ball, and then are gone, their exoskeletons, as intricate as everything else the good Lord makes, easily crunched in the beak of a crow or swallow, a seagull or a cowbird."

Now the preacher's blue sleeves thrash and bits of spittle from his mouth spark in the lectern light, and the choir below him sways, with Joryleen in it. "And Caleb said, 'Let's go, let us go up at once, and possess it'—'We can take 'em, giants or not. Let's go do it!' " And the tall coffee-colored man reads, in a voice vibrant and rapid, taking many voices: " 'And all the congregation lifted up their voice, and cried; and the people wept that night. And all the children of Israel murmured against Moses and against Aaron: and the whole congregation said unto them, Would God that we had died in the land of Egypt! or would God we had died in this wilderness!' "

He looks gravely out at the congregation, his spectacles circles of pure blind light, and repeats, " 'Would to God that we had died in Egypt!' So why *did* God bring us out of slavery into this wilderness"—he consults his book—" 'to fall by the sword, that our wives and our children should be a prey'? A prey! Hey, this is *se*rious! Let's hustle our asses— our oxes and asses—back to Egypt!" He glances into the book, and reads a verse aloud: " 'They said to one another, Let us make a captain, and let us return to Egypt.' That Pharaoh, he wasn't so bad. He fed us, though not much. He gave us cabins to sleep in, down by the marsh with all the mosquitoes. He sent us welfare checks, pretty regular. He gave us jobs dishing up fries at McDonald's, for the minimum wage. He was friendly, that Pharaoh, compared to those giants, those humongous sons of Anak."

He stands erect, dropping his impersonation for the moment. "And what did Moses and his brother Aaron do about all this talk? It says right here, in Numbers fourteen, five: 'Moses and Aaron fell on their faces before all the assembly of the congregation of the children of Israel.' They gave up. They said to the people, the people they were supposed to be leading on behalf of the Almighty Lord, they said, 'Maybe you're right. We've had it. We've been wandering out of Egypt too long. This wilderness is just too much.'

"And Joshua—you remember him, the son of Nun, of the tribe of Ephraim, he was one of the twelve on that scouting party, along with Caleb—and Joshua stood up and said, 'Wait a minute. Wait a minute, brethren. This is good land those Canaanites have. Don't be afraid of those Canaanites, for they'—and I'm reading now—'are bread for us: their defense is departed from them, and the Lord is with us: fear them not.'" Solemnly, slowly, the preacher repeats, " 'The Lord is with us: fear them not.' And how did those average Israelites react when those two brave warrior-men stood up and said, 'Let's go. Don't be afraid of those Canaanites'? They said, 'Stone them. Stone those noisy rascals.' And they picked up stones—some considerably sharp and ugly flint lying around in that desert wilderness—and were set to crush the heads and mouths of Caleb and Joshua, when something *amazing* happened. Let me read to you what happened: 'And the glory of the Lord appeared in the tabernacle of the congregation before all the children of Israel. And the Lord said unto Moses, "How long will this people provoke me? and how long will it be ere they believe me, for all the signs which I have showed among them?" ' Manna from Heaven had been a sign. Water from the rock of Horeb had been a sign. The voice from the burning bush had been a clear sign. The pillars of cloud by day and of fire by night had been signs. Signs, signs around the clock, twenty-four/seven, as the saying is now.

"Still, the people had no faith. They wanted to go back to Egypt and that friendly Pharaoh. They preferred the devil they knew to the God they didn't. They still had a soft spot for that golden calf. They wouldn't mind going back to being slaves. They wanted to give up their civil rights. They wanted to forget their sorrows in dope and disgraceful behavior on Saturday nights. The good Lord said, 'I can't *stand* this people.' This tribe of Israel. And he asked Moses and Aaron, as if just for the information, 'How long shall I bear with this evil congregation, which murmur against me?' He doesn't wait for the answer; he answers Himself. The Lord, He slays *all* the scouts except for Caleb and Joshua. He tells *all* the others, that evil congregation, 'Your carcasses shall fall in this wilderness.' He sentences the others, all twenty years old or older, who had murmured against him, to forty years in this wilderness—'and your children shall wander in the wilderness forty years, and bear your whoredoms, until your carcasses be wasted in the wilderness.' Think of it. Forty years, with no time off for good behavior." He repeats, "With no time off for good behavior, because you have been an *evil* congregation."

A male voice in the congregation cries out, "Right on, Reverend! Evil!"

"No time off, be*cause*," continues the Christian imam, "you lacked the *faith*. Faith in the power of the Lord Almighty. That was your iniquity—let me give you the wonderful old word in all four of its syllables, *in-ick-qui-tee*: 'visiting the iniquity of the fathers upon the children unto the third and fourth generation.' Moses tries to soften Him up, the mouthpiece pleading with his client. 'Pardon, I beseech thee,' he says it right here in the Book, 'the iniquity of this people according unto the greatness of thy mercy, and as thou hast forgiven this people, from Egypt even until now.'

" 'No way,' the Lord says back. 'I'm tired of all this forgiving I'm supposed to do. I want some glory for a change. I want your carcasses.' "

The preacher slumps in the pulpit a little wearily, and

rests his elbows informally on the massive holy book with gilded edges. "My friends," he confides, "you can see what Moses was driving at. What was so terrible, what was so"—he parts with a smile, pronouncing—"*in-ick-qui-tuss*, about going into enemy territory, scouting out the situation, coming home and giving an honest, cautious report? 'Things don't look good. These Canaanites and giants have a good tight grip on the milk and honey. We better back off.' It sounds just like good common sense, doesn't it? 'Don't cross the man. He has the stocks and bonds, he has the whip and chains, he controls the means of pro-duc-*shun*.' "

Several voices call out, "That's right. Good sense. Don't cross the man."

"And to drill home his point, the Lord sent down plagues and pestilences, and the people mourned, and decided too late to go up into the mountains and face the Canaanites, who didn't look so bad now, and Moses, that good old mouthpiece, that savvy lawyer, advised them, 'Don't go. You shall not prosper. The Lord is not with you.' But these wrongheaded Israelites, they went up anyway, and what do we read, in the last verse of Numbers fourteen? 'Then the Amalekites came down, and the Canaanites which dwelt in that hill, and smote them, and discomfited them, even unto Hormah.' 'Even unto Hormah'—that's a long way. It's a long way to Hormah.

"You see, my friends, the Lord *had* been with them. He gave them a chance to go forward with Him in all of His glory, and what did they do? They hesitated. They betrayed Him with their hesitations—their caution, their *cow-ar-diss*—and Moses and Aaron betrayed Him by letting themselves be swayed, as politicians do when the polls come in—pollsters and spokesmen, they had them even then, in the days of the Bible—and for that they were held back from the Promised Land, Moses and Aaron left there on that mountain looking over into the land of Canaan like children with their faces pressed to the window of the candy store. They couldn't pass through. They were im*pure*. They hadn't measured up. They didn't let the Lord act through them. They had good human intentions, but they didn't trust enough in the Lord. The Lord is trustworthy. He says He'll do the impossible, He'll do it, don't tell Him He can't."

Ahmad finds himself getting excited along with the rest of the congregation, which is stirring and murmuring, relaxing from straining to follow every turn in the sermon, even the little pigtailed girls in the pew beside him, switching their heads back and forth as if to ease a pain in their necks, one of them looking up into Ahmad's face like a bug-eyed dog wondering if this human being is worth begging at. Her eyes shine as if reflecting a treasure she has spotted within him.

"*Faith*," the preacher is proclaiming in a voice roughened by oratory, gritty like coffee overloaded with sugar. "They didn't have *faith*. That is why they were an evil congregation. That is why the Israelites were visited by pestilence and shame and defeat in battle. Abraham, the father of the tribe, had faith when he lifted up his knife to sacrifice his only son, Isaac. Jonah had faith in the belly of the whale. Daniel had faith in the lion's den. Jesus on the cross had faith—he asked the Lord why He had abandoned him but then in the next breath he turned to the thief on the cross next to him and promised that man, that evil man, that 'hardened criminal,' as the sociologists say, that that very day he would dwell with him in Paradise. Martin Luther King had faith on the Mall in Washington, and in that hotel in Memphis where James Earl Ray martyred Reverend King—he had gone there to support the striking sanitation workers, the lowest of the low, the untouchables that haul our trash. Rosa Parks had faith in that bus in Montgomery, Alabama." The preacher's body leans out, growing taller, and his voice changes tune as a new thought strikes him. "She took a seat in the front of the bus," he says at conversational pitch. "That's what the Israelites didn't do. They were afraid to sit at the front of the bus. The Lord said to them, 'There it is, right behind the driver, the land of Canaan full of milk and honey, that seat's for you,' and they said, 'No thanks, Lord, we like it at the back of the bus. We have a little game of craps going, we have our little pint of Four Roses to pass around, we have our little crack pipe, our heroin needle, we have our under-age crackhead girlfriends to bear our illegitimate children that we can leave in a shoebox at the disposal and recycling facility on the edge of town—don't send us up that hill, Lord. We no match for those giants. We no match for Bull Connor and his police dogs. We'll just stay in the back of the bus. It's nice and dark there. It's cozy.' " He returns to his own voice and says, "Don't be like them, brothers and sisters. Tell me what you need."

"Faith," a few voices weakly offer, uncertain.

"Let me hear it again, louder. What do we all need?"

"Faith," comes the more unified reply. Even Ahmad pronounces the word, but so no one can hear, except the little girl next to him.

"Better, but not loud enough. What do we have, brothers and sisters?"

"Faith!"

"Faith in what? Let me hear it so those Canaanites quake in their big goatskin boots!"

"Faith in the Lord!"

Two

"Yes, oh yes," individual voices add. A few women here and there are sobbing. The mother, still young and comely, in Ahmad's pew has gleaming cheeks, he sees.

The preacher is not quite done with them. "The Lord of who?" he asks, answering himself with an excitement almost boyish: "The Lord of Abraham." He takes a breath. "The Lord of Joshua." He takes another. "The Lord of King David."

"The Lord of Jesus," a voice from the back of the old church puts forth.

"The Lord of Mary," cries a female voice.

Another ventures, "The Lord of Bathsheba."

"The Lord of Zipporah," calls a third.

The preacher decides the time to close has come. "The Lord of us all," he booms, leaning as close into the microphone as a rock star. He is wiping the shine from his tall bald head with a white handkerchief. He is filmed with sweat. It has made his starched collar wilt. He has been in his kafir way wrestling with devils, wrestling even with Ahmad's devils. "The Lord of us all," he repeats, mournfully. "Amen."

"Amen," many say, in relief and emptiness. There is silence, and then a businesslike sound of muffled pacing as four men in their suits march two abreast up the aisle to receive wooden plates while the choir with a massive rustle stands and readies itself to sing. A small robed man who has made up for his shortness by growing his kinky hair into a tall puff lifts his arms in readiness as the grave men in pastel polyester suits take the plates the preacher has handed them and fan out, two down the center aisle and two on the sides. They expect money to be placed in the plates, which have red felt bottoms to soften the rattle of coins. The unexpected word "impure" returns from the sermon; Ahmad's insides tremble with the impure trespass of his witnessing these black unbelievers at worship of their non-God, their three-headed idol; it is like seeing sex among people, pink scenes glimpsed over the shoulders of boys misusing their computers at school.

Abraham, Noah: these names are not totally strange to Ahmad. The Prophet in the third sura affirmed: *We believe in God, and in what hath been sent down to us, and what hath been sent down to Abraham, and Ishmael, and Isaac, and Jacob, and the tribes, and in what was given to Moses, and Jesus, and the Prophets, from their Lord. We make no difference between them.* These people around him are too in their fashion People of the Book. *Why disbelieve ye the signs of God? Why repel believers from the way of God?*

The electric organ, played by a man the back of whose neck shows rolls of creased flesh as if to form another face, makes a trickle of sound, then jabs out a swoop like a splash of icy water. The choir, Joryleen among them, in the front row, begins to sing. Ahmad has eyes only for her, the way she opens her mouth so wide, the tongue inside so pink behind her small round teeth, like half-buried pearls. "What a friend we have in Jesus," he understands the opening words to say, slowly, as if dragging the burden of the song up from some cellar of sorrow. "All our sins and griefs to bear!" The congregation behind Ahmad greets the words with grunts and yips of assent: they know this song, they like it. From the side aisle a kafir man taller than most, in a lemon-yellow suit, with a big broad-knuckled hand that makes the collection plate look the size of a saucer, passes it into the row where Ahmad sits. Ahmad passes it on quickly, depositing nothing; it tries to fly out of his hand, the wood is so surprisingly light, but he brings it down to the level of the little girl next to him, her scrabbly brown hands, not quite a baby's, reaching to snatch it away and pass it on. She, who has been looking up at him with bright dog-eyes, has inched over so that her wiry small body touches his, leaning so softly she may think he will not notice. Still feeling himself a trespasser, he stiffly ignores her, looking straight ahead as if to read the words from the mouths of the robed singers. "What a *priv*-i-lege to carry," he understands, "everything to God in prayer."

Ahmad himself loves prayer, the sensation of pouring the silent voice in his head into a silence waiting at his side, an invisible extension of himself into a dimension purer than the three dimensions of this world. Joryleen has told him she would be singing a solo, but she stays in her row, between a fat older woman and a skinny one the color of dried leather, all jiggling slightly in their shimmery blue robes, their mouths pretty much in unison, so he cannot tell which voice is Joryleen's. Her eyes stay on the puff-haired director and not once stray toward Ahmad, though he has risked Hellfire to accept her invitation. He wonders if Tylenol is in the evil congregation at his back; his shoulder hurt for a day where Tylenol had gripped it. ". . . All because we do not carry," the choir sings, "everything to God in prayer." These women's voices all together, with the deeper ones of the men standing in the row behind, have a stately frontal quality, like an army advancing without fear of attack. The many throats are massed into an organ sound, unanswerable, plaintive, far removed from an imam's single voice intoning the music of the Qur'an, a music that enters the spaces behind your eyes and sinks into a silence of your brain.

The electronic organist slips into a different rhythm, a hippity-hop studded with a knocking noise, a wooden percussion produced at the back of the choir, by an instrument, a set of sticks, that Ahmad cannot see. The congregation greets the shift of tempo with mutters of approval, and the choir begins to keep the rhythm with its feet, its hips. The organ makes a gulping, dipping sound. The song is shedding the clothing of its words, which become harder to understand—something about trials and temptations and trouble anywhere. The skinny dried-up woman next to Joryleen steps forward and, in a voice that sounds like a man's, a mellow man's, asks the congregation, "Can we find a friend so faithful, who will all our sorrows share?" Behind her the chorus is chanting the one word, "Prayer, prayer, prayer." The organist is bouncing up and down, seemingly going his own way but keeping in touch. Ahmad hadn't known the organ had so many notes on the keyboard, high ones and low ones, all in clusters hurrying upward, upward. "Prayer, prayer, prayer," the chorus keeps chanting, letting that fat organist have his solo say.

Then comes Joryleen's turn; she steps forward into a spatter of clapping, and her eyes skim right across Ahmad's face before she turns the full-lipped oval of her own face toward the crowd beyond his pew and higher, in the balcony. She takes a breath; his heart stops, fearful for her. But her voice unspools a luminous thread: "Are we weak and heavy laden, cumbered with a load of care?" Her voice is young and frail and pure, with a little quaver to it before her nervousness settles. "Precious Savior, still our refuge," she sings. Her voice relaxes into a brassy color, with a rasping edge, then rises in sudden freedom to a shriek like that of a child pleading to be let into a locked door. The congregation murmurs approval of these liberties. Joryleen cries out, "Do-hoo thy friends despise, for-horsake thee?"

"Hey, well, do they?" the fat woman next to her calls out, chiming in as if Joryleen's solo is a warm bath become too inviting to stay out of. She jumps in not to jostle Joryleen but to join her; hearing this other voice beside her, Joryleen tries a few off notes, harmonizing, her young voice getting bolder, transported into self-forgetfulness. "In his arms," she sings, "in his arms, in his arms he'll take and shield thee; thou wilt find, oh mercy yes, a solace there."

"Yes, a solace; yes, a solace," the fat woman echoes, and steps out into a roar of recognition, of love from the crowd, for her voice takes them deep into and then right out of the bottom of their lives, Ahmad feels. Her voice has been seasoned in the suffering that for Joryleen is mainly ahead, a mere shadow on her young life. With that authority, the fat woman, her face as broad as a stone idol's, begins again, with "What a friend." Dimples appear not just below her cheeks but at the corners of her eyes, the sides of her broad flat nose, as her nostrils flare at a fierce slant. The hymn has by now been so pounded into the veins and nerves of those gathered here that it can be accessed at any point. "All our sins, I mean *all* our sins and griefs—hear that, Lord?" The choir, Joryleen among them, hang on undismayed while this fat ecstatic snaps her arms back and forth, swings them for a moment in the mock-comic jaunty triumph of someone striding down a gangplank after crossing a stormy sea, and shoots out a pointing hand to the writhing reaches of the balcony, shouting, "Hear that? Hear that?"

"We hearin' it, sister," comes back a man's voice.

"Hear what, brother?" She answers the question: "*All* our sins and griefs to bear. Think of those sins. Think of those griefs. They're our babies, isn't that right? Sins and griefs, our natural-born babies." The chorus keeps dragging the tune along, but faster now. The organ clambers and jounces, the percussion sticks keep knocking out of sight, the fat woman shuts her eyes and slaps the word "Jesus" across the blindly continuing beat, shortening it to "Jeez. Jeez. Jeez," and breaking into, as if another song is leaking in, "Thank you, Jesus. Thank you, Lord. Thank you for the love, all day, all night." As the choir sings, "O what needless pain we bear," she sobs, "Needless, needless. We need to take it to Jesus, we need to, *need* to!" When the choir, still under the control of the small man with the high puff of hair, arrives at the last line, she does too, singing it, "Everything, *every-thing*, every little old thing to God in prayer. Yeaahuyess."

The choir, Joryleen's the widest-open, freshest mouth in it, stops singing. Ahmad finds his eyes heated and his stomach in such a stir he fears he might vomit, here among these yelping devils. The false saints in the soot-darkened tall windows look down. The face of a scowling white-bearded one burns with a passing beam of sun. The little girl has snuggled into his side without his noticing; suddenly heavy, she has fallen asleep in the heart of the huge, belting music. The whole rest of the family, down the length of the pew, smiles at him, at her.

He doesn't know if he should wait for Joryleen outside the church, as the worshippers in their pastel spring outfits push out into the April air, which is turning watery and chill as clouds overhead tarnish darker. Ahmad's indecision is prolonged while, half hiding behind a curbside locust tree that survived the demolition that created the lake of rubble, he satisfies himself that Tylenol was not in the crowd. Then, just as he decides to sneak away, there she is, coming up to him, serving up all her roundnesses like fruit on a plate. She wears a silver bead, holding a tiny reflection of the sky, in one nostril-wing. Beneath the blue robe all along there were the same sort of clothes she wears to high school, not dress-up church clothes. He remembers her telling him she doesn't take religion all that seriously. "I saw you," she teases. "Sitting with the Johnsons, no less."

"The Johnsons?"

"That family you were with. They are big church people. They own do-it-yourself laundry places downtown and over in Passaic. You've heard of the black *boor-shwa-zee*? That's them. What you staring at, Ahmad?"

"That little thing in your nose. I didn't notice it before. Just those little rings on the edge of your ear."

"It's new. You don't like it? Tylenol likes it. He can hardly wait till I get a tongue stud."

"Piercing your tongue? That's horrible, Joryleen."

"Tylenol says the Lord loves a sporty woman. What does your Mr. Mohammed say?"

Ahmad hears the mockery but nevertheless feels tall standing next to this short, ripe girl; he looks down past her face, with its gleam of mischief, to the tops of her breasts, exposed by a loose-necked springtime blouse and still glazed with the excitement and exertion of her singing. "He advises women to cover their ornaments," he tells her. "He says good women are for good men, and unclean women for unclean men."

Joryleen's eyes widen and she blinks her lids, taking this unsmiling solemnity as part of him, which she might have to deal with. "Well, I don't know where that leaves me," she says cheerfully. "Their notion of unclean was pretty broad in those there days," she adds, and brushes back some moisture from her temple, where the hair is fine like a boy's mustache before he thinks to shave. "How'd you like my singing?"

He takes thought, while the chattering congregants stroll past, their duty done for the week, and the in-and-out sun makes feathery weak shadows beneath the emergent locust leaves. "You have a beautiful voice," Ahmad tells her. "It is very pure. The uses to which it is being put, however, are not pure. The singing, especially of the very fat woman—"

"Eva-Marie," Joryleen supplies. "She's the *most*. She never gives it less than her everything."

"Her singing seemed to me very sensual. And I did not understand many of the words. In what way is Jesus such a friend to all of you?"

"What a friend, what a friend," Joryleen pants lightly, in imitation of the way the choir broke up the hymn's phrases suggesting the repetitive (as he understood them) motions of sexual intercourse. "He just is, that's all," she insists. "People feel better, thinking he's right there. If he isn't there caring, who is, right? The same thing, I 'spect, with your Mohammed."

"The Prophet is many things to his followers, but we do not call him our friend. We are not so cozy, as your clergy-man said."

"Hey," she says, "let's not talk this stuff. Thanks for coming, Ahmad. I never thought you would."

"You have been gracious to me, and I was curious. It is helpful, up to a point, to know the enemy."

"Enemy? Whoa. You didn't have no enemies there."

"My teacher at the mosque says that all unbelievers are our enemies. The Prophet said that eventually all unbeliev-ers must be destroyed."

"Oh, man. How'd you get this way? Your mother's just a freckle-faced mick, right? That's what Tylenol says."

"Tylenol, Tylenol. How close are you, may I ask, to this fount of wisdom? Does he consider you his woman?"

"Oh, that boy's just trying things out. He's too young to get fixed up with any one lady friend. Let's walk along. We're getting too many looks."

They walk along the northern edge of the empty acres waiting to be developed. A painted big sign shows a four-story parking garage that will bring shoppers back to the inner city, but for two years nothing has been built, there is only the picture, more and more scribbled over. When the sun, slanting from the south above the new glass buildings downtown, comes through the clouds, a fine dust can be seen lifting from the rubble, and when the clouds return the sun becomes a white circle like a perfect hole burned through, exactly the size of the moon. Feeling the sun on one side of him makes him conscious of the warmth on the other, the warmth of Joryleen's body moving along, a system of overlapping circles and soft parts. The bead above her nostril-wing gleams a hot pinpoint; sunlight sticks a glistening tongue into the cavity at the center of her scoop-necked blouse. He tells her, "I am a good Muslim, in a world that mocks faith."

"Instead of being good, don't you ever want to *feel* good?" Joryleen asks. He believes she is sincerely curious; in his severe faith he is a puzzle to her, a curiosity.

"Perhaps the two go together," he offers. "The feeling and the being."

"You came to my church," she says. "I could go to your mosque with you."

"That would not do. We could not sit together, and you could not attend without a course of instruction, and a demonstration of sincerity."

"Wow. That may be more than I have time for. Tell me, Ahmad, what do you do for *fun*?"

"Some of the same things you do, though 'fun,' as you put

it, is not the point of a good Muslim's life. I take lessons twice a week in the language and lessons of the Qur'an. I attend Central High. I am on the soccer team in the fall—indeed, I scored five goals this past season, one a penalty shot—and do track in the spring. For spending money, and to help out my mother—the freckle-faced mick, as you call her—"

"As Tylenol called her."

"As the two of you evidently call her—I clerk at the Shop-a-Sec from twelve to eighteen hours a week, and this can be 'fun,' observing the customers and the varieties of costume and personal craziness that American permissiveness invites. There is nothing in Islam to forbid watching television and attending the cinema, though in fact it is all so saturated in despair and unbelief as to repel my interest. Nor does Islam forbid consorting with the opposite sex, if strict prohibitions are observed."

"So strict nothing happens, right? Turn left here, if you're walking me home. You don't have to, you know. We're getting into worse neighborhoods. You don't want to be hassled."

"I wish to see you home." He goes on, "They exist, the prohibitions, for the benefit less of the male than of the female. Her virginity and purity are central to her value."

"Oh, my," Joryleen says. "In whose eyes? I mean, who's doing this valuing?"

She is leading him, he feels, close to the edge of betraying his beliefs, just in responding to her questions. In class, he observed at the high school, she talked well, so that the teachers became engaged with her, not realizing that she was leading them from the set lessons and wasting classroom time. She has a wicked streak. "In the eyes of God," he tells her, "as revealed by the Prophet: 'Enjoin believing women to turn their eyes away from temptation and to preserve their chastity.' That's from the same sura that advises women to cover their ornaments, and to draw their veils over their bosoms, and not even to stamp their feet so their hidden ankle bracelets can be heard."

"You think I show too much tit—I can tell by where your eyes go."

Just hearing the word "tit" from her lips stirs him indecently. He says, staring ahead, "Purity is its own end. As we were discussing, it is both being good and feeling good."

"What about all them virgins on the other side? What happens to purity when those young-men martyrs get there, all full of spunk?"

"Their virtue enjoys its reward, while remaining pure, in the context God has created. My teacher at the mosque thinks that the dark-eyed virgins are symbolic of a bliss one cannot imagine without concrete images. It is typical of the sex-obsessed West that it has seized upon that image, and ridicules Islam because of it."

They continue in the direction she indicated. The neighborhood grows shaggier around them; bushes are untended, houses unpainted, sidewalk squares in places tilted and cracked by tree roots underneath; the little front yards are speckled with litter. The rows of houses lack a few, like teeth knocked out, the gaps fenced in but the thick chain-link fencing cut and twisted under the invisible pressure of people who hate fences, who want to get somewhere quick. The row houses in some blocks become a single long building with many peeling doors and four-step stairs, old and wooden or new and concrete. Overhead, high twigs interlace with electric wires carrying electricity across the city, a sagging harp that dips through gaps lopped by tree crews. Spatters of blossom and unfolding leaf, in color between yellow and green, appear luminous against the cloud-blotched sky.

"Ahmad," Joryleen says with a sudden exasperation, "suppose none of it is true—suppose you die and there's nothing there, nothing at all? What's the point of all this purity then?"

"If none of it is true," he tells her, his stomach clenching at the thought, "then the world is too terrible to cherish, and I would not regret leaving it."

"Man! You are one in a million, no kidding. They must love you to death over at that mosque."

"There are many like me," he tells her, both stiffly and gently, half rebuking. "Some are"—he does not want to say "black," since the word though politically correct does not sound kind—"what you call your brothers. The mosque and its teachers give them what the Christian U.S. disdains to—respect, and a challenge that asks something of them. It asks austerity. It asks restraint. All America wants of its citizens, your President has said, is for us to buy—to spend money we cannot afford and thus propel the economy forward for himself and other rich men."

"He ain't my President. If I could vote this year I'd vote to kick him out, in favor of Al Sharpton."

"It makes no difference which President is in. They all want Americans to be selfish and materialistic, to play their part in consumerism. But the human spirit asks for self-denial. It longs to say 'No' to the physical world."

"You scare me when you talk like that. It sounds like you hate life." She goes on, revealing herself as freely as if she is singing, "The way I feel it, the spirit is what comes out of the body, like flowers come out of the earth. Hating your body is like hating yourself, the bones and blood and skin and shit that make you you."

Two

As when standing above that glistening trail of a disappeared worm or slug, Ahmad feels tall, tall enough to be dizzy, looking down at this short round girl whose indignation at his yearning for purity gives her voice and lips a lively quickness. Where her lips meet the other skin of her face there is an edge, a little line like the circle cocoa leaves on the inside of a cup. He thinks of sinking himself into her body and knows from its richness and ease that this is a devil's thought.

"Not *hate* your body," he corrects her, "but not be a slave to it either. I look around me, and I see slaves—slaves to drugs, slaves to fads, slaves to television, slaves to sports heroes that don't know they exist, slaves to the unholy, meaningless opinions of others. You have a good heart, Joryleen, but you're heading straight for Hell, the lazy way you think."

She has halted on the sidewalk, in a bleak, treeless stretch, and he thinks it is her anger at him, her disappointment near tears, that has stopped her, but then realizes that this drab doorway is hers, with its four wooden steps stained gray as if with never-ending rain. He at least lives in a brick apartment building on the north side of the boulevard. He feels guilty about her disappointment, since in inviting him to walk with her she laid herself open to expectation.

"You're the one, Ahmad," she says, turning to go in, planting a foot on the first drab step, "don't know where he's heading. You're the one don't know which fucking end is up."

Sitting at the heavy old round brown table that he and his mother call "the dining table" though they never dine at it, Ahmad studies the Commercial Drivers' License Home Study Course booklets, four of them, each stapled together.

Shaikh Rashid helped him send away to Michigan for them, writing the check for $89.50 on the mosque account. Ahmad always thought truck-driving was something for simpletons like Tylenol and his gang at school, but in fact there is a confusing amount of expertise to it, such as all the hazardous materials that have to be publicly identified one from another by means of four different placards measuring ten and three-quarters inches and placed in a diamond shape. There are flammable gases like hydrogen and poisonous/toxic gases like compressed fluorine; there are flammable solids like wetted ammonium picrate and spontaneously combustible ones like white phosphorus and ones spontaneously combustible when wet like sodium. Then there are real poisons like potassium cyanide and infectious substances like the anthrax virus and radioactive substances like uranium and corrosives like battery fluid. All this has to be trucked, and any spills of a certain quantity (depending on toxicity, volatility, chemical durability) must be reported to the DOT (Department of Transportation) and EPA (Environmental Protection Agency).

Ahmad is sickened, thinking of the paperwork, the shipping papers bristling with numbers and codes and prohibitions. Poisons should never be loaded with animal or human food; hazardous materials even in a tightly sealed canister should never ride up front with the driver; beware of heat, leaks, and sudden changes in speed. Besides hazardous substances there are ORM (Other Regulated Materials) that might have an anesthetic or irritating or noxious effect on a driver and his passengers, such as monochloroacetone or diphenylchlorarsine, and a material that might damage the vehicle if leaked, like the liquid corrosives bromine, soda lime, hydrochloric acid, sodium-hydroxide solution, and

Two

battery acid. All across this land, Ahmad now realizes, hazardous materials are hurtling, spilling, burning, eating roadways and truck beds—a chemical deviltry making manifest materialism's spiritual poison.

Then, the booklets tell him, there is, in shipping liquids by bulk in tanker trucks, outage, also called ullage, the amount by which the cargo falls short, so that the tank will not burst when its contents expand during shipping—if, say, ambient temperature goes as high as one hundred thirty degrees. And also, with tank vehicles, the driver must beware of liquid surge, more acute and dangerous in the case of so-called smooth-bore tanks than in that of those with inside baffles or complete compartments. Even in these, however, sideways surge can overturn a truck taking a curve too sharply. Forward surge can push a truck out into traffic at a red light or stop sign. Yet sanitation regulations forbid baffles in a tanker transporting milk or fruit juice; baffles make the tanks harder to clean, and hence invite contamination. Transportation is full of dangers that Ahmad has never before contemplated. It excites him, however, to see himself—like the pilot of a 727 or the captain of a supertanker or the tiny brain of a brontosaurus—steering a great vehicle through the maze of dire possibilities to safety. He is pleased to find in the trucking regulations a concern with purity almost religious in quality.

Somebody knocks at the door, at quarter of eight at night. The noise, not far from the table where Ahmad studies by the light of a battered bridge lamp, jolts him from his focus on ullage and tonnage, surge and flow. His mother quickly emerges from her bedroom, which is also her painting studio, and goes—rushes, even—to answer the knock, fluffing up her light red hair—nape-length, henna-enhanced—as

: 75 :

she goes. She greets mysterious interruptions more hopefully than Ahmad. He is still, ten days after attending the infidel church service, nervous about having trespassed on Tylenol's territory; it is not impossible that the bully and his gang will waylay him sometime, even at night, calling him out from his own apartment.

Nor is it impossible, though unlikely, that an emissary from Shaikh Rashid knocks. His master has few disciples. He has seemed on edge lately, as if something weighs upon him; he feels to Ahmad like a finely honed element in a structure on which too much tension is imposed. This past week the imam showed a short temper with his pupil in a discussion of a verse from the third sura: *Let not the infidels deem that the length of days we give them is good for them! We only give them length of days that they may increase their sins! and a shameful chastisement shall be their lot.* Ahmad dared ask his teacher if there wasn't something sadistic in the taunt, and in the many verses like it. He ventured, "Shouldn't God's purpose, as enunciated by the Prophet, be to convert the infidels? In any case, shouldn't He show them mercy, not gloat over their pain?"

The imam presented half a face, the lower half being hidden by a trimmed beard flecked with gray. His nose was thin and high-arched and the skin of his cheeks pale, but not pale as Anglo-Saxons or Irish were, freckled and quick to blush, like Ahmad's mother (a tendency the boy has regrettably inherited), but pale in a waxy, even, impervious Yemeni way. Within his beard, his violet lips twitched. He asked, "The cockroaches that slither out from the baseboard and from beneath the sink—do you pity them? The flies that buzz around the food on the table, walking on it with the dirty feet that have just danced on feces and carrion—do you pity them?"

Ahmad did, in truth, pity them, being fascinated by the vast insect population teeming at the feet of godlike men, but, knowing that any qualifications or signs of further argument would anger his teacher, responded, "No."

"No," Shaikh Rashid agreed with satisfaction, as a delicate hand tugged lightly at his beard. "You want to destroy them. They are vexing you with their uncleanness. They would take over your table, your kitchen; they will settle into the very food as it passes into your mouth if you do not destroy them. They have no feelings. They are manifestations of Satan, and God will destroy them without mercy on the day of final reckoning. God will rejoice at their suffering. Do thou likewise, Ahmad. To imagine that cockroaches deserve mercy is to place yourself above *ar-Raḥīm*, to presume to be more merciful than the Merciful."

It seemed to Ahmad that, as with the facts of Paradise, his teacher resorted to metaphor as a shield against reality. Joryleen, though an unbeliever, did have feelings; they were there in how she sang, and how the other unbelievers responded to the singing. But it was not Ahmad's role to argue; it was his to learn, to submit to his own place in Islam's vast structure, visible and invisible.

His mother may have hurried to the door in expectation of one of her male friends, but her voice in Ahmad's hearing backs off, puzzled and yet not alarmed, respectful. A polite, weary voice slightly familiar to Ahmad is announcing itself as Mr. Levy, the guidance counselor at Central High School. Ahmad relaxes; it is not Tylenol or anybody from the mosque. But why Mr. Levy? Their conference left Ahmad uneasy; the counselor communicated dissatisfaction with Ahmad's plans for his future and a desire to interfere.

How has he gotten this far, to the door? The apartment building is one of three erected twenty-five years ago to displace row houses so run-down and drugs-plagued that the administrators of New Prospect thought that ten-story stacks of mixed-income housing had to be an improvement. In addition, they calculated, the land taken under the right of eminent domain could be used for a park with recreational areas and, in the bargain, a curving parkway speeding commerce with towns where a "better element" prevailed. Yet, as with draining malarial land, problems returned: the sons of former drug dealers took up the trade, and addicts used the park benches and bushes and the apartment-house stairways, and raced back and forth in the hallways at night. The original plan called for a security guard at each entrance, but the city had to effect budget cuts, and the little offices with television monitors showing halls and doorways were erratically manned. *Back in 15 minits*, a hand-lettered sign would say for hours at a time. This time of evening, residents and visitors usually walked right in. Mr. Levy must have walked in and studied the mailboxes and taken the elevator and knocked on their door. Here he was, standing in the space this side of the door, off the kitchen, describing himself in a louder, more formal voice than he had used with Ahmad in the guidance conference. Then, he had seemed insinuating, lazy, and bone-weary. Ahmad's mother's face is flushed and her voice high and quick; she is excited by this visit from a representative of the distant bureaucracy that hovers above their lonely lives.

Mr. Levy senses her excitement and tries to put a calm face on things. "I apologize for invading your privacy," he says to a point midway between the standing mother and the sitting son, who does not get up from the brown table. "But when I tried the phone number on Ahmad's school records, I got a recording saying it had been disconnected."

"We had to, after Nine-Eleven," she explains, still a little breathless. "We were getting hate calls. Anti-Muslim. I had the number changed and unlisted, even if it does cost a couple dollars a month more. It's worth it, I tell you."

"I'm sorry to hear that, Mrs.—Ms.—Mulloy," the guidance counselor says, and he does seem sorry, above and beyond his usual sad look.

"There were just one or two calls," Ahmad interposes. "No big deal. Most people were cool. I mean, I was only fifteen when it happened. Who could blame me?"

His mother, with that infuriating way she has of making something of nothing, says, "It was more than one or two, I can tell you, Mr. Levine."

"Levy." He still wants to explain why he has shown up. "I could have called Ahmad to my office at the school, but it was you I wanted to speak to, Ms. Mulloy."

"Teresa, please."

"Teresa." He comes to the table and looks over Ahmad's shoulder. "At it already, I see. Studying for the CDL. As you realize, I'm sure, until you're twenty-one you can't get better than a 'C' rating. No tractor trailers, no hazardous materials."

"Yeah, I know," Ahmad says, pointedly looking down at the page he was trying to study. "But it's interesting, it turns out. I wanted to learn it all, while I'm at it."

"Good for you, my friend. For a young man as bright as you are, it should all be pretty simple."

Ahmad isn't afraid of arguing with Mr. Levy. He tells him, "There's more to it than you'd think. There's a lot of strict rules, and then there's all the parts of the truck and what you should do for maintenance. You don't want your truck to break down, it can be dangerous."

"O.K., you keep at it, son. Don't let it get in the way of your schoolwork, though; there's still a month to go, with a lot of exams. You want to graduate, don't you?"

"Yes, I do." He doesn't want to argue over everything, though in truth he resents the hint of a threat. They're dying to graduate him, get rid of him. And graduate into what? An imperialist economic system rigged in favor of rich Christians.

Mr. Levy, hearing his surly tone, asks, "Do you mind if I talk a minute with your mother?"

"No. Why would I? And what if I did?"

"You want to see me?" the woman affirms, to cover up her son's rudeness.

"Very briefly. Again, Mrs.—Ms.—whatever: Teresa!—I'm sorry to bother you, but I'm the kind of guy, when something is bothering me, my mind won't let me rest until I take action."

"Would you like a cup of coffee, Mr.—?"

"Jack. My mother called me Jacob, but people call me Jack." He looks at her face, with its flush and freckles and protuberant, overeager eyes. She seems anxious to please. School personnel don't get the respect from parents they used to, and with some of the parents you're an enemy like the police, only laughable because you don't have a gun. But this woman, though of a generation younger than his, is old enough, he guesses, to have had a parochial education and learned respect from the nuns. "No thanks," he tells her. "I'm a lousy sleeper anyway."

"I can do decaf," she promises, too eagerly. "Can you stand instant?" Her eyes are a pale green, like the glass bottles Coke used to come in.

"I'm tempted," he allows. "If it can be quick. Where can we go, to stop bothering Ahmad here? The kitchen?"

"It's too messy. I haven't cleared the dishes yet. I'd hoped to get to my painting while I still had some energy left. Let's go into my studio. I have a hot plate."

"Studio?"

"I call it that. It's also the room I sleep in. Ignore the bed. I have to multi-task, so Ahmad has *his* privacy in *his* room. We shared a room for years, maybe too long. These cheap apartments, the walls are like paper."

She opens the door she came out of, ten minutes ago. "Wow!" Jack Levy says, entering. "I guess Ahmad told me you painted, but—"

"I'm trying to work bigger, and brighter. Life's so short, I suddenly figured, why keep fussing at the details? Perspective, shadows, fingernails—people don't notice, and your peers, the other painters, accuse you of being just an illustrator. Some of my regulars, like a gift shop in Ridgewood that's sold me for ages, are a little bewildered by this new direction of mine, but I tell them, 'I can't help it, it's the way I've got to go.' If you don't grow, you die, right?"

Stepping around the carelessly made bed, its blanket tugged up roughly, he surveys the walls with a respectful squint. "You really sell this stuff?"

He regrets his phrasing; she goes defensive. "Some, not all. Not even Rembrandt and Picasso sold *all* their work, right away."

"Oh, no, I didn't mean . . ." he blusters. "They're very striking; you just don't expect it, walking in."

"I'm ex*peri*menting," she says, mollified and willing to go on, "with straight out of the tube. The viewer, that way, mixes the colors with his eye."

"Terrific," Jack Levy says, hoping to conclude this part of the conversation. He is out of his element.

She has got a kettle of water heating on the little electric coil set on a bureau whose top is crusty with spilled or wiped-off oil colors. He finds her paintings pretty wild but he likes the atmosphere in here, the messiness and the icy-clear fluorescent lights overhead. The smell of paints speaks to him, like the fragrance of wood shavings, of a bygone time when people made things by hand, hunched over in their own cottages. "Maybe you'd prefer herbal tea," she says. "Chamomile makes me sleep like a baby." Her eyes glance his way, testing. "Except when I wake up four hours later." *Needing to go pee*, she doesn't say.

"Yeah," he says. "That's the problem."

Cut short and knowing it, she blushes and tends to the water, which already is sending a plume of steam out through the hole in its hinged spout cap. "I forget what you said about what kind of tea. Chamomile or what?"

He resists this woman's New Age side. Next thing she'll be pulling out her crystals and *I Ching* sticks. He says, "I thought we had agreed on instant decaf, even though it always tastes scalded."

Her color stays high under her sifting of freckles. "If you feel that way about it, maybe you don't want anything."

"No, no, Miss—Mrs.—" He gives up trying to name her. "Anything wet and hot would be fine. Anything you want. You're being very gracious. I didn't expect—"

"I'll get the decaf and check on Ahmad. He hates studying when I'm not in and out of the living room; he feels he's not getting credit, you know?"

Teresa disappears, and when she comes back with a stubby jar of brown powder in her hand—a short-nailed, firm-fleshed hand that does things—Jack has turned off the hot plate so the water wouldn't boil away. Her mothering has taken some minutes; he could hear her in the other room bantering in a light, probing, female voice, and her son's scarcely deeper voice whining and groaning back at her with those inarticulate high-school denials he knows too well— as if the very existence of adults is a cruel and needless trial they're being put to. Jack tries to pick up on this: "So you see your son as a pretty typical, average eighteen-year-old?"

"Isn't he?" Her maternal side is a sensitive side; her beryl-green eyes bulge out at him between colorless lashes that must get mascara from time to time, but not today or yesterday. The hair at her hairline is a lighter, softer tint than the metallic red up top. The set of her lips, the plump upper one lifted a bit as with someone listening hard, tells him that he has used up her initial gush of friendliness. She comes on strong, then gets impatient, is his take.

"Maybe," he tells her. "But something's throwing him off." Jack gets down to the business he came for. "Listen. He doesn't want to be a truck driver."

"He doesn't? He thinks he does, Mr.—"

"Levy, Teresa. Like in 'Down by the levee' but spelled differently. Somebody's putting pressure on Ahmad, for whatever reason. He can do better than be a trucker. He's a smart, clean-cut kid, with a lot of inner-directedness. What I want him to have are some catalogues for colleges around here where it's not too late for admission. Princeton and Penn, it's way too late, but New Prospect Community College— you have to know where that is, up past the falls—and Fairleigh Dickinson and Bloomfield, he might get in, and could commute to any of them if you can't swing room and board. The thing would be to get him started somewhere and, depending how he does, hope to transfer up. Any college these days, the way the politics of it are, wants diversity, and your boy, what with his self-elected religious affiliation, and, pardon me for saying it, his ethnic mix, is a kind of minority's minority—they'll snap him up."

"What would he study at college?"

"What anybody studies—science, art, history. The story of mankind, of civilization. How we got here, what now. Sociology, economics, anthropology even—whatever turns him on. Let him feel his way. Few college students nowadays know what they want to do at first, and the ones that do get their minds changed. That's the purpose of college, to let you change your mind, so you can handle the twenty-first century. Me, I can't. When I was in college, who ever heard of computer science? Who knew about genomes and how they can track evolution? You, you're a lot younger than I, maybe you can. These new-style paintings of yours—you're making a start."

"They're very conservative, really," she says. "Abstraction's old hat." The open set of her lips has closed; his remark about painting was dumb.

He hurries to finish his pitch. "Now, Ahmad—"

"Mr. Levy. Jack." She has become a different person, sitting with her too-hot decaf on a kitchen stool bought unpainted and never varnished. She lights a cigarette and props one foot, in a crêpe-soled blue canvas shoe, on a rung and crosses her legs. Her pants, tight white jeans, bare her ankles. Blue veins wander through the white skin, Irish-white skin; the ankles are bony and lean, considering the soft heft of the rest of her. Beth's weight has had twenty more years than this woman's to settle low, drooping over her shoes and taking all the anatomy out of her ass. Jack, though he used to be a two-packs-a-day Old Golds man, has grown unused to people smoking, even in the school's faculty room, and the smell of burning tobacco is deeply familiar to him but verges on being scandalous. The stylized acts of lighting up, inhaling, and hurling smoke violently out of her pursed lips give Terry—how her paintings are signed, big and legibly, with no last name—an edge. "Jack, I appreciate your interest in Ahmad and would have been more so if the school had shown any interest in my son before a month before graduation."

"We're swamped over there," he interrupts. "Two thousand students, and half of them it would be kind to call dysfunctional. The squeakiest wheels get the attention. Your son never made trouble, was his mistake."

"Regardless, at this phase of his development he sees what college offers, those subjects you name, as part of godless Western culture, and he doesn't want more of it than he absolutely can't avoid. You say he never made trouble, but it was more than that: he sees his *teachers* as the troublemakers, worldly and cynical and just in it for the paycheck—the short hours and summer vacations. He thinks they set poor examples. You've heard the expression, 'above it all'?"

Levy merely nods, letting this now-cocky woman run on. What she might tell him about Ahmad could be a help.

"My son is above it all," she states. "He believes in the Islamic God, and in what the Koran tells him. I can't, of course, but I've never tried to undermine his faith. To someone without much of one, who dropped out of the Catholic package when she was sixteen, his faith seems rather beautiful."

Beauty, then, is what makes her tick—attempts at it on the wall, all that sweet-smelling paint drying, and letting her boy hang out to dry in grotesque, violent superstition. Levy asks, "How did he get to be so—so good? Did you set out to raise him as a Muslim?"

"No, Christ," she says, dragging deep, playing the tough girl, so that her roused eyes seem to burn along with the tip of the cigarette. She laughs, having heard herself. "How do you like that for a Freudian slip? 'No, *in nomine Domini.*' Islam meant nothing to me—less than nothing, to be accurate: it had a negative rating. And it meant not much more to his father. Omar never went to a mosque that I could see, and whenever I'd try to raise the subject he'd clam up, and look sore, as if I was pushing in where I had no business. 'A woman should serve a man, not try to own him,' he'd say, as if he were quoting some kind of Holy Writ. He'd made it up. What a pompous, chauvinistic horse's ass he was, really. But I was young and in love—in love mostly with him being, you know, exotic, third-world, put-upon, and my marrying him showing how liberal and liberated I was."

"I know the feeling. I'm a Jew, and my wife was a Lutheran."

"Was? Did she convert, like Elizabeth Taylor?"

Jack Levy snarls out a chuckle and, still clutching his unwanted college catalogues, admits, "I shouldn't have said 'was.' She never changed, she just doesn't go to church. Her sister on the other hand works for the government in Washington and is very involved in church, like all those born-againers down there. It may be just that around here the only Lutheran church is the Lithuanian, and Elizabeth can't see herself as a Lithuanian."

" 'Elizabeth' is a pretty name. You can do so much with it. Liz, Lizzie, Beth, Betsy. All you can do with Teresa is Terry, which sounds like a boy."

"Or like a male painter."

"You noticed. Yeah, I sign that way because female artists have always seemed smaller than the male ones, no matter how big they painted. This way, I make them guess."

"You can do a lot with 'Terry.' Terry cloth. Terri-ble. Terri-fy. And there's Terrytoons."

Two

"What's that?" she asks in a startled voice. As laid-back as she wants to appear, this is a shaky woman, who married what her harp brothers and father would have called a nigger. Not a mother who'd give a lot of firm guidance; she'd let the kid take charge.

"Oh, something from long ago—animated cartoons at the movie show. You're too young to remember. One of the things when you're ancient, you remember things nobody else does."

"You're not ancient," she says automatically. Her mind switches tracks. "Maybe on television I saw some, when I used to watch with little Ahmad." Her mind switches tracks again. "Omar Ashmawy was handsome. I thought he was like Omar Sharif. Did you ever see him in *Doctor Zhivago*?"

"Only in *Funny Girl*. And I went to see Streisand."

"Of course." She smiles, that short upper lip of hers exposing imperfect Irish teeth, the eyeteeth crowded. She and Jack have reached a stage when anything they say to each other is pleasing, their senses ratcheted up. Sitting with her legs crossed on the high unpainted stool, she preens, stretching her neck and doing a slow shimmy with her back, as if easing out a kink caused by standing at her easel. How seriously can she work at this stuff? He guesses she could slap out three a day if she tried.

"Handsome, huh? Does your son—"

"And he's a fantastic international bridge player," she says, not jumping her own track.

"Who? Mr. Ashmawy?" he asks, though of course he knows who she means.

"No, the other one, silly. Sharif."

"Does your son, I tried to ask him, have a picture of his father in his room?"

"What a strange question, Mr. —"

"Come *on*. Levy. Like a levy of taxes. School taxes, let's say. Or those things that keep the Mississippi from over-flowing. Get an association, that's what I do with names. You can do it, Terrytoons."

"What *I* started to say, Mr. Down-by-the-Levee, was you must be a mind reader. Just this year, Ahmad took the pho-tographs in his room of his father and put them face-down in drawers. He announced it was blasphemy to duplicate the image of a person God had made—a kind of counterfeiting, he explained to me. A rip-off, like those Prada bags the Nigerians sell on the street. My intuition tells me this terri-ble teacher at the mosque put him up to it."

"Speaking of terri-ble," Jack Levy says quickly. Forty years ago he thought of himself as a wit, quick on the verbal trigger. He even daydreamed about joining a team of joke writers for one of the Jewish comedians on television. Among his peers at college he had been a wise guy, a fast talker. "How terrible?" he asks. "Why terrible?"

Signalling with her hands and eyes toward the other room, where Ahmad might be sitting listening while pre-tending to study, she drops her voice, so Jack has to move a step closer. "Ahmad often returns disturbed from one of their sessions," she says. "I don't think the man—I've met him, but just barely—shows enough conviction to satisfy Ahmad. I know my son is eighteen and shouldn't be so naïve, but he still expects adults to be absolutely sincere and sure of things. Even supernatural things."

Levy likes the way she says "my son." There's a homier feeling here than his interview with Ahmad had led him to expect. She may be one of these single women trying to get by on sheer brass, but she's also some kind of nurturer. "The reason," he tells her, in a conspiratorially lowered voice,

"I asked about a picture of his father is that I wondered if his . . . if this faith of his had to do with a classic overestimation. You know—not there, you can do no wrong. You see a lot of that in, in"—why did he keep putting his foot in it?—"black families, the kids idealizing the absent dad and directing all their anger at poor old Mom, who's knocking herself out trying to keep a roof over their heads."

Teresa Mulloy does take offense; she sits so erect on the stool he feels the hard wood circle of the seat biting into her tightened buttocks. "Is that how you see us single moms, Mr. Levy? So thoroughly undervalued and downtrodden?"

Single moms, he thinks. What a cutesy, sentimentalizing, semi-militant phrase. How tedious it makes conversation these days, every possible group except white males on the defensive, their dukes up. "No, not at all," he backtracks. "I see single moms as terrific, Terry—they're all that's holding our society together."

"Ahmad," she says, loosening up a little immediately, the way a responsive woman does, "has *no* illusions about his father. I've made it very clear to him what a loser his father was. An opportunistic, clueless loser, who hasn't sent us a postcard, let alone a fucking check, for fifteen years."

Jack likes the "fucking"—loosening up fast. She was wearing instead of a painter's smock a man's blue work shirt, the tail hanging down and her breasts shaping the pockets from behind. "We were a disaster," she confides, her voice still kept low, out of Ahmad's hearing. As if stretching within the extra room of this confession, she arches her back, kittenishly, perched on the high bare stool, pushing her breasts out an inch farther. "He and I were crazy, thinking we ought to marry. We each thought the other had the answers, when we didn't even speak the same language, literally. Though his

English wasn't bad, to be fair. He'd studied it in Alexandria. That was another thing I fell for, his little bit of an accent, almost a lisp, kind of British. He sounded so refined. And always tidy, shining his shoes, combing his hair. Thick jet-black hair like you never see on an American, a little curl behind the ears and at the neck, and of course his skin, so smooth and even, darker than Ahmad's but perfectly matte, like a cloth that's been dipped, olive-beige with a pinch of lampblack in it, but it didn't come off on your hand—"

My God, Levy thinks, *she's getting carried away, she's going to describe his purple third-world prick to me.*

She feels his distaste and halts herself, saying, "Don't worry about any overestimation on Ahmad's part. He despises his father, as he should."

"Tell me, Terry. If his father was around, do you think Ahmad'd be settling for driving a truck for a job after graduation, with his SAT scores?"

"I don't know. Omar couldn't have done even that. He would have gotten to daydreaming and drifted off the road. He was a hopeless driver; even then, supposed to be a submissive young wife, I'd take the wheel of the car whenever I was in it. I said to him, 'It's my life, too.' I'd ask him, 'How are you going to be an American if you can't drive a car?' "

How had Omar gotten to be the subject? Is Jack Levy the only person in the world who cares about the boy's future? "You've got to help me," he tells his mother earnestly, "to get Ahmad's future more in line with his potential."

"Oh, Jack," she says, gesturing airily with her cigarette and swaying slightly on her stool, a sibyl on her tripod, pronouncing. "Don't you think people *find* their potential, like water does its level? I've never believed in people being pots of clay, to be shaped. The shape is inside, from the start. I've treated Ahmad as an equal since he was eleven, when he began to be so religious. I encouraged him at it. I'd pick him up at the mosque after school in the winter months. I must say, this imam of his almost never came out to say hello. He hated shaking my hand, I could tell. He never showed the slightest interest in converting *me*. If Ahmad had gone the other way, if he had turned against the God racket all the way, the way I did, I would have let that happen, too. Religion to me is all a matter of attitude. It's saying *yes* to life. You have to have *trust* that there's a purpose, or you'll sink. When I paint, I just *have* to believe that beauty will emerge. Painting abstract, you don't have a pretty landscape or bowl of oranges to lean on; it has to come purely out of *you*. You have to shut your eyes, so to speak, and take a *leap*. You have to say *yes*." Having pronounced to her satisfaction, she leans far over to a worktable and crushes out her cigarette in an ashy jar-lid. The effort stretches her shirt tight across her breasts and makes her eyes protrude. She turns those eyes, their glassy pale green, on her guest and adds as an afterthought, "If Ahmad believes in God so much, let God take care of him." She softens what sounds callous and flip in this with a pleading tone: "Your life isn't something to be *controlled*. We don't control our breathing, our digestion, our heartbeat. Life is something to be lived. Let it *happen*."

It has become weird. She has sensed his trouble, his desolation at four a.m., and is ministering to him, her voice massaging him. He likes it, up to a point, when women start undressing their minds in front of him. But he has stayed too long already. Beth will be wondering; he told her he had to swing by Central High for some college materials. This was not a lie; now he has distributed these materials. "Thanks for the decaf," he says. "I feel sleepy already."

"Me, too. And I got to be at work by six."

"Six?"

"The early shift at Saint Francis's. I'm a nurse's aide. I never really wanted to be a nurse, it was too much chemistry and then too much administration; they get to be as pompous as doctors. Nurse's aides do what nurses used to do. I like hands-on—dealing with people right down there at the level of their real needs. Bedpan level. You didn't think I made a living out of *these*?" She gestures, with those short-nailed hands that do things, at her gaudy walls.

"No," he admits.

She breezes on. "It's my hobby, my self-indulgence—my bliss, as that man on television used to say a few years ago. Some get bought, sure, but I hardly care. Painting is my *passion*. Don't you have a passion, Jack?"

He backs off; she is beginning to look possessed, a priestess on her tripod with snakes in her hair. "Not really." He gets out of bed in the morning as if pushing aside a blanket of lead, and bulls head-down into his day of waving kids good-bye as they slide off into the world's morass. "Have you ever thought," he can't help adding, "with your nursing, of urging Ahmad to become a doctor? He has a dignity, a presence. I'd trust him with my life, if I were sick."

Her eyes narrow, turning shrewd and—a word his mother used to use, mostly of other women—*common*. "It's a long expensive haul, Jack, a medical education. And the docs I know do nothing but complain about the paperwork and being pushed around by the insurance companies. It used to be a profession where you got a lot of respect and made a fair amount of money. But medicine isn't the field it used to be. It's going to get socialized one way or another eventually, and doctors will be paid like schoolteachers."

Two

He laughs at this little kick. She has a number of nimble moves. "And that's not good," he acknowledges.

"Let him wait for his passion," she counsels the guidance counselor. "For the moment it's trucks, getting on the move. He says to me, 'Mom, I need to see the world.' "

"As I understand the Commercial Driver's License, all he'll see until he's twenty-one is New Jersey."

"That's a start," she says, and nimbly slides off the stool. She has left undone the two top buttons of her paint-smeared man's work shirt, so he sees the tops of her breasts bounce. This woman has a lot of *yes* in her.

But the interview is over; it is eight-thirty. Levy lugs the three unwanted college catalogues back through the room where the boy is still studying, and halts at the heavy old dark round table—some kind of inheritance, it reminds him of the heavy sad stuff his parents and grandparents had in the house he grew up in, out on Totowa Road. Approached from behind, Ahmad's neck looks vulnerably thin, and the tops of his tidy, tight-whorled ears show a few freckles lifted from his mother. Levy gingerly sets the catalogues on the table's edge and touches the boy's shoulder, through the white shirt, to get his attention. "Ahmad, look these over some-time when you have a chance, and see if anything here piques your interest enough to discuss it with me. It's not too late to change your mind about applying."

The boy feels the touch and responds, "Here's something interesting, Mr. Levy."

"What?" He feels closer and easier with the boy, having met his mother.

"Here's a typical question of the kind they're going to ask."

Levy read over his shoulder:

55. You are driving a tank truck and the front wheels begin
    to skid. Which of these is most likely to occur?
        a. You will counter steer as necessary to maintain
           control.
        b. Liquid surge will straighten the trailer out.
        c. Liquid surge will straighten the tractor out.
        d. You will continue in a straight line and keep
           moving forward no matter how much you steer.

"Sounds like a pretty bad situation," Levy admits.

"Which do you think the answer is?"

Ahmad has felt the man approach, and then the presumptuous, poisonous touch on the shoulder. Now he is aware of, too close to his head, the man's belly, its warmth carrying out with it a smell, several smells—a compounded extract of sweat and alcohol, Jewishness and Godlessness, an unclean scent stirred up by the consultation with Ahmad's mother, the embarrassing mother he tries to hide, to keep to himself. The two adult voices had intertwined flirtatiously, disgustingly, two aged infidel animals warming to each other in the other room. Mr. Levy, having bathed in her babble, her insatiable desire to press upon the world her sentimental vision of herself, now thinks himself entitled to play with her son a paternal, friendly role. Pity and presumption prompt this unseemly, odorous closeness. Yet the Qur'an urges courtesy upon the faithful; this Jew, though self-invited, is a guest in Ahmad's tent.

The intruder lazily responds, "I don't know, my friend. Liquid surge isn't something I deal with very often. Let me opt for 'a,' the counter steering."

In a quiet voice that conceals the small surge of triumph within him, Ahmad says, "No, 'd' is the answer. I looked it up on the answer sheets they give you."

The belly next to his ear gives off a rumble of disquiet, and the unseen face above it grunts. "Huh. Don't bother to steer. That's sort of what your mother was just telling me. Relax. Follow your bliss."

"After a while," Ahmad explains, "the truck will lose speed on its own."

"The will of Allah," Mr. Levy says, trying to be funny, or friendly: trying to insert himself where Ahmad's insides are clenched shut, filled with the All-Encompassing.

The interface of Central High and its formerly extensive grounds with the city's private property has grown more complicated in the years since its playing fields stretched behind it, unfenced, toward a street of Victorian houses so varied and widely spaced as to be suburban. This area, to the northwest of the spectacular City Hall, was a domain of the middle class that pulled its money from the mills along the river, a short walk from the working-class tenements on the lower side of the then-bustling downtown. But the near-suburban houses became, as Jack Levy thinks of it, housing. Cost-cutting contractors broke them into apartments and subdivided their wide lawns or else tore them down to make room for solid blocks of low-rent row houses. The pressure of population and the encroachments of vandalism bore upon the grassy vacancies of school property and eventually caused the football field, which in the spring became a track-meet site, and the baseball grounds, whose outfield became in football season a junior-varsity gridiron, to be moved, in what seemed to various city boards a shrewd and profitable rearrangement, a fifteen-minute bus ride away, to the purchased land of an old dairy farm, Whelan & Sons Dairy, whose milk had contributed calcium to the bones of generations of New Prospect youngsters. The inner-city fields became congested slums.

The great high school and its several outbuildings were then walled off by Italian bricklayers whose work was later topped by glinting coils of razor wire. The immurement was piecemeal, a running response to various complaints and incidents of damage and explosions of spray-painted graffiti. The defaced, rusting fortifications created areas of unintended privacy, such as some square yards of cracked concrete alongside the half-buried yellow-brick edifice housing the giant boilers, originally coal-burning, that send steam, furiously knocking, into every classroom. One yellow-brick wall holds a basketball backboard whose hoop has been bent at a nearly vertical angle by boys imitating the dunk-and-hang style of NBA professionals. Twenty paces away, in the main building, double doors equipped with crash bars inside are in warm weather left propped open; they give onto steel stairs leading down to the basement floor with its locker rooms, boys' and girls' on either end, and, in between, the cafeteria and the wood and machine shops for the voke students. Underfoot, the cracks in the concrete hold crabgrass and mullein and dandelions and ridges of the minute particles, shining like coffee grounds, of the underlying earth which ants have brought to the surface. Where the concrete has been thoroughly undermined and pulverized, taller weeds, purslane and snakeroot and bedstraw and a species of daisy, have taken root and extend spindly stems up into the lengthening daylight.

In this gritty and unpoliced area, good for nothing with its deformed basketball hoop but to sneak a smoke or a sniff or a swig or to arrange showdowns between warring boys, Tylenol confronts Ahmad, who is still in his track shorts. A school-operated bus has brought him to the parking lot from practice on the former farm fifteen minutes away. Today he has ten minutes to shower and change and run the seven blocks to the mosque for his biweekly Qur'an lesson; he hoped to save some steps by cutting through to the double doors that should be open. This late after school, the area is usually empty, except for a few ninth-graders who accept the hoop at its ruined angle and use it for shooting baskets anyway. But today a cluster of blacks and Latinos, the gang allegiances declared by the blue and red of the belts on their droopy, voluminous drawers and their headbands and skull-fitting do-rags, are promiscuously mingled, as if the benign weather has declared a truce.

"Hey. You Arab." Tylenol stands square before him, flanked by several others wearing tight blue muscle shirts. Ahmad feels vulnerable, near-naked in his running shorts, his striped socks and feather-light cleats and sleeveless shirt sweat-soaked back and front in dark butterfly shapes; he has a sense of himself, his long limbs bare, as beautiful, beauty being an affront to the brutes of the world.

"Ahmad," he corrects, and stands there still with the heat of exertion, the heart-bursting sprints and jumps, rising from his pores. He feels luminous, and Tylenol's deepset little eyes wince, looking at him.

"Hear you went to church to hear Joryleen sing. How come?"

"She asked me to."

"Shit she did. You're an Arab. You don't go there."

"I did, though. People were friendly. One family shook my hand and gave me big smiles."

"They didn't know about you. You was there under false pretenses."

Ahmad stands lightly braced, his feet in their weightless shoes spread for balance, against Tylenol's coming assault.

But the pained squint becomes a smirk. "People seen you two walkin' after."

"After church, yes. So?"

Now, surely, the assault will come. Ahmad plans to feint left with his head and then sink his right hand into Tylenol's soft stomach, and then sharply lift his knee. But his enemy lets his smirk tear open into a grin. "So nothin', 'cordin' to her. She had somethin' she wanted me to tell you."

"Oh, yes?" The other boys, the blue-shirted minions, are listening. Ahmad's plan is that, having left Tylenol gasping and doubled up on the crumbling concrete, he will dodge between these astonished others for the relative safety of the school.

"She says she hates you. Joryleen says she don't give a flying fuck about you. You know what a flying fuck is, Arab?"

"I've heard the phrase." He feels his face go stiff, as if something warm is slowly coating it.

"So I don't care about you and Joryleen no more," Tylenol concludes, leaning in closer, almost as if amorous. "We laugh about you, the two of us. Especially when I fuck her. We fuck a lot, lately. A flying fuck is when you do it to yourself, like all you Arabs do. You all faggots, man."

The little audience around them laughs, and Ahmad knows from the heat on his face that he is blushing. This infuriates him to the point that when he blindly pushes through the muscular bodies toward the doors to the locker room, late now for his shower, late for his lesson, no one moves to stop him. Instead, there are whistles and hoots behind him, as if he is a white girl with pretty legs.

. . .

Two

The mosque, the humblest of the several in New Prospect, occupies the second floor above a nail salon and a check-cashing facility, in a row of small shops that includes a dusty-windowed pawn shop, a secondhand bookstore, a shoe-repair man and sandal-maker, a Chinese laundry down a little flight of steps, a pizza joint, and a grocery store specializing in Middle Eastern foods—dried lentils and fava beans, hummus and halvah, falafel and couscous and tabouli moldering in plain printed packages that look strange, in their lack of pictures and bold lettering, to Ahmad's American eyes. For four or so blocks to the west, the so-called Arab section, begun with the Turks and Syrians who worked as tanners and dyers in the old mills, stretches along this part of Main Street, but Ahmad never ventures there; his exploration of his Islamic identity ends at the mosque. The mosque took him in as a child of eleven; it let him be born again.

He opens a flaking green door, number 2781½, between the nail salon and the establishment, its big window masked by long blond Venetian blinds, that advertises CHECKS CASHED: *Minimal Fee.* Narrow stairs lead upward to *al-masjid al-jāmi'*, the place of prostration. The green door and the windowless long flight of stairs frightened him the first times he came here, searching for something he had heard about in the chatter of his black classmates concerning their mosques, their preachers who "didn't take none of the man's shit." Other boys his age became choir boys or joined the Cub Scouts. He thought he might find in this religion a trace of the handsome father who had receded at the moment his memories were beginning. His flighty mother, who never went to mass, and deplored the restraints of her own religion, humored him by driving him, those first times and afterwards, when her schedule permitted, until he was a teen-ager and relatively safe on the streets, to this mosque on the second floor. The large hall converted to worship was once a dance studio, and the imam's office has replaced the foyer where pupils in tap and ballroom dancing, accompanied by parents if they were children, waited for their lessons. The lease and conversion of the space dated from the last decade of the last century, but the close air still bears, Ahmad imagines, echoes of a piano being thumped and a whiff of awkward, unholy effort. The worn, wavery boards where so many labored steps were rehearsed are covered by large Oriental rugs, rug upon rug, which in turn show some wear.

A caretaker, a shrivelled elderly Lebanese with a bent back and lame leg, vacuums the rugs and tidies the imam's office and the children's nursery created to satisfy Western baby-sitting habits, but the windows, high enough to discourage spying, whether upon dancers or worshippers, are beyond the crippled caretaker's reach and semi-opaque with accumulated grime. Clouds are all that can be glimpsed through them, and these darkly. Even on Friday's *salāt al-Jumʿa*, when a sermon is preached from the *minbar*, the hall of prostration is underutilized, while the thriving modernistic mosques of Harlem and Jersey City fatten on fresh emigrants from Egypt, Jordan, Malaysia, and the Philippines. The Black Muslims of New Prospect, and the apostate adherents of the Nation of Islam, keep to their own lofts and storefront sanctuaries. Shaikh Rashid's hope of starting, in one of his third-floor spaces, a *kuttab* for teaching the Qur'an to flocks of elementary-school-age children, hangs short of fulfillment. Lessons that Ahmad seven years ago began in the company of eight or so others, in age from nine to thirteen, are now carried on by him as the only pupil. He is alone with the teacher, whose soft voice in any case carries best to a small audience. Ahmad is not utterly comfortable with his master, but, as the Qur'an and the Hadith enjoin, reveres him.

For seven years Ahmad has been coming twice a week, for an hour and a half, to learn the Qur'an, but he lacks opportunity in the rest of his time to use classical Arabic. The eloquent language, *al-lugha al-fushā*, still sits awkwardly in his mouth, with all its throat syllables and dotted emphatic consonants, and baffles his eyes: the cursive print, with its attendant spattering of diacritical marks, looks small to him, and to read it from right to left still entails a switch of gears in his head. As the lessons, having slowly marched through the holy text, undergo review, recapitulation, and refinement, Shaikh Rashid reveals his preference for the shorter, early Meccan suras, poetic and intense and cryptic compared with the prosy stretches in the book's first half, wherein the Prophet set about governing Medina with particularizing laws and mundane advisements.

Today the teacher says, "Let us turn to 'The Elephant.' It is the one hundred and fifth sura." Since Shaikh Rashid doesn't wish to pollute his student's carefully acquired classical Arabic with the sounds of a modern colloquial tongue, *al-lugha al-ʿāmmiyya*, in his rapid Yemeni dialect, he conducts the lessons in a fluent but rather formal English, speaking with some distaste, his violet lips, framed in his neat beard and mustache, pursed as if to maintain an ironical remove. "Read it to me," he tells Ahmad, "with some rhythmic feeling, please." He shuts his eyes the better to listen; his lowered lids show a few purple spider veins, vivid in the waxy-white face.

Ahmad recites the invocatory formula *"bi-smi llāhi r-rah-*

māni r-raḥīm" and, tensely because of his master's demand for a feeling rhythm, tackles aloud the long first line of the sura: *"a-lam tara kayfa faʿala rabbuka bi-aṣḥābi 'l-fīl."* His eyes still closed as he leans back against the cushions of the spacious silver-gray high-backed wing chair in which he sits at his desk and receives his student, who perches at the corner of his desk on a Spartan chair of molded plastic such as might be found in the luncheonette of a small-city airport, the shaikh admonishes, "Ṣ, ḥ: two distinct sounds, not 'sh.' Pronounce them as in, oh, 'asshole.' Forgive me; that is the sole word in the devils' language that comes to mind. On the glottal stop, don't overdo it; classical Arabic is not some African click-language. Sweep the sound in gracefully, as though it's second nature. Which it is, of course, for native speakers, and students sufficiently diligent. Maintain the rhythm, despite difficult sounds. Stress the last syllable, the rhyming syllable. Remember the rule? Stress falls on a long vowel between two consonants, or on a consonant followed by a *short* vowel followed by *two* consonants. Proceed, please, Ahmad." Even the master's pronunciation of "Ahmad" has the soft knife-edge, the soulful twist, of the pharyngeal fricative.

   "—a-lam yajʿal kaydahum fī taḍlīl—"

"Strengthen that '*līl*,'" Shaikh Rashid says, his eyes still closed, trembling as if with a weight of jelly behind them. "You can hear it even in the Reverend Rodwell's quaint nineteenth-century translation: 'Did He not make their guile to go astray?'" His eyes half open as he explains, "The men or companions, that is, of the elephant. The sura supposedly refers to an actual event, an attack on Mecca by Abraha al-ḥabashī, the governor, as it happens, of Yemen, the lavender land of my warrior ancestors. Armies in those days, of course, had to have elephants; elephants were the Sherman M1 tanks, the armored Humvees, of the time; let's hope they were equipped with thicker skins than the unfortunate Humvees supplied to Bush's brave troops in Iraq. The historical event was supposed to have occurred at about the time the Prophet was born, in 570 of the Common Era. He would have heard his relatives—not his parents, since his father died before he was born and his mother when he was six, but perhaps his grandfather, 'Abd al-Muṭṭalib, and his uncle, Abū Ṭālib—talking about this fabled battle, by the firelight of the Hashemite camps. For a time the infant was entrusted to a Bedouin nurse, and perhaps from her, it has been thought, he imbibed the heavenly purity of his Arabic."

"Sir, you say 'supposedly,' yet the sura asks in the first verse, 'Have you not seen?'—as if the Prophet and his audience *have* seen it."

"In his mind's eye," the teacher sighs. "In his mind's eye, the Prophet saw many things. As to whether the attack by Abraha was historical, scholars, equally devout and equally convinced that the Qur'an was of divine inspiration, differ. Read me the last three verses, which are especially profoundly inspired. Keep your breath flowing. Favor your nasal passages. Let me hear the desert wind."

"wa arsala 'alayhim ṭayran abābīl," Ahamad intones, trying to drop his voice into a place of gravity and beauty deeper in his throat, so he feels the holy vibration in his sinuses. *"tarmīhim b-ḥijāratin min sijjīl,"* he continues, gathering a walled-in resonance in at least his own ears, *"fa-ja'alahum ka-'aṣfin ma'kūl."*

"Better," Shaikh Rashid indolently concedes, waving in dismissal his soft white hand, whose fingers appear sinuously long, though his body as a whole, clothed in a delicately embroidered caftan, is slight and small. Beneath it he wears the white undertrousers called the *sirwāl*, and, level on his tidy head, the white brimless lacy cap, the *'amāma*, that identifies him as an imam. His black shoes, tiny and obdurate as a child's, peep out of the caftan's hem when he lifts them and rests them on the padded footstool in the same opulent fabric, containing the glints of a thousand silver threads, that covers the thronelike wing chair from which he delivers his teaching. "And what do these superb verses tell us?"

"They tell us," Ahmad ventures, blushing with the shame of sullying the holy text with a clumsy paraphrase, which furthermore depends less on his sight-reading of the ancient Arabic than on a surreptitious study of English translations, "they tell us that God loosed flocks of birds, hurling them against stones of baked clay, and made the men of the elephant like blades of grass that have been eaten. Devoured."

"Yes, more or less," said Shaikh Rashid. "The 'stones of baked clay,' as you put it, presumably formed a wall which then came down, under the barrage of birds, which remains somewhat mysterious to us, though presumably as clear as crystal in the graven prototype of the Qur'an that exists in Paradise. Ah, Paradise; one can hardly wait."

Ahmad's blush slowly fades, leaving on his face a crust of unease. The shaikh has closed his eyes again in reverie. When the silence stretches painfully, Ahmad asks, "Sir, are you suggesting that the version available to us, fixed by the first caliphs within twenty years of the Prophet's death, is somehow imperfect, compared with the version that is eternal?"

The teacher pronounces, "The imperfections must lie within ourselves—in our ignorance, and in the records that the first disciples and scribes made of the Prophet's utterances. The very title of our sura, for example, may be a mistranscription of Abraha's royal monarch, Alfilas, which a dropped ending left as *al-Fīl*—'the elephant.' One presumes that the flocks of birds are a metaphor for some sort of missiles hurled by catapult, or else we have the ungainly vision of winged creatures, less formidable than the Roc of *The Thousand and One Nights* but presumably more numerous, crunching their beaks upon the clay bricks, the *bi-ḥijāratin*. Only in this verse, the fourth, you will notice, are there any long vowels that do not come at the end of a line. Though he spurned the title of poet, the Prophet, especially in these early Meccan verses, achieved intricate effects. But, yes, the version handed down to us, while it would be blasphemy to call it imperfect, is, because of our mortal ignorance, in sore need of interpretation, and interpretations, in the course of fourteen centuries, differ. The exact meaning of the word *abābīl*, for example, remains after all this time conjectural, since it occurs nowhere else. There is a term in Greek, dear Ahmad, for such a unique and therefore undeterminable word: *hapax legomenon*. In the same sura, *sijjīl* is another mystery-word, though it occurs three times in the sacred book. The Prophet himself foresaw difficulties, and in the seventh verse of the third sura, 'The Imrans,' admits that some expressions are clear—*muḥkamāt*—but others are understood only by God. These unclear passages, the so-called *mutashābihāt*, are sought out by the enemies of the true faith, those 'with an evil inclination in their hearts,' as the Prophet expressed it, whereas the wise and faithful say, 'We believe in it; it is all from our Lord.' Am I boring you, my pet?"

"Oh, no," Ahmad answers, truly; for as his teacher murmurs casually on, the student feels an abyss is opening within him, a chasm of the problematical and inaccessibly ancient.

The shaikh, tilting forward in his great chair, is taking on a vehement energy of discourse, with indignant gestures of his long-fingered hands. "The atheist Western scholars in their blind wickedness allege the Sacred Book to be a shambles of fragments and forgeries slapped together in expedient haste and arranged in the most childish order possible, that of sheer bulk, the longest suras first. They claim to find endless obscurities and cruces. For example, there has been a recent, rather amusing controversy over the scholarly dicta of a German specialist in ancient Middle Eastern tongues, one Christoph Luxenberg, who maintains that many obscurities of the Qur'an disappear if the words are read not as Arabic but as Syriac homonyms. Most notoriously, he asserts that, in the magnificent suras 'Smoke' and 'The Mountain,' the words that have traditionally been read as 'virgins with large dark eyes' actually mean 'white raisins' of 'crystal clarity.' Similarly, the enchanting youths, likened to scattered pearls, cited in the sura called 'Man' should be rendered 'chilled raisins'—referring to a cooling raisin drink served with elaborate courtesy in Paradise while the damned drink molten metal in Hell. I fear this particular revision would make Paradise significantly less attractive for many young men. What say you to that, as a comely young man?" With an animation almost humorous, the teacher accentuates his forward tilt, resting his feet on the floor so that his black shoes flick out of sight; his lips and eyelids open in expectation.

Startled, Ahmad says, "Oh, no. I thirst for Paradise," though the abyss within him continues to widen.

"It is not merely attractive," Shaikh Rashid pursues,

"some distant place pleasant to visit, like Hawaii, but something we long for, long for ardently, is it not so?"

"Yes."

"So that we are impatient with this world, so dim and dismal a shadow of the next?"

"Yes, exactly."

"And even if the dark-eyed houris are merely white raisins, does that lessen your appetite for Paradise?"

"Oh, no, sir, it does not," Ahmad answers, as these other-worldly images swirl in his head.

Where some might take these provocative moods of Shaikh Rashid to be satiric, and indeed a dangerous flirtation with Hellfire, Ahmad has always taken them to be maieutic, a teasing-forth, from his student, of necessary shadows and complications, thus enriching a shallow and starkly innocent faith. But today the rub of maieutic irony feels sharper, and the boy's stomach chafes, and he wants the lesson to end.

"Good," the teacher pronounces, his lips snapping shut in a tight bud of flesh. "My own sense of it has always been that the houris are metaphors for a bliss beyond imagining, a bliss chaste and unending, and not literal copulation with physical women—warm, rounded, slavish women. Surely copulation as commonly experienced is the very essence of earthly transience, of vain joy. "

"But . . . ," Ahmad blurts, blushing again.

"But—?"

"But Paradise must be real, a real place."

"Of course, dear boy—what else? And yet, to continue briefly with this matter of textual perfection, even in the tamer declarations of the suras ascribed to the Prophet's Medina governance, infidel scholars claim to discover awkwardness. Could you read for me—I know, the shadows are lengthening, the spring day outside our windows is pathetically dying—read for me, please, verse fourteen from the sixty-fourth sura, 'Mutual Deceit.' "

Ahmad fumblingly finds the page in his dog-eared copy of the Qur'an, and makes his way aloud through *"yā ayyuhā 'lladhīna āmanū inna min azwājikum wa awlādikum 'aduwwan lakum fa 'hdharūhum, wa in ta'fū wa tasfahū wa taghfirū fa-inna 'llāha ghafūrun rahīm."*

"Good. I mean, good enough. We must work harder, of course, on your accent. Can you tell me, Ahmad, quickly, what it means?"

"Uh, it says that in your wives and children you have an enemy. Beware of them. But if you, uh, forgive and pardon and are lenient, God is forgiving and merciful."

"But your wives and children! What is 'enemy' about them? Why would they need forgiveness?"

"Well, maybe because they distract you from *jihād*, from the struggle to become holy and closer to God."

"Perfect! What a beautiful tutee you are, Ahmad! I could not have put it better myself. *'ta'fū wa tasfahū wa taghfirū'*— *'afā* and *safaha*, abstain and turn away! Do without these women of non-Heavenly flesh, this earthly baggage, these unclean hostages to fortune! Travel light, straight into Paradise! Tell me, dear Ahmad, are you afraid of entering into Paradise?"

"Oh, no, sir. Why would I be? I look forward to it, as do all good Muslims."

"Yes. Of course they do. We do. You gladden my heart. For next session, kindly prepare 'The Merciful' and 'The Event.' In numerical terms, suras fifty-five and fifty-six— side by side, conveniently. Oh, and Ahmad—?"

"Yes?" The spring day has passed, beyond the upward-

looking windows, into evening, an indigo sky too stained by
the mercury-vapor lights of inner-city New Prospect to
show more than a handful of stars. Ahmad tries to remember if his mother's hours at the hospital will permit her to be
home. Otherwise, perhaps there will be a cup of yogurt in
the refrigerator, or he else must risk the doubtful cleanness
of the Shop-a-Sec's snack provisions.

"I trust you will not be returning to the kafir church in the
center of town." The shaikh hesitates, and then speaks as if
quoting a sacred text: "The unclean can appear to shine, and
devils do good imitations of angels. Keep to the Straight
Path—*ihdinā 's-sirāta 'l-mustaqīm*. Beware of anyone, however pleasing, who distracts you from Allah's pure being."

"But the entire world," Ahmad confesses, "is such a
distraction."

"It need not be. The Prophet himself was a worldly man:
merchant, husband, father of daughters. Yet he became in
his forties the vehicle God chose through which to deliver
His final and culminating word." The cell phone that lives
deep in the shaikh's overlapping garments suddenly sounds
its trilling, semi-musical plea, and Ahmad seizes the moment
to flee out into the evening, out into the world with its
homeward rush of headlights and its sidewalk scents of fry-
ing food and of branches pale with blossoms and sticky
catkins overhead.

Corny as they are, and as many times as he has partici-
pated in them, commencements at Central High bring Jack
Levy near to tears. They all begin with "Pomp and Circum-
stance" and the stately procession of seniors in their swinging black robes and perilously perched mortarboard hats,

and end in the brisker, grinning, parent-greeting, high-fiving parade back up the aisle to the tunes of "Colonel Bogey's March" and "When the Saints Go Marchin' In." Even the most rebellious and recalcitrant student, even those with FREE AT LAST spelled out in white tape on their mortarboards or a sassy sprig of paper flowers interwoven with the tassel cord, appears subdued by the terminal nature of the ceremony and the timeworn pieties of the speeches. Contribute to America, they are told. Take your places in the peaceful armies of democratic enterprise. Even as you strive to succeed, be kind to your fellow-man. Think, in spite of all the scandals of corporate malfeasance and political corruption with which the media daily dishearten and sicken us, of the common good. Real life now commences, they are informed; the Eden of public education has swung shut its garden gate. A garden, Levy reflects, of rote teaching dully ignored, of the vicious and ignorant dominating the timid and dutiful, but a garden nevertheless, a weedy patch of hopes, a rough and ill-tilled seedbed of what this nation wants itself to be. Ignore the armed cops stationed here and there in the back of the auditorium, and the metal detectors at every entrance that isn't locked and chained. Look instead at the graduating seniors, at the smiling earnestness with which they perform, to loyal applause denied to none of them, not the dullest and most delinquent, their momentary march across the stage, under the Roxyesque proscenium, between banks of flowers and potted palms, to receive their diplomas from the hand of slick Nat Jefferson, head of the New Prospect school system, while their names are chanted into the mike by the acting high-school principal, tiny Irene Tsoutsouras. The diversity of names is echoed by that of the footgear displayed beneath the bouncing hems of their robes as they saunter forth in tattered Nikes, or strut by on stiletto heels, or shuffle past in loose sandals.

Jack Levy begins to choke up. The docility of human beings, their basic willingness to please. Europe's Jews dressing up in their best clothes to be marched off to the death camps. The male and female students, men and women suddenly, shaking Nat Jefferson's practiced hand, something they have never done before and will never do again. The broad-shouldered black administrator, a master surfer of local political waves as voting power has shifted from white to black and now to Hispanics, refreshes his smile for each and every graduating face, showing a special graciousness, in Jack Levy's eyes, to the white students, a distinct minority here. *Thank you for sticking with us*, his warmly prolonged handshake says. *We're going to make America / New Prospect / Central High work.* In the middle of the seemingly endless list, Irene reads out, *"Ahmad Ashmawy Mulloy."* The boy moves elegantly, tall but not ungainly, enacting his part but not overacting—too dignified to play, like some of the others, to partisans in the audience with waves and giggles. He has few partisans—sparse handclaps spatter. Situated in a front row between two other faculty members, Levy with a furtive knuckle attacks the incipient tears tickling both sides of his nose.

The benediction is offered by a Catholic priest and, as a sop to the Muslim community, an imam. A rabbi and a Presbyterian had delivered the invocations, both of them, for Jack Levy's money, at excessive length. The imam, in a caftan and tight turban of an electrically pure whiteness, stands at the lectern and twangs out a twist of Arabic as if sticking a dagger into the silent audience. Then, perhaps translating, he offers up in English, "Knower of the Hidden and the

Manifest! the Great! the Most High! God is the Creator of all things! He is the One! the Conquering! He sendeth down the rain from Heaven: then flow the torrents in their due measure, and the flood beareth along a swelling foam. And from the metals which are molten in the fire for the sake of ornaments or utensils, a like scum ariseth. As to the foam, it is quickly gone: and as to what is useful to man, it remaineth on the Earth. To those who graduate today, we say, rise above the foam, the scum, but dwell instead usefully upon the Earth. To those whom the Straight Path leads into danger, we repeat the words of the Prophet: 'Say not of those who are slain on God's path they are Dead; nay, they are Living!' " Levy studies the imam—a slight, impeccable man embodying a belief system that not many years ago managed the deaths of, among others, hundreds of commuters from northern New Jersey. From the higher vantages in New Prospect, crowds gathered to see smoke pour from the two World Trade Towers and recede over Brooklyn, that clear day's only cloud. When Levy thinks of embattled Israel and of Europe's pathetically few remaining synagogues needing to be guarded by police day and night, his initial good will toward the imam dissolves: the man in his white garb sticks like a bone in the throat of the occasion. Levy doesn't mind Father Corcoran's nasally nailing the triple Lord's blessing on the lid of the long ceremony; Jews and Irish have been sharing America's cities for generations, and it was Jack's father's and grandfather's generation, not his, that had to endure the taunt of "Christ-killer."

"Well, mon, we made it," the teacher on his right says. The speaker is Adam Bronson, an emigrant from Barbados who taught business math to tenth- and eleventh-graders. "Always I thank God when the school year gets by with no killings."

Two

"You watch too much news," Jack tells him. "We're no Columbine; that was Colorado—the Wild West. Central is safer now than when I was a kid here. The black gangs had zip guns, and there were no security gates or security guards. The hall monitors were supposed to be the security. They were lucky if they weren't pushed down the stairs."

"I could not at first believe when I came here," Adam tells him, in his hard-to-understand accent, music from a gentle island, a steel-drum pealing from a distance, "the policemen in the halls and cafeteria. In Barbados we shared books falling apart and used both sides of tablet paper, every scrap, education was so precious to us. We never dreamed of mischief. Here in this grand building you need guards as if in a jail, and the students do everything destructive. I do not understand this American hatred of decent order."

"Think of it as love of freedom. Freedom is knowledge."

"My students do not believe they will ever need business math in their heads. They imagine the computer will do everything for them. They think the human mind is on eternal holiday, and from now on has nothing else to do but absorb entertainment."

The faculty falls two by two into the procession, and Adam, paired with a teacher from across the aisle, steps ahead of Levy but then turns and continues the conversation. "Jack, tell me. There is something I am embarrassed to ask anyone. Who is this J-Lo? My students keep referencing him."

"Her. Singer. Actress," Jack calls ahead. "Hispanic. Very well turned out. Great ass, apparently. I can't tell any more. There comes a time in life," he explains, lest the Barbadian think him curt, "when celebrities don't do for you what they used to."

The teacher he has been paired with in the recessional is,

he now notices, a woman, Miss Mackenzie, twelfth-grade English, first name Caroline. Lean, square-jawed, a fitness freak, she wears her graying hair in an old-fashioned page-boy, the bangs cut level with her eyebrows. "Carrie," Jack says warmly. "What's this I hear about your assigning *Sexus* to your seniors?" She lives with another woman up in Paramus, and Levy feels he can josh her as he would another man.

"Don't be dirty, Jack," she says, not giving him a smile. "It was one of his memoirs, the one with Big Sur in the title. I had it on the optional list, nobody had to read it."

"Yeah, but what did those that did make of it?"

"Oh," her flat, incipiently hostile voice tells him, through the din and shuffle and recessional music, "they take it in stride. They've already seen it all, at home."

The entire human agglomeration of this gala event—graduates, teachers, parents, grandparents and uncles and aunts, nieces and nephews—pushes out of the auditorium into the front hall, where the athletic trophies stand watch in long cases like a dead Pharaoh's treasure, sealed in, the magical past, and out the broad front doors, thrown open to the sunshine of early June and the dusty vista of the lake of rubble, and down the great front steps, gabbing and cat-calling in their triumph. Once this grand granite staircase gave onto an ample green lap of lawn and symmetrical shrubs; but the demands of the automobile nibbled and then slashed at this margin, widening Tilden Avenue (defiantly thus renamed by the solidly Democratic board of aldermen in the wake of the 1877 theft of the Presidency by a Republican-dominated electoral commission colluding with a South anxious to have all Northern military protection of its Negro population lifted) so that now the lowest course of

granite impinges directly upon a sidewalk, a sidewalk sepa-
rated from the asphalt street by a narrow strip of sod that is
green only for a few weeks, before summer's baking heat and
a host of heedless footsteps beat its burst of vernal growth
into a flat mat of dead grass. Beyond the curb the asphalt
avenue, as rumpled as a hastily made bed with its patched
and repatched potholes and the tarry swales created by the
constant weight of rushing cars and trucks, has been closed
to traffic by orange-striped barricades for this hour, to give
the graduation crowd a place to stand and bask in self-
congratulation and to wait for the recent graduates to
turn in their gowns within the building and make their final
partings.

Milling in this crowd, in no hurry to go home and face the
start of a summer in the company of his wife, and morosely
feeling after his merry exchange with Carrie Mackenzie that
he is missing out in an anything-goes society, Jack Levy
bumps into Teresa Mulloy. Freckled and flushed in the heat,
she wears an already wilted orchid pinned to the rumpled
jacket of a pale linen suit. He greets her gravely: "Congrat-
ulations, Ms. Mulloy."

"Hello!" she responds, making an exclamatory occasion of
it, and lightly touching his forearm, as if to re-establish the
burgeoning intimacy of their last encounter. She tells him,
breathlessly grabbing the first words that come to her, "You
must have a wonderful summer ahead of you!"

The thought takes him aback. "Oh—same old same old,"
he tells her. "We don't do much. Beth has only a few weeks
off from the library. I try to pick up some pin money tutor-
ing. We have a son in New Mexico and we visit him for a
week in usually August; it's hot but not muggy the way it is
here. Beth has a sister in Washington, but that's even mug-

gier, so she used to come up to us and we'd go for a week or
so to the mountains somewhere, one side or other of the
Delaware Water Gap. But now she's so damn busy, always
some emergency or other, that this summer . . ." *Shut up,
Levy. Don't talk it to death.* Maybe it was good that the "we"
slipped out, reminding this woman he has a wife. He thinks
of them, actually, as being on the same continuum, with
their fair skins and tendency to plumpness, but Beth twenty
years farther along. "What about you? You and Ahmad."

Her outfit is staid enough—eggshell-colored linen suit
over a white chemise—yet colorful touches suggest a free
spirit, an artist as well as a mother. Clunky turquoise rings
weigh down those short-nailed, firm-fleshed hands of hers,
and her arms, showing haloes of fuzz candescent in the sunlight, hold a clicking horde of gold and coral bracelets. Most
surprisingly, a large silk scarf, patterned in angular abstract
shapes and staring circles, is knotted beneath her chin and
covers the hair of her head but for the blurred edge, with a
few stray reddish filaments, where it meets the Irish-white
bulge of her brow. Watching Levy's eyes with her own, and
seeing them fix on her jauntily demure head scarf, she laughs
and explains, "He wanted me to wear it. He said if there was
one thing he wanted for his graduation it was his mother not
looking like a whore."

"My goodness. But, anyway, it's oddly becoming. And the
orchid was his idea too?"

"Not really. The other boys do it for their mothers, and he
would have been embarrassed not to. He has this conformist
streak."

Her face with its protuberant green eyes, pale as beach
glass, seems in the scarf to look at him around a corner; its
covering poses a provocation, implying a dazzling ultimate

nakedness. Her head scarf speaks of submission, which stirs him. He moves closer in the press of the crowd, as if taking her under his protection. She tells him, "I spotted some other scarved mothers, Black Muslims quite dramatic in all their white, and some of the graduating daughters of the Turks—as a girl we called them 'Turks,' the dark men at the mills, but of course they all weren't. I was thinking, *I bet I have the reddest hair underneath*. The nuns would be thrilled. They said I flaunted my charms. At the time I wondered what charms were, and how you could flaunt them. They were just *there*, it seemed to me. My so-called charms."

She shares his tendency to babble, here in this excited crowd. He says quietly, meaning it, "You were a good mom, to humor Ahmad."

Her face loses its gleam of mischief. "He's asked so little, really, over the years, and now he's leaving. He's always seemed so alone. He did this Allah thing all by himself, with no help from me. Less than help, really—I resented that he cared so much about a father who didn't do squat for him. For us. But I guess a boy needs a father, and if he doesn't have one he'll invent one. How's that for cut-rate Freud?"

Does she know she is doing this to him, making him want her? Beth would never think to bring in Freud. Freud, who encouraged a century to keep on screwing. Levy says, "Ahmad looked handsome up there, in his robe. I'm sorry I began too late to get to know your son. I feel a fondness for him, though I suspect it's not reciprocated."

"You're wrong, Jack—he appreciates your wanting to raise his sights. Maybe he'll do it himself later. For now he's barreling ahead on the trucker's license. He passed the written exam and in two weeks takes the physical exam. For Passaic County it's over in Wayne. They need to make sure you're not color-blind and have enough peripheral vision. Ahmad has beautiful eyes, I've always thought. Inky. His father had lighter eyes, oddly, sort of gingerbread color. I say 'oddly' because you'd think Omar's would be the darker, with my pale ones in there."

"I see a shadow of your green in Ahmad's."

She ignores this flirtation and goes on, "But they're not twenty-twenty. Ahmad's. More like twenty-thirty—astigmatism—but he was always too vain to wear glasses. You'd think with all this piety he wouldn't be vain, but he is. Maybe it's not vanity, it's more that he thinks Allah would give you glasses if He wanted you to wear them. He had trouble seeing the ball in baseball; that was one of the reasons he took up track as his spring sport."

This tumble of sudden specifics about a boy not too different in Jack Levy's mind from the hundreds he deals with every year, intensifies his suspicion that this woman wants to see him again. He says to her, "I guess he won't be needing those college catalogues I dropped off a month ago."

"I hope he can still find them: his room is a mess except for the corner where he prays. He should have returned them to you, Jack."

"*No problema, señora.*" He notices around them, in the jostling, jubilant, but already dwindling crowd, other people glancing in their direction and giving them a little room, sensing that something is cooking here. He feels himself incriminated by Terry's overanimation as he tenaciously tries to match his smile to that on her round, bright, freckle-starred face.

The shadow of a big dark-hearted cloud sweeps the sunshine away and casts dullness upon the scene—the lake of rubble, the street from which traffic is barred, the bravely, brightly clad mob of parents and relatives, the civic façade of Central High School, its portals pillared and its windows barred, the height of it like the backdrop of an opera set dwarfing the singers of a duet.

"That was rude of Ahmad," his mother says, "not to return them to you at the school. Now it's too late."

"Like I said, no problem. Why don't I come by sometime and pick 'em up?" he asks. "I'll give a call ahead to make sure you're there."

As a kid, living over on Totowa Road when it was still pretty rural but for the new ranch houses, walking to school in the winter, Jack would sometimes venture out, to test his nerve, onto the ice of a marshy pond, long since built over, that he passed on the way. The water was not deep enough to drown in—cattails and grassy hummocks betrayed its shallow depth—but if he broke through, his good leather school shoes would be soaked and muddied and maybe even ruined, and in a family whose finances were as pinched as his family's, that would have been a disaster. At the silver edge of the cloud, sunshine breaks through, scintillating on Terry's silk head scarf, and he listens with trepidation for the ice to crack.

III

THE PHONE RINGS. Beth Levy struggles to extri-
cate herself from her favorite chair, a rocker recliner
called a La-Z-Boy, covered in a dull-brown vinyl imitating
creased cowhide and equipped with a lever-operated padded
leg rest, in which she has been sitting eating a plate of
oatmeal-raisin cookies—low in calories compared with
chocolate-chip or sandwich creams—while watching *All My
Children* on WABC before switching channels to *As the World
Turns*, on at two. She has often thought of putting a longer
cord into the jack so she can carry the phone over to her
chair and rest it on the floor for this part of her day, the days
when she doesn't go into the Clifton Library, but she never
remembers to ask Jack to buy the longer cord at the telephone store, which is way off in the mall on Route 23. When
she was a girl you just called AT&T and they sent a man in
a gray (or was it green?) uniform and black shoes who fixed
everything for a few dollars. It was a monopoly, and she
knows this was a bad thing—calling long-distance, you were

charged for every minute, and now she can talk to Markie or Herm for hours and it costs next to nothing — but also now there is no fixing phones. You throw them out, just like old computers and yesterday's paper.

Also, at some level she doesn't want to make her life any physically easier for herself than it already is; she needs every pitiful ounce of exercise she gets. When she was younger and married, she spent all the morning running around making beds and vacuuming and putting dishes away, but she became so expert she can do these things almost in her sleep; just sleepwalking through a room she makes the beds and tidies things up, though it's true she doesn't vacuum the way she once did — the new machines are lighter and she knows are supposed to be more efficient, but she never has the right brush for the end of the hose and finds the little storage compartment the vacuum part carries around inside itself difficult to unlatch; it's almost like a puzzle putting things together, compared with the old uprights that you just switched on and that set up vacuumed breadths on the carpet like a lawnmower on the lawn, with the sweet little light in front, like a snowplow at night. She hardly noticed any exertion, doing housework. But then she had less weight to move around — it is her cross to bear, her mortification, as religious people used to say.

A lot of her colleagues at the Clifton Library and all the young people who come in and out have cell phones right in their purses or clipped on their belts, but Jack says it's a racket, the charges add up, like on cable TV, which was something she wanted, not him. The so-called electronic revolution, to hear Jack tell it, has brought about a wealth of schemes for painlessly extracting money from us in monthly charges for services we don't need, but with cable the picture is certainly clearer—no ghosts, no wobble and twitch—and the choices are so much more there was no comparison; he himself turns on the History Channel some nights. Though he claims books are much better and deeper, he almost never finishes one through. About cell phones he actually told her, right to her face, that he doesn't want to be reached all the time, especially if he's in a tutorial—if she has a health emergency she should call 911, not him. This isn't very subtle. There's a level, she knows, at which he wouldn't mind if she were dead. It would be two hundred forty pounds less on his shoulders. On the other hand she knows he will never leave her: his Jewish sense of responsibility and a sentimental loyalty, which must be Jewish too. If you've been persecuted and reviled for two thousand years, being loyal to your loved ones is just good survival tactics.

They *are* special, the Bible wasn't wrong about that. At work in the library, they make all the jokes and have the ideas. Until she and Jack met at Rutgers, it was as if she had never been touched by human electricity before. The other women he had known, including his mother, must have been very clever. Very Jewish-intellectual. He thought she was funny, so relaxed and light-hearted and, though he never quite said it, naïve. He told her she had grown up wrapped in the Lutheran Daddy-Bear God. He peeled back the covering on her nerves and thrust himself at her; he bore into her, all over, thinner himself then, and full of himself, a born teacher it turned out, glib, quick, thinking he might become a gag writer for Jack Benny, or was it Milton Berle at that point?

Who knows where he is now, out somewhere on this impossibly sticky hot summer day when she can hardly move. She'd rather be at work, where they at least have

Three

effective air-conditioning; the one tucked in their bedroom window mostly just makes noise, and he has always begrudged the electricity for one downstairs. Men, they roam, participating in the society. She had always tended to be quiet, certainly next to Hermione, prattling away with her theories and ideals. Their parents drove her crazy, she said, always stodgily accepting whatever the unions and the Democrats and *The Saturday Evening Post* dished out, whereas Elizabeth found their stodgy passivity comforting. She had always been drawn to quiet places, parks and cemeteries and libraries before they became noisy, some of them even with background music like restaurants, half of what people checked out were tapes and now DVDs. As a girl she had loved living on Pleasant Street, within an easy walk of Awbury Park, so much green space and, a little beyond, the Arboretum off Chew, the weeping beech like a great green igloo around you and her notion of Heaven somehow caught up in the swaying tops of those tall, tall trees, the poplars showing white undersides in the slightest breeze as if there were live spirits inside, you can see how primitive people worshipped trees once. The other direction took you, by the trolley that ran on Germantown Avenue just a block away, to Fairmont Park, which was truly endless, with the Wissahickon flowing through, the stop at the Lutheran Theological Seminary with its sweet old stone buildings and the seminarians so young and handsome and dedicated; you could see them on the walks, in the shade, there wasn't all this guitar music and women clergymen and talk about same-sex marriages then. The young people in the library talk out like they're in their own living rooms, it's the same at the movies, there are no manners any more, television has ruined everybody's. When she and Jack fly to New Mexico

: 123 :

to visit Markie in Albuquerque, the disrespectful way the other passengers wear shorts and what look like pajamas on the plane: television has made people at home now everywhere, not caring how they look, women absolutely as fat as she wearing shorts; they must never look in the mirror.

Working four days a week at the library, she can't watch enough of the midday serials to follow every twist of the plot, but the plots, three or four plots intertwined the way they do it now, move slowly enough she doesn't feel left out. It's become a habit with her lunch, to take the sandwich or the salad, or the microwaved leftovers from a few nights ago, Jack never seems to finish what's on his plate any more, and for dessert a bit of cheesecake or a few cookies, oatmeal-raisin if she's on a binge of being virtuous, and settle in the chair and let it wash over her, all the young actors and actresses, usually two or three at a time in one of those sets that look too large, with everything new-bought, to be a real room, with a stagy echo in the air, and that kind of tingling music they all use, not organ music as in the old radio serials but a synthesized, she supposes is the word, sound almost like a harp at moments and then at others like a xylophone with violins, everything on tiptoe to convey suspense. The music underlines the dramatic confessional or confrontational utterances that leave the actors staring at each other in stunned close-up, their eyeballs glazed with sorrow or animosity, little bridges constantly being crossed in the endless lattice of their relationships: "I really don't give a damn about Kendall's welfare. . . ." "Surely you knew that Ryan never wanted to have children; he was terrified of the family curse. . . ." "My whole life seems just out of my reach. I don't know who I am or what I think any more. . . ." "I can see it in your eyes; everybody loves a winner. . . ." "You've got to love yourself enough to walk away from that man. Let your mother have him if that's what she wants—they deserve each other. . . ." "I truly, deeply hate myself. . . ." "I feel lost in the desert. . . ." "I never paid for sex in my life, and I'm not starting now." And then a less angry, frightened voice, directly at the viewer: "A woman's curves can mean chafing. The makers of Monistat understand this intimate problem, and are therefore introducing a new, wholly unprecedented product."

To Beth it seems the young female actresses talk in a new way, the words curling under at the ends of sentences, back into their throats like the start of a gargle, and they seem more natural, or less unnatural and plasticky, than the young men, who look more like mere actors than the women do actresses—more like Ken, Barbie's opposite-sex partner, than the girls do Barbie. When there are three characters on the screen it is usually two women undercutting each other over a boy-man who stands there squirming with a frozen jaw, and if there are four, one man is older with beautifully grayed hair, like the Before head in commercials for Grecian Formula, and the crosscurrents in the air thicken until the swelling, eerie music rescues them momentarily by signalling that it is time for another cluster of "messages." Beth is fascinated to think that this is life, all this competing to the point of murder, sex and jealousy and financial greed driving them to it, these supposedly ordinary people in the typical Pennsylvania community of Pine Valley. She's from Pennsylvania and never knew a place like it. How has she missed life, so much of it? "My whole life seems just out of my reach," one character on *All My Children* once said, maybe Erin. Or Krystal. The remark went right through Beth like an arrow. Loving parents; a happy though not quite conven-

tional marriage; a wonderful only child; intellectually interesting, physically untaxing work checking out books and
looking up subjects on the Internet: the world has conspired
to make her soft and overweight, insulated against the passion and danger that crackle wherever people truly rub
against one other. "Ryan, I want so much to help you, I'd do
truly anything; I'd poison your mother for you if you asked."
Nobody says such things to Beth; the most extreme thing
that ever happened to her was her parents' refusing to show
up at her civil wedding to a Jew.

The men-boys who receive these burning vows are usually
slow to answer. There is an eerie, full quality to the silence
in the gap of non-conversation. Beth often fears they
have forgotten their lines, but then they say the next thing,
after *such* a long pause. To a degree not true of evening
programs—cop shows, comedies, news hours with their
bantering desk of four (one male and one female newscaster,
a peppy sports reporter, and, the butt of their humor and
good-natured grousing, the slightly goofy weatherman)—
the daytime soap operas take place against a background of
thick, teeming silence, a silence that all the erotic declarations, tense confessions, false assurances, and seething ani-
mosities cannot blot out, nor can the otherworldly chiming
music and the sudden intervention of the lame pop song that
does for a closing theme. A terrifying silence is the ground
that holds them all there, like magnets on a refrigerator
door, the cast in its echoing three-sided rooms and Beth in
her extra-wide armchair, vexed with herself because she did
not bring quite enough oatmeal cookies on her plate and
now the phone won't stop ringing so she must abandon her
La-Z-Boy island of perfect padded comfort even as David,
the impossibly handsome cardiologist ominously uttering

charged words to Maria, the gorgeous brain surgeon whose husband, the Pulitzer Prize–winning journalist Edmund, was murdered in an earlier episode Beth unfortunately missed.

She rises in stages, first pulling the lever to lower the foot-rest and, fighting the rocker motion, transferring her feet to the floor and gripping the left arm of the chair with both hands to tug herself almost up, and finally, with an audible exclamation, heaving her weight onto her braced knees, which slowly, excruciatingly straighten, while she catches her breath. At the start of the process, she thought to place the empty plate on the chair arm safely onto the side table, but she forgot the television remote in her lap, and it falls to the floor. She sees it there, the numbered buttons of its little rectangular panel down with the spots of coffee and spilled food that have accumulated over time on the pale-green carpet. Jack warned her that the carpet would show dirt, but pale wall-to-wall was in that year, the carpet sales-man said. "It gives a cool, contemporary look," he assured her. "It expands the space." Everybody knows Orientals are best for spots blending in, but when could she and Jack ever afford an Oriental? There's a place on Reagan Boulevard where you can get them secondhand at a bargain price, but she and Jack never go that way together, it's where mostly blacks shop. Anyway, used, you don't know what the previous people have spilled that's hidden in the fibers, and the idea is distasteful, like carpets in hotel rooms. Beth can't bear to think of turning her body around and bending over to pick up the remote—her sense of balance is getting worse with age—and there must be some urgent reason why the person on the phone doesn't hang up. For a while they had an answering machine attached, but there were so many crank calls from parents whose children didn't get into the colleges Jack advised that they had the machine taken out. "If I'm there, I'll cope," he said. "People aren't so damn nasty when they get an actual voice on the other end."

Beth takes another step, leaving the people on television to stew in their own abundant juices, and totters to the table by the wall and plucks up the telephone. The new style of telephone stands upright in its cradle, and a little panel below the perforations to listen at supposedly gives you the name and number calling. It says OUT OF AREA, so it's either Markie or her sister in Washington or some telemarketer calling from wherever they call from—it can be as far away as India. "Hello?" The perforations at the other end of the receiver don't come to her mouth the way the old phones did, the hefty simple ones of honest black Bakelite that rested face-down in a cradle, and Beth tends to raise her voice because she doesn't trust it.

"Beth, it's Hermione." Herm always sounds ostentatiously brisk, busy, as if to shame her younger, indolent, self-pampered sister. "What took you so long? I was about to hang up."

"Well, I wish you had."

"That's not very nice to say."

"I'm not like you, Herm. I'm not still fast on my feet."

"Who's that talking in the background? Is somebody there?" Her words jump on things, one after another. Yet her bluntness, almost rude, is a welcome leftover from the Pennsylvania-Dutch manner of their girlhood. It reminds Beth of home, of northwest Philadelphia with all its humid greenery and trolley cars and corner grocery stores stacked with Maier's and Freihofer's bread.

"It's the television. I was looking for the clicker to turn it

Three

off"—she doesn't want to admit she was too lazy and unwieldy to bend over and pick it up—"and couldn't find the gosh-darn thing."

"Well, go find it. It can't be far. I can wait. We can't talk with all that babbling. What were you watching anyway, in the middle of the day?"

Beth puts the receiver down without answering. *She sounds like Mother*, she thinks, plodding over to where the remote—curiously similar to the telephone in look and feel, matte black and packed with circuitry: a pair of mismatched sisters—lies on its back on the pale-green wall-to-wall. The salesman called it celadon. With a groan of effort, gripping the chair arm with one hand and reaching down with the other in an exertion that reawakens in her little-used muscles the sensation of an exercise, an *arabesque penchée*, learned in ballet lessons when she was eight or nine, at Miss Dimitrova's Studio, above a cafeteria downtown on Broad Street, she retrieves the thing and points it at the television screen, where *As the World Turns* is winding up on Channel Seven, under a cloud of tingling, ominous music. Beth recognizes Craig and Jennifer, in heated conference, and wonders what they are saying even as she clicks them off. They turn into a little star that lingers less than a second.

In ballet class she had been the more lithe and promising sister; Hermione, Miss Dimitrova would say in her scornful White Russian way, lacked *ballon*. "Light, *light*," she would shout, the ligaments jumping in her scrawny throat. "*Vous avez besoin de légèreté! Conceive that you are des oiseaux!* You are the creatures of air!" Hermione, gawkily tall for her age and already, it was clear, destined to be plain, was the heavy-footed plodder then, and Beth the one who felt, *en faisant des pointes*, birdlike, whirling with her skinny arms extended.

: 129 :

"You're panting," Hermione accuses her when Beth returns to the phone and drops her body with a grunt onto the little hard chair that came in from the kitchen table when Mark was no longer around to eat with his parents. A maple reproduction Shaker, the chair has such a narrow seat that she has to aim her bottom at it; a few years ago she half missed and the chair tipped and dumped her onto the floor. She could have broken her pelvis if she weren't so well upholstered, Jack said. But he wasn't amused at first. He rushed over to her horrified and, when she made clear she wasn't injured, looked disappointed. Hermione asks sharply, "You weren't watching some special announcement, were you?"

"On the television? No—is there one?"

"No, but"—her hesitation is fraught, like the pauses in soap operas—"there are leaks. Things get out before they should."

"What's getting out?" Beth asks, knowing that bland ignorance was the way to open up Hermione, with her itch to lord it over her sister.

"Nothing, darling. I of course can't say." But, unable to bear Beth's silence, she goes on, "Internet chatter is up. We think something's brewing."

"Oh, dear," Beth says docilely. "How's the Secretary taking it?"

"The poor saint. He's *so* conscientious, the whole country on his shoulders, I'm honestly afraid it might kill him. He has high blood pressure, you know."

"He looks pretty healthy on TV. I wonder, though, if he could use a slightly different haircut. It makes him look belligerent. It puts the Arabs and the liberals on the defensive." She can't chase from her mind the image of one more oatmeal-raisin cookie—how it would crumble in her mouth, her saliva leaving the raisins for her tongue to find and fiddle with before she bites down. She used to settle with a cigarette for a phone chat; then the Surgeon General kept telling her it was bad for her, so she gave it up and gained thirty pounds the first year. Why should the government care if the people died? It didn't own them. That many less to govern, she would think they'd be relieved. But, oh yes, lung cancer was a drain on Medicare, and cost the economy millions of productive work-hours. "I suspect," Beth offers helpfully, "a lot of this chatter is just high-school and college kids making mischief. Some of them, I know, call themselves Mohammedans just to annoy their parents. There's this boy at the high school Jack has been advising. He thinks he's a Muslim because his deadbeat father was, at the same time ignoring this hardworking Irish-Catholic mother he lives with. Think of what our parents would have said if we'd brought home Muslim men to marry."

"Well, you did the next-best thing," Hermione tells her, paying her back for the haircut criticism.

"Poor Jack," Beth continues, rising above the slur, "he's been knocking himself out to get this boy out of the grip of his mosque. They're like Baptist fundamentalists, only worse, because they don't care if they die." A born peacemaker—maybe all younger sisters are—she reverts to Hermione's favorite subject. "Tell me what he's especially worried about these days. The Secretary."

"Ports," came the ready answer. "Hundreds of container ships go in and out of our American ports every day, and nobody knows what's in a tenth of them. They could be bringing in atomic weapons labelled Argentinean cowhides or something. Brazilian coffee—who's sure it's coffee? Or think of these huge tankers, not just the oil, but, say, liquid propane. That's how they ship propane, liquefied. But think of what would happen in Jersey City or under the Bayonne Bridge if they got to it with just a few pounds of Semtex or TNT. Beth, it would be a conflagration: thousands dead. Or the New York subways—look at Madrid. Look at Tokyo a few years ago. Capitalism has been so *open*—that's how it has to be, to make it work. Think of a few men with assault rifles in a mall anywhere in America. Or in Saks or Bloomingdale's. Remember the old Wanamaker's? How we used to go there as children with such happy hearts? It seemed a paradise, especially the escalators and the toy department on the top floor. All that's gone. We can never be happy again—we Americans."

Beth feels sorry for Hermione, taking everything so much to heart, and says, "Oh, don't most people just bumble along still? There's always some kind of danger in life. Plagues, wars. Tornadoes out in Kansas. People keep going. You go on living until you're made to stop, and then you're unconscious."

"That's it, that's just it, Betty, they're working on stopping us. Everywhere, anywhere—all it takes is a little bomb, a few guns. An open society is so *defenseless*. Everything the modern free world has achieved is so *fragile*."

Only Hermione still called her Betty, and only then when she was miffed. Jack and her college friends called her Beth, and after she was married even her parents tried to switch over. To erase the little slip-up, Hermione courts her, trying to enlist her in her own infatuation with the Secretary. "He and these experts we have try to think day and night of worst-case scenarios. For instance, Beth, computers. We've built them into the system so that everybody's dependent, not just libraries but industry, and banks, and brokerage houses, and the airlines, and nuclear-power plants—I could go on and on."

"I don't doubt it."

Hermione entirely misses the sarcasm, going on, "There could be what they call a cyberattack. They have these worms that get by the firewalls and plant these applets, they call them, that send back covert messages describing the network they've penetrated and paralyzing everything, scrambling what they call the routing tables and getting by the gateway protocols so that not just the stock market and traffic lights but everything freezes—the power grids, the hospitals, the Internet itself, can you imagine? The worms would be programmed to spread and spread until even that television you were watching would go on the fritz, or else show nothing but Osama bin Laden on all the channels."

"Herm, honey, I haven't heard anybody say 'on the fritz' since Philadelphia. Aren't these worms and viruses being sent out all the time, and the source turns out to be some pathetic maladjusted teen-ager sitting in his grubby room in Bangkok or the Bronx? They make a little mess for a while but they don't bring the world down. They get caught and put in jail, eventually. You're forgetting all the clever men, and women too, that design these firewalls or whatever. Surely they can keep ahead of a few fanatic Arabs—it's not as if they invented the computer like we did."

"No, but they invented zero, as you may not know. They don't need to invent the computer to wipe us out with it. The Secretary calls it cyberwar. That's what we're in, like it or not, cyberwar. The worms are already out there running around; the Secretary every day has to sift through hundreds of reports that tell him about attacks."

"The cyberattacks."

"That's right. You think it's funny, I can tell from your voice, but it's not. It's deadly serious, Betty."

This Shaker chair is beginning to hurt. They must have had different body types back then, the Quakers and the Puritans: different philosophies about comfort and necessity. "I don't think it's funny, Herm. Of course very bad things can happen, some already have, but—" She forgets what the "but" was to preface. She thinks of walking with the portable phone into the kitchen and reaching into the cookie drawer. She loves the texture of these particular ones; that only one old-fashioned corner store left on Eleventh Street sells. Jack picks them up for her. She wonders when Jack will be back; his tutorials seem to take longer than they used to. "But I'm not aware of too many cyberattacks lately."

"Well, thank the Secretary for that. He gets reports even in the middle of the night. It's aging him, it honestly is. He's getting white hairs above his ears, and hollows under his eyes. I feel helpless."

"Hermione, doesn't he have a wife? And umpteen children? I saw them in the paper, all going to church at Easter."

"Yes, of course he does. I know that. I know where I stand. Our relationship is purely official. And, since you're being so provocative—and this is *very* confidential—one of the areas we get most reports from is northern New Jersey. Tucson, and the Buffalo area, and northern New Jersey. He's very tight-lipped—he *has* to be—but there are some imams, if I'm pronouncing it right, that distinctly bear watching. They all preach terrible things against America, but some of them go beyond that. I mean, in advocating violence against the state."

"Well, at least it's imams. If the rabbis start in, Jack'll have to join up. Though he never goes to temple. He might be happier if he did."

Hermione's exasperation breaks out: "*Really*, I wonder sometimes what Jack makes of you; you don't take *any*thing seriously."

"That was part of the attraction," Beth tells her. "He's a depressive, and he liked my being such a lightweight."

There is a pause in which she feels her sister resisting the obvious rejoinder: she is no lightweight now. "Well," Hermione sighs down there in Washington. "I'll let you get back to your soap opera. My other phone is blinking red; he wants something."

"It's been good to talk," Beth lies.

Her older sister has taken the place of her mother in not letting her forget how much is wrong with her. Beth has let herself, as they say, "go." A scent rises to her nostrils from the deep creases between rolls of fat, where dark pellets of sweat accumulate; in the bathtub her flesh floats around her like a set of giant bubbles, semi-liquid in their sway and sluggish buoyancy. How has this happened to her? As a girl she had eaten what she pleased; it had never seemed to her that she ate more than other people, and still doesn't: the food just sticks to her more. Some people have bigger cells than others, she has read. Different metabolisms. Maybe it was being marooned in this house, and the house before it—on Eighteenth Street, and the one before that, a half-mile closer to the downtown, before the neighborhood became too bad—marooned by a man who abandoned her without appearing to. At the high school each day earning his living, who could fault him for that? As a young wife she used to sympathize, but as she aged she came to see how he dramatized everything, leaving in the winter dark and not home until long after dark with his extracurricular duties, his problem students, his emergency sessions with delinquent parents. He would come home depressed because of all the problems he couldn't solve, the poor lives lived in New Prospect to no purpose and now being passed on to the children: "Beth, they don't give a fuck. They never knew structure. They can't imagine a life that goes beyond the next fix, the next binge, the next scrape with the cops or the bank or the INS. The poor kids, they've never had the luxury of being kids. You see them come into the ninth grade with a little hope left in them, a trace of that eagerness second-graders have, a belief that if you learn the rules and do the drills you'll be rewarded; and by the time they graduate, if they do, we've knocked it all out of them. Who's 'we'? America, I suppose, though it's hard to put your finger exactly on where it goes wrong. My grandfather thought capitalism was doomed, destined to get more and more oppressive until the proletariat stormed the barricades and set up the workers' paradise. But that didn't happen; the capitalists were too clever or the proletariat too dumb. To be on the safe side, they changed the label 'capitalism' to read 'free enterprise,' but it was still too much dog-eat-dog. Too many losers, and the winners winning too big. But if you don't let the dogs fight it out, they'll sleep all day in the kennel. The basic problem the way I see it is, society tries to be decent, and decency cuts no ice in the state of nature. No ice whatsoever. We should all go back to being hunter-gatherers, with a hundred-percent employment rate, and a healthy amount of starvation."

Then Jack comes home depressed because the problems beyond solving are getting to be boring, and his gestures at solving them a mere routine, a shtik, a job, a con job. "What really gets me," he would say, "is they refuse to grasp how

Three

bad off they are. They think they're doing pretty good, with some flashy-trashy new outfit they've bought at half-price, or the latest hyper-violent new computer game, or some hot new CD everybody has to have, or a ridiculous new religion when you've drugged your brain back into the Stone Age. It makes you seriously wonder if people deserve to live—if the massacre masterminds in Rwanda and Sudan and Iraq don't have the right idea."

And by letting herself get fat she has disqualified herself from cheering him up like she used to. He never would say so. He would never be rude. She wonders if that is the Jewish in him—the sensitivity, the burden, a sense of superiority really that tries to keep his sorrow to himself, getting up early and going to the window rather than wake her up with it by staying in bed. They have had a good life together, Beth decides, pushing herself up from the tiny hard wood-seated Shaker chair, bracing herself with a hand on the back, taking care not to tip it with her weight. That would be a pretty sight, sprawled on the floor with a broken pelvis, unable even to reach down and tug her bathrobe down for the paramedics when they came.

She must get out of her bathrobe and go do some shopping. They are running out of basics—soap, laundry detergent, paper towels, toilet paper, mayonnaise. Cookies and snacks. She can't ask Jack to buy all these things on top of picking up the microwave meals from ShopRite or take-out from the Chinese place whenever they keep her at the library until six. And cat food. Where *is* Carmela? The cat doesn't get stroked enough, she sleeps all day under the sofa, depressed, and runs around like a wild thing at night. It was wrong in a way to get her spayed, but then if you don't it's wall-to-wall kittens.

She and Jack have had a good life together, Beth tells herself, getting a living pushing pencils—tapping computer keys now—and being pleasant and helpful to people. This was more than Americans in the old days had been allowed to do, slaving in the mills when cities still made things; people are so afraid of the Arabs, but it's the Japanese and Chinese and Mexicans and Guatemalans and those others in these low-wage platforms who are doing us in, putting our workforce out of work. We come to this country and pen the Indians into reservations and build skyscrapers and superhighways and then everybody wants a piece of our domestic markets, like a whale being gutted by sharks in that Hemingway story; but that was a marlin. The same idea. And Hermione has been fortunate too, landing an important Washington job with one of the administration's key players, but it's ridiculous the way she goes on about her boss—the savior of us all, to hear her tell it. You get a spinster mentality from stopped-up hormones, like those nuns and priests who turn out to be so cruel and wanton, not believing any of what they've been preaching, to judge from their actions, molesting these poor trusting little children trying to be good Catholics. Getting married and learning the sorts of thing men do, the way they smell and behave, at least is normal: it releases frustrations and quenches ridiculous romantic ideas. On her way to the stairs and her bedroom to change into street clothes (but what? is the problem; nothing is going to disguise a hundred extra pounds, nothing is going to make her look snappy on the street again), Beth thinks she wouldn't mind peeking into the kitchen to see if there's something to nibble in the refrigerator even if she did just have lunch. As if to suppress that impulse she lets herself flop back into the La-Z-Boy, and levers up the foot-rest to ease the throb in her ankles. Dropsical, the doctor calls them, where Jack once could circle them with his thumb and middle finger. No sooner stuck there in the chair's embrace, she realizes she needs to go pee. Well, ignore it and the need goes away, her life's experience has taught her.

Now, where did that TV remote get to? She picked it up and clicked the TV off, and then her memory is blank. It's frightening, how often her mind is blank. She checks both chair arms and with an effort peers over the arms to the celadon carpet that man sold her, thinking for the second time that day of Miss Dimitrova and her stretching exercises. It must have been balanced on an arm and then slid down into the crevice beside the cushion when she just flopped herself here instead of going upstairs to dress. The fingers of her right hand explore the tight crevice, the vinyl imitating cowhide from the old Wild West days that probably weren't so wonderful if you were there, and then those of the left hand the crevice on the other side, and they do encounter it—the cool matte length of the channel clicker. It would all be easier if her body wasn't so much in the way, pushing the cushion so tight against the chair arm she had to be careful of catching a nail on a seam or something metal. Hairpins and coins and even needles and pins collect in these cracks. Her mother was always sewing or mending something in that old skirted plaid armchair by the window at home to catch the light, the deep wooden sill with its dotted-swiss curtains and tray of geraniums and view of greenery so lush it kept its moist places right through the middle of the day. She points the remote and clicks it to Channel Two, CBS, and the summoned electrons slowly gather, making sounds and an image. The background music on *As the World Turns* is subtly more orchestral, less wispily pop, than that on *All My Children*—woodwinds and deep strings mixed in with the more ghostly sounds, a knocking like hoofbeats fading in the distance. Beth can tell from the excited music and the expressions on the faces of the young actor and actress who have just spoken—angry, eyebrow-knitting, even frightened expressions—that what they have just said to one another was momentous, pivotal, a parting or a murder agreed upon, but she has missed it; she has missed the world turning. Beth could almost cry.

But life is strange, the way it comes to the rescue. Carmela, out of nowhere, comes and jumps up on her lap. "Where has Baby *been*?" Beth asks in a high ecstatic voice. "Mama has *missed* you!" In the next minute, though, she impatiently pushes the cat, settling in on the expanse of warm flesh to purr, off her lap, and struggles to rise again from the La-Z-Boy. Suddenly, there are too many things to do.

Two weeks after his day of graduation from Central High, Ahmad passed his commercial-driver's-license test at the testing facility in Wayne. His mother, who had allowed him in so many respects to raise himself, accompanied him, in the battered maroon Subaru station wagon she uses for driving to the hospital and for hauling her paintings to the gift shop in Ridgewood and what other display venues she has, including various amateur shows in churches and school auditoriums. Winter salt has eaten away at the lower edges of the chassis, and her careless driving and the hastily opened doors of other cars in parking lots and spiral-ramped garages has taken a toll on the sides and fenders. The front right fender, victim of a misunderstanding at a four-way stop sign, was patched with Bondo body filler by one of her boyfriends, a significantly younger man who dabbled in junk sculpture and moved to Tubac, Arizona, before the patch could be smoothed and painted. So it stays a raw and rough putty color, and in other spots, mostly the hood and roof, the paint, exposed outdoors to all weathers, has faded from maroon to the tint of a peach. His mother seems to Ahmad to flaunt her poverty, her everyday failure to blend into the middle class, as if such failure were intrinsic to the artistic life and the personal freedom so precious to infidel Americans. She contrives, with her bohemian wealth of bangles and odd clothing, such as the factory-blotched jeans and vest of purple-dyed leather she wore on this day, to embarrass him whenever they venture together into public.

That day in Wayne, she flirted with the elderly man, this miserable minion of the state, who administered the exam. She said, "I have no idea why he thinks he wants to drive a truck. It's an idea he picked up from his imam—not his mama, his imam. The dear child calls himself a Muslim."

The man behind the desk at the MVC Regional Service Center in Wayne looked troubled by this gush of maternal confiding. "There can be steady money in it," he brought out, after thought.

Ahmad perceived that words came painfully to the public servant, spending a resource within him that he felt to be precious and in short supply. His face, foreshortened as he crouched at his desk, under his winking fluorescent tubes, was subtly deformed, as if it had once been rippled by a harsh emotion and then frozen. This was the sort of hopeless creature his mother lavished her flirtations upon, at the expense of her son's dignity. The man was so dimly alive in his spider web of regulations that he failed to appreciate how Ahmad, though old enough to apply for Class C CDL, was not yet quite man enough to disown his mother. Conscious merely of the woman's impropriety and possible mockery, the man snatched from the applicant's hand the completed physical examination form and had Ahmad thrust his face into a box that had him read, one eye at a time, letters in various colors, telling red from green and both from amber. The machine measured his fitness to drive another machine, and this administrator of the test had been frozen into a kind of wrath because doing his job day after day had transformed him into yet another machine, an easily replaced element in the workings of the merciless, materialist West. It was Islam, Shaikh Rashid had more than once explained, that had preserved the science and simple mechanisms of the Greeks when all Christian Europe had in its barbarism forgotten such things. In today's world, the heroes of Islamic resistance to the Great Satan were former doctors and engineers, adepts in the use of such machines as computers and airplanes and roadside bombs. Islam, unlike Christianity, has no fear of scientific truth. Allah had formed the physical world, and all its devices when put to holy use were holy. Thus Ahmad, with such reflections, received his truckers' license. Class C required no road test.

Shaikh Rashid is pleased. He tells Ahmad, "Appearances can deceive. Though I know our mosque appears, to youthful eyes, shabby and fragile in its external trappings, it is woven of tenacious strands and built upon truths set deep in the hearts of men. The mosque has friends, friends as powerful as they are pious. The head of the Chehab family, just the other day, told me that his prospering business has need for a young truck driver, with no unclean habits and firmly of our faith."

"My rating is only a 'C,' " Ahmad tells him, backing a step from what he senses is too easy and swift an entry into the adult world. "I can't drive out of state or carry hazardous materials."

He has been enjoying, in the weeks since graduation, living with his mother in a condition of idleness, working his desultory, harshly lit hours at the Shop-a-Sec, faithfully performing his daily salat, venturing to a movie or two and marvelling at the expenditure of Hollywood ammunition and the beauty of its explosions, and running in his old track shorts through the streets, sometimes into the region of row houses where he had walked that Sunday noon with Joryleen. He never sees her, just girls of similar color with her way of sauntering, knowing they are being watched. As he flies through the run-down blocks, he remembers Mr. Levy's vague talk of college and its vague but grand subject matter, "science, art, history." The guidance counselor has come by the apartment, actually, once or twice, but, though friendly enough to Ahmad, was quick to leave, as though forgetting what he came for. Without listening carefully to the answer, he asked Ahmad how his plans are coming and whether he intends to stick around here or to go out and see the world, the way a young man should. This sounded curious coming from Mr. Levy, who has lived in New Prospect all of his life, except for college and the spell in the Army that American men used to have to do. Though the doomed American war against Vietnamese self-determination was progressing at this time, Mr. Levy was never assigned to leave the United States, remaining in desk jobs, a fact he feels guilty about, since even though the war was a mistaken one it offered a chance to prove his courage and to show his love for his country. Ahmad knows this because his mother talks to him now and then about Mr. Levy—what a nice man he seems to be, though not a very happy one, and underappreciated by the school administrators, and no longer of much importance to his wife or his son. His mother lately is unusually talkative and inquisitive; she takes more interest in Ahmad than he has come to expect, asking him, whenever he goes out, when he is coming back, and sometimes acting annoyed when he answers, "Oh, sometime."

"And when might that be, exactly?"

"Mother! Get off my case. Pretty soon. I might poke around over at the library."

"Would you like some money for a movie?"

"I *have* money, and I just saw a couple movies, one with Tom Cruise and one with Matt Damon. They were both about professional assassins. Shaikh Rashid is right— movies are sinful and stupid. They are foretastes of Hell."

"Oh, my, how holy we're getting to be! Don't you have any friends? Don't boys your age usually have girlfriends?"

"Mom. I'm not gay, if that's what you're implying."

"How do you know?"

He was shocked. "I know."

"Well, all *I* know," she said, combing her hair back from her forehead with the bent fingers of her left hand in a swift gesture acknowledging the dishevelled nature of this conversation and signalling a willingness to end it, "is I never know when you're going to pop back in."

Now, with somewhat the same testy tone, Shaikh Rashid answers, "They don't *want* you to drive out of state. They don't want you to carry hazardous materials. They wish you to transport furniture. The Chehabs' firm is Excellency Home Furnishings, on Reagan Boulevard. You must have noticed it, or heard me mention the Chehab family."

"The Chehabs?" At times Ahmad fears that, wrapped in his sensation of God standing beside him—so close as to

Three

make a single, unique holy identity, *closer to him than his neck-vein*, as the Qur'an expresses it—he notices fewer mundane details than other people, unreligious people.

"Habib and Maurice," the imam clarifies, with an impatience that bites off his words as precisely as his beard is trimmed. "They are Lebanese, non-Maronite, non-Druze. They came to this country as young men in the 'sixties, when it looked as if Lebanon might become a satellite of the Zionist entity. They brought some capital with them and put it into Excellency. Inexpensive furniture, new and used, for the blacks, was the basic idea. It has proved successful. Habib's son, informally called Charlie, has been selling merchandise and performing deliveries, but they wish him to play a more significant role in the office, now that Maurice has retired to Florida, save for a few summer months, and Habib's diabetes takes an increasing toll on his stamina. Charlie will—what's the phrase?—show you the ropes. You'll like him, Ahmad. He's very American."

The Yemeni's feminine gray eyes narrow in amusement. To him, Ahmad is American. No amount of zeal and Qur'an studies can change his mother's race or his father's absence. The lack of fathers, the failure of paternity to keep men loyal to their homes, is one of the marks of this decadent and rootless society. Shaikh Rashid—a man slight and slim as a dagger, with a dangerous slyness about him, implying at moments that the Qur'an may not have eternally pre-existed in Paradise, to which the Prophet during one night-journey travelled on the supernatural horse Buraq—does not offer himself as a father; there is in his regard of Ahmad something fraternal and sardonic, a splinter of hostility.

But he is right, Ahmad does like Charlie Chehab, a thick-set six-footer in his middle thirties, his swarthy face deeply

: 145 :

creased, with a broad and flexible mouth much in motion. "Ahmad," he says, giving the syllables equal weight, broadening the second "a" as in "Baghdad" or "mad." He asks, "So what're you mad about?" Expecting no answer, he goes on, "Welcome to Excellency, so called. My dad and uncle didn't quite know English when they named it; they thought it meant something excellent." His face as he talks expresses complicated mental currents like disdain, self-disparagement, suspicion, and (with lifted eyebrows) a good-humored awareness of himself and his listener being placed somehow in a compromised situation together.

"We knew English," his father beside him protests. "We knew English from the American School in Beirut. 'Excellency' means something classy. Like 'new' in New Prospect. Doesn't mean prospect is new *now*, it was new *then*. If we call it 'Chehab Furnishings,' people ask, 'What means that, "Chehab"?' " He softly hawks the "ch," a sound Ahmad associates with his Qur'an lessons.

Charlie stands a good foot taller than his father, and easily encircles the older, paler man's head in his arm and gives him a fond hug, a harmless enactment of a wrestling hold. Thus cradled, old Mr. Chehab's head looks like a giant egg, hairless on top and thinner-skinned than his rubber-faced son's. The father's face is somewhat translucent and puffy, perhaps because of the diabetes Shaikh Rashid had mentioned. Mr. Chehab's pallor is glassy but his manner is not sickly; though older than, say, Mr. Levy, he seems younger, plump and excitable and willing to be amused, even by his own son. He appeals to Ahmad: "America. I don't understand this hatred. I came here a young man, married but my wife had to be left behind, just me and my brother, and nowhere was there the hatred and shooting of my own country, everybody in tribes. Christian, Jew, Arab, indifferent, black, white, in between — everybody get along. If you have something good to sell, people buy. If you have job to do, people do it. Everything is clear, on surface. Makes business easy. From the beginning, no trouble. We thought in the Old World to set our prices high, then be bargained down. But nobody understands, even poor *zanj* come in to buy sofa or easy chair, they pay the price on sticker just like in grocery store. But few come. We understand, and put on the furniture prices we expect getting — lower prices — and more come. I say to Maurice, 'This is honest and friendly country. We will have no problems.' "

Charlie has released him from his hug, looks Ahmad in the eye, for the new employee was his height though thirty pounds lighter, and winks. "Papa," he says, with a snarl of patience. "There are problems. The *zanj* weren't given any rights, they had to fight for them. They were being lynched and not allowed in restaurants, they even had separate drinking fountains, they had to go to the Supreme Court to be considered human beings. In America, nothing is free, everything is a fight. There is no *ummah*, no *shari'a*. Let the young man here tell you, he's just out of high school. Everything is war, right? Look at America abroad — war. They forced a country of Jews into Palestine, right into the throat of the Middle East, and now they've forced their way into Iraq, to make it a little U.S. and have the oil."

"Don't believe him," Habib Chehab tells Ahmad. "He says this propaganda, but he knows he has it good here. He is good boy. See, he smiles."

And Charlie does more than smile; he laughs, throwing back his head so the horseshoe arc of his upper teeth is displayed, and the grainy muscle of his tongue, like a broad worm. His flexible lips close upon a contemplative smirk; his eyes, watchful beneath his thick brows, study Ahmad.

"How do you feel about all this, Madman? The imam tells us you're very pious."

"I seek to walk the Straight Path," Ahmad admits. "In this country, it is not easy. There are too many paths, too much selling of many useless things. They brag of freedom, but freedom to no purpose becomes a kind of prison."

The father interrupts, speaking loudly. "You have never known a prison. In this country, people have no fear of prison. Not like Old World. Not like Saudis, not like Iraq before. "

Charlie says soothingly, "Papa, the U.S. has the biggest prison population in the world."

"Not bigger than Russia's. Not than China's, if we knew."

"Plenty big, though—going on two million. The young black women don't have enough guys to go around. They're all in jail, for Chrissake."

"They are for criminals, the prisons. Three, four times a year they break into store. If don't find money they smash the furniture and make shit everywhere. Disgusting!"

"Papa, they're underprivileged. To them, we're rich."

"Your friend Saddam Hussein, he knows prisons. The Communists, they knew prisons. In this country, the average man knows nothing about prisons. The average man has no fear. He does his job. He obeys the laws. They are easy laws. Don't steal. Don't kill. Don't fuck another Mrs."

A number of Ahmad's classmates back at Central High broke the law and were sentenced in juvenile court, for having drugs and breaking-and-entering and DWI. The worst of them thought of court and jail as part of normal life, holding no terrors; they were already reconciled to it. But his wish to contribute this information to the debate is stifled by Charlie's saying, with a clever stretched expression that simultaneously seeks peace and yearns to make his clinching point, "Papa, what about our little concentration camp down at Guantánamo Bay? Those poor bastards can't even have lawyers. They can't even get imams who aren't snitches."

"They are enemy soldiers," Habib Chehab says sulkily, wishing the discussion to end but unable to surrender. "They are dangerous men. They wish to destroy America. That is what they say to reporters, even though they are better fed by us than ever by the Taliban. They think Nine-Eleven was a great joke. It is war for them. It is jihad. That is what they say themselves. What they expect, Americans to lie down flat under feet and make no self-defense? Even bin Laden, he expects being fought back."

"Jihad doesn't have to mean war," Ahmad offers, his voice shyly cracking. "It means striving, along the path of God. It can mean inner struggle."

The elder Chehab looks at him with new interest. His eyes are not as dark a brown as his son's; they are golden marbles, in watery eye-whites. "You are good boy," he says solemnly.

Charlie claps his strong arm around Ahmad's thin shoulders as if to express solidarity among the three of them. "He doesn't say that to everyone," he confides to the new recruit.

This interview takes place at the back of the establishment, where a countertop separates some steel desks and, beyond them, a pair of frosted-glass office doors from the rest of the building. All the rest of the space serves as a showroom—a nightmare room containing chairs, end tables, coffee tables, table lamps, standing lamps, sofas, easy chairs, dining tables and chairs, footstools, sideboards, chandeliers hanging thick as jungle vines, wall sconces in various metallic or enamelled finishes, and large and small mirrors from stark to ornate, their frames gilded or silvered amalgams of leaves and chunky flowers and carved ribbons and eagles in profile, with lifted wings and clasping talons; American eagles stare back above Ahmad's startled reflection, a lean boy of mixed parentage in white shirt and black jeans.

"Downstairs," says the short, plump father, with his gleaming arched nose and pockets of tired dark skin below his golden eyes, "we have the outdoor furniture, lawn and porch, wicker and folding, and even some aluminum cabanas, screened to set yourself off from the bugs in the back yards, for when the family wants a change of air. Upstairs is for bedroom furniture, the beds and bedside tables and bureaus, dressing tables for the lady, armoires for where there aren't enough closets, chaise longues for the lady to put up her feet, upholstered side chairs and stools for the same relaxed mood, little table lamps softer, you know, to go with what should happen in a bedroom."

Charlie, perhaps seeing Ahmad blush, says gruffly, "Used, new, we don't make that much of a distinction. The price tag tells the story, and the condition of the piece. Furniture isn't like a car; it doesn't have a lot of secrets. What you see is what you get. Where you and I come in is, anything over a hundred dollars we deliver free in any part of the state. People love that. It's not like we get many drop-in customers from Cape May, but people love the idea of free."

"And rugs," says Habib Chehab. "They want Oriental rugs, as if Lebanese are from Armenia, from Iran. So we keep selection downstairs, and any on floor you can buy and we clean. There are special carpet places along Reagan, but people believe in our bargains."

Three

"They believe in us, Papa," Charlie says. "We have a good name."

Ahmad smells arising from all this massed equipment for living the mortal aura, absorbed into the cushions and carpets and linen lampshades, of organic humanity, its pathetic six or so positions and needs repeated in a desperate variety of styles and textures between the mirror-crammed walls but amounting to the same daily squalor, the wear and boredom of it, the closed spaces, the floors and ceilings constantly measuring finitude, the silent stuffiness and hopelessness of lives without God as a close companion. The spectacle revives a sensation buried in the folds of his childhood—the false joy of shopping, the tempting counterfeit lavishness of man-made plenty. He would go with his mother up the escalators and through the perfumed aisles of the last, failing emporium downtown or, trotting to keep up with her energetic strides, embarrassed by the mismatch of her freckles with his own dun skin, across tar parking lots into the vast spaces of hastily slapped-up hangars in the "big box" style, where packaged goods were stacked up to the exposed girders. On those trips, narrowly aimed at replacing a certain irreparable home appliance or some boys' clothing his relentless growing demanded or, before Islam rendered him immune, a long-coveted electronic game obsolete within a season, the mother and son were besieged on all sides by attractive, ingenious things they didn't need and could not afford, potential possessions that other Americans seemed to acquire without effort but that for them were impossible to squeeze from the salary of a husbandless nurse's aide. Ahmad tasted American plenty by licking its underside. *Devils*, these many gaudy packages seemed to be, these towering racks of today's flimsy fashion, these shelves of chip-power expressed in murderous cartoons prodding the masses to buy, to consume while the world still had resources to consume, to gorge at the trough before death closed greedy mouths forever. In all this wooing of the needy into debt, death was the bottom line, the counter where the diminishing dollars clattered. Hurry, buy now, since the afterlife's pure and plain joys are an empty fable.

There were goods for sale in the Shop-a-Sec, of course, but mostly bags and boxes of salty, sugary, deleterious food, and plastic fly-swatters, and pencils, made in China, with useless erasers; but here in this great showroom Ahmad feels himself about to be enlisted in the armies of trade, and despite the near presence of the God of whom all material things form the mere shadow, he is excited. The Prophet himself was a merchant. *Man never wearies of praying for good things*, says the forty-first sura. Among these good things the world's manufacture must be included. Ahmad is young; there is plenty of time, he reasons, for him to be forgiven for materialism, if forgiveness is needed. God is closer than the vein in his neck, and He knows what it is to desire comfort, else He would not have made the next life so comfortable: there are carpets and couches in Paradise, the Qur'an affirms.

Ahmad is taken to see the truck, his future truck. Charlie leads him beyond the desks, down a corridor dimly lit by a skylight strewn with the shadows of fallen twigs and leaves and winged seeds. The corridor holds a water cooler, a calendar whose numbered squares are scribbled solid with delivery dates, and what Ahmad will come to understand is a dingy time clock, with a rack for each employee's repeatedly punched time cards on the wall beside it.

Charlie opens another door and there the truck waits,

Three

backed up to a thick-planked loading porch beneath a projecting roof. A tall orange box with each edge reinforced by riveted metal strips, the truck shocks Ahmad, coming upon it for the first time; his impression from the loading platform is of a great blunt-headed animal that is coming too close, nosing up against the platform as if to be fed. Its orange side, dulled a bit by road dirt, bears in a slanting indigo script outlined in gold the word *Excellency* and then, beneath, in block capitals, HOME FURNISHINGS, and, smaller, the store's address and phone number. The truck has double tires behind. Its bulky chrome side-mirrors protrude. Its cab is attached to its box of a body with no space between. It is grand, but friendly. "It's a trusty old beast," Charlie says. "A hundred ten thousand miles and no major problems. Come on down and get acquainted. Don't jump, use these steps over here. The last thing we need is you breaking an ankle your first day on the job."

Ahmad feels this area is somehow already familiar. In the future he will come to know it well—the loading platform, the parking lot with its cracked concrete baking in the shimmering summer heat, the surrounding low brick buildings and cluttered backs of row houses, a rusting Dumpster in one corner from some long-defunct enterprise, the half-heard oceanic sound of traffic waves swishing by on the four-lane boulevard. This space will always have something magic about it, something peaceful not of this world, a strange quality of being under magnification from some high vantage. It is a place God has breathed upon.

Ahmad descends the flight of four thick-planked steps and stands on the same level with the truck. A badge on the driver's door says *Ford Triton E-350 Super Duty*. Charlie opens that door and says, "Here you go, Madman. Climb in."

The cab holds a leathery warm reek of male bodies and stale cigarette smoke and cold coffee and the meat of Italian sandwiches eaten on the move. Ahmad is surprised, after the hours studying the booklets for the CDL with all their talk of double-clutching and downshifting on perilous slopes, by the lack of a stick shift on the floor. "How do we shift gears?"

"We don't," Charlie tells him, his face creasing sourly, but his voice neutral enough. "It's automatic. Just like in your friendly family car."

His mother's embarrassing Subaru. His new friend senses an embarrassment, and says reassuringly, "Gears give you one more thing to worry about. One kid we took on, a couple of drivers ago, stripped the gears shifting into reverse going downhill."

"But on steep hills, shouldn't you shift down? Instead of riding the brake and wearing out the pads."

"Go ahead; you can shift down on the steering stalk. But this part of Jersey isn't that big into hills. It's not like we're West Virginia."

Charlie knows the states; he is a man of the world. He walks around the cab and in one easy swoop, his arms stretching like a monkey's, ascends into the passenger's seat. To Ahmad it feels that someone has jumped into bed with him. Charlie pulls a half-red pack of cigarettes from the pocket of his shirt—a coarse tough cloth like denim, but a military green instead of blue—and adroitly snaps it so that several tan-tipped cigarettes pop out an inch. He asks Ahmad, "A smoke steady your nerves?"

"Thanks, sir, no. I don't smoke."

"Really? That's smart. You'll live forever, Madman. You can cut the 'sir.' 'Charlie' will do. O.K.: let's see you drive this heap."

"Right now?"

Charlie snorts, making an explosion of smoke in the corner of Ahmad's vision. "You'd rather next week? What'd you come here for? Don't look so anxious. It's a piece of cake. Morons do it, all the time; believe me. This isn't rocket science."

It is eight-thirty in the morning—too early, Ahmad feels, for an initiation. But if the Prophet entrusted his body to the fearsome horse Buraq, Ahmad can ascend to the high black seat, cracked and stained and split by previous occupants, and steer this towering orange box on wheels. The engine, when the key turns it over into combustion, has a deep pitch, as if the fuel is a thicker, lumpier substance than gasoline. "It takes diesel?" Ahmad asks.

Charlie exhales more sputtery smoke: it keeps coming from deep in his lungs. "You kidding, kid? You ever driven diesel? Stinks up the place, and takes forever for the engine to warm up. You can't just get in and put the pedal to the metal. One thing to keep in mind, though: there's no rearview mirror over the dash. Don't panic when out of habit you look and there's nothing there. Use your side mirrors. Another thing, remember everything takes longer—takes longer to stop, and longer to get going. At stoplights, you're not winning any dig-out races; don't try. She's like an old lady: don't push her, but don't underestimate her either. Take your eye off the road for a second, and she can kill. But don't let me scare you. O.K., let's give it a try. Let's go. Wait: make sure you put it in reverse. We've had more than one collision with the platform. That same driver I mentioned before. You know what I've learned over the years? There's nothing so stupid people won't go ahead and do it. Back up, do a three-point, head straight out of the lot, that's Thirteenth Street, and go right on Reagan. You can't go left; there's a cement divider, but, like I say, there's nothing so stupid people won't do it, so I mention it."

Charlie is still talking as Ahmad eases the truck back, backs it a tidy half-circle, and in forward gear heads out of the lot. He discovers that, this high off the ground, he floats, looking down upon the tops of cars. As he heads out onto the boulevard, he takes the corner too short and drags the back tires up over the curb, but hardly feels it. He has been transposed to another scale, to another plane. Charlie is busy stubbing out his cigarette in the dashboard ashtray and doesn't mention the bump.

After a few blocks, Ahmad's eyes acquire the habit of darting left to the long-side mirror, and then through the passenger window to the right-hand mirror. The orange, chrome-edged reflections of Excellency's own sides that he glimpses no longer alarm him but become parts of him, like the shoulders and arms that figure in his peripheral awareness as he walks down the street. In his dreams since childhood he would sometimes be flying down hallways or skimming sidewalks a few feet off the ground, and sometimes would awake with an erection or, more shamefully still, a large wet spot on the inside of his pajama fly. He had consulted the Qur'an for sexual advice in vain. It talked of uncleanness but only in regard to women, their menstruation, their suckling of infants. In the second sura, he found the mysterious words, *Your wives are your field: go in, therefore, to your field as ye will; but do first some act for your souls' good: and fear ye God, and know that ye must meet Him.* In the verse before that, he read that women are a pollution. *Separate yourselves therefore from women and approach them not, until they be cleansed. But when they are cleansed, go in unto them as God hath ordained for you. Verily God loveth those who turn to Him, and loveth those who seek to be clean.* Ahmad feels clean in the truck, cut off from the base world, its streets full of dog filth and blowing shreds of plastic and paper; he feels clean and free, flying his orange box kite behind him in the side mirrors.

"Don't pass on the right," Charlie suddenly admonishes him, in a voice sharp with alarm. Ahmad slows, not having realized he was overtaking cars to his left, in the lane next to the traffic divider, a solid, sullied string of Jersey barriers.

"Why are they called Jersey barriers?" he asks. "In Maryland, what are they called?"

"Don't change the subject, Madman. Driving a truck, you can't sit there and daydream. You got life and death in your hands, not to mention repairs that'll jack up the insurance premiums if you goof. No hot-dogging and farting around with cell phones like people do in cars. You're bigger; you got to be better."

"Really?" Ahmad makes an attempt to tease the older man, his Lebanese-American brother, out of his grimly serious mood. "Shouldn't cars get out of my way?"

Charlie doesn't see that Ahmad is teasing. He keeps his eyes on the road, through the windshield, and says, "Don't be stupid, kid: they can't. It's like animals. You don't hold rats and rabbits to the same standard as lions and elephants. You don't hold Iraq to the same standard as the U.S. Bigger, you better be better."

This political note strikes Ahmad as strange, slightly out of tune. But he is in bed with Charlie, and submissively settles himself for the ride.

. . .

"Jesus," says Jack Levy. "This is what life is all about. I'd forgotten, and never expected anybody to remind me." Thus guardedly, in these circumstances, without naming her, he pays tribute of a sort to his wife, who long ago had had her turn at showing him what life was all about.

Teresa Mulloy, naked beside him, agrees, "It is," but then adds, in self-protection, "but it doesn't last." Her face, with its round shape and slightly protuberant eyes, is flushed so that her freckles blend in, pale brown on pink.

"What does?" Jack asks. She doesn't really want him to agree with such a careless shrug. Her rosy flush becomes the high color that follows the sting of a rebuke, a facing of her defenselessness in this dead-end adventure, another married boyfriend. He will never leave his fat Beth, and would she want him to in any case? He is twenty-three years older than she, and she needs a man to last her the rest of her life.

Summer in New Jersey has attained July's steady swelter, but even so, feeling the air as cool on their love-flushed skins, the lovers have drawn up the top sheet, rumpled and damp from having been beneath their bodies. Jack sits up against the pillow, exposing the slack muscles and gray froth of his chest, and Terry, with lovable bohemian immodesty, has pulled her side of the sheet no higher, so her breasts, white as soap where the sun never touches them, jut free for him to admire and to feel the heft of again if he desires. He loves plump, though it can get to be too much. The fragrances of paint thinner and linseed oil lull Jack here in his mistress's bed. As Terry said, she is working bigger and brighter. When in fucking she sits on his lap, impaling herself on his erection, he feels the colors reflected from her walls flow down her sides along with his hands, her elongating, rib-filled, preening, Irish-white sides. With Beth, he can't imagine her weight on his pelvis, or her legs spread far enough apart; they have run out of positions, except for the spoon, and even there her huge ass pushes him away like a jealous child in their bed.

"The thing is," Jack goes on, hearing in Terry's silence a withdrawal from some tactlessness on his part, "while it's going on it doesn't matter that it doesn't last—Mother Nature says, 'Who cares?' It feels like it's forever. I adore your tits, have I said that lately?"

"They're starting to droop. You should have seen them when I was eighteen. Bigger, even, and stuck straight out."

"Terry, please. Don't get me excited again. I got to go." Beth's, too, he could remember, had been like inverted bowls, the size for breakfast cereal, with nipples hard as a single blueberry in his mouth.

"Where to now, Jack?" Terry's voice is weary. A mistress knows the man to be a liar, where the wife only guesses.

"A tutorial. A real one, across town. I have the car; she needs it in an hour and a half to get to the library." He is uncertain, in the gap his post-orgasmic daze leaves in his head, of how much of what he says is true. Beth needs the car eventually, he knows.

Terry, hearing his uncertainty, complains, "Jack, you're always rushing off. Do I have body odor or something?"

This is cruel, because Beth indeed does; it fills up the bed at night, a caustic exhalation from her deep creases, and adds to his nocturnal unease and dread.

"No way," he says, having picked up this much slang from his students. "Not even—" He halts, on the edge of over-stepping.

"My cunt. Say it."

"Not even there," he concedes. "Especially there. You're

sweet. You're my sugar plum." But if truth be known he is wary of having his face too long between her legs, for fear of Beth's smelling the other woman through their good-night kiss—a mere peck, but their enduring custom for thirty-six years of marriage.

"Tell me about my cunt, Jack. I want to hear it. Loosen up."

"Please, Terry. This is grotesque."

"Why, you prim prick? You Jewish priss. What's grotesque about my cunt?"

"Nothing, nothing," he concedes, beaten down. "It's perfect, it's gorgeous, it—"

"It? What? What is all these nice things? Perfect and gorgeous."

"Your cunt."

"Good. Go on." Perhaps her point is that he uses it, as he uses her, without paying enough attention, without taking in the whole picture—the aroma, the incidentals, her ache of loneliness when he pulls out, her awareness of being used, and used squeamishly at that.

"—is wet," he goes on, "and fuzzy, and soft as a flower inside, and stretchy—"

"Oh," she says, "stretchy. This is interesting. And it likes—tell me what it likes."

"It likes being kissed, and licked, and played with, and entered—don't make me go on any more, Terry. It kills it for me. I'm crazy about you, you know that. You're the nicest—"

"Don't tell me," she says angrily, and throws back the sheet and jackknifes out of bed, her buttocks jiggling and beginning, as she said of elsewhere, to droop. Her buttocks are developing puckers. As if sensing his eyes on her backside, she turns in the bathroom doorway, flashing her little

patch of cedar color; the whole doughy softness of her—
white bread without the crust—is exposed, he feels, defiantly, an invitation to kindness that he has failed to accept
heartily enough. The sight of her, so naked and female, so
sensitive and lumpy, dries his mouth, sucking the air of his
usual clothed, conscientious life quite out of him. She com-
pletes his sentence for him: "—the nicest thing since Beth
before she got pig-fat. You're happy enough to fuck me, but
you don't want to say 'fuck' for fear she'll somehow hear it.
It used to be you'd fuck and run because you were afraid
Ahmad might come back any minute, but now he's gone at
his job all day you always have some other excuse not to
hang around even a minute. Just enjoy me, that's all I ever
asked, but, no, Jews have to have guilt, it's their way of showing how special they are, how superior to everybody else,
God gets sore at just *them*, with their putrid precious
covenant. You make me sick, Jack Levy!" She slams the bathroom door, but it catches on a woolly bathroom rug and
shuts reluctantly, not before in the slice of the light being
angrily flicked on he sees her Irish ass, never kissed by the
desert sun, jiggle.

Jack lies there feeling mournful, wanting to get his clothes
back on but knowing this would prove her point. When she
finally comes out of the bathroom, having washed him away
with a shower, she picks up her underwear from the floor
and in measured fashion puts it on. Her breasts swing as she
bends down, and these are the first pieces of her she covers,
catching them up in the gossamer cups of her bra and reaching with a grimace behind to do the fasteners. Then she
steps into her underpants, steadying herself with an extended
arm and a shapely firm hand on the bureau top that is covered with lined-up tubes of painter's oils. She tugs with one

hand and then with both the bit of nylon smartly up; the cedar-colored patch of frizzy hair puffs out, in its moment of capture, above the elastic waistband like the head on an impatiently poured beer. Her bra is black but her thong panties are lilac. Their elastic waist is low, exposing the pearly swell of her belly to the depth of the most daring hip-huggers, though what she next puts on are a pair of ordinary old high-waisted jeans, with a dab or two of paint on the front. A ribbed jersey and a pair of canvas sandals, and she will be completely armored, ready to face the street and its opportunities. Another man might steal her. Jack fears that each time he sees her naked might be the last. A desolation sweeps through him sharp enough to make him cry out, "Don't put all that crap back on! Come back to bed, Terry. Please."

"You don't have time."

"I have time. I just remembered, the tutorial isn't until three. The kid's a loser anyway, from over in Fair Lawn, his parents think I can tutor him into Princeton. I can't. Pretty please?"

"Well . . . maybe a second. For just a snuggle. I hate it when we quarrel. We shouldn't have anything to quarrel about."

"We quarrel," he explains to her, "because we care about each other. If we didn't care we wouldn't quarrel."

She undoes the snap on her jeans, sucking in her gut and looking comically pop-eyed for a second, and quickly slithers back beneath the wrinkled sheet in her black and lilac underthings. There is a light-hearted whorishness in the outfit, like the teeny-slut look affected by some of the bolder girls at Central High, which startles a furtive throb from his penis. He tries to ignore it, putting his arm around her shoulders—the downy hairs at the nape of her neck are still damp from her shower—and pulling her closer to him in chaste companionship. "How is Ahmad doing?" he asks.

Terry answers warily, feeling the transition abrupt from whore to mother. "He seems to be doing fine. He likes the people he works for—a Lebanese father and son, who do a kind of good-cop / bad-cop routine on him. The son is apparently something of a character. Ahmad loves the truck."

"The truck?"

"It could be any truck, but this one is *his* truck. You know how love is. Every morning he checks the tire pressure, the brakes, all these fluids. He tells me about them—engine oil, radiator coolant, windshield-washer fluid, battery, power steering, automatic transmission . . . I think that's all. He checks the fan belts for tightness and I don't know what all else. He says the mechanics at the service stations, for the scheduled check-ups, are too rushed and hungover to do it right. The truck even has a name—Excellency. Excellency Home Furnishings. They thought it meant something excellent."

"Well," Jack admits, "it almost does. It's witty." His hard-on is growing back as he lies there trying to think of Terry as a mother and a professional person, a nurse's aide and an abstract painter, an intelligent many-sided individual he would be glad to know even if she weren't of the opposite gender. But his thoughts have taken off from her silken underclothes, lilac and black, and the easy, even careless way she deals with him sexually—all that experience, all those boyfriends accumulated in the fifteen years since Ahmad's father failed to crack America's riddle and fled. Even back then she was a Catholic-raised girl who didn't mind shacking up with a raghead, a Mussulman. She was a wild one, a rule-breaker. Terri-ble. A holy Terr-or. He asks her, "Who told you about Jews and the covenant?"

"I don't know. Some guy I knew once."

"You knew him in what sense?"

"I knew him. Jack, look, don't we have a deal? You don't ask, and I don't tell. I've been abandoned and single in the best years a woman is supposed to have. Now I'm forty. Don't begrudge me a little past."

"In my head I don't, of course. But, like we were saying, when you care, you get possessive."

"Is that what we were saying? I didn't hear that. All I heard was you thinking about Beth. Pathetic Beth."

"She's not so pathetic at the library. She sits behind the reference desk and moves around on the Internet much better than I can do."

"She sounds wonderful."

"No, but she's a person."

"Great. Who isn't? You're saying I'm not?"

An Irish temper makes you appreciate Lutherans. His prick feels the change in Teresa's climate, and is beginning to wilt again. "We all are," he soothes her. "You especially. But as to the covenant, here's one Jew who never felt it. My father hated religion, and the only covenants I heard about were in neighborhoods that wouldn't let Jews in. How religious is Ahmad these days?"

She relaxes a little, slumping down into her pillow. His gaze travels an inch farther down into the black bra. The freckled skin of her upper chest looks a bit crêpey, exposed to sun damage year after year, in contrast to the soap-white strip this side of the bra's edge. Jack thinks, *So another Jew has been here before me.* Who all else? Egyptians, Chinamen, God knows. A lot of these painters she knows are kids half her age. To them she'd be a mother who fucks. Maybe that's why her own kid is queer, if he is.

She is saying, "It's hard to say. He never talked much about it. Poor little guy, he used to look so frail and scared when I'd drop him off at the mosque, going up those stairs all by himself. When I'd ask him afterwards how it had gone, he'd say 'Great' and clam up. He'd even blush. It was something he couldn't share. With the job, he told me, it's hard for him to always get to the mosque on Fridays, and this Charlie who's always with him doesn't seem to be all that observant. But, you know, really, all in all Ahmad seems more relaxed — just the way he talks to me, more of a man's manner, looking me level in the eye. He's pleased with himself, earning money, and, I don't know, maybe I'm imagining this, more open to new ideas, not closed into this very, in my opinion, limited and intolerant belief system. He's getting fresh input."

"Does he have a girlfriend?" Jack Levy asks, grateful to Terry for warming to a subject other than his own failings.

"Not as far as I know," she says. He loves that Irish mouth of hers when she gets pensive, forgetting to close her lifted upper lip, with its little blister of flesh in the middle. "I think I would know. He comes home tired, lets me feed him, reads the Koran or lately the newspaper — this stupid war on terror — so he can talk with this Charlie about it, and goes to bed in his room. His sheets" — she regrets bringing up the subject, but goes ahead with it — "are unspotted." She adds, "They weren't always."

"How would you know if he has a girl?" Jack presses.

"Oh, he'd talk about it, if only to get my goat. He's always hated my having male friends. He'd want to go out nights, and he doesn't."

"It doesn't seem quite right. He's a good-looking kid. Could he be gay?"

The question doesn't faze her; she has thought about it. "I could be wrong, but I think I'd know that, too. His teacher at the mosque, this Shaikh Rashid, is kind of creepy; but Ahmad's aware. He reveres him but distrusts him."

"You say you've met the man?"

"Just once or twice, picking up Ahmad or dropping him off. He was very smooth and proper with me. But I could feel hatred. To him I was a piece of meat—un*clean* meat."

Unclean meat. Jack's hard-on has revived. He makes himself focus, a minute or so longer, before sharing this possibly inconvenient development. There is a pleasure, which he had forgotten, in just *having* the thing—the firm, stout, importunate stalk, the pompous little freshly appointed center of your being, bringing with it the sensation of there being *more* of you. "The job," he resumes. "Does he put in long hours?"

"It varies," Terry says. Her body gives off, perhaps in response to an emanation from his, a mix of tingling scents, soap at the nape of her neck foremost. The subject of her son is losing her interest. "He gets off when he's delivered the furniture. Some days it's early, most days it's late. Sometimes they drive as far as Camden, or Atlantic City."

"That's a long way to go, to deliver a piece of furniture."

"There aren't just deliveries; there are pickups, too. A lot of their furniture is secondhand. They make bids on people's estates and truck the stuff off. They have a kind of network; I don't know how much the Islamic thing matters. Most of their customers around New Prospect are black families. Some of their homes, Ahmad says, are surprisingly nice. He loves seeing the different areas, the different lifestyles."

"See the world," Jack sighs. "See New Jersey first. That's what I did, only I left out the world part. Now, missy"—he clears his throat—"you and I have a problem."

Teresa Mulloy's protuberant, beryl-pale eyes widen in mild alarm. "Problem?"

Jack lifts the sheet and shows her what has happened below his waist. He hopes he has shared enough life in general with her for her to share this with him.

She stares, and lets the tip of her tongue curl up to touch the plump center of her upper lip. "That's not a problem," she decides. *"No problema, señor."*

Charlie Chehab often rides with Ahmad, even when Ahmad could handle by himself the furniture to be loaded or unloaded. The boy is growing stronger with the lifting and hauling. He has asked that his paychecks—nearly five hundred a week, at twice what Shop-a-Sec paid per hour—be made out to Ahmad Ashmawy, though he still lives with his mother. Because his Social Security and driver's license both list his last name as Mulloy, she has gone with him downtown to the bank, in one of the new glass buildings, to explain, and to make out new forms for a separate account. That is how she is these days: she makes no resistance to him, though she never made much. His mother is, he sees now, looking back, a typical American, lacking strong convictions and the courage and comfort they bring. She is a victim of the American religion of freedom, freedom above all, though freedom to do what and to what purpose is left up in the air. *Bombs bursting in air*—empty air is the perfect symbol of American freedom. There is no *ummah* here, both Charlie and Shaikh Rashid point out—no encompassing structure of divine law that brings men rich and poor to bow down shoulder to shoulder, no code of self-sacrifice, no exalted submission such as lies at the heart of Islam, its very name. Instead there is a clashing diversity of private self-seeking, whose catchwords are *Seize the day* and *Devil take the hindmost* and *God helps those who help themselves*, which translate to *There is no God, no Day of Judgment; help yourself.* The double sense of "help yourself"—self-reliance and "grab what you can"—amuses the shaikh, who, after twenty years among these infidels, takes pride in his fluency in their language. Ahmad sometimes has to suppress a suspicion that his teacher inhabits a semi-real world of pure words and most loves the Holy Qur'an for its language, a shell of violent shorthand whose content is its syllables, the ecstatic flow of "l"s and "a"s and guttural catches in the throat, savoring of the cries and the gallantry of mounted robed warriors under the cloudless sky of Arabia Deserta.

Ahmad sees his mother as an aging woman still in her heart a girl, playing at art and love—for she is alive lately with a preoccupation in which her son detects a new lover, though this one, unlike the run of them, does not come around to the apartment and vie with Ahmad for dominance of the premises. *She may be your mother but I fuck her,* their manner said, and this too was American, this valuing of sexual performance over all family ties. The American way is to hate one's family and flee from it. Even the parents conspire in this, welcoming signs of independence from the child and laughing at disobedience. There is not that bonding love which the Prophet expressed for his daughter Fatimah: *Fatimah is a part of my body; whoever hurts her, has hurt me, and whoever hurts me has hurt God.* Ahmad does not hate his mother; she is too scattered to hate, too distracted by her pursuit of happiness. Though they still live together in that apartment perfumed with the sweet and acrid odors of oil paints, she has as little to do with the self he presents to the daytime world as do the pajamas, greasy with sweat, that he sleeps in at night and sheds before the shower through which he hurries into the morning purity of the working day, and his mile walk to work. For some years it has been awkward, their bodies sharing the limited space of the apartment. Her ideas of healthy behavior include appearing before her son in her underwear or a summer nightie that allows the shadows of her private parts to show through. On the summer street she wears halters and miniskirts, blouses unbuttoned at the top and low-slung jeans tightest where she is fullest. When he rebukes her attire as improper and provocative, she mocks and teases him as if he is flirting with her. Only at the hospital, with pale-green scrubs, decently baggy, worn over her indiscreet street clothes, does she meet the Prophet's injunction to women, in the twenty-fourth sura, to throw veils over their bosoms and to display their ornaments only to their husbands and fathers and sons and brothers and slaves and eunuchs and, the Book emphasizes, *children who note not women's nakedness.* As a child of ten or less, he more than once, to patch over the lack of a babysitter, waited for her at Saint Francis's and would rejoice to see her flushed with the hurry of her job, muffled below the waist in scrub pants and thick-soled running shoes, with no bangles to break the silence. A tense moment was reached when, at fifteen, he became taller than she, and sprouted a dark down on his upper lip: still under forty, she still foolishly hoped to catch a man, to pluck a rich doctor from the midst of his harem of comely young attendants, and her teen-age son was betraying her as middle-aged.

From Ahmad's standpoint she looked and acted younger

than a mother should. In the countries of the Mediterranean and the Middle East, women withdrew into wrinkles and a proud shapelessness; an indecent confusion between a mother and a mate was not possible. Praise Allah, Ahmad never dreamed of sleeping with his mother, never undressed her in those spaces of his brain where Satan thrusts vileness upon the dreaming and the daydreaming. In truth, insofar as the boy allows himself to link such thoughts with the image of his mother, she is not his type. Her flesh, mottled with pink and dotted with freckles, seems unnaturally white, like a leper's; his taste, developed in his years at Central High, is for darker skins, cocoa and caramel and chocolate, and for the alluring mystery of eyes whose blackness, opaque at first glance, deepens to the purple of plums or the glinting brown of syrup—what in the Qur'an figure as *large dark eyeballs, kept close in their pavilions.* The Book promises: *And theirs shall be the dark-eyed houris, chaste as hidden pearls: a guerdon for their deeds.* Ahmad regards his mother as a mistake that his father made but that he never would.

Charlie is married, to a Lebanese woman Ahmad sees rarely, coming into the store toward closing hour, at the end of her own day's work, which was performed in a legal office where tax forms are filled out for those who cannot do it for themselves, and where paper intercessions are made with the governments of the city, the state, and the nation as each exacts its tribute from all citizens. There is a mannish air to her Western dress and pants suits, and only her olive complexion and thick, untrimmed eyebrows distinguish her from a kafir. Her hair bushes out to several inches all around her head, but in the photograph Charlie keeps on his desk she is wearing an extensive head scarf that conceals every hair, and smiles above the faces of two small children. He never speaks of her, yet speaks of women often, especially the women who appear on television commercials.

"Did you see the one on the Levitra ad for guys who can't get it up?"

"I rarely watch television," Ahmad tells him. "Now that I am no longer a child, it does not interest me."

"Well, it should—how can you know what the corporations that run this country are doing to us if you don't? The one in the Levitra ad is my idea of absolute pussy, purring away about her 'guy' and how he likes 'quality' in his erections—she doesn't say 'erections' but that's what the whole ad is about, pricks getting hard enough, erectile dysfunction is the biggest thing the drug-makers have hit upon since Valium—and the way she gazes off into the middle distance and gets misty-eyed, you can just see, see through a woman's eyes, this big stiff prick of his, hard as a rock, and her mouth does this funny little thing—she has a *great* mouth—it kind of ripples, the tiny little muscles in the lips, so you know she's picturing it, thinking of blowing it—the *per*fect mouth for cocksucking—and then, looking, you know, all kind of misty and smug and sexually satisfied, she turns to the guy— some male model, probably gay in his real life—and, quick as a wink, says, '*Look* at that!' and touches his cheek where he was making a dimple, listening sheepishly to her talking about how great he is. You wonder how the hell they did it— how many takes on videotape before she thought of it, or if the scriptwriter for the commercial thought of it and wrote it out ahead of time—but it seems so spontaneous, you wonder how they got her to look so sexed-up. She really has that happily fucked look women get, you know? And it's not just the soft focus."

This, Ahmad thinks to himself a little mournfully, is male

talk, which he, in his severe white shirt and black jeans, skirted the edges of in high school, and which his father might have provided in measured and less obscene fashion, had Omar Ashmawy waited to play a father's role. Ahmad is grateful to Charlie for including him in the club of male friendship. Fifteen or more years older than he, and married though he doesn't sound it, Charlie seems to assume that Ahmad knows everything he knows, or that if not he wants to know it. The boy finds it easier to talk to Charlie sideways, staring ahead through the truck windshield and with his hands on the wheel, than he does face to face. He tells him, blushing in exposing his piety, "I do not find that television encourages clean thoughts."

"Hell, no. Wake up: it's not meant to. Most of it is just crap they put out to fill in between the commercials. That's what I'd love to be doing, if I didn't have Dad's business to keep from going under. His brother got it going with him and now sits down there in Florida bleeding us dry with his cut. I'd love to make commercials. Planning it out, putting together the elements—the director, the cast, the sets, the script; those things have to have a script—and then socking John Q. Public with it, right in the kisser, so he can't ever think straight again. Your gut to his gut, telling him what he can't live without. What else do they give us, these media moguls? The news is sob-sister stuff—Diane Sawyer, the poor Afghani babies, boo-hoo-hoo—or else straight propaganda; Bush complains about Putin turning into Stalin, but we're worse than the poor old clunky Kremlin ever was. The Commies just wanted to brainwash you. The new powers that be, the international corporations, want to wash your brains away, period. They want to turn you into machines for consuming—the chicken-coop society. All this entertainment—Madman, it's crap, the same crap that kept the masses zombified in the Depression, only then you stood in line and paid a quarter for the movie, where today they hand it to you free, with the advertisers paying a million a minute for the chance to mess with your heads."

Ahmad, steering, tries to agree: "It is not on the Straight Path."

"You kidding? It's the Yellow Brick Road, paved with insidious intentions." *In-sid-i-ous*, Ahmad thinks, recalling the last time he was preached at. In the side of his field of vision he sees sparks of saliva spray from Charlie's mouth in his hurry to speak. "Sports," the man spits out. "They pay zillions for the rights to televise sports. It's reality without being real. The money has ruined the professional leagues; nobody sticks with their team any more, they jump ship for another fifteen mill when already they can't count the money they have. There used to be team loyalty and some regional identification, but the morons in the stands don't know what they're missing. They think this has always been it, greedy players and records broken every year. Barry Bonds—he's better than Ruth, better than DiMaggio, but who can love that juiced-up surly bastard? Fans now don't know about love. They don't care about it. Sports are like video games; the players are holograms. You listen to these radio talk shows and want to say to these Cheeseheads or Jetheads or whatever who spout off endlessly, 'Oh, please, get a fucking life.' My God, the poor saps have all these statistics memorized, as if *they're* getting paid A-Rod's salary. And the so-called comedies the networks dish up—Jesus— who's laughing? It's slop. And Leno and Letterman, more slop. But the commercials, they are fantastic. They're like Fabergé eggs. When somebody in this country wants to sell you something, they really buckle down. They get intense. You watch the same commercial twenty times, you see how every second has been weighed out in gold. They're full of what physicists call *information*. Would you know, for example, that Americans were as sick as they are, full of indigestion and impotence and baldness, always wetting their pants and having sore assholes, if you didn't watch commercials? I know you say you never watch it, but you really shouldn't miss this Ex-Lax commercial with this cute dish with long straight hair and Waspy long teeth who looks out through the camera and tells you, just *you*, sitting there with your bag of Fritos, that she has a weakness for junk food—skinny as a rail, with a weakness for junk food supposedly—and has to battle constipation sometimes? How old is she? Twenty-five if that, and as buff as Lance Armstrong, and you can bet she hasn't missed taking a dump for a day in her life, but the Ex-Lax CEO wants the old ladies out there not to be ashamed of their plugged-up colons. 'Look,' he's saying to them, the Ex-Lax CEO is saying, 'even a snappy Waspy chick like this can't always take a shit, or keep her underpants dry on the golf course, or her hemorrhoids from ruining her day in the bleachers; so, Grandma, you're not some old piece of crud on the trash heap, you're in the same boat with these young glamour pusses!' "

"It is a society that fears getting old," Ahmad agrees, gently braking in anticipation of a far-off green light's turning red before the truck gets there. "Infidels do not know how to die."

"No," Charlie says, his unstoppable voice halting, and sounding cautious. "Who does?" he asks.

"True believers," Ahmad tells him, since he has asked. "They know that Paradise awaits the righteous." Gazing through Excellency's tall and dirty windshield at the oil-stained macadam and red taillights and blaring blobs of reflected sun that compose a summer day along a truck route in New Jersey, he quotes the Qur'an: *"God giveth you life, then causeth you to die: then will He assemble you on the day of resurrection: there is no doubt of it."*

"Absolutely," Charlie says. "Good stuff. 'No doubt of it.' Me, if a good reason came up, I'd be happy to cash it in. You, you're too young. You got all your life ahead of you."

"Not so," Ahmad says. He did not hear in Charlie's gruff response the quaver of doubt, the silken shimmer of irony, which he detects in the voice of Shaikh Rashid. Charlie is a man of the world, but Islam is solidly part of that world. Lebanese are not fine-honed and two-edged like Yemenis or handsome and vanishing like Egyptians. He shyly points out, "Already I have lived longer than many martyrs in Iran and Iraq."

But Charlie is not done with the women he sees on television commercials. "And now," he says, "the drug cartels have made such a killing with Viagra and so on they're selling sex enhancement, as they call it, to women. There's one commercial—you may not have seen it, it doesn't come on too often—showing a woman, kind of sensible and plain, a schoolteacher, you figure, or an office manager for some middle-grade tech company, not the upper end, with this little frown on her face so you know something's missing in her life, and the music adds an undercurrent, kind of a minor-key nagging, and the next thing you know you see her floating along swathed in this filmy stuff, barefoot; she better be barefoot, because when you look she's walking on water, trailing ripples, there off the beach where it's just a couple of inches deep, but even so she's not sinking in, and has a new hairdo, and better makeup, so she's gone all misty in the face, like that terrific cocksucker I was describing—I think they have some dilator they put in the eyes of these women to make them look that way—and then you get the reason, the logo of this new 'hormone enhancer,' they call it. The message is, she's been laid. She's been knocking herself silly with multiple orgasms. They would never have admitted that in commercials ten, fifteen years ago—that women want it, they want it a lot; being fucked is a relaxant and a beauty aid. How about you, Madman? You getting a lot lately?"

"A lot of what?" Ahmad's attention perhaps has wandered. They have come off the Turnpike at Bayway and are in some anonymous downtown with a lot of double parking that creates tight spots for Excellency to squeeze through.

"Poontang," Charlie says with exasperation, sucking in his breath as the orange truck scrapes past a lumbering school bus loaded with staring little faces. "Pussy," he clarifies. When Ahmad, blushing, offers no response, Charlie announces in a tone of quiet resolve, "We gotta get you laid."

The towns of northern New Jersey are enough alike—storefronts and sidewalks and parking meters and neon signs and quickly passed patches of civic green space—to create even in a moving vehicle a sensation of being stuck. The territories he and Charlie together drive through, with their summer scents of softened tar and spilled motor oil and of onions and cheese exhaled from small eateries out into the street, are much the same until they get south of South Amboy or the Sayreville exit on the Jersey Pike. Yet as one small city yields to the next Ahmad comes to see that no two are identical, and each has social variety within it. In some neighborhoods large houses sprawl in the shade back from the roadway on lush rising lawns populated by squat trim shrubs like security guards. Excellency makes few deliveries to such homes, but passes them on its way to inner-city rows where the front steps spring up straight from the sidewalk, without even the merest excuse for a front yard. Here those awaiting delivery tend to live: darker-skinned families with voices and televisions sounding from back rooms, out of sight, as if chamber after chamber of linked family members telescope out from the vestibule. Sometimes there are signs of Islamic practice—prayer mats, women in hijabs, framed images of the twelve imams including the Hidden Imam with his featureless face, identifying the household as Shia. These homes affect Ahmad with uneasiness, as do the city neighborhoods where shops advertise in mixed Arabic and English and mosques have been created by substituting a crescent for the cross on a deconsecrated Protestant church. He does not like to linger and chat, as Charlie does, making his way in whatever dialect of Arabic is offered, with laughter and gestures to bridge gaps in comprehension. Ahmad feels his pride of isolation and willed identity to be threatened by the masses of ordinary, hard-pressed men and plain, practical women who are enrolled in Islam as a lazy matter of ethnic identity. Though he was not the only Muslim believer at Central High, there were no others quite like him—of mixed parentage and still fervent in the faith, a faith chosen rather than merely inherited from a father present to reinforce fidelity. Ahmad was native-born, and in his travels through New Jersey he takes interest less in its pockets of a diluted Middle East than in the American reality all around, a sprawling ferment for which he feels the mild pity owed a failed experiment.

This fragile, misbegotten nation had a history scarcely

expressed in the grandiose New Prospect City Hall and the lake of developers' rubble on whose opposite shores stand, with their caged windows, the high school and the sooty black church. Each town bears in its center relics of the nineteenth century, civic buildings of lumpy brown stones or soft red brick with jutting cornices and round arched entryways, ornate proud buildings outlasting the flimsier twentieth-century constructions. These older, ruddier buildings express a bygone industrial prosperity, a wealth of manufacture, machinery and railroads harnessed to the lives of a laboring nation, an era of internal consolidation and welcome to the world's immigrants. Then there is an underlying earlier century, which made the succeeding ones possible. The orange truck rumbles past small iron signs and overlookable monuments commemorating an insurgency that became a revolution; from Fort Lee to Red Bank, its battles had been fought, leaving thousands of boys asleep beneath the grass.

Charlie Chehab, a man of many disparate parts, knows a surprising amount about that ancient conflict: "New Jersey's where the Revolution got turned around. Long Island had been a disaster; New York City was more of the same. Retreat, retreat. Disease and desertions. Just before the winter of 'seventy-six–'seventy-seven, the British moved down from Fort Lee to Newark, then to Brunswick and Princeton and Trenton, easy as a knife through butter. Washington straggled across the Delaware with an army in rags. A lot of them, believe it or not, were barefoot. Barefoot, and winter coming on. We were *toast*. In Philadelphia, everybody was trying to leave except the Tories, who sat around waiting for their buddies the redcoats to arrive. Up in New England, a British fleet took Newport and Rhode Island without a fight. It was *over*."

Three

"Yes, and why wasn't it?" Ahmad asks, wondering why Charlie is telling this patriotic tale with such enthusiasm.

"Well," he says, "several things. *Some* good things were happening. The Continental Congress woke up and stopped trying to run the war; they said, 'O.K., let George do it.' "

"Is that where the phrase comes from?"

"Good question. I don't think so. The other American general in charge, a silly prick called Charles Lee—Fort Lee is named after him, thanks a bunch—let himself be captured in a tavern in Basking Ridge, leaving Washington in total charge. At this point Washington was lucky to have an army at all. After Long Island, see, the British had gone easy on us. They let the Continental Army retreat and get across the Delaware. That proved to be a mistake, for, as they must have taught you at school—what the fuck *do* they teach you at school, Madman?—Washington and a plucky band of threadbare freedom fighters crossed the Delaware on Christmas Day and routed the Hessian troops garrisoned in Trenton, and took a whole bunch of prisoners. On top of that, when Cornwallis brought down a big force from New York and thought he had the Americans trapped south of Trenton, Washington snuck off through the woods, around the Barrens and the Great Bear Swamp, and marched north to Princeton! All this with soldiers in rags who hadn't slept for days! People were tougher then. They weren't afraid to die. When Washington ran into a British force south of Princeton, an American general named Mercer was captured, and they called him a damn rebel and told him to beg for quarter, and he said he wasn't a rebel and refused to beg, so they bayoneted him to death. They weren't such nice guys, the British, as *Masterpiece Theatre* lets on. When things looked their worst at Princeton, Washington on a white horse—this is honest truth, on a truly white horse—

led his men into the heart of the British fire and turned the tide, and ran after the retreating redcoats shouting, 'It's a fine fox chase, my boys!' "

"He sounds cruel," Ahmad said.

Charlie made that negative American noise in his nose, *aahnn*, signifying dismissal, and said, "Not really. War is cruel, but not the men who wage it necessarily. Washington was a gentleman. When the battle at Princeton was over, he stopped and complimented a wounded British soldier on what a gallant fight they had put up. In Philadelphia, he protected the Hessian prisoners from the pissed-off crowds, who would have killed them. See, the Hessians, like most professional European soldiers, were trained to give quarter only in certain circumstances, and to take no prisoners otherwise—that's what they did on Long Island, they butchered us—and they were so amazed at the humane treatment they got instead that a quarter of them stayed here when the war was over. They intermarried with the Pennsylvania Dutch. They became Americans."

"You seem very enamored of George Washington."

"Well, why not?" Charlie considers, as if Ahmad has sprung a trap. "You have to be, if you care about New Jersey. Here's where he earned his spurs. The great thing about him, he was a learner. He learned, for one thing, to get along with the New Englanders. From the standpoint of a Virginia planter, the New Englanders were a bunch of unkempt anarchists; they had blacks and red Indians in their ranks as if these guys were white men, just like they had them on their whaling ships. Washington himself, actually, for that matter, had a big black buck for a sidekick, also called Lee, no relation to Robert E. When the war was over, Washington freed him for his services to the Revolution. He had learned to think of slavery as a bad thing. He wound up encouraging black enlistment, after resisting the idea initially. You've heard the word 'pragmatic'?"

"Of course."

"That was Georgie. He learned to take what came, to fight guerrilla-style: hit and hide, hit and hide. He retreated but he never gave up. He was the Ho Chi Minh of his day. We were like Hamas. We were Al-Qaida. The thing about New Jersey was," Charlie hurries to add, when Ahmad takes a breath as if he might interrupt, "the British wanted it to be a model of pacification—winning hearts and minds, you've heard of that. They saw what they did on Long Island was counterproductive, recruiting more resistance, and were trying to play nice here, to woo the colonists back to the mother country. At Trenton, what Washington was saying to the British was, 'This is real. This is beyond nice.' "

"Beyond nice," Ahmad repeats. "That could be the title of a TV series for you to direct."

Charlie doesn't acknowledge the playful idea. He is selling something. He goes on, "He showed the world what can be done against the odds, against a superpower. He showed— and this is where Vietnam and Iraq come in—that in a war between an imperialist occupier and the people who actually live there, the people will eventually prevail. They know the terrain. They have more at stake. They have nowhere else to go. It wasn't just the Continental Army in New Jersey; it was the local militias, little sneaky bands of locals all across New Jersey, acting on their own, picking off British soldiers one by one and disappearing, back into the countryside—not playing fair, in other words, by the other guy's rules. The attack on the Hessians was sneaky, too—in the middle of a blizzard, and on a holiday when not even soldiers ought to have to work. Washington was saying, 'Hey, this is *our* war.' About Valley Forge: Valley Forge gets all the publicity, but the winters after that he camped out in New Jersey—in Middlebrook in the Watchung Mountains, and then in Morristown. In Morristown, the first winter was the coldest in a century. They chopped down six hundred acres of oak and chestnut trees to make huts and have firewood. There was so much snow that winter the provisions couldn't get through and they nearly starved."

"For the state of the world now," Ahmad offers, to get in step with Charlie, "it might have been better if they had. The United States might have become a kind of Canada, a peaceable and sensible country, though infidel."

Charlie's surprised laugh becomes a snort in his nose. "Dream on, Madman. There's too much energy here for peace and sensible. Contending energies—that's what the Constitution allows for. That's what we get." He shifts in his seat and shakes out a Marlboro. Smoke envelops his face as he squints through the windshield and appears to reflect upon what he has told his young driver. "The next time we're south on Route Nine we ought to swing over to Monmouth Battlefield. The Americans fell back, but stood up to the British well enough to show the French they were worth supporting. And the Spanish and Dutch. All of Europe was out to cut England down to size. Like the U.S. now. It was ironical: Louis Seize spent so much supporting us he taxed the French to the point where they revolted and cut off his head. One revolution led to another. That happens." Charlie exhales heavily and in a graver, surreptitious voice pronounces, as if not sure Ahmad should hear the words, "History isn't something over and done, you know. It's now, too. Revolution never stops. You cut off its head, it grows two."

Three

"The Hydra," Ahmad says, to show he is not completely ignorant. The image recurs in Shaikh Rashid's sermons, in illustration of the futility of America's crusade against Islam, and was first encountered by Ahmad in watching children's television, the cartoons on Saturday mornings, while his mother slept late. Just he and the television in the living room—the electronic box so frantic and bumptious with the hiccups and pops and crashes and excited high-pitched voices of cartoon adventure, and its audience, the watching child, utterly quiet and still, the sound turned down to let his mother sleep off her date last night. The Hydra was a comic creature, all its heads chattering with each other on their undulating necks.

"These old revolutions," Charlie continues confidentially, "have much to teach our jihad." Ahmad's lack of a response leads the other to ask in a quick, testing voice, "You are with the jihad?"

"How could I not be? The Prophet urges it in the Book." Ahmad quotes: *"Mohammed is Allah's apostle. Those who follow him are ruthless to the unbelievers but merciful to one another."*

Still, the jihad seems very distant. Delivering modern furniture and collecting furniture that had been modern to its dead owners, he and Charlie ride Excellency through a sweltering morass of pizzerias and nail salons, thrift outlets and gas stations, White Castles and Blimpies. *Krispy Kreme* and *Lovely Laundry, Rims and Tires* and 877-TEETH-14, *Starlite Motel* and *Prime Office Suites, Bank of America* and *Metro Information Shredding, Testigos de Jehovah* and *New Christian Tabernacle:* signs in a dizzying multitude shout out their potential enhancements of all the lives crammed where once there had been pastures and water-powered factories. The thick-walled, eternity-minded structures of municipal purpose still stood, preserved as museums or apartments or quarters for civic organizations. American flags flew everywhere, some so tattered and faded they had evidently been forgotten on their flagstaffs. The world's hopes had centered here for a time, but the time was past. Ahmad sees through Excellency's high windshield clots of males and females his age gathering in gabbling idleness, idleness with an edge of menace, the brown skins of the females bared by skimpy shorts and tight elastic halters, and the males arrayed in tank tops and grotesquely droopy shorts, earrings and wool skullcaps, clownish jokes they play on themselves.

A kind of terror at the burden of having a life to live hits Ahmad through the dusty windshield glare. These doomed animals gathered in the odor of mating and mischief yet have the comfort of their herded kindred, and each harbors some hope or plan of a future, a job, a destination, an aspiration if only to rise in the ranks of dope dealers or pimps. Whereas he, Ahmad, with abilities that Mr. Levy had told him were ample, has no plan: the God attached to him like an invisible twin, his other self, is a God not of enterprise but of submission. Though he endeavors to pray five times a day, if only in the truck body's rectangular cave with its stacked blankets and packing pads, or in a patch of gravel behind a roadside eating place where he can spread his mat for a cleansing five minutes, the Merciful and Compassionate has illuminated no straight path into a vocation. It is as if in the delicious sleep of his devotion to Allah his future has been amputated. When, in the long lulls of devouring the miles, he confesses his disquiet to Charlie, the usually talkative and well-informed man seems evasive and discomfited.

"Well, in less than three years you'll be getting the Class A CDL and can drive any load—hazmat, trailer rigs—out of state. You'll be making great money."

"But to what end? As you say, to consume consumer goods? To feed and clothe my body that will eventually become decrepit and worthless?"

"That's a way to look at it. 'Life sucks, and then you die.' But doesn't that leave out a lot?"

"What? 'Wife and kids,' as people say?"

"Well, with wife and kids on board, it's true, a lot of these big, meaning-of-it-all existential questions take a back seat."

"You have the wife and kids, and yet you rarely speak of them to me."

"What's to say? I love 'em. And what about love, Madman? Don't you feel it? Like I say, we got to get you laid."

"That is a kind wish on your part, but without marriage it would go against my beliefs."

"Oh, come on. The Prophet himself was no monk. He said a man could have four wives. The girl we'd get you wouldn't be a good Muslim; she'd be a hooker. It wouldn't matter to her and shouldn't matter to you. She'd be a filthy infidel with or without whatever you did to her."

"I do not desire uncleanness."

"Well, what the hell do you desire, Ahmad? Forget fucking, I'm sorry I brought it up. What about just being alive? Breathing the air, seeing the clouds? Doesn't that beat being dead?"

A spatter of sudden summer rain from the sky—cloudless, an overall pewter gray shot through with smothered sunlight—speckles the windshield; at the touch of Ahmad's hand the wipers begin their cumbersome flapping. The one on the driver's side leaves a rainbow arc of unswept moisture, a gap in its rubber blade: he makes a mental note to replace that faulty blade. "It depends," he tells Charlie. "Only the unbelievers fear death absolutely."

"What about daily pleasures? You love life, Madman,

don't deny it. Just the way you come to work early every morning, eager to see what's on our schedule. We've had other kids on the truck who didn't see a thing, didn't give a damn, they were dead behind the eyes. All they cared about was stopping at the junk-food chains to eat a ton and take a piss and, when the day was over, going out and getting high with their buddies. You, you got potential."

"I have been told that. But if I love life, as you say, it is as a gift from God that He chose to give, and can choose to take away."

"O.K., then. As God wills. In the meantime, enjoy the ride."

"I am."

"Good boy."

One July day, on the way back to the store, Charlie directs him to swing into Jersey City, through a warehouse region rich in chain-link fences and glittering coils of razor wire and the rusting rails of abandoned freight-car spurs. They proceed past new glass-skinned tall apartment buildings being erected in place of old warehouses, to a park on a point from which the Statue of Liberty and lower Manhattan loom close. The two men—Ahmad in black jeans, Charlie in a loose olive-drab coverall and yellow work boots—attract suspicious glances from older, Christian tourists as they all stand out on a concrete viewing platform. Children who have just been in the domed Liberty Science Center dart in and out and jump on the low iron fence that guards the drop to the river. A breeze and swarms of sparkle like dazzling gnats come in off the Upper Bay. The world-famous statue, copper-green across the water, presents a rather diminished side view at this angle, but lower Manhattan thrusts forward like a magnificently bristling snout. "It's nice," Charlie observes, "to see those towers gone." Ahmad is too busy absorbing the sight to respond; Charlie clarifies, "They were ugly—way out of proportion. They didn't belong."

Ahmad says, "Even from New Prospect, from the hill above the falls, you could see them."

"Half of New Jersey could see the damn things. A lot of the people killed in them lived in Jersey."

"I pitied them. Especially those that jumped. How terrible, to be so trapped by crushing heat that jumping to certain death is better. Think of the dizziness, looking down before you jump."

Charlie says hurriedly, as if reciting, "Those people worked in finance, furthering the interests of the American empire, the empire that sustains Israel and inflicts death every day on Palestinians and Chechnyans, Afghans and Iraqis. In war, pity has to be put on hold."

"Many were merely guards and waitresses."

"Serving the empire in their way."

"Some were Muslims."

"Ahmad, you must think of it as a war. War isn't tidy. There is collateral damage. Those Hessians George Washington woke from their sleep and shot were no doubt good German boys, sending their pay home to Mother. An empire sucks the blood of subject peoples so cleverly they don't know why they're dying, why they have no strength. The enemies around us, the children and fat people in shorts giving us their dirty little looks—have you noticed?—do not see themselves as oppressors and killers. They see themselves as innocent, absorbed in their private lives. Everyone is innocent—they are innocent, the people jumping from the towers were innocent, George W. Bush is innocent, a simple reformed drunk from Texas who loves his nice wife and naughty daughters. Yet, out of all this innocence, somehow evil emerges. The Western powers steal our oil, they take our land—"

"They take our God," Ahmad says eagerly, interrupting his mentor.

Charlie stares for a second, then agrees slowly, as if this had not occurred to him. "Yes. I guess so. They take from Muslims their traditions and a sense of themselves, the pride in themselves that all men are entitled to."

This is not quite what Ahmad said, and sounds a bit false, a bit forced and far removed from the concrete living God who stands beside Ahmad as close as the sunshine warming the skin of his neck. Charlie stands opposite him with knitted thick eyebrows and his flexible mouth clenched in a sort of pained stubbornness; he has a soldier stiffness to him, a cancellation of the genial road companion habitually lodged in the side of Ahmad's vision. Seen frontally, Charlie, who neglected to shave this morning, and whose eyebrows meet above the creased bridge of his nose, fails to harmonize with the expansive loveliness of the day—the sky cloudless but for a puffy far scatter over Long Island, the ozone at the zenith so intense it seems a smooth-walled pit of blue fire, the accumulated towers of lower Manhattan a single gleaming mass, speedboats purring and sailboats tilting in the bay, the cries and conversation of the tourist crowd making a dapple of harmless sound around them. *This beauty*, Ahmad thinks, *must mean something*—a hint from Allah, a foreshadow of Paradise.

Charlie is asking him a question. "Would you fight them, then?"

Ahmad has missed what "them" refers to, but says "Yes" as if answering a roll call.

Charlie appears to repeat himself: "Would you fight with your life?"

"How do you mean?"

Charlie is insistent; his brows bear down. "Would you *give* your life?"

The sun leans on Ahmad's neck. "Of course," he says, trying to lighten the exchange with a flicking gesture of his right hand. "If God wills it."

The slightly false and menacing Charlie collapses, and is replaced by the good-natured motormouth, the ersatz older brother, who grins to put the exchange behind them, tucking it away. "Just what I thought," he says. "Madman, you're a good brave kid."

At times, as the summer wears on, its August bringing later sunrises and earlier dusks, Ahmad is considered competent enough, enough a trustworthy member of the Excellency team, to handle on his own, with a dolly in the truck, a day of deliveries. He and two black minimum-wagers— "the muscle," Charlie calls them—have the truck loaded by ten, and Ahmad is off with a list of addresses, a sheaf of invoices, and his set of full-color Hagstrom maps from Sussex County all the way down to Cape May. The deliveries one day include an old-fashioned item, a horsehair-stuffed leather ottoman, to a town on the Upper Shore, south of Asbury Park; it will be his longest drive of the day and his last destination. He takes the Garden State past Route 18, skirting the eastern edge of the U.S. Naval Ammunition Depot, and exits at 195 East, toward Camp Evans. By means of lesser roads, over misty low terrain, he works his truck toward the sea; the salty wild smell strengthens and there is even a sound—the precisely spaced breathing of the surf.

The Shore is a region of architectural oddities, of buildings in the shape of elephants or cookie jars, windmills and plaster lighthouses. A long-settled state, it holds in its cemeteries, Charlie has more than once boasted, tombstones cut to imitate a giant shoe or a light bulb or one man's beloved Mercedes; there are, in pine barrens and along mountain roads, a number of allegedly haunted mansions and insane asylums, which flit through Ahmad's mind as daylight gradually fades. Excellency's headlights pick out seaside cottages in tight rows, with scruffy front yards of lightly grassed sand. Motels and night spots name themselves with neon signs whose defective connections sizzle in the dusk. Ornately carpentered houses built as vacation homes for well-to-do large families with their numerous servants have been reduced to offering ROOMS and BED & BREAKFAST and VACANCY. Even in August this is not a bustling resort. Along what seems to be the main street one or two restaurants are plywooded shut, their oysters and clams and crabs and lobsters still advertised but no longer served up steaming.

From the bleached boardwalks that do for sidewalks, clusters of people stare at his high square orange truck as if its appearance is an event; they look, in their medley of bathing suits and beach towels and tattered shorts and T-shirts imprinted with hedonistic slogans and jibes, like refugees who were given no time to gather their effects before fleeing. Children among them wear towering hats of plastic foam, and those who might be their grandparents, having forsaken all thought of dignity, make themselves ridiculous in clinging outfits of many colors and patterns. Sunburned and overfed, some sport in complacent self-mockery the same foam carnival hats as their grandchildren wear, tall and striped ones as in the books by Dr. Seuss or headgear shaped like open-mouthed sharks or lobsters extending a giant red mitt of a claw. *Devils.* The guts of the men sag hugely and the monstrous buttocks of the women seesaw painfully as they tread the boardwalk in swollen running shoes. A few steps from death, these American elders defy decorum and dress as toddlers.

Searching for the address on the last invoice of the day, Ahmad steers the truck through a grid of streets back from the beach. There are no curbs or sidewalks. The macadam's edges crumble into patches of sunbaked grass. The houses are shingled and small and close together, with an air of minimum upkeep and seasonal rental; about half of them display signs of life within—lights, a flickering television screen. Children's bright beach toys litter some yards; surfboards and inflatable Nessies and SpongeBobs wait on screened porches for the next day's oceanic romp.

Number 292, Wilson Way. The cottage shows no exterior signs of habitation, and the front windows are masked by drawn Venetian blinds, so Ahmad is startled when the front door pops open seconds after he presses the chiming doorbell. A tall man with a narrow head made to seem narrower still by his close-set eyes and tight-cropped black hair stands behind the screen door. Unlike the crowds near the beach, he is dressed in sun-repellent clothes, in gray trousers and a long-sleeved shirt the indeterminate color of an oil stain, buttoned at his wrists and throat. His stare is not friendly. There is a wiry tension to his whole body; his stomach is admirably flat.

"Mr."—Ahmad consults his invoice—"Karini? I have a delivery from Excellency Home Furnishings in New Prospect." He consults the invoice again. "An ottoman in multi-colored dyed leather."

"In New Prospect," the flat-stomached man repeats. "No Charlie?"

Ahmad is slow to understand. "Uh—I drive the truck now. Charlie is busy in the office, learning the business in the office. His father is sick with diabetes." Ahmad fears these superfluous sentences will not be understood, and he blushes, there in the dark.

The tall man turns and repeats the words "New Prospect" to the others in the room. There are three others, Ahmad sees—all men. One is short and heavyset and older than the other two, who are not much older than Ahmad. All are dressed not in resort clothes but as if for manual labor, sitting on the rented furniture as if waiting for the work to begin. They respond with mutters of approval in which Ahmad thinks he hears, buried among the inflections, the words *fulūs* and *kāfir*; the tall man observes him listening and asks him sharply, *"Enta btehki 'arabī?"*

Ahmad blushes and tells him, *"La'—ana aasif. Inglizi."*

Satisfied, and a shade less tense, the man says, "Bring in, please. All day we wait."

Excellency Home Furnishings doesn't sell many otto-mans; they belong, like New Prospect's City Hall, to a more ornate age. Wrapped in a thick transparent plastic to protect its delicate skin of tinted leather patches sewn together in an abstract six-sided pattern, the item, pre-owned but well preserved, is a stuffed cylinder solid enough to take a sitting man's weight but soft enough to support pleasantly the slippered feet of one stretched at his ease in an armchair. It makes a lightweight armful, slightly rustling as Ahmad carries it from the truck across the crabgrass to the front room, where the four men sit in the light of a single wan table lamp. None offer to take the burden from his arms.

"On floor is O.K.," he is told.

Ahmad sets the thing down. "It should go very nicely in here," he says, to break the silence in the room, and, standing up, "Would you please sign here, Mr. Karini?"

"Karini not here. I sign for Karini."

"None of you is Mr. Karini?" The three men smile the quick, hopeful smile of those who have not understood what has been asked.

"I sign for Karini," the leader of the group insists. "I am colleague of Karini." Without further resistance Ahmad lays the invoice on the end table with the dim lamp and indicates with the pen where to sign. The nameless lean man signs. The signature is thoroughly illegible, Ahmad observes, and he notices for the first time that one of the Chehabs, father or son, has scrawled "NC" on the invoice—no charge, significantly less than the hundred-dollar minimum for free delivery.

As he closes the screen door behind himself, more lights come on in the cottage's front room, and as he walks across the sandy lawn to his truck he hears an excited gabble of Arabic, with some laughter. Ahmad climbs up into the driver's seat of the truck and revs the engine to make sure they hear him depart. He moves down Wilson Way to the first intersection and turns right, parking in front of a cottage that looks unoccupied. Quickly, quietly, his breathing shallow in his chest, Ahmad walks back along a path worn in the grass in place of a sidewalk. No car or person is moving on the scruffy little street. He goes to the window at the side of 292's front room, where a struggling hydrangea bush with parched lavender blooms offers some concealment, and carefully peeks in.

The ottoman has been disrobed of its plastic protection and set up on a tile-top coffee table in front of a worn plaid sofa. With a retractable touch-knife the size of a silver dollar, the leader has cut the stitches on one of the triangular patches that form a six-sided star, a snowflake of red and green, in the circular leather top. When this triangle has become a big-enough loose flap, the leader's lean hand can insert itself down the inside and extract, pinched between two long fingers, quantities of green American currency. Ahmad cannot read, through the dying hydrangea bush, the denominations, but, to judge from the reverence with which the men are counting and arranging the bills on the tile-top table, the denominations are high.

IV

CHARLIE'S UNCLE and Habib Chehab's brother, Maurice, rarely comes up from Florida, but the heat and humidity of Miami in July and August drive him north for those months. He stays off and on at Habib's home in Pompton Lakes and shows up occasionally at Excellency Home Furnishings, where Ahmad sees him—a man much like his brother, only bigger and more formal, given to seersucker suits, white leather shoes, and shirts and neckties rather too obviously coördinated. He formally shakes Ahmad's hand the first time they meet, and the boy has an unpleasant sensation of being sized up, by eyes more guarded than Habib's, with even more gold in them, and less quick to break into a twinkle of amusement. He is the younger brother, it turns out, though he has the overweening manner of an older. Ahmad, an only child, is fascinated by brotherhood—its advantages and disadvantages, the quality it imparts of being in some sense duplicated. Had he been blessed with a brother, Ahmad would feel less alone, perhaps, and rely less on the God he carries with him, in his pulse and thoughts. Whenever he and Maurice see each other in the store, the portly, smooth man in his pale clothes gives Ahmad a slightly smiling nod that says, *I know you, young man. I have your number.*

Ahmad's glimpse of the dollars he delivered to the four men in the cottage on the Upper Shore stays with him as something partaking of the supernatural, that featureless vastness which yet deigns, by Its own unfathomable will, to reach into our lives. He wonders if he dares confess his discovery to Charlie. Was Charlie aware of the contents of the ottoman? How many others of the pieces of furniture they have delivered and collected were similarly loaded in their crevices and interior hollows? And to what purpose? The mystery savors of the events reported in the newspapers, the headlines he barely skims, of political violence abroad and domestic violence locally, and in the nightly newscasts that he clicks through while channel-surfing the stations on his mother's obsolete Admiral.

He has taken to searching television for traces of God in this infidel society. He watches beauty pageants where luminous-skinned and white-toothed girls, along with one or two token entrants of color, compete in charming the master of ceremonies with their singing or dancing talents and their frequent if hasty expressions of gratitude to the Lord for their blessings, which they intend to devote, when their singing days in bathing suits are done, to their fellow-man in the form of such lofty vocations as doctor, educator, agronomist, or, holiest calling of all, homemaker. Ahmad discovers a specifically Christian channel featuring deep-voiced, middle-aged men in suits of unusual colors, with wide, reflective lapels, who leave off their impassioned rhetoric ("Are you ready for Jesus?" they ask, and "Have you received Jesus in your hearts?") to break suddenly into sly flirtation with the middle-aged female members of the audience, or else jump back, snapping their fingers, into song. Christian song interests Ahmad, above all gospel choruses in iridescent robes, the fat black women bouncing and rolling with an intensity that at times appears artificially induced but at others, as the choruses go on, appears to be genuinely kindled from within. The women hoist high their hands along with their voices and clap in a rocking, infectious manner that spreads even to the smattering of whites among them, this being one area of American experience, like sports and crime, where darker skins unquestionably prevail. Ahmad knows, from Shaikh Rashid's dry, half-smiling allusions, of the Sufi enthusiasm and rapture that had anciently afflicted Islam, but finds not even a faint echo of it in the Islamic channels beamed from Manhattan and Jersey City — just the five calls to prayer broadcast over a still slide of the great mosque of Mohammed Ali in Saladin's Citadel, and solemn panels of bespectacled professors and mullahs discussing the anti-Islamic fury that has perversely possessed the present-day West, and sermons delivered by a turbanned imam seated at a bare table, relayed by a static camera from a studio strictly devoid of images.

It is Charlie who broaches the subject. One day in the cab of the truck, as they pass through an unusually empty piece of northern New Jersey, between an extensive cemetery and a surviving piece of the Meadows — cattails and shiny-leaved reeds rooted in brackish water — he asks, "Something eating you, Madman? You seem quiet lately."

"I am generally quiet, no?"

"Yeah, but this is different. At first it was 'Show me' quiet, now it's more a 'What's up?' kind of quiet."

Ahmad does not have so many friends in the world that he

can risk losing one. There is no going back from this juncture, he knows; he has little to go back to. He tells Charlie, "Some days ago, when I was doing deliveries alone, I saw a strange thing. I saw men removing wads of money from that ottoman I delivered to the Shore."

"They opened it in front of you?"

"No. I left, and then crept back and looked in the window. Their manner made me suspicious, and curious."

"You know what curiosity did to the cat, don't you?"

"It killed it. But ignorance can also kill. If I am to deliver, I should know what I am delivering."

"Why so, Ahmad?" Charlie says, almost tenderly. "I saw you as not wanting to know more than you can handle. In truth, ninety-nine percent of the time the furniture you are delivering is just that—furniture."

"But who are that fortunate one percent who win a bonus?" Ahmad feels a tense freedom, now that the juncture is behind them. It is like, he imagines, the release and responsibility a man and a woman feel when they first take off their clothes together. Charlie, too, seems to feel this; his voice sounds lighter, having shed a level of pretense.

"The fortunate," he says, "are true believers."

"They believe," Ahmad guesses, "in jihad?"

"They believe," Charlie carefully restates, "in action. They believe that something can be done. That the Muslim peasant in Mindanao need not starve, that the Bangladeshi child need not drown, that the Egyptian villager need not go blind with schistosomiasis, that the Palestinians need not be strafed by Israeli helicopters, that the faithful need not eat the sand and camel dung of the world while the Great Satan grows fat on sugar and pork and underpriced petroleum. They believe that a billion followers of Islam need not have their eyes and ears and souls corrupted by the poisonous entertainments of Hollywood and a ruthless economic imperialism whose Christian-Jewish God is a decrepit idol, a mere mask concealing the despair of atheists."

"Where does the money come from?" Ahmad asks, when Charlie's words—not so different, after all, from the world-picture that Shaikh Rashid more silkily paints—have run their course. "And what are the recipients to do with these funds?"

"The money comes," Charlie tells him, "from those who love Allah, both within the U.S. and abroad. Think of those four men as seeds placed within the soil, and the money as water to keep the soil moist, so that some day the seeds will split their shells and bloom. *Allāhu akbar!*"

"Does the money," Ahmad persists, "come somehow through Uncle Maurice? His arrival here seems to make a difference, though he disdains the daily workings of the store. And your good father—how much is he part of all this?"

Charlie laughs, indulgently; he is a son who has grown beyond his father but continues to honor him, as Ahmad has done to his own. "Hey, who are you, the CIA? My father is an old-fashioned immigrant, loyal to the system that took him in and let him prosper. If he knew any of what you and I are discussing, he would report us to the FBI."

Ahmad in his new capacity tries a joke: "Who would swiftly mislay the report."

Charlie does not laugh. He says, "These are important secrets that you have extracted from me. They are life-and-death stuff, Madman. I'm wondering right now if I've made a mistake, telling you all this."

Ahmad seeks to minimize what has passed between them.

He realizes that he has swallowed knowledge that cannot be coughed back up. *Knowledge is freedom*, it said on the front of Central High. Knowledge can also be a prison, with no way out once you're in. "You've made no mistake. You've told me very little. It was not you who led me back to the window to see the money being counted. There could be many explanations for the money. You could have denied knowledge of it, and I would have believed you."

"I could have," Charlie concedes. "Perhaps I should have."

"No. It would have put falsity between us, where there has been trust."

"Then you must tell me this: are you with us?"

"I am with those," Ahmad says slowly, "who are with God."

"O.K. Good enough. Be as silent as God about this. Do not tell your mother. Do not tell your girlfriend."

"I have no girlfriend."

"That's right. I promised to do something about that, didn't I?"

"You said I should get laid."

"Right. I'll work on it."

"Do not, please. It is not yours to work on."

"Friends help each other out," Charlie insists. He reaches over and squeezes the young driver's shoulder, and Ahmad does not entirely like it; it reminds him of Tylenol's bullying grip that time in the high-school hall.

The boy states, with a new-won man's dignity, "One more question, and then I will say nothing until I am spoken to on these matters. Is there a plan developing, with these seeds that are being watered?"

Ahmad knows Charlie's facial expressions so well he does

not have to look sideways in the truck to see the man's rubbery lips work around as if exploring the shape of his own teeth, and then heavily exhale in an exaggerated sigh of exasperation. "Like I said, there are always a number of projects under consideration, and how they develop is somewhat hard to predict. What does the Book say, Madman? *And the Jews plotted, and God plotted. But of those who plot, God is the best.*"

"In these plots, will I ever have a part to play?"

"You might. Would you like that, kid?"

Again, Ahmad feels a juncture being reached, and a gate closing behind him. "I believe I would."

"You believe? You got to do better than that."

"As you say, individual events are not easy to predict. But the lines are clear."

"The lines?"

"The lines of battle. The armies of Satan versus those of God. As the Book affirms, *Idolatry is worse than carnage.*"

"Right. *Right*," Charlie agrees, and slaps his thigh as if to wake himself up, there in the passenger's seat. "I like that. Worse than carnage." He is a naturally talkative and humorous man, and it has been hard for him to keep a straight face, talking with Ahmad like two men walking through a cemetery where they may some day lie. "One thing to keep in mind," he adds. "There's an anniversary coming up, in September. And the people who call the shots—our generals, so to speak—have an old-fashioned thing about anniversaries."

Jacob and Teresa have made love and bring the sheets up over their naked bodies. The breeze through her bedroom windows is cool. September is drawing near; single yellow leaves, like isolated sparks, show in the wearying greenery. They both, he reflects after his warm bath in her flesh, could lose a few pounds. Her skin, where it is not freckled, is almost too pale, like that of a plastic doll except that it yields under his thumb, leaving a pink dent slow to erase itself. His shaggy arms and chest pain him with their slack, rumpled look; at home the bathroom mirror shows him the beginnings of puckery pseudo-breasts, and his stomach under its twin black swirls of hair has developed another fold. On his chest, the white hairs have no curl, and stick out like wavery antennae: an old man's hairs.

Terry cuddles against him, her snub nose snuggled into his armpit. His love for her stirs within him like the start of nausea.

"Jack?" she breathes.

"What?" He sounds ruder than he had intended.

"What makes you so sad?"

"I'm not sad," he says. "I'm fucked. You really do it. I thought my old chassis was ready for the junk heap, but you get those spark plugs firing. You're gorgeous, Terry."

"Cut the malarkey, as my father used to say. You haven't answered my question. Why are you sad?"

"Maybe I was thinking, Labor Day's coming. It's going to be harder to work us in." He has learned to express his difficulties in deceiving his wife without mentioning Beth's name, which Terry hates to hear, for some reason that eludes him. If the truth were known, Beth should be the jealous and indignant one.

Terry smells his very thought. "You're so afraid of Beth's finding out," she spitefully says. "So what if she did? Where can she go? Who would want her, in the shape she's in?"

"Is that the point?"

Four

"No? So what is the point, baby? You tell me."

"Not hurting people?" he suggests.

"You don't think I hurt? You think being fucked and deserted the next minute doesn't hurt?"

Jack sighs. The fight is on, the same old fight. "I'm sorry. I'd like to be with you more." Leaving before he gets bored suits him, actually. Women can be boring. They make everything personal. They're so wrapped up in self-preservation, self-presentation, self-dramatization. With men you don't have to keep maneuvering, you just punch. Dealing with a woman is like jujitsu, looking for the trip.

She senses the threatening run of his thoughts and says, mollifyingly if grumpily, "She probably guesses anyway."

"How would she do that?" Though of course Terry is right.

"Women know," she tells him smugly, bragging up her gender, cuddling closer to him, and toying annoyingly with the hair on his rumpled slack belly. She says, "I keep telling myself, 'Love him less. For your own good, girl. For his good, too.' "

But as Terry says this, she feels an inner sliding and glimpses the relief she might experience if he indeed were to become less to her—if her tacky relationship with this melancholy old loser of a guidance counselor were in fact to end. At the age of forty she has parted from a number of men, and how many of them would she want back? With each break, it seems to her in retrospect, she returned to her single life with a fresh forthrightness and energy, like facing a blank, taut, primed canvas after some days away from the easel. The broken circle of her, an arc of it held open in hope of a phone call from a certain man, a knock on the door, an invasion and transformation from without, would close again. This Jack Levy, smart as he is, and even sensitive at times, is a heavy case. A guilty Jewish gloom weighs him down, and her too, if she lets it. She needs somebody nearer her own age, and unmarried. These married men are always more married than they let on at first. They even try to marry *her*, without letting go of the legal one first.

"How's Ahmad doing?" he asks her, pseudo-paternally.

He keeps asking her about Ahmad, though as far as she's concerned she wants to move on from mothering to something she's better at. "With me on night duty lately," she says, "and him doing deliveries until after dark many days, we hardly overlap. He's gotten fuller in the face and the rest of him more muscular, what with all this lifting he does—this Charlie he loves so much just comes along for the ride, as far as I can tell. These Lebanese, they get the last penny's worth out of their help. The blacks they hire keep quitting on them, Ahmad did mention. Lately they seem to have promoted him—at least he comes home later and, the few times I see him, acts preoccupied."

"Preoccupied?" Jack says, preoccupied himself—worrying about big Beth, no doubt. Face it: much as she would miss Jack's flattery in bed when they get there, he would be good riddance. Maybe she needs another artist, even if he's like the last, Leo: Leo the un-lion-hearted, utterly stuck on himself, a dripper and scrubber channeling Pollock sixty years too late, quick to push and slap back when he's de-inhibited on liquor or meth, but at least he made her laugh and didn't try to lay a guilt trip on her, implying he could have been a better mother of Ahmad than she was. Or maybe she should go out with a resident, like that new little guy with a blinky stammer on his way to be a neurosurgeon; but, face it, she is too old for a resident now, and in any case they always pass up the nurses they fuck and go for the proctologist's daughter. Still, just the thought of the world of men out there, even at her age, even in northern New Jersey, hardens her heart against this lugubrious, boringly well-intentioned, stale-smelling man. She resolves to put him behind her.

"Secretive," she clarifies. "Maybe he's found a girl. I hope so. Isn't he way overdue?"

Jack says, "Kids today have more to worry about than we did. At least than I did—I shouldn't talk as if we're the same age."

"Oh, go ahead. Help yourself."

"It's not just AIDS and the rest; there's a certain hunger for, I don't know, the absolute, when everything is so relative, and all the economic forces are pushing instant gratification and credit-card debt at them. It's not just the Christian right—Ashcroft and his morning revival meeting down in D.C. You see it in Ahmad. And the Black Muslims. People want to go back to simple—black and white, right and wrong, when things aren't simple."

"So my son is simple-minded."

"In a way. But so is most of mankind. Otherwise, being human is too tough. Unlike the other animals, we know too much. They, the other animals, know just enough to get the job done and die. Eat, sleep, fuck, have babies, and die."

"Jack, everything you say is depressing. That's why you're so sad."

"All I'm saying is that kids like Ahmad need to have something they don't get from society any more. Society doesn't let them be innocent any more. The crazy Arabs are right—hedonism, nihilism, that's all we offer. Listen to the lyrics of these rock and rap stars—just kids themselves, with smart agents. Kids have to make more decisions than they used to, because adults can't tell them what to do. We don't *know* what to do, we don't have the answers we used to; we just futz along, trying not to think. Nobody accepts responsibility, so the kids, some of the kids, take it on. Even at a dump like Central High, where the demographics are stacked against the whole school population, you see it—this wish to do right, to be good, to sign up for something—the Army, the marching band, the gang, the choir, the student council, the Boy Scouts even. The Boy Scout leader, the priests, all they want is to bugger the kids, it turns out, but the kids keep showing up, hoping for some guidance. In the halls, their faces break your heart, they're so hopeful, wanting to be *good*, to amount to something. They expect something of themselves. This is America, we all expect something, even the sociopaths have some sort of a good opinion of themselves. You know what they wind up being, the worst discipline cases? They wind up being cops and high-school teachers. They want to please society, though they say they don't. They want to be worthy, if we could just tell them what worth is." His discourse, delivered in a rapid, edgy mutter from within his hairy chest, lurches: "Shit, forget what I just said. The priests and Boy Scout troop leaders don't *only* want to bugger them; they want to be good, too. But they can't, the little boys' bottoms are just too inviting. Terry, tell me: why am I going on like this?"

Her inner sliding brings her to: "Maybe because you sense that this is your last chance."

"My last chance at what?"

"At sharing yourself with me."

"What are you saying?"

"Jack, it's no good. It's hurting your marriage and isn't doing me any good either. It did at first. You're a great guy—

just not *my* guy. After some of the jerks I've been dealing with, you're a saint. I mean it. But I got to deal with reality, I've got to think about my future. Already, Ahmad's gone—all he needs from me is some food in the refrigerator."

"*I* need you, Terry."

"You do and you don't. You think my painting's a crock—"

"Oh no. I love your painting. I love it that you have this extra dimension. Now, if Beth—"

"If Beth had an extra dimension, she'd break through the floor." She laughs at this image, sitting up in bed so her breasts bounce free of the sheet, their top half freckled, the half with the nipple untouched by the sun no matter how many other men have put their lips and fingers there.

The Irish in her, he thinks. That's what he loves, that's what he can't do without. The moxie, the defiant spark of craziness people get if they're sat on long enough—the Irish have it, the blacks and Jews have it, but it's died in him. He wanted to be a comic but he's become a humorless enforcer of a system that doesn't believe in itself. All those mornings waking up too early, he was giving himself time to die in. Learn to die in your spare time. What did Emerson say about being dead? At least you're done with the dentist. That struck him forty years ago, when he could still read something that mattered. This zaftig redhead isn't dead yet, and she knows it. But he has to protest to her, of Beth, "Let's leave her out of it. She can't help the shape she's in."

"Oh, *crap*. If she can't, who can? As to leaving her out of it, I'd have loved to, Jack, but you can't. You bring her with you. There's a look on your face, a look that says, 'So help me, dear Lord, this is just for an hour.' You treat me like a fifty-minute class period at school. I can feel you waiting for

the buzzer." *This is the way*, she thinks. This is the way
to repel him, to make herself repulsive—attack his wife.
"You're *married*, Jack. You're too fucking married for me."

"No." It comes out as a whimper.

"You *are*," Terry tells him. "I tried to forget it, but you
wouldn't let me. I give up. For my own sake, Jack, I got to
give up. Let me go now."

"What about Ahmad?"

This surprises her. "What about him?"

"I worry about him. Something's fishy with this furniture
store."

Her temper is getting short; it has not been helped by
Jack's lying there in the sweaty warmth of her bed as if he
was still her lover and had some rights of tenancy. "So
what?" she says. "Something's fishy everywhere these days. I
can't live Ahmad's life for him, and I can't live yours. I wish
you well, Jack, I truly do. You're a sweet, sad man. But if you
call me or come around after you go out the door today, it'll
be harassment."

"Hey, don't," he says brokenly, just wanting things back
the way they were an hour ago, she greeting him with a wet
kiss that carried down to their groins, the apartment door
not even closed behind them. He liked having a woman on
the side. He liked her baggage: her being a mother, her
being a painter, her being a nurse's aide, forgiving of other
people's bodies.

She gets out of the bed that smells of them both. "Let go,
Jack," she tells him, standing just out of his arm's reach.
With a wary quickness she bends down to retrieve some of
her clothes where she dropped them. Her tone is getting
pedagogic, scolding. "Don't be a leech. I bet you're a leech
on Beth, too. Sucking, sucking the life out of a woman, drag-

ging her down into your feeling so sorry for yourself. No wonder she eats. I've given what I can, Jack, and *must* move on. Please. Don't make it hard."

He begins to resent and resist this cunt's scolding tone. "I can't believe this is happening, for no reason," he says. He feels soft, too limp and damp to get out of her bed; her image of a leech has penetrated him. Maybe she's right; he's a burden on the world. He stalls. "Let's give ourselves some time to think about it," he says. "I'll call you in a week."

"Don't you dare."

This imperious command gets his goat; he snaps, "What's your reason again? I missed it."

"You teach school, you've heard of a clean slate."

"I'm a guidance counselor."

"Well, give yourself some guidance. Clean up your act."

"If I got rid of Beth, what would happen then?"

"I don't know. Nothing much, probably. Anyway, how would you get rid of her?"

Indeed, how? Terry's bra is back on, and her jeans are being angrily tugged up, his inert nakedness becoming increasingly shameful and abject. He says, "O.K. Enough said. Sorry if I've been thick." Still he keeps lying there. A melody from long ago, when the downtown bristled with movie marquees, enters his head—a cascading, slippery tune. He croons the concluding phrase: "Deedee-dit-*da*-dat-*daaa*."

"What's that?" she asks, angry though she has won.

"Not a Terry tune. Another kind, Warner Brothers. At the end a stuttering pig would pop out of a drum and say, "Th-th-that's all, folks!"

"You're not cute, you know."

He kicks off the sheet. He likes the feel of being a naked

hairy animal, spent genitals flopping, yellow-soled feet smelling cheesy; he likes the flare of alarm in the other animal's glassy bulging eyes. Standing naked, his creased and sagging sexagenarian self, Jack Levy tells her, "I'll miss the hell out of you." As the cool air licks his skin, he remembers reading years ago how that paleontologist Leakey, who found the world's oldest human in the Olduvai Gorge, claimed that a naked human being could run down and kill bare-handed any prey, even a toothed predator, smaller than he. He feels that potential within him. He could wrestle this smaller member of his own species to the floor and strangle her. "You were my last—" he begins.

"Your last what? Piece of ass? That's your problem, not mine. You can hire it, you know." Her freckled face is pink with defiance. She doesn't get it, that she doesn't have to fight him, being crude and spelling everything out. He knows when he's flunked the course. He feels his exposed flesh as dead weight.

"Hey, Terry, easy. My last reason to live, I was going to say. My last reason for joie de vivre."

"Don't do a sentimental kike number on me, Jack. I'll miss you, too." Then she has to add hurtfully, "For a while."

Charlie greets Ahmad one morning early in September saying, "This is your lucky day, Madman!"

"How so?"

"You'll see." Charlie has been sober yet brusque lately, as if something is eating at him, but whatever this surprise is pleases him so simply that, seen from the side, the corner of his restless mouth tucks into his cheek with a smile. "First, we got a ton of deliveries, one of them way down to Camden."

Four

"Do they need both of us? I don't mind doing it alone."
He has come to prefer it. In the solitude of the cab he is not
alone, God is with him. But God is Himself alone, He is the
ultimate of solitude. Ahmad loves his lonely God.

"Yep, they do. One's a Hide-A-Bed, they weigh a fucking
ton with all that internal metal, and the Camden delivery is
an eighty-eight-inch all-actual-leather nail-head sofa, with
flared arms. But you mustn't lift by the arms; they crack
right off, as one of your predecessors and I discovered.
Marked down from over a thousand, for the waiting room of
a fancy clinic for disturbed children."

"Disturbed?"

"Who isn't, right? Anyway, with the two matching armchairs it's a two-grand deal, and we don't get those every day
of the week. Watch that oil truck on your left; I think the
bastard's stoned."

But Ahmad already has his eye on the speeding, grimy
Getty tanker, wondering if the driver is taking sufficient
account of liquid surge and other factors requiring caution.
September brings with it an extra danger on the streets and
highways, as returning vacationers jostle and joust for their
old place in the pack. "Excellency is heading upscale," Charlie is saying, "with all these new houses selling for a million
up. Have you noticed, on the quiz shows, the audience no
longer laughs when you say you're from New Jersey? We're
getting to be Connecticut South, only a tunnel away from
Wall Street. My dad and uncle, they thought modest—
stained poplar and stapled vinyl for the masses—but now we
get these white-collar commuters from Montclair and Short
Hills who think nothing of forking over two grand for a
bone leather sectional or three for an Old World–style dining suite, say, with a matching Gothic-style curio cabinet
and everything carved oak. Stuff like that moves these days;

it never used to. We'd take the odd quality piece at an estate clearance and have it on the floor for years. There's new money even in poor old New Prospect."

"It is good," Ahmad says cautiously, "that business thrives." He dares to add, seeking harmony with Charlie's upbeat mood, "Perhaps the new customers expect to find a cash bonus tucked into the cushions."

Charlie's profile doesn't acknowledge any joke. He keeps his tone offhand. "We've done our payouts for now. Uncle Maurice has headed back to Miami. Now we're the ones waiting for delivery." His tone becomes less offhand; he says, "Madman, you don't talk about your job here with anybody, do you? The details. Anybody ever quiz you? Your mother, say? Any guys that she dates?"

"My mother is too self-absorbed to spare me much curiosity. She is relieved I have steady employment, and contribute now to our expenses. But we come and go in our apartment as strangers." This is not quite true, it occurs to him. The other night, during an unusual, well-cooked dinner together at the old round table where he used to study, she asked him if he had ever felt anything "fishy" at the furniture store. Not at all, he told her. He is learning to lie. To be honest with Charlie, he tells him, "I think recently my mother has suffered one of her romantic sorrows, for the other night she produced a flurry of interest in me, as if remembering that I was still there. But this mood of hers will pass. We have never communicated well. My father's absence stood between us, and then my faith, which I adopted before entering my teen years. She is a warm-natured woman, and no doubt cares for her hospital patients, but I think has as little talent for motherhood as a cat. Cats let the kittens suckle for a time and then treat them as enemies. I am not yet quite

Four

grown enough to be my mother's enemy, but I am mature enough to be an object of indifference."

"How does she feel about your not having a girlfriend?"

"I think she is relieved, if anything. An attachment to my life would complicate hers. Another woman, however young, might begin to judge her and hold her to a certain standard of conventional behavior."

Charlie interrupts: "There's a left turn coming—I think not this light but the next—where we get Route 512 to Summit, where we drop off the dinette set with the cinnamon finish. So you haven't gotten laid yet?" He takes Ahmad's silence to confirm his assertion, and says, "Good." The dimpling smile has returned to his profile. Ahmad is so used to seeing Charlie in profile that it shocks him when the man turns in the shadows of the cab and shows him both sides of his face. Having done this, Charlie returns his gaze to the shifting lights seen through the windshield. "You're right about Western advertisers," he says, picking up an old thread between them. "They push sex because it means consumption. First the liquor and flowers that go with dating, and then the breeding and the buying that goes with that, baby food and SUVs and—"

"Dinette sets," Ahmad supplies.

When Charlie is not kidding he is so serious he invites teasing. The lone eye in his profile blinks and his mouth makes a swigging motion, as if he has tasted a sour truth. "A bigger house, I was going to say. These young couples spend and go deeper and deeper into debt, which is just what the Jewish usurers want. It's the 'buy now, pay later' trap—very seductive." But he did hear the teasing; he goes on, "Sure, we're merchants. But Dad's idea was, reasonable prices. Don't encourage the customer to buy more than he can afford. Bad for him, and eventually bad for us. We didn't even accept credit cards until a couple years ago. Now we do. One must join the system," he says, "until the moment."

"The moment?"

"The moment to give it a blow from within." He sounds impatient. He seems to think Ahmad knows more than he does.

Ahmad asks him, "When does such a moment arrive?"

Charlie ponders. "It arrives when it has been created. It can be never, or can be sooner than we think."

Ahmad feels he is balanced on a scaffolding of straws, in the dizzying space of their shared faith, revealed when the other man spoke of the Jewish usurers. Having been admitted, the boy feels, to a rare level of Charlie's confidence, he in turn confides, "I have a God to whom I turn five times a day. My heart needs no other companion. The obsession with sex confesses the infidels' emptiness, and their terror. "

Charlie says, perking up, "Hey, don't knock it till you've tried it. Here we are. Number eight eleven Monroe. One cinnamon dinette set, coming up. One table, four chairs."

The house is a hybrid colonial, red brick and white wood, on a well-watered small lawn. The young lady of the house, Chinese-American, comes out on her flagstone walk to greet them. As the two men carry in chairs and an oval table, her two children, a kindergarten-age girl in hot-pink overalls with duckling appliqués and a male toddler in a food-stained T-shirt and a sagging diaper, stare and cavort as if another set of siblings is being delivered. The young mother in her happiness of fresh acquisition offers to tip Charlie a ten, but he waves it away, giving her a lesson in American equality. "It's been our pleasure," he tells her. "Enjoy."

There are fourteen more deliveries that day, and by the time they get back from Camden long shadows have crept across Reagan Boulevard, and the other stores are closed. They approach from the west. Next to Excellency Home Furnishings, on the other side of Thirteenth Street, there is a tire store that used to be a service station, with the gas island still in place though the pumps are gone, and next to it a funeral home, converted from a private mansion before this section of town went commercial, with a deep porch and white awnings and a discreet sign, UNGER & SON, out on the lawn. They park the truck in the lot and wearily clump up onto the resounding loading platform, into the back door and the hall, where Ahmad punches his card on the time clock. "Don't forget, you have a surprise," Charlie tells him.

The reminder surprises Ahmad; in the course of the long day he has forgotten. He has outgrown games.

"It's waiting upstairs," says Charlie in a voice too soft to be heard by his father, who is working late in his office. "Let yourself out the back when you're done. Put the alarm on when you go."

Habib Chehab, bald as a mole in his musty underworld of furniture new and used, emerges from behind his office door. He looks pale even after a summer of Pompton Lakes, with a sickly puffiness to his face, but he says cheerfully to Ahmad, "How's the boy?"

"I can't complain, Mr. Chehab."

The old man contemplates his young driver, feeling a need to say something additional, to cap a summer's worth of faithful service. "You the best boy," he says. "Hundreds of miles, two, three hundred miles many days, not a dent, not a scrape. No speeding ticket, either. Excellent."

"Thank you, sir. It's been my pleasure"—a phrase, he realizes, he heard from Charlie earlier in the day.

Mr. Chehab looks at him curiously. "You going to stay with us, now Labor Day here?"

"Sure. What else? I love driving."

"I just thought, boys like you—bright, obedient—go for more education."

"People have suggested it, sir, but I don't feel the need yet." More education, he feared, might weaken his faith. Doubts he had held off in high school might become irresistible in college. The Straight Path was taking him in another, purer direction. He couldn't explain this very well. Ahmad wonders how much the old man knows of the smuggled cash, of the four men in the Shore cottage, of his own son's anti-Americanism, of his brother's connections in Florida. It would be strange if he were totally ignorant of these currents; but, then, families, as Ahmad knows from his own family of two, are nests of secrets, of eggs that lightly touch but hold each its own life.

As the two men move toward the back door to the parking lot and their own separate cars—Habib's Buick, Charlie's Saab—Charlie repeats his instructions to Ahmad about activating the alarm and closing the door with its oiled double lock. Mr. Chehab asks, "The boy stays?"

Charlie puts a hand on his father's back to urge him forward. "Papa, I've given Ahmad an assignment to do upstairs. You trust him to close up, don't you?"

"Why ask? He is good boy. Like family."

"Actually," Ahmad hears Charlie explaining to his father on the loading porch, "the kid has a date and wants to freshen up and put on clean clothes."

Date? Ahmad thinks. He has already figured out the surprise Charlie has for him: it will be a hassock, like the one he delivered, stuffed with money, an end-of-summer bonus. But as if to make Charlie's lie to his father good, Ahmad does, in the little lavatory next to the water cooler, scrub the day's grime from his hands and splash water on his face and neck before making his way toward the stairs, in the middle of the store, up to the second floor. With silent steps he climbs them. The second floor displays beds and dressers, side tables and armoires, mirrors and lamps. These things bulk in the dim light of a distant bedside lamp, while the headlights of the evening rush flicker at the high windows. Unlit lampshades knife into the shadows with their acute angles; overhead fixtures dangle spiderlike. There are padded headboards, and headboards of florid wooden shapes, and others of parallel rods of brass. Bare mattresses, side by side on both sides, present a pair of receding planes raised up by the thickness of box springs mounted on metal frames. As he moves between the two receding planes, his heart beats and his nose is touched by forbidden cigarette smoke and his ears by a familiar voice. "Ahmad! They didn't tell me it would be *you*."

"Joryleen? Is that *you*? They didn't tell me anything."

The black girl steps out from behind the low-lit lampshade, under which the smoke from her cigarette, suddenly doused in an ashtray improvised from a candy bar's tinfoil wrap, stands up like a piece of sculpture, slowly twisting. As his eyes adjust he sees that she is wearing a red vinyl miniskirt and tight black top with a low oval neckline like that of a ballet leotard. Her roundnesses have been poured somehow into a new mold, narrower at the waist; her jaw is leaner. Her hair is cut shorter and splashed with blond bleach, the way it never was at Central High. Looking lower, he sees she is wearing white boots with zigzag stitching and long pointed toes, the new kind with lots of spare room in the front. "All I was told was to wait for this boy that needs to be devirginated."

"To be laid, I bet he said."

"Yes, he did, come to think of it. You don't hear that word all the time; you hear lots of others. He said he was your boss and here was where you worked. Tylenol was who he originally talked to, but he wanted then to see me and tell me how sweet I should be to this certain boy. He was a tall kind of Arab, with a shifty twitchy mouth. I said to myself, 'Joryleen, don't you trust that man,' but his cash was good. Nice clean bills."

Ahmad is struck; he would not have described Charlie as an Arab or as shifty. "They're Lebanese. Charlie's been raised pure American. He's not exactly my boss, he's the son of the owner, and we deliver furniture in a truck together."

"You know, Ahmad, pardon my saying it, but I would have figured you back in school for something a little above that. Something where you could use your head more."

"Well, Joryleen, I could say the same about you. The last time I had a good look, you were dressed up in choir robes. What you doing in that hooker outfit, talking about devirginating people?"

Defensively she tips back her head, pushing out her mouth, with its greasy shine of a coral-colored lipstick. "It's not something permanent," she explains. "Just a few favors Tylenol asks me to do for people till we get set up and can have a house of our own and all." Joryleen looks around her and changes the subject. "You mean a bunch of Arabs have all this on their own? Where their money come from?"

"You don't understand business. You borrow from the bank to create an inventory, and then the interest gets figured into your expenses. That's called capitalism. The Chehabs came over here in the 'sixties, when everything was easier."

"I guess it was," she says, and sits down bouncily on a

bare mattress, its pattern of cushioned diamond shapes cov- ered in a silvery brocade. Her little red miniskirt, smaller than a cheerleader's, allows him to see her thighs, spread fat from the pressure of the mattress edge. He thinks of only her underpants coming between her bare bottom and the fancy ticking; the thought constricts his throat. Everything about her seems to gleam—her hot-pink lipstick, her short hair moussed up into little points like porcupine quills, the gold sparkles sprinkled in the grease around her eyes. She says, to fill his silence, "Those were easy times, compared to nowadays and its job market."

"Why doesn't Tylenol get a job for this money he wants?"

"He thinks too big for any old job. He has plans to be a big man some day and meanwhile asks me to put a little bread on the table. He doesn't ax me to work the street, just oblige somebody now and then, usually some white man. When we're fixed up and settled down he's gone to treat me like a queen, he says." Since high school she has pierced one eye- brow for a little ring to add to the nostril-bead and the silver row of rings that looks like a caterpillar feeding on the upper curve of her ear. "So, Ahmad. No more just standing there staring your face off. What would you like? I could give you a blow job right the way we are and cut down on the mess, but I think your Mr. Charlie had his heart set on your get- ting a real piece of ass, which involves a scumbag and a wash- up afterwards. He paid me for the full deal, depending on how it suited you. He anticipated you might be shy."

Ahmad whimpers. "Joryleen, I can't stand to hear you talk like this."

"Talk like what way, Ahmad? You still have your head up there in Arab Neverland? I'm just trying to be clear. Let's get some clothes off and pick one of these beds. Boy, do we have the beds!"

"Joryleen, you keep those clothes on. I respect you the way you used to be, and anyway don't want to be devirginated, until a lawful marriage to a good Muslim woman, like the Qur'an says."

"She's out there in Neverland, baby, and I'm right here and ready to take you around the world."

"What does that mean, 'take you around the world'?"

"I can show you. You don't even have to take off that faggy white shirt, just your black pants. Those are *evil* tight pants of yours; they used to get me to creaming."

And, her face at the level of his fly, Joryleen opens her lips, not as wide as when she used to sing, but wide enough so he can see in. The moist inner membranes and gums gleam at the base of her teeth, the perfect pearly arc of them, with the fat pale tongue behind. The whites of her eyes enlarge as she looks a question up into his face.

"Don't you be disgusting," he says, though the flesh behind his fly has responded.

Joryleen turns pettish, teasing. "You want me to have to return the money your Mr. Charlie gave? You want Tylenol to beat the shit out of me?"

"Is that what he does?"

"He tries not to mark me up. The older pimps tell him you're just spiting your own self when you do that." She stops looking up at him and gently butts him below his belt, twisting her head there like a dog drying off. She looks up again. "Come on, you pretty thing. You like me, I can see you do." With both sets of long-nailed fingertips she touches the bulge behind his fly.

He jumps back, alarmed less by Joryleen's caress than by the devil of assent and submission rising within him, stiffening one part of his body and causing a dazed relaxation elsewhere, as if his blood has been injected with a thickening

Four

substance; she has roused a sugary reality within him, that of a man coming into his own in the service of the seed he carries. Women are his fields, *on couches with linings of brocade shall they recline, and the fruit of the two gardens shall be within easy reach.* He tells Joryleen, "I like you too well to treat you like some whore."

But she is in a crooning mood, amused and challenged by her balky customer. "Just let me take him into my mouth," she says. "That's no sin in the old Koran. That's just natural affection. We're made for it, Ahmad. And we won't stay made forever. We get old, we get sick. Be your plain self with me for an hour, and you'll be doing us both a favor. Wouldn't you like to play with my nice big tits? I see you looking down my blouse every time we got close at school."

He holds himself back from her, his calves pressing against the mattress of the next bare bed, but is too dazed by the storm in his blood to protest when in a zigzag set of gestures she tugs her close-fitting top out of her little skirt, pulls it up over her blotchily bleached head of short hair, and, arching her back, uncouples her webby black bra. The brown of her breasts is dark as eggplants in the circles around the meat-colored nipples. Having them there out in the air, purple and rose, looking less enormous than they seemed half concealed, makes her feel, somehow, more like the old friendly Joryleen he used to, slightly, know, her smile both cocky and tentative out by the lockers.

He says, with a thick tongue and dry throat, "I don't want you telling Tylenol what we did and didn't do."

"O.K., I won't, I promise. He doesn't like to hear what I do with the tricks anyway."

"I want you to take off the rest of your clothes and we'll just lie together a while and talk."

That he has taken even this much initiative seems to subdue her. She crosses her legs and takes off one pointy white boot and then the other and stands, the top of her spiky blond-spotted head no higher, now that she is barefoot, than the base of Ahmad's throat. Joryleen bumps against his chest, balancing on one leg and now the other, to pull down her red vinyl skirt and filmy black underpants. This done, she keeps her chin and eyelids lowered, waiting, crossing her arms in front of her breasts as if nudity makes her more modest.

He stands back and says, "Little Miss Popular," marvelling at the real, bare, vulnerable Joryleen. "We'll leave my clothes on," he tells her. "Let me see what I can find for a blanket and some pillows."

"It's pretty hot and stuffy up here," she says. "I'm not sure we need a blanket."

"A blanket *under* us," he explains. "To protect the mattress. You know what a good mattress costs?" Most are protected in thick plastic, but that would make an unpleasant, skin-adhesive surface to lie down on.

"Hey, let's move this show along," she complains. "I'm all undressed—suppose somebody comes up?"

"I'm surprised you care," he says, "if you turn all those tricks." He has taken on a responsibility, to create a bower for him and a mate; the sensation excites him but makes him anxious. Turning at the head of the stairs, he sees her, sitting calmly in the lamplight, light another cigarette, and the smoke make that rippling structure in the conical glow. He runs downstairs, rapidly so she won't evaporate. Amid the furniture in the main showroom he finds no blankets, but he takes two patterned pillows from a chenille-covered sofa and carries up along with them a small Oriental rug, four by six. These hurried tasks cool him off a little, but his legs still tremble.

Four

" 'Bout time," she greets him. He arranges the pillows and rug on the mattress, and she stretches herself out on the rug's intertwining pattern, bordered in blue—the traditional image, Habib Chehab has explained to him, of an oasis garden, encircled by a river. Joryleen, one arm cocked behind her head on the chenille pillow, exposes a shaved armpit. "Man, this is kinky," she says as he lies down, shoeless but otherwise clothed, beside her.

His shirt will get wrinkled, but he figures this is part of what this will cost him. "Can I put my arm around you?" he asks.

"Oh, Christ, sure. You're entitled to a lot more than that."

"Just this," he tells her, "is as much as I can stand."

"O.K. Ahmad: now, you relax."

"I don't want to do anything that strikes you as repulsive."

This makes her smile, and then laugh, so he feels her expressed breath warm on the side of his neck. "That would be harder than you'd like to know."

"Why do you do it? Let Tylenol send you out like this."

She sighs, again a gust of life on his neck. "You don't know much yet about love. He's my man. Without me, he doesn't have much. He'd be pathetic, and maybe I love him too much for him to know that. For a black man grown up poor in New Prospect, having a woman to peddle around is no disgrace—it's a way to prove your manhood."

"Yeah, but what are *you* getting to prove?"

"That I can deal with shit, I guess. It's just for a while. I don't do drugs, that's how the girls get hooked, they do the drugs so they can stand the shit, and then the habit becomes the main shit. All I'll do is grass, and a puff of crack now and then; nobody's breakin' into my veins. I can walk away, when circumstances change."

"Joryleen: how would they change?"

She offers, "He gets set up with some other connection. Or I say I won't do it any more."

"I don't think he will let you go easily now. You yourself say you're all he has."

She confesses the truth of this with her silence, a silence that adds a density to her body under his arm. Lightly she presses her belly against his, and her breasts are like sponges of warm water held at the level of his shirt pocket, deepening the wrinkles. At a far reach of him, her toenails— painted plain red, he noticed when she took off her pointy white boots, whereas her fingernails are painted silver and green divided the long way—scratch at his ankles in playful interrogation. These touches from her are wonderfully welcome, washing across his senses with the odors of her hair and scalp and sweat and the velvet abrasion of her voice, close to his ear. He hears in her breath a huskiness with its own tremble. "I don't want to talk about me," she tells him. "That kind of talk scares me." She must be aware, if less intensely than he, of the congested knot of arousal below his waist, but in obedience to the pact he has imposed upon her she does not touch it. He has never had power over anybody before, not since his mother, without a husband, had to worry about keeping him alive.

He persists, "What about all that church singing you were doing? How does that fit in?"

"It doesn't. I don't do it any more. My mother doesn't understand why I've dropped out. She says Tylenol is a bad influence. She doesn't know how right she is. Listen: the deal is you can fuck me, but not grill me."

"I just want to be with you, as close as I can."

"Oh, boy. I've heard that before. Men, they are all heart. Let's hear about you, then. How's old Allah doing? How do you like being holy, now that school's out and we're in the real world?"

His lips move an inch from her forehead. He has decided to be open with her, about this thing in his life that his instinct is to protect from everyone, even from Charlie, even from Shaikh Rashid. "I still hold to the Straight Path," he tells Joryleen. "Islam is still my comfort and guide. But—"

"But what, baby?"

"When I turn to Allah and try to think of Him, it is borne in upon me how alone He is, in all the starry space He has willed into existence. In the Qur'an, He is called the Loving, the Self-Subsistent. I used to think of the love; now I'm struck by the self-subsistence, in all that emptiness. People are always thinking of themselves," he tells Joryleen. "Nobody thinks of God—if He suffers or not, if He likes being what He is. What does He see in the world, to take any pleasure in it? And to even think of such things, to try to make such pictures of God as a kind of human being, my master the imam would tell me was blasphemy, deserving an eternity of Hellfire."

"My goodness, what a lot to take on in your own brain. Maybe He gave us each other, so we wouldn't be as alone as He is. That's in the Bible, pretty much."

"Yeah, but what are we? Smelly animals, really, with a little bunch of animal needs, and shorter lives than turtles."

This—his mentioning turtles—makes Joryleen laugh; when she laughs, her whole naked body jiggles against his, so he thinks of all those intestines, and stomach and things, packed in: she has all that inside her, and yet also a loving spirit, breathing against the side of his neck, where God is as close as a vein. She says to him, "You better get on top of all those weird ideas you have, or they gone to drive you crazy."

His lips move within an inch of her brow. "At times I have this yearning to join God, to alleviate His loneliness." No sooner are the words out of his mouth than he recognizes them as blasphemy: in the twenty-ninth sura it is written, *Allah does not need His creatures' help.*

"To die, you mean? You're scaring me again, Ahmad. How's that prick been poking me doing? We talk it all away?" She touches him, quickly, expertly. "No, man, we didn't. He's still there, wanting what he wants. I can't stand it—can't stand the suspense. Don't you do a thing. Allah can blame me. I can take it, I'm just a woman, dirty anyway." Joryleen puts her hands one on each of his buttocks through the black jeans and by pulling him rhythmically into her pushing softness draws him up and up into a convulsive transformation, a vaulting inversion of his knotted self like that, perhaps, which occurs when the soul passes at death into Paradise.

The two young bodies cling together, panting climbers who have attained a ledge. Joryleen says, "There, now. You got a mess in your pants but we didn't have to use any scumbag and you're still a virgin for that bride of yours with the head scarf."

"The hijab. There may never be such a bride."

"Why you say that? You've got the working parts, and a good nature besides."

"A feeling," he answers her. "You may be the closest to a bride I get." He lightly accuses her, "I didn't ask you to do that, making me come."

"I like to earn my money," she tells him. He is sorry to feel her relax into conversation, receding from the tight, moist seam that made them one body. "I don't know where you get that bad feeling from, but that Charlie friend of yours has some sort of game going. Why'd he arrange this hook-up, when you didn't ax for it?"

"He thought it was something I needed. And maybe I did. Thank you, Joryleen. Though, as you said, it was unclean."

"It's almost like they're fattening you up."

"Who is, for what?"

"Sugar, I don't know. You heard my advice. Get away from that truck."

"Suppose I told you to get away from Tylenol?"

"That's not so easy. He's my man."

Ahmad tries to understand. "We seek attachments, however unfortunate."

"You got it."

The mess in his underpants is drying, growing sticky; still, he resists when she tries to roll out from under his arm. "Got to go," Joryleen says.

He hugs her tighter, a little cruelly. "Have you earned your money?"

"Haven't I? I felt you shoot off, real big."

He wants to join her in uncleanness. "We didn't fuck, though. Maybe we should. Charlie would want me to."

"Getting the idea, huh? Too late this time, Ahmad. Let's keep you pure for now."

Night has descended outside the furniture store. They are two beds away from the single lit lamp, and by its dim light her face, on the pillow of white chenille, is a black oval, a perfect oval holding its sparkles and the silvery small movements of her lips and eyelids. She is lost to God but is giving her life for another, so that Tylenol, that pathetic bully, can live. "Do one more thing for me," Ahmad begs. "Joryleen, I can't bear to let you go."

"What kind of thing?"

"Sing to me."

"Boy. You're a man, all right. Always wanting one more thing."

"Just a little song. I loved it, in the church, being able to pick your voice out from all the others."

"And now somebody's taught you how to sweet-talk. I got to sit up. You can't sing lying down. Lying down's for other things." This was needlessly coarse of her to say. Her breasts there in the light from the lone lamp in that ocean of mattresses have crescents of shadow beneath their rounded weight; she is eighteen, but already gravity tugs them down. He has an urge to reach out and touch the jut of her meat-colored nipples, to pinch them even, since she is a whore and used to worse, and wonders at this itch of cruelty within him, fighting that tenderness which would seduce him away from his innermost loyalty. *He that fights for Allah's cause*, the twenty-ninth sura says, *fights for himself*. Ahmad closes his eyes as he sees from the tensing little muscles of her lips, with that delicate welt of flesh that runs around their edges, that she is about to sing.

" 'What a friend we have in Jesus,' " she croons, quaveringly and without the jumping syncopation of the version he heard in church, " 'all our sins and griefs to bear . . . ' " As she sings she reaches out a pale-palmed hand and touches his brow, an upright square brow bent on carrying more faith than most men can bear, and, her fingers with their two-toned nails straying, pinches the lobe of his ear in conclusion. " '. . . take it to the Lord in prayer.' "

He watches her briskly put her clothes back on: bra first, then, with a comical wriggle, her skimpy underpants; next, her snug jersey, short enough to let a strip of belly show, and the scarlet miniskirt. She sits on the edge of the bed to put on her long-toed boots, over some thin white socks he hadn't noticed her taking off. To protect the leather from her sweat, and her feet from the smell.

What time is it? The dark comes earlier every day. Not much past seven; he has been with her less than an hour. His mother might be home, waiting to feed him. She has more time for him, lately. Reality calls: he must get up and smooth any shadow of their shapes out of the plastic-wrapped mattress and restore the carpet and cushions to their places downstairs and lead Joryleen among the tables and armchairs, past the desks and the water cooler and the time clock, and let them both out the back door into the night, busy with headlights less now of workers coming home than of people out hunting for something, for dinner or for love. Her singing and his coming have left him so sleepy that the thought, as he walks the dozen blocks home, of going to bed and never waking up has no terror for him.

Shaikh Rashid greets him in the language of the Qur'an: *"fa-inna ma'a 'l-'usri yusrā."* Ahmad, his classical Arabic rusty after three months of skipping his lessons at the mosque, deciphers the quote in the head and ponders it for hidden meanings. *Every hardship is followed by ease.* He recognizes it as from "Comfort," one of the early Meccan suras placed late in the Book because of their shorter length but dear to his master because of their compressed, enigmatic nature. Sometimes called "The Opening," it addresses, in God's voice, the Prophet himself: *Have We not lifted up your heart and relieved you of the burden which weighed down your back?*

His encounter with Joryleen had been arranged for the

Friday before Labor Day, so it was not until the next Tues-
day that Charlie Chehab asked him at work, "How'd it go?"

"Fine" was Ahmad's queasy reply. "It turns out I knew her,
slightly, at Central High. She has been led sorely astray
since."

"She do the job?"

"Oh, yes. The job is done."

"Good. Her thug promised she could do it nicely. What a
relief. To me, I mean. It didn't feel natural, you still having
your cherry. Don't know why I took it so personally, but I
did. Feel like a new man?"

"Oh, yes. I see life through a new veil. A new lens, I should
say."

"Great. *Great*. Until your first piece of ass, you really
haven't lived. I got mine when I was sixteen. Two, actually—
a pro with a Trojan, and a girl from the neighborhood bare-
back. But that was when things were wilder, before AIDS.
Your generation is smart to be cautious."

"We were cautious." Ahmad blushed at the secret he was
hiding from Charlie, that he was still pure. But he had no
wish to disappoint his mentor by sharing this truth. There
had perhaps been too much sharing between them, in the
closeness of the cab as Excellency processed New Jersey
beneath its whirring wheels. Joryleen's advice to get away
from that truck rankles.

An air of apprehension, of nervous multi-tasking, clung to
Charlie this morning. The quick creasing of his face, the flitting expressions of his mobile mouth, seemed excessive in
his office behind the showroom, where morning coffee was
consumed and the day's plan was sketched. Unwashed olive
coveralls waited here, and yellow slickers for days of delivering in the rain; they hung on their hooks like flayed skins.

Charlie announced, "I ran into Shaikh Rashid over the long weekend."

"Oh, yes?" Of course, Ahmad reflected, the Chehabs were significant members of the mosque; there was nothing strange in an encounter.

"He'd like to see you over at the Islamic Center."

"To chastise me, I fear. Now that I work, I neglect the Qur'an, and my Friday attendance has fallen off, though I never fail, as you have noticed, to fulfill salat, wherever I can spend five minutes in an unpolluted place."

Charlie frowned. "You can't do just you and God, Madman. He sent His Prophet, and the Prophet created a community. Without the *ummah*, the knowledge and practice of belonging to a righteous group, faith is a seed that bears no fruit."

"Is that what Shaikh Rashid told you to say to me?" It sounded more like Shaikh Rashid than Charlie.

The man grinned—that sudden, engaging exposure of his teeth, like a child caught out in a trick. "Shaikh Rashid can speak for himself. But he isn't calling you to him to rebuke you—quite the contrary. He wants to offer you an opportunity. Shut my big mouth, I'm speaking out of turn. Let him tell you himself. We'll end deliveries early today, and I'll drop you at the mosque."

Thus he has been delivered to his master, the imam from Yemen. The nail salon below the mosque, though well equipped with chairs, holds one bored Vietnamese manicurist reading a magazine, and the CHECKS CASHED window, through its long Venetian blinds, affords a narrow glimpse of a high counter, protected by a grille, behind which a heavyset white man yawns. Ahmad opens the door between these places of business, the scabby green door numbered 2781½, and climbs the narrow stairs to the foyer where once the customers of the departed dance studio would wait for their lessons. The bulletin board outside the imam's office still holds the same computer-printed notices for classes in Arabic, for counseling in holy, proper, and seemly marriage in the modern age, and for lectures in Middle Eastern history by this or that visiting mullah. Shaikh Rashid, in his caftan embroidered with silver thread, comes forward and clasps his pupil's hand with an unusual fervor and ceremoniousness; he seems unchanged by the summer past, though in his beard perhaps a few more gray hairs have appeared, to match his dove-gray eyes.

To his initial greeting, while Ahmad is still puzzling over its meaning, Shaikh Rashid adds, "*wa la 'l-ākhiratu khayrun laka mina 'l-ūlā. wa la-sawfa yu'ṭīka rabbuka fa-tarḍā.*" Ahmad dimly recognizes this as from one of the short Meccan suras of which his master was so fond, perhaps that one called "The Brightness," to the effect that the future, the life to come, holds a richer prize for you than the past. *You shall be gratified with what your Lord will give you.* In English Shaikh Rashid says, "Dear boy, I have missed our hours studying Scripture together, and talking of great matters. I, too, learned. The simplicity and strength of your faith instructed and fortified my own. There are too few like you."

He leads the young man into his office, and settles himself in the tall wing chair from which he does his teaching. "Well, now," he addresses Ahmad, when both are seated in their accustomed positions around the desk, upon whose surface nothing rests but a well-worn, green-bound copy of the Qur'an. "You have travelled in the wider, infidel world—what our friends the Black Muslims call 'the dead world.' Has it modified your beliefs?"

"Sir, I am not aware that it has. I still feel God beside me, as close as the vein in my neck, cherishing me as only He can."

"Did you not witness, in the cities you visited, poverty and misery that led you to question His mercy, and inequalities of wealth and power that cast doubt on His justice? Did you not discover that the world, in its American portion, emits a stench of waste and greed, of sensuality and futility, of the despair and lassitude that come with ignorance of the inspired wisdom of the Prophet?"

The dry flourishes of this imam's rhetoric, delivered by a two-edged voice that seems to withdraw even as it proffers, afflict Ahmad with a familiar discomfort. He tries to answer honestly, somewhat in Charlie's voice: "This isn't the fanciest part of the planet, I guess, and it has its share of losers, but I enjoyed being out in it, really. People are pretty nice, mostly. Of course, we were usually delivering something they wanted, and they thought would make their lives better. Charlie was good fun to be with. He knows a lot about state history."

Shaikh Rashid leans forward, resting his shoes on the floor, and presses the fingertips of his fine small hands together, perhaps to suppress their tremor. Ahmad wonders why his teacher should be nervous. Perhaps he is jealous of another man's influence upon his student. "Yes," he says. "Charlie is 'fun,' but is possessed of serious purpose as well. He informs me that you have expressed a willingness to die for jihad."

"I did?"

"In an interview in Liberty State Park, in view of lower Manhattan, where the twin towers of capitalist oppression were triumphantly brought down."

"That was an interview?" How strange, Ahmad thinks, that the conversation, in the open air, has been reported here, in the closed space of this inner-city mosque, whose windows have a view of only brick walls and dark clouds. The sky today is close and gray in wispy layers that may produce rain. At that earlier interview, the day had been harshly bright, the cries of children in holiday packs ricocheting between the glitter of the Upper Bay and the glaring white dome of the Science Center. Balloons, gulls, sun. "I will die," he confirms, after silence, "if it is the will of God."

"There is a way," his master cautiously begins, "in which a mighty blow can be delivered against His enemies."

"A plot?" Ahmad asks.

"A way," Shaikh Rashid repeats, fastidiously. "It would involve a *shahīd* whose love of God is unqualified, and who impatiently thirsts for the glory of Paradise. Are you such a one, Ahmad?" The question is put almost lazily, while the master leans back and closes his eyes as if against too strong a light. "Be honest, please."

Ahmad's rickety feeling, of being supported over a gulf of bottomless space only by a scaffold of slender and tenuous supports, has returned. After a life of barely belonging, he is on the shaky verge of a radiant centrality. "I believe I am," the boy tells his teacher. "But I have no warrior skills."

"It has been seen to that you have all the skills you need. The task would involve driving a truck to a certain destination and making a certain simple mechanical connection. Exactly how would be explained to you by the experts that arrange these matters. We have, in our war for God," the imam lightly explains, with an amused small smile, "technical experts equal to those of the enemy, and a will and spirit overwhelmingly greater than his. Do you recall the twenty-fourth sura, *al-nūr*, 'The Light'?"

Four

His eyelids close, showing their tiny purple veins, in the effort of remembering and reciting. *"wa 'l-ladhīna kafarū a'māluhum ka-sarābi biqiʿatin yaḥsabuhu 'z-ẓamʾānu māʾan ḥattā idhā jāʾahu lam yajidhu shayʾan wa wajada 'llāha ʿindahu fa-waffāhu ḥisābahu, wa 'llāhu sarīʿu 'l-ḥisāb."* Opening his eyes to see a guilty incomprehension on Ahmad's face, the shaikh, with his thin off-center smile, translates: " 'As for the unbelievers, their works are like a mirage in a desert. The thirsty traveller thinks it is water, but when he comes near he finds that it is nothing. He finds Allah there, who pays him back in full.' A beautiful image, I have always thought—the traveller thinks it is water, but he finds only Allah there. It dumbfounds him. The enemy has only the mirage of selfishness, of many small selves and interests, to fight for: our side has a single sublime selflessness. We submit to God and become one with Him, and with one another."

The imam shuts his eyes again as in a holy trance, his closed lids shuddering with the pulse of the capillaries within them. His voice emerges from his mouth cogently, however. "Your translation to Paradise would be instant," he states. "Your family—your mother—would receive compensation, *iʿāla*, for her loss, even though she is an unbeliever. The beauty of her son's sacrifice may perhaps persuade her to convert. All things are possible with Allah."

"My mother—she has always supported herself. Could I name another, a female friend my age, to receive the compensation? It might help her to achieve freedom."

"What is freedom?" Shaikh Rashid asks, his eyes opening and breaking the skin of his trance. "As long as we are in our bodies, we are slaves to our bodies and their necessities. How I envy you, dear boy. Compared with you, I am old, and it is to the young that the greatest glory of battle belongs. To sacrifice one's life," he continues, as his eyelids

: 235 :

half shut, so just a wet gray glitter shows, "before it becomes a tattered, exhausted thing. What an endless joy that would be."

"When," Ahmad asks after letting these words sink into a silence, "will my *istishhād* take place?" His self-sacrifice: it is becoming a part of him, a live, helpless thing like his heart, his stomach, his pancreas gnawing away with its chemicals and enzymes.

"Your heroic sacrifice," his master quickly amplifies. "Within a week, I would say. The details are not mine to specify, but a week would approximate an anniversary and send an effective message to the global Satan. The message would be, 'We strike when we please.' "

"The truck. Would it be the one I drive for Excellency?" Ahmad can grieve, if not for himself, for the truck—its cheerful pumpkin orange, its ornate script lettering, the vantage from its driver's seat that puts the world of obstacles and dangers, of pedestrians and other vehicles, just on the other side of the tall windshield, so that clearances are easier to gauge than when driving an automobile, with its long and bloated hood.

"A truck like it, which should give you no trouble in driving a short distance. The Excellency truck itself would of course incriminate the Chehabs, if any identifiable fragments remain. The hope is that none will. In the first World Trade Center bombings, you may be too young to remember, the rented truck was traced with laughable ease. This time, the physical clues will be obliterated—sunk, as the great Shakespeare puts it, full fathom five."

"Obliterated," Ahmad repeats. The word is not one he often hears. A strange layer, as of a transparent, disagreeable-tasting wool, has come to enwrap him and act as an impediment to the interaction of his senses with the world.

In contrast, Shaikh Rashid has come sharply out of his trance, sensitive to the boy's queasy mood, quickly insisting to him, "You will not be there to experience it. You will already be in Jannah, in Paradise, at that instant, confronting the delighted face of God. He will greet you as His son." The shaikh bends forward earnestly, changing gears. "Ahmad, listen to me. You do not have to do this. Your avowal to Charlie does not obligate you, if your heart quails. There are many others eager for a glorious name and the assurance of eternal bliss. The jihad is overwhelmed by volunteers, even in this homeland of evil and irreligion."

"No," Ahmad protests, jealous of this alleged mob of others who would steal his glory. "My love of Allah is absolute. Your gift is one I cannot refuse." Seeing a kind of flinch on his master's face, a clash of relief and sorrow, a disconcerted gap, in his usual composed surface, through which his mere humanity flashes, Ahmad relents, joining him in humanity with the joke, "I would not have you think that our hours studying the Eternal Book were wasted."

"Many study the Book; few die for it. Few are given your opportunity to prove its truth." From this stern high plane Shaikh Rashid relents in turn: "If there is any uncertainty in your heart, dear boy, speak it now, without penalty. It will be as if this conversation has never taken place. I ask from you only silence, a silence in which someone with more courage and faith may carry out the mission."

The boy knows he is being manipulated, yet accedes to the manipulation, since it draws from him a sacred potential. "No, the mission is mine, though I feel shrunk to the size of a worm within it."

"Good, then," the teacher concludes, leaning back, lifting

up his little black shoes, and resting them in view on the silver-threaded footstool. "You and I will not speak of this again. Nor will you visit here again. Word has reached me that the Islamic Center may be under surveillance. Inform Charlie Chehab of your heroic resolve. He will arrange that you soon receive detailed instruction. Give him the name of this *sharmoota* whom you value above your mother. I cannot say that I approve: women are our fields, but our mother is the Earth itself, from which we drew existence."

"Master, I would rather entrust the name to you. Charlie has a connection with her that might lead him to disrespect my intent."

Shaikh Rashid resents such a complication, which mars the purity of his pupil's submission. "As you wish," he says stiffly.

Ahmad prints JORYLEEN GRANT on a piece of notepaper, just as he saw it, not many months ago, inscribed in ballpoint on the edges of the pages of a thick high-school textbook. They were nearly equals then; now he is headed for Jannah and she for Jahannan, the pits of Hell. She is the only bride he will enjoy on Earth. Ahmad notices in writing that the trembling has passed out of his teacher's hands into his own. His soul feels like one of those out-of-season flies that, trapped in winter in a warm room, buzz and insistently bump against the glass of a window saturated with the sunlight of an outdoors wherein they would quickly die.

The next day, a Wednesday, he wakes early, as if at a shout that quickly dies away. In the kitchen, in the dark before six o'clock, he encounters his mother, who is back on the morning shift at Saint Francis. She wears, chastely, a beige street

Four

dress and a blue cardigan thrown across her shoulders; her footsteps pad silently in the white Nikes she wears for the miles she traverses the hospital's hard floors. He gratefully senses that her recent mood—the short temper and distraction caused by one of those obscure disappointments whose atmospheric repercussions have bothered him since early childhood—is lifting. She wears no makeup; the skin beneath her eyes is blanched, and her eyes are reddened by her swim in the waters of sleep. She greets him with surprise: "Well, you're an early bird!"

"Mother—"

"What, darling? Don't make it long, I'm on duty in forty minutes."

"I wanted to thank you, for putting up with me all these years."

"Why, what a strange thing to say! A mother doesn't put up with her child; the child is her reason for being."

"Without me, you would have had more freedom to be an artist, or whatever."

"Oh, I'm as much of an artist as I have talent for. Without you to care for, I might have just sunk myself in self-pity and bad behavior. And you've been such a good boy, really— never giving me real trouble, like I hear about at the hospital all the time. And not just from the other nurse's aides but from the *doctors*, with all that education they have and the lovely homes. They give their children *every*thing, and yet they turn out horribly—self-destructive and other-destructive. I don't know how much credit to give your Mohammedanism. Even as a baby, you were so trusting and easy. Everything I suggested, you thought was a good idea. It worried me, even, you seemed so easily led, I was afraid you'd be influenced by the wrong people as you grew

: 239 :

older. But look at you! A man of the world, earning good money just as you said you would, and handsome besides. You have your father's lovely lanky build, and his eyes and sexy mouth, but nothing of his cowardice, always looking for a shortcut."

He does not tell of the shortcut to Paradise he is about to take. He tells her instead, "We don't call it Mohammedanism, Mother. That sounds as if we worshipped Mohammed. He never claimed to be God; he was just God's prophet. The only miracle he ever claimed was the Qur'an itself."

"Yes, well, darling, Roman Catholicism is full of these fussy distinctions too, about all these things nobody can see. People make them up out of hysteria and then they get passed on as gospel. Saint Christopher medals and not touching the wafer with your teeth and saying the mass in Latin and no meat on Fridays and crossing yourself constantly, then it all got tossed out by Vatican Two as cool as you please—stuff that people had believed for two thousand years! The nuns put such ridiculous stock in all of it, and expected us children to, too, but all I saw was a beautiful world around me, for however briefly, and I wanted to make images of its beauty."

"In Islam, that's called blasphemy, trying to usurp God's prerogative of creation."

"Well, I know. That's why there aren't any statues or paintings in mosques. To me that seems unnecessarily bleak. God gave us eyes to see what, then?"

She talks while rinsing her cereal bowl and slapping it into the drainer in the sink, and hurrying her toast up out of the toaster and slapping on jam between gulps of coffee. Ahmad tells her, "God is supposed to be beyond description. Didn't the nuns say that?"

"Not really, that I remember. But, then, I only had three years of parochial school before switching to public, where they were supposed not to mention God, for fear some Jewish child would go home and tell his atheist lawyer parents." She looks at her watch, thick-faced like a diver's watch, with big numbers she can see while taking a pulse. "Darling, I love having a serious conversation, maybe you could convert me, except there are all these baggy hot clothes they make you wear, but now I'm truly getting late and must run. I don't even have time to swing you by work, I'm so sorry, and anyway you'd be the first one there. Why don't you finish up your breakfast and the dishes and then walk over to the store, or even run? It's only ten blocks."

"Twelve."

"Remember how you used to run everywhere in those little track shorts? I was so proud, you looked so sexy."

"Mother, I love you."

Touched, even stricken, sensing some abyss of need within him but able only to dart to the edge and away, Teresa pecks a kiss on her son's cheek and tells Ahmad, "Well, of course, you sweet thing, and I do you. What is it the French say? *Ça va sans dire*. It goes without saying."

He is blushing, stupidly, hating his own hot face. But he must get this out: "I mean, all those years, there I was obsessing about my father, and *you* were the one taking care of me." *Our mother is the Earth itself, from which we drew existence.*

Her hands flit over herself to check that everything is in place; she looks at her watch again, and he can feel her mind flying, flying away. Her response makes him doubt that she heard what he said. "I know, dear—we all make mistakes in relationships. Can you possibly see to your own supper

: 241 :

tonight? The Wednesday-evening sketch group is starting up again, we have a model tonight—you know, we each kick in ten dollars to pay her and have five-minute poses followed by a longer sitting, you can bring pastels but they discourage oils. Anyway, Leo Wilde called the other day and I promised to go with him. You remember Leo, don't you? I used to go out with him, a little. Stocky, wears his hair in a ponytail, funny little granny glasses—"

"I re*mem*ber him, Mother," Ahmad says coldly. "One of your losers."

He watches her rush out the door, hears her rapid padded steps in the hall and the muffled heave of the elevator answering her call. At the sink he washes his dirty bowl and orange-juice glass with a new zeal, the thoroughness of a last time. He leaves them in the drainer to dry. They are utterly clean, like a desert morning, the crescent moon sharing the sky with Venus.

At Excellency, out on the lot, with the freshly loaded orange truck between themselves and the office window from which old, bald Mr. Chehab might see them talking and sense a conspiracy, he tells Charlie, "I'm in."

"I heard. Good." Charlie gives Ahmad a look, and it's as if his Lebanese eyes are new to the boy, crystalline in complexity, this part of us not quite flesh, brittle with its amber rays and granulations, the area around the pupil paler than the dark-brown ring rimming the iris. Charlie has a wife and children and a father, Ahmad realizes; he is tied to this world in a way Ahmad isn't. His substance is knottier. "You sure, Madman?"

"As God is my witness," Ahmad tells him. "I burn to do it."

Four

It always faintly embarrasses him, he does not know why, when God arises between himself and Charlie. The man makes one of his intricate quick mouths, a pinching of the lips together and then puffing them out, as if something inside has been regretfully kept from escaping.

"Then you'll need to meet some specialists. I'll arrange it." He hesitates. "It's a little tricky, it may not happen tomorrow. How're your nerves?"

"I have placed myself in God's hand, and feel very serene. My own will, my own cravings, are at rest."

"Right." Charlie lifts his fist and punches Ahmad on the shoulder with it, in a gesture of solidarity and mutual con-gratulation such as when football players bump helmets, or basketball players exchange high-fives even as they back-pedal into their defensive positions. "All systems go," Char-lie says; his wry smile and wary eyes mix in an expression in which Ahmad recognizes the mixed nature—Mecca and Medina, the rapt inspiration and the patient working-out— of any holy enterprise on Earth.

Not the next day but the next, a Friday, Charlie, sitting in the passenger seat, directs the truck to leave the lot and go right on Reagan, then left at the light up on Sixteenth down to West Main, into that section of New Prospect, extending some blocks west of the Islamic Center, where emigrants from the Middle East, Turks and Syrians and Kurds packed into steerage on the glamorous transatlantic liners, settled generations ago, when the silk-dyeing and leather-tanning plants were in full operation. Signs, red on yellow, black on green, advertise in Arabic script and Roman alphabet *Al Madena Grocery*, *Turkiyem Beauty*, *Al-Basha*, *Baitul Wahid Ahmadiyya*. The older men visible on the streets have long since discarded the gallabiya and the fez for the dusty-black

: 243 :

Western-style suits, shapeless with daily wear, favored by the Mediterranean males, Sicilians and Greeks, who preceded them in this neighborhood of tight-to-the-street row houses. The younger Arab-Americans, idle and watchful, have adopted the bulky running shoes, droopy oversize jeans, and hooded sweatshirts of black homeys. Ahmad, in his prim white shirt and his black jeans slim as two stovepipes, would not fit in here. To these co-religionists, Islam is less a faith, a filigreed doorway into the supernatural, than a habit, a facet of their condition as an underclass, alien in a nation that persists in thinking of itself as light-skinned, English-speaking, and Christian. To Ahmad these blocks feel like an underworld he is timidly visiting, an outsider among outsiders.

Charlie seems at ease here, cheerfully exchanging jabber for jabber as he directs Ahmad to park the truck in a jammed parking lot behind a Pep Boys and the Al-Aqsa True Value hardware store. He pleadingly holds up ten fingers to the True Value clerk who has emerged, arguing that nobody in his right mind could refuse him ten minutes of off-street parking; to clarify his point, a ten-dollar bill changes hands. Walking away, he mutters to Ahmad, "Out on the street the damn truck sticks out like a circus van."

"You do not wish to be observed," Ahmad deduces. "But who would observe?"

"You never know" is the unsatisfactory reply. They walk, at a pace brisker than Charlie's usual one, along a back alley running parallel to Main and haphazardly lined with razor-wire-topped chain-link fences, asphalt lots forbiddingly marked PRIVATE PROPERTY and CUSTOMERS ONLY, and the porches and front steps of housing meekly fitted into back-lot slices of urban space, their original wooden sides covered

with aluminum clapboards or metal sheets patterned to imitate bricks. Non-domestic structures of real, time-darkened
brick serve as warehouses and back-lot workplaces for the
shops that front on Main Street; some are now boarded-up
shells, with every exposed window smashed by methodical
delinquents, and from others emerge the glow and clangor
of small-scale manufacture or repair still being carried forward. One such building, of a brick painted a dour tan, has
rendered its metal-sashed windows opaque with an interior
coating of the same tan paint. Its wide overhead garage door
is down, and the tin sign above, advertising in clumsy hand-
painted letters COSTELLO'S MACHINE SHOP *All Repairs and
Body Work*, has faded and rusted into near-illegibility. Charlie raps on a small side door of quilted metal, with a shiny
new brass lock. After a considerable silence, a voice from
within asks, "Yes? Who?"

"Chehab," Charlie says. "And the driver."

He speaks so softly that Ahmad doubts he has been heard,
but the door does open, and a scowling young man steps
aside. Ahmad is coping with his sensation that he has seen
this man before when Charlie roughly, with fear's rigid
touch, takes his arm and pushes him inside. The interior
space smells of oil-soaked concrete and an unexpected substance that Ahmad recognizes from two summers spent, in
his mid-teens, as a junior member of a lawn crew: fertilizer.
The caustic dry odor of it parches his nose and sinuses; there
are also the scents of an acetylene welding torch and of clos-
eted male bodies needing to be bathed and aired. Ahmad
wonders if the men—two of them, the younger slender one
and a stockier older, who turns out to be the technician—
were among the four in the cottage on the Jersey Shore. He
saw them for only a few minutes, in an unlit room and then

through a dirty window, but they exuded this same sullen tension, as of distance runners who have trained too long. They resent being asked to talk. But they owe Charlie the deference paid a supplier and an arranger, at a level above them. Ahmad they regard with a kind of dread, as if, so soon to be a martyr, he is already a ghost.

"*Lā ilāha illā Allāh*," he greets them, as a reassurance. Only the younger—and though young he is older than Ahmad by some years—replies in kind, "*Muḥammad rasūlu Allāh*," muttering the formula as if tricked into an indiscretion. Ahmad sees that no merely human response, no nuance of sympathy or humor, is expected of them; they are operatives, soldiers, units. He straightens his posture, seeking their good opinion, shouldering his similar role.

Traces of the building's former life as Costello's Machine Shop linger in the cloistered, layered air: overhead, beams, chains, and pulleys for hoisting engines and axles; workbenches and arrays of small drawers whose pulls are blackened by greasy fingers; pegboards painted with the silhouettes of absent tools; scraps of wire and sheet metal and rubber tubing left where the last hand set them aside at the end of the last repair; drifts of discarded oil cans and gaskets and traction belts and emptied parts packages in the corners, behind oil drums used as trash cans. In the center of the concrete floor, under the only bright lights, with extension cords feeding into its cab like the tubes sustaining a patient on life support, sits a truck much the size and shape of Excellency. Instead of being a Ford Triton E-350, it is a GMC 3500, not orange but a bleak white, the way it came from the factory. On its side has been lettered, in carefully but not professionally done black block letters, the words WINDOW SHADES SYSTEMS.

Ahmad dislikes the truck at first sight; the vehicle has a furtive anonymity, a generic blankness. It has a hard-used, slummy look. At the side of the New Jersey Turnpike he has often seen ancient sedans from the 'sixties and 'seventies, bloated and two-tone and chrome-laden, broken down, with some hapless family of color clustered waiting for the state police to come and rescue them and tow away their shabby bargain. This bone-white truck savors of such poverty, such pathetic attempts to keep up in America, to join the easy seventy-miles-per-hour mainstream. His mother's maroon Subaru, with its Bondo-patched fender and its red enamel abraded by years of acid New Jersey air, was another pathetic attempt. Whereas bright-orange Excellency, its letters gold-edged, has a spruce jolliness to it—as Charlie said, a circus air.

The older, shorter of the two operatives, who is fractionally more friendly, beckons Ahmad to come look with him into the cab's open door. His hands, the fingertips stained with oil, flow toward an unusual element between the seats—a metal box the size of a cigar box, its metal painted a military drab, with two terminal knobs on the top and insulated wires trailing from these back into the body of the truck. Since the space between the driver's and passenger's seats is deep and awkward to reach down into, the device rests not on the floor but on an inverted plastic milk crate, duct-taped to the crate's bottom for security. On one side of the detonator—for such it must be—there is a yellow contact lever, and in the center, sunk a half-inch in a little well where a thumb would fit, a glossy red button. The color-coding smacks of military simplicity, of ignorant young men being trained along the simplest possible lines, the sunken button guarding against accidental detonation. The man explains to Ahmad, "This switch safety switch. Move to right"—*snap*—"like this, device armed. Then push button down and hold—*boom*. Four thousand kilos ammonium nitrate in back. Twice what McVeigh had. That much needed to break steel tunnel sheath." His black-tipped hands shape a circle, demonstrating.

"Tunnel," Ahmad repeats, stupidly, nobody having spoken to him before now of a tunnel. "What tunnel?"

"Lincoln," the man answers, with slight surprise but no more emotion than a thrown switch. "No trucks allowed in Holland."

Ahmad silently absorbs this. The man turns to Charlie. "He knows?"

"He does now," Charlie says.

The man gives Ahmad a gap-toothed smile, his friendliness growing. His flowing hands describe a larger circle. "Morning rush," he explains. "From Jersey side. Right-hand tunnel only one for trucks. Newest built of three, nineteen fifty-one. Newest but not strongest. Older construction better. Two-thirds through, weak place, where tunnel makes turn. Even if outer sheath hold and keep out water, air system destroyed and all suffocate. Smoke, pressure. For you, no pain, not even panic moment. Instead, happiness of success and God's warm welcome."

Ahmad recalls a name dropped weeks ago. "Are you Mr. Karini?"

"No, no," he says. "No no no. Not even friend. Friend of friend—all fight for God against America."

The younger operative, not much older than Ahmad, hears the word "America" and utters a heated long Arabic sentence that Ahmad does not understand. Ahmad asks Charlie, "What did he say?"

Charlie shrugs. "The usual."

"You sure this will work?"

"It'll do a ton of damage, minimum. It'll deliver a statement. It'll make headlines all over the world. They'll be dancing in the streets of Damascus and Karachi, because of you, Madman."

The older unidentified man adds, "Cairo, too." He smiles that engaging smile of square, spaced, tobacco-stained teeth and strikes his chest with his fist and tells Ahmad, "Egyptian."

"So was my father!" Ahmad exclaims, yet in exploration of the bond can only think to ask, "How do you like Mubarak?"

The smile fades. "Tool of America."

Charlie, as if joining in a game, asks, "The Saudi princes?"

"Tools."

"How about Muammar al-Qadaffi?"

"Now, too. Tool. Very sad."

Ahmad resents Charlie intruding in the conversation between what are, after all, the key players, the technician and the martyr; it is as if, his martyrdom assured, he can be brushed aside. A tool. He asserts himself, asking, "Osama bin Laden?"

"Great hero," the man with oil-blackened fingers answers. "Cannot be caught. Like Arafat. A fox." He smiles, but has not forgotten the point of this meeting. He says to Ahmad in his most careful English, "Show me what you will do."

The boy is beset by a freezing sensation, as if reality has shed a layer of its bulky disguise. He overcomes his distaste for the ugly plain truck, dispensable like him. He reaches toward the detonator, his face stretched into a question.

The stocky technician smiles and reassures him, "Is O.K. Not connected. Show me."

The small yellow lever, L-shaped in cross-section, touches his hand, it seems, rather than his hand touching it. "I turn this switch to the right"—it stiffly resists, and then sucks, as if magnetized, into its off position, ninety degrees away— "and push this button down in here down." Involuntarily he closes his eyes, feeling it sink half an inch.

"And hold down," his teacher repeats, "until—"

"*Boom*," Ahmad supplies.

"Yes," the man agrees; the word hangs in the air like a mist.

"You are very brave," the younger, taller, and thinner of the two strangers says, in an English virtually accent-free.

"He is a faithful son of Islam," Charlie tells him. "We all envy him, right?" Again Ahmad feels irritation with Charlie, for acting proprietorial where he has no ownership. Only the doer owns this deed. Something preoccupied and bossy in Charlie's approach casts doubt on the absolute nature of *istishhād* and the exalted, dread-filled condition of the *istishhādī*.

Perhaps the technician feels this slight failure of accord among the warriors, for he rests a paternal hand on Ahmad's shoulder, soiling the boy's white shirt with oily fingerprints, and explains to the others, "His way is good. To be hero for Allah."

Back in the cheerfully orange truck, Charlie confides to Ahmad, "Interesting to see their minds work. Tools, hero: no shades in between. As if Mubarak and Arafat and the Saudis don't all have their special situations and their own intricate games to play."

Again, Charlie strikes a note that feels, to Ahmad in his newly elevated and simplified sense of himself, slightly false. Relativism seems cynical. "Perhaps," he offers in polite contradiction, "God Himself is simple, and employs simple men to shape the world."

"Tools," Charlie says, staring humorlessly ahead through the windshield, which Ahmad wipes every morning but which becomes dirty anyway by the end of the day. "We're all tools. God bless brainless tools—right, Madman?"

A certain simplicity does lay hold of Ahmad in the troughs between surges of terror and then of exaltation, collapsing back into an impatience to be done with it. To have it behind him, whatever "him" will then be. He exists as a close neighbor to the unimaginable. The world in its sunstruck details, the minute scintillations of its interlocked workings, yawns all about him, a glistening bowl of busy emptiness, while within him a sodden black certainty weighs. He cannot forget the transformation awaiting him, behind, as it were, the snapped camera's shutter, even as his senses still receive their familiar bombardment of sights and sounds, scents and tastes. The luster of Paradise leaks backward into his daily life. Things will feel big there, on a cosmic scale; in his childhood, only a few years into this life, falling asleep, he would experience a sensation of hugeness, every cell a world, and this demonstrated to his childish mind religion's truth.

His workload at Excellency has lightened, and he is left with stretches of idleness in which he should read the Qur'an, or study the pamphlets, readily available from overseas sources, composed and printed to prepare a *shahīd*—the ablutions, the mental cleansing of the spirit—for his end, or her end, for women now, their loose black burqas well concealing their explosive vests, are permitted, in Palestine, the privilege of martyrdom. But his mind is too a-flutter to sink into study. His whole existence has become enraptured as perhaps the Prophet's was in accepting Gabriel's dictation of the divine suras. Ahmad's every minute has taken on the intimate doubleness of prayer, the self-release of turning aside and addressing a self not his own but that of Another, a Being as close as the vein of his neck. More than five times a day he finds the opportunity, most often in the store's barren parking lot, to spread his mat in the eastward direction and touch his forehead to the earth, each time receiving, through the concrete, the close comfort of submission. The slaglike dark weight nagging within him skews his view of the world, and bedecks each twig and telephone wire with jewels he has never before noticed.

Saturday morning, before the store has opened, he sits on a step of the loading platform, observing a black beetle struggling on his back on the concrete of the parking lot. The day is September eleventh, still summer. The early sun slants off the rough, pale surface with a mildness that holds in it the heat of the coming day as a seed not yet germinated holds in it the eventual blossom. The concrete in its cracks has permitted weeds to flourish, the tall weeds of the dying season, with their milky spittle and fine-haired leaves, wet with autumn's heavy dew. The sky above is cloudless, but for some dry shreds of cirrus and a disintegrating jet trail. Its pure blue is still somehow soft, powder-blue, from its recent immersion in darkness and stars. The beetle's tiny black legs wave in the air, groping for a purchase with which to right itself, casting sharp shadows elongated by the sun at its morning slant. The legs of the small creature wiggle and writhe in a kind of fury, then subside into a semblance of thought, as if the beetle seeks to reason a way out of its predicament. Ahmad wonders, *Where did this bug come from?* How did it fall here, seeming unable to use its wings? The struggle resumes. How precise the shadows of its legs are, cast with an all-loving fidelity by photons that have traveled ninety-three million miles to this exact spot!

Ahmad rises from his seat on the coarse plank step and stands over the insect in lordly fashion, feeling huge. Yet he shies from touching this mysterious fallen bit of life. Perhaps it has a poisonous bite, or, like some miniature emissary from Hell, it will fasten onto his finger and never let go. Many a boy—Tylenol, for one—would simply crush this irritating presence with his foot, but for Ahmad the option does not exist: it would produce a broadened corpse, a squashed tangle of tiny parts and spilled vital fluid, and he does not wish to contemplate any such organic horror. He looks around him briefly for a tool, for something stiff with which to flip the insect over—the dark little cardboard, for instance, used to give the two parts of a Mounds bar integrity, or to reinforce a double Reese's Peanut Butter Cup—but he sees nothing suitable. Excellency Home Furnishings tries to keep its private lot litter-free. The African-American "muscle" and Ahmad himself have been sent out into it with a green garbage bag, on clean-up duty. He spots no happenstance spatula lying loose but, on a sudden inspiration, remembers the driver's license in his wallet, a plastic rectangle in which a scowling and unflattering image of himself is embedded with some numerical data important to the state of New Jersey and a hologrammatical, counterfeit-repellent image of its Great Seal. With this, he manages, after a few tentative, squeamish attempts, to flip the tiny creature at his mercy over onto its legs. Sunlight strikes sparks of iridescence, purple and green, from the biform shell of folded wings. Ahmad goes back to his porch on the step to enjoy the good results of his rescue, his merciful intervention in the natural order. Fly away, fly away.

But the bug, right side up, its shiny body minutely hoisted on its six legs above the rough concrete, merely creeps a fraction of its length and then remains still. Its antennae searchingly wave, then they too stop. For five minutes that partake of the eternal, Ahmad watches. He returns his license with its burden of coded information to his wallet. Cars blaring rap music rush by out of sight on Reagan Boulevard, the noise swelling and receding. An airplane gaining altitude out of Newark rattles in the hardening sky. The beetle, paired with its microscopically shrinking shadow, remains still.

It had been on its back in its death throes and now is dead, leaving behind a largeness that belongs not to this world. The experience, so strangely magnified, has been, Ahmad feels certain, supernatural.

V

THE SECRETARY is in a bad mood that makes his loyal undersecretary cringe. His moods sweep through Hermione like a power boat's backwash through a hovering jellyfish. For one thing, he, she knows, *hates* being pulled back to his office on a Sunday; it disrupts his cherished afternoons of leisure with Mrs. Haffenreffer and their family, whether spent at a late-season Orioles game up in Baltimore or on a stroll through Rock Creek Park, with all those children suited up for a run except for the fifth, the youngest, who at age three still gets to ride in the jogging stroller. Miss Fogel cannot be jealous of his wife and family; she almost never sees them and they are an invisible part of him, like the parts properly concealed inside his blue suit and boxer shorts. But in her mind she sometimes accompanies him, imagining a more relaxed, husbandly presence than the tense battler against shadows who shows up in his cramped corner office. Hermione intuits that, now that summer's swampy heat at last has lifted and the buttonwoods and plane trees around the Mall are tinged in their broad leaves by a dignified dullness, the Secretary yearns to be out of doors. She can tell from the tension bulging out the back of his very dark suit coat. Men in American jobs used to wear blue or brown suits—Daddy would leave the house on Pleasant Street to take the trolley in the same brown pin-stripe, with a vest, for a week at a time—but now the only serious color is black, or navy blue close to black, in mourning for the bygone days of cheap freedom.

He has been wrought up, lately, by the common and yet well-publicized lapses in airport security. It seems that every sleazy reporter and headline-grabbing House Democrat who wants to can triumphantly brandish knives, blackjacks, and loaded revolvers which have successfully ridden through the X-ray scanners of carry-on luggage. The two of them, Secretary and undersecretary, have stood shoulder to shoulder with the security details, being slowly hypnotized by the endless procession of ghostly suitcase interiors irradiated in unreal colors—cyanic greens, fleshy peach tones, sunset magentas, and the telltale midnight blue of metal. Automobile and house keys fanned like card hands, with their rings and little chains and souvenir gizmos; the unblinking blank stare of wire-frame reading glasses in cloth cases; zippers like the skeletons of miniature snakes; bubble-clusters of coins left bunched in pants pockets; constellations of gold and silver jewelry; the airy chains of eyelets in sneakers and shoes; the tiny metal knobs and cogs in travelling alarm clocks; hair dryers, electric razors, Walkmans, miniaturized cameras: all contribute their deep-blue diatoms to the pale swim of tweaked cathode rays. Small wonder that dangerous weapons again and again waft past eyes glazed by eight hours of deciphering two-dimensional images of packed accou-

trements, searching for the tumor of malice, the abrupt silhouette of deadly intent, within an oceanic stream of the
everyday blandness of American lives boiled down to their
basic nuggets—the equipment necessary for a few days' stay
in another city or state in the materialist comfort that is our
globally abnormal norm. A pair of nail scissors or knitting
needles—while these are being spotted and confiscated,
four-inch knives pass as shoe shanks seen on edge, and a
petite pistol of mostly hard plastic sneaks through taped into
a pewter porringer supposedly being transported, if its dark
orb is challenged, as a present for a baby being baptized
tomorrow in Des Moines. The inspection always ends, has
to end, with the Secretary clapping the underpaid watchdogs
on their uniformed shoulders and telling them to carry on;
they are defending democracy.

He turns in his black suit from the radiant window looking over the Ellipse and the Mall, trampled meadows where
those sheep the citizenry graze in their jogging suits and
polychrome shorts and running shoes configured like space
ships in 'thirties comic books. "I'm wondering," he confides
to Hermione, "if we should put the Mid-Atlantic region
back on the orange level of alert."

"Sir, begging your pardon," she says, "but I talk with my
sister in New Jersey, and I'm not sure the people know what
to do different as the levels go up."

The Secretary chews this over a moment, with his powerful, rueful masseters, then asserts, "No, but the authorities
do. They up their own levels; they have a whole menu of
emergency measures in front of them." Yet even as he utters
this reassurance he feels irritation—she can tell by the way
his fine eyes narrow under their thoroughly masculine but
beautifully formed brunette brows—at the gaps that exist

between his single isolated will and the myriad assorted offi-cers, efficient and indifferent, corrupt and sterling, who, like frayed neuron-endings, make contact or not with the vast, sluggish, carefree populace.

Helplessly Hermione offers, "But I think people *do* like the sensation that steps are being taken, by a whole govern-ment department devoted to their homeland security."

"My trouble is," the Secretary blurts, helpless in turn, "I love this damn country so much I can't imagine why any-body would want to bring it down. What do these people have to offer instead? More Taliban—more oppression of women, more blowing up statues of Buddha. The mullahs in northern Nigeria are telling people not to let their children be given polio vaccine, and then the kids are brought in paralyzed to the health-aid clinic! They wait until they're totally paralyzed to bring them in, after they've gone all the way with the local mumbo-jumbo."

"They fear losing something, something precious to them," Hermione says, trembling on the edge of a new degree (the degrees are subtle, and are negotiated within the strict proprieties of a thoroughly Republican and Christian administration) of intimacy. "So precious they will sacrifice their own children to it. It happens in this country, too. The marginal sects, where some charismatic leader seals them off from common sense. The children die, and then the parents cry in court and are acquitted—they're children themselves. It's frightening, the power of abuse adults have over their children. It makes me glad, frankly, I never had any."

Is this a plea? A complaint that, standing together though they are on the lip of a splendid Sunday in the capital of the greatest nation on Earth, she is a spinster and he a married man bound by the vows of his religion to be as one, spiritu-

Five

ally and legally, with the mother of his own children? They should be *her* children. In the workings of the national government, spending twelve, fourteen hours a day in the same room or adjacent rooms, they are just as much one as if legally married. His wife hardly knows him, compared with Hermione. This thought gives her so much satisfaction that she must quickly erase an inadvertent smile from her face.

"Damn!" he explodes, his mind having been moving on its own track and coming up against the sore matter that has brought him back to his office on this day supposedly of rest. "I *hate* losing an asset. We got so few in the Muslim community, that's one of our weaknesses, that's how they caught us with our pants down. We don't have enough Arabic speakers, and half of those we do have don't think like we do. There's something weird about the language—it makes them feeble-minded, somehow. Their Internet chatter— *Heaven will split asunder beneath the Western river. The light shall be admitted.* What the fuck kind of sense does that make? Pardon my French, Hermione."

She murmurs forgivingly, marking the new level of intimacy.

He goes on, "Our problem is, the asset was holding out on us, keeping too many cards in his own hands. He wasn't following procedure. He had some vision of a great revelation and round-up, like in the movies, starring guess who? Him. We know about the money conduit in Florida, but the bagman has vanished. He and his brother own a cut-rate furniture store up in northern New Jersey, but nobody answers any phones or comes to the door. We know something about a truck, but don't know where it is or who's doing the driving. The explosives team, we got two out of the four, but they aren't talking, or else the translator isn't telling us what they're saying. They all cover for each other, even the ones on our payroll, you can't trust your own recruits any more. It's an unholy mess, and wouldn't you know the body turns up on a Sunday morning!"

In their native Pennsylvania, she knows, people could be trusted. A dollar is still a dollar there, a meal a meal, a deal a deal. Rocky looks like a boxer should, and dishonest men smoke cigars, wear checked suits, and wink a lot. She and the Secretary have wandered far from that elemental land of genial sincerity, of row houses numbered with stained glass in unchanging fanlights, of miners' sons who become star quarterbacks, of pork sausage sizzling in its own fat and scrapple drenched in maple syrup—foods that make no pretense of not being loaded with lethal cholesterol. She longs to comfort the Secretary, to press her lean body like a poultice upon his ache of overwhelming responsibility; she wants to take his meaty weight, which strains against his *de rigueur* black suit, upon her bony frame, and cradle him on her pelvis. Instead, she asks, "Where is the store?"

"A city called New Prospect. Nobody ever goes there."

"My sister lives there."

"Yeah? She should get out. It's full of Arabs—Arab-Americans, so-called. The old mills brought them in and then slowly folded. The way things are going, there won't be a thing America makes. Except movies, which are getting crappier every year. My wife and I—you've met Grace, haven't you?—used to love them, we used to go all the time, before the kids came and we had to get sitters. Judy Garland, Kirk Douglas—they gave good honest value, every performance, one hundred ten percent. Now all you hear about these kid movie actors—the women don't like being called actresses any more, everybody's an *actor*—is drunk driving and who's pregnant out of wedlock. They make these poor black teen-age girls think it's just the thing, to bring a baby into the world without any father. Except Uncle Sam. He gets the bills, and no thanks from them: welfare's their right. If there's anything wrong with this country—and I'm not saying there is, compared to any other, France and Norway included—is we have too many rights and not enough duties. Well, when the Arab League takes over the country, people'll learn what duties are."

"Exactly so, sir." The "sir" is meant to recall him to himself, his own duties in the present emergency.

He hears her. He turns back to moody contemplation of the capital's Sunday calm, with its distant prospect of the Tidal Basin and the smooth white knob, like an observatory with no opening for the telescope, of the Jefferson Memorial. People blame Jefferson now for holding on to his slaves and fathering children by one of them, but they forget the economic context of the times and the fact that Sally Hemmings was very pale. *It's a heartless city*, the Secretary thinks, a tangle of slippery power, a scattering of great white buildings like the field of icebergs that sank the *Titanic*. He turns and tells his undersecretary, "If this thing in New Jersey blows up, there'll be no sitting on fat-cat boards for me. No speaker's fees. No million-dollar advance on my memoirs." It was the sort of confession a man should make only to his wife.

Hermione is shocked. He has come closer to her but has fallen in her estimation. She tells him a shade tartly, trying to recall this beautiful, selfless public servant to himself, "Mr. Secretary, no man can serve two masters. Mammon is one; it would be presumptuous of me to name the other."

The Secretary takes this in, blinks his surprisingly light

blue eyes, and swears, "Thank God for you, Hermione. Of course. Forget Mammon." He settles at his exiguous desk and vehemently punches beeping triplets of code numbers into the electric console, and leans back in his ergonomically correct chair to bark into the speaker-phone.

Hermione doesn't usually phone on a Sunday. She prefers weekdays, when she knows Jack isn't likely to be there. She has never had much to say to Jack, which used to slightly hurt Beth's feelings; it was as if Herm were carrying on their parents' ridiculous Lutheran anti-Semitic prejudices. Also, Beth has deduced, on a weekday her "big" sister has the excuse of her red light blinking on her other phone when she thinks Beth is rambling on too long. But today she calls while church bells are ringing, and Beth is glad to hear her voice. She wants to share her good news. "Herm, I've gone on this diet and in just five days I've lost twelve pounds!"

"The first pounds are the easiest," Hermione says, always putting down anything Beth does or says. "At this point you're just losing water, which will come right back. The real test comes when you can see the difference and decide to pig out to celebrate. Is this the Atkins diet, by the way? They say it's dangerous. He was about to be sued by a thousand people, that's why his sudden death seemed so fishy."

"It's just the carrot-and-celery diet," Beth tells her. "Whenever I have the urge to nibble, I go for one of these baby carrots they sell everywhere now. Remember how carrots used to come into Philly from the Delaware truck farms, in a tied bunch with the dirt and sand still on them? Oh, how I used to hate that feeling of biting down on grains of sand— it sounded so loud in your head! No danger of that with these baby ones; they must come out of California and are all peeled down to exactly the same size. The only trouble is, if they sit too long in the sealed pack they come out slimy. The trouble with *celery* is, after a couple of stalks this ball of string collects in your mouth. But I'm determined to stick with it. It's easier to nibble cookies, God knows, but every bite adds on calories. A hundred thirty each, I was shocked to read on the package! The print is so fine, it's diabolical!"

That Hermione hasn't yet cut her short seems odd; Beth knows she's boring on the subject of doing without food, but it's all she can think about, and talking about it out loud holds her to it, keeps her from backsliding, despite her faint spells and stomach cramps. Her stomach doesn't understand what she's doing to it, why it's being punished, not knowing it's been her worst enemy for years, lying there under her heart crying out to be filled. Carmela won't lie on her lap any more, she's become so jumpy and irritable.

"What does Jack make of all this?" Hermione asks. Her voice sounds level and grave, a little halting and solemn, weighing her words. This prospect of a new, slim, presentable sister is something they both could be giggling about, the way they used to when sharing their room in the Pleasant Street house, sharing the sheer joy of being alive. As she got more serious and studious, Hermione stopped knowing how to giggle; she found it hard to lighten up. Beth wonders if that is the reason she never found a husband— Herm didn't know how to make men forget their troubles. She lacked *ballon*, as Miss Dimitrova had said.

Beth lowers her voice. Jack is in the bedroom reading and he may have read himself to sleep. Central High has started up again, and he has volunteered to teach a course on civics, saying he needs more exposure to these kids he is supposed to counsel. He claims they are getting away from him. He claims he is too old, but that's his depression talking. "He doesn't say much," she tells Hermione in answer to her question. "I think he's afraid to jinx it. But he *has* to be pleased; I'm doing it for *him*."

Herm asks, shooting her down again, "Is that ever a good idea, to do something because you think your husband wants it? I'm just asking—I've never been married."

Poor Herm, this has to be on her mind all the time. "Well, you're"—Beth stops her tongue; she had been about to say that Hermione was as good as married, to that bull-headed linebacker of a boss of hers—"as wise as anybody else, any other woman. I'm doing it for myself, too. I feel so much better, with just the twelve pounds off. The girls at the library can see the difference—they're very supportive, though at their age I couldn't imagine my figure ever getting out of hand. I said I'd like to help with the shelving instead of just sitting on my fat ass behind the desk Googling for kids too lazy to learn to Google for themselves."

"How does Jack like the change in his diet?"

"Well, I've tried not to change his, still giving him meat and potatoes. But he says he'd just as soon have simple salads with me. The older he gets, he says, the more eating anything disgusts him."

"That's the Jew in him," Hermione cuts in.

"Oh, I don't think so," Beth says, haughtily.

Hermione is then so silent Beth wonders if the connection has been broken off. Terrorists are blowing up oil pipes and power plants in Iraq, nothing is utterly secure any more. "How's the weather down there?" Beth asks.

"Still hot, once you leave the building. September in the District can be still muggy. The trees don't turn with all that color we used to get in the Arboretum. Spring is the season here, with the cherry blossoms."

"Today," Beth says, as her starved stomach gives a pang that makes her grip the back of the kitchen chair for support, "I felt fall in the air. The sky is so absolutely clear, like"—*like the day of Nine-Eleven*, she started to say, but stopped, thinking it might be tactless to mention that to an undersecretary of Homeland Security, the fabled blue sky that has become mythic, a Heavenly irony, part of American legend like the rockets' red glare.

They must be thinking the same thoughts, for Hermione asks, "Do you remember you mentioned this young Arab-American Jack had taken such an interest in, who instead of taking Jack's advice to go to college had gotten a license to drive a truck because the imam at his mosque had asked him to?"

"Vaguely. Jack hasn't mentioned him for a while."

"Is Jack there?" she asks. "Could I talk to him?"

"To Jack?" She has never wanted to talk to Jack before.

"Yes, to your husband. Please, Betty. It may be important."

Betty, yet. "Like I was saying, he may be having a nap. We went out walking earlier, to give me exercise. The exercise is just as important as the dieting. It reshapes the body."

"Could you please go see?"

"If he's awake? Maybe it's something I could pass on to him, if he is. Having a nap."

"I don't think so. I'd rather talk to him myself. You and I can have our chat this week, when you're watching your serials."

"I've given them up, too—I associate them too much with nibbling. And they were getting scrambled up in my mind, all these characters. I'll go see if he's awake." She is mystified and cowed.

"Betty, even if he's not—could you wake him up?"

"I'd hate to do that. He sleeps so poorly at night."

"I need to ask him some things right *now*, honey. They can't wait. I'm sorry. Just this once." Ever the older sister, knowing more than she does, telling her what to do. Reading her mind again, over the telephone, Hermione fondly admonishes Beth, in a voice that sounds like their mother's, "Now, no matter what happens, don't you fall off your diet."

On Sunday night, Ahmad fears he will not be able to sleep, on what is to be the last night of his life. The room around him is unfamiliar. It is one, Shaikh Rashid assured him, standing with him in the room earlier that evening, where no one can find him.

"Who would be looking for me?" Ahmad asked. His small, slight mentor—it was strange for Ahmad, as the two of them stood close together in collusion, to feel how much taller he had become than his master, who during Qur'an lessons augmented his height with that of the high-backed chair with the silver threads—gave one of his quick, knifing shrugs. The man this evening wore not his usual shimmering embroidered caftan but a gray Western-style suit, as if dressed for a business trip among the infidels. How else explain his shaving off his beard, the precisely trimmed gray-flecked beard? It had concealed, Ahmad saw, a number of small scars, traces on his waxy white skin of some disease, eradicated in the West, contracted by a child in Yemen. With these roughnesses was revealed something disagreeable about his violet lips, a sulky masculine set to them that had lurked unemphasized when they moved so rapidly, so seductively, in a recess of facial hair. The shaikh was not wearing his turban or his lacy white 'amāma; a receding hairline was bared.

Five

Shrunken in Ahmad's eyes, he asked, "Your mother will not miss you and activate the police?"

"She has night duty this weekend. I left a note for her to see when she comes in, saying I am spending the night with a friend. She may suppose it is a girlfriend. She nags me on the subject, suggesting I should have one."

"You will spend the night with a friend who will prove more true than any disgusting *sharmoota*. The eternal, inimitable Qur'an."

A copy bound in limp rose-colored leather, with English and Arabic *en face*, rested on the bedside table in this narrow, barely furnished room. It was the only thing new and expensive in the room—a "safe" room close enough to the center of New Prospect for its one window to provide a glimpse of the City Hall's mansard steeple. The building with its multicolored fish-scale shingles loomed above the lesser buildings like some fantastic sea-dragon frozen in the moment of breaching. The evening sky behind it was ribbed with rolls of cloud tinted a rosy pink by a sun setting out of sight. The solar image, its orange blare of reflection, was caught in the spire's Victorian gills of glass—windows on an interior spiral stair closed decades ago to tourists. As Ahmad strained to see from his own window, the thin old panes dirty and wavy and bearing small bubbles of antique manufacture, he saw the dying sunlight seeming to melt the highest corner of one of the rectilinear glass-skinned civic additions. The City Hall's mansard steeple holds a clock, and he feared its chiming would keep him awake all of the night, making him a less efficient *shahīd*. But its mechanical music—a brief phrase tolling the quarter-hour, the last, upward note lingering like an inquisitively lifted eyebrow, and with every fourth quarter a fuller phrase preceding the doleful count of the hour—

: 267 :

proves to be lulling, reassuring him, when the shaikh at last left him alone, that this room is indeed safe.

The previous residents of this little chamber have left few clues to their passage. Some scuff marks on the baseboards, two or three cigarette burns on the windowsills and bureau top, the shine left by repeated use of the doorknob and key-slot, a certain faint animal scent in the scratchy blue blanket. The room is religiously clean, more extremely so than Ahmad's room in his mother's apartment, which still holds unholy possessions—electronic toys with dead batteries, out-of-date sports and automotive magazines, clothes meant to express, in their severity and snug fit, his teen-age vanity. His eighteen years have accumulated historical evidence, which will become, he imagines, of great interest to the news media: cardboard-framed photos of children squinting in May sunshine on the brownstone steps of the Thomas Alva Edison Elementary School, Ahmad's dark gaze and unsmil-ing mouth embedded in the ranks of other faces, most black and some white, all lumped in the child labor of becoming loyal and literate Americans; photos of the track team, in which Ahmad Mulloy is older and fractionally smiling; track-meet ribbons, their cheap dye rapidly faded; a felt Mets pennant from a ninth-grade bus trip to a game in Shea Stadium; a beautifully calligraphed roll of the names in his Qur'an class before it dwindled to just him; his Class C driver's certificate; a photograph of his father, wearing a for-eigner's eager-to-please grin, a thin mustache that must have seemed quaint even in 1986, and shiny, centrally parted hair, obsequiously slicked down where Ahmad wore his own hair, identical in texture and thickness, brushed proudly upright, with a whiff of mousse. His father's face, it will be broadcast, was more conventionally handsome than the son's, though a shade darker. His mother, like televised victims of floods and tornadoes, will be much interviewed, at first incoherently, in shock and tears, and later more calmly, speaking in sorrowful retrospect. Her image will appear in the press; she will become momentarily famous. Perhaps there will be a spike in the sale of her paintings.

He is glad the safe room is clean of all clues to his person. This room is, he feels, his decompression chamber for the violent ascent before him, on an explosion as swift and strong as the muscular white horse Buraq.

Shaikh Rashid seemed reluctant to leave. He too, shaven and wearing a Western suit, was engaged in a departure. He fidgeted about the tiny room, tugging open reluctant bureau drawers, and making sure that the bathroom contained washcloths and towels for Ahmad's ritual ablutions. Fussily, he pointed out the prayer rug on the floor, its woven-in mihrab giving the eastern direction of Mecca, and emphasized how he had placed in the miniature refrigerator an orange, and plain yogurt, and bread for the boy's breakfast in the morning—very special bread, *khibz el-ʿAbbās*, the bread of Abbas, made by the Shiites of Lebanon in honor of the religious celebration Ashoura. "It is made with honey," he explained, "and sesame and anise seeds. It is important that you be strong tomorrow morning."

"I may not be hungry."

"Make yourself eat. Is your faith still strong?"

"I believe so, master."

"With this glorious act, you will become my superior. You will leap ahead of me on the golden rolls kept in Heaven." His fine gray eyes, with their long lashes, appeared to water and weaken as he looked down.

"You have a watch?"

"Yes." A Timex he bought with his first paycheck, a clunky one like his mother's. It has big numbers and phosphorescent hands to read at night, when the truck cab had been hard to see in, though easy to see out of.

"It is accurate?"

"I believe so."

There is a plain chair in the room, its legs wired together since the rungs are no longer held by glue. Ahmad thought it would be discourteous to take the room's one chair, and instead, allowing himself a foretaste of the exalted status he will earn, lay down on the bed, lacing his hands together behind his head to show that he had no intention of falling asleep, though in truth he did feel suddenly tired, as if the tawdry room had somewhere in it a leak of soporific gas. He was not comfortable under the shaikh's concerned gaze, and wished now the man would go. He yearned to savor his solitary hours in this clean, safe room, alone with God. The curious way in which the imam looked down upon him reminded Ahmad of how he himself stood above the worm and the beetle. Shaikh Rashid was fascinated by him, as if by something repellent yet sacred.

"Dear boy, I have not coerced you, have I?"

"Why, no, master. How could you?"

"I mean, you have volunteered out of the fullness of your faith?"

"Yes, and out of hatred of those who mock and ignore God."

"Excellent. You do not feel manipulated by your elders?"

It was a surprising idea, though Joryleen also had expressed it. "Of course not. I feel wisely guided by them."

"And your path tomorrow is clear?"

"Yes. I am to meet Charlie at seven-thirty at Excellency

Home Furnishings, and we are to drive together to the loaded truck. He will accompany me in it part of the way to the tunnel. Then I am on my own."

Something ugly, a disfiguring little twist, crossed the shaikh's clean-shaven face. Without his beard and richly embroidered caftan, he appeared disconcertingly ordinary— slight of frame, a bit tremulous in manner, a bit withered, and no longer young. Stretched out on the rough blue blanket, Ahmad was conscious of his superior youth, height, and strength, and of his teacher's fear of him, as one is afraid of a corpse. Shaikh Rashid, hesitating, asked, "And if Charlie by some unforeseen mischance were not to be there, could you proceed with the plan? Could you find the white truck by yourself?"

"Yes. I know the alley. But why would Charlie not be there?"

"Ahmad, I am sure he will be. He is a brave soldier in our cause, the cause of the true God, and God never deserts those who wage war on His behalf. *Allāhu akbar!*" His words mixed with the distant musical phrases of the City Hall clock. Everything had a distance to it by now, a receding vibration. The shaikh went on, "In a war, if the soldier beside you falls, even if he is your best friend, even if he has taught you all you know about soldiering, do you run and hide, or do you march on, into the guns of the enemy?"

"You march on."

"Exactly. Good." Shaikh Rashid lovingly yet warily gazed down upon the boy on the bed. "I must leave you now, my prize pupil Ahmad. You have studied well."

"I thank you for saying so."

"Nothing in our studies, I trust, has led you to doubt the perfect and eternal nature of the Book of Books."

"No, indeed, sir. Nothing." Though Ahmad had sometimes sensed that his teacher in his studies had been infected with such doubts, now was not the time to question him, it was too late; we must each meet death with what faith we have created within, and stored up against the Event. Was his own faith, he had asked himself at times, an adolescent vanity, a way of distinguishing himself from all those doomed others, Joryleen and Tylenol and the rest of the lost, the already dead, at Central High?

The shaikh was hurried and troubled, yet had difficulty in leaving his pupil, searching for the final word. "You have your printed instructions for the final cleansing, before . . ."

"Yes," said Ahmad when the older man could not finish.

"But most important," Shaikh Rashid urged, "is the Holy Qur'an. If your spirit were to weaken in the long night ahead of you, open it, and let the only God speak to you through His last, perfect prophet. Unbelievers marvel at the power of Islam; it flows from the voice of Mohammed, a manly voice, a voice from the desert and the marketplace—a man among us, who knew earthly life in all its possibilities and yet hearkened to a voice from beyond, and who submitted to its dictation though many in Mecca were quick to ridicule and revile him."

"Master: I will not weaken." Ahmad's tone verged on impatience. When the other man at last was gone, and the chain lock secured, the boy stripped to his underwear and performed ablutions in the tiny bathroom, where the basin nudged the shoulder of anyone sitting on the toilet. On the inside of the basin a long brown stain testifies to years of a faucet dripping rusty water.

Ahmad takes the room's one chair to the room's only table, a bedside table of varnished maple scarred by ash-colored troughs of cigarettes allowed to burn down beyond its top's bevelled edge. Reverently he opens the gift Qur'an. Its flexible gilt-edged pages fall open to the fiftieth sura, "Qāf." He reads, on the left-hand side where the English translation is printed, a distinct echo of what Shaikh Rashid has said:

They marvel forsooth that one of themselves hath come to them charged with warnings. "This," say the infidels, "is a marvelous thing:

What! when dead and turned to dust shall we . . . ? Far off is such a return as this?"

The words speak to him, yet make insufficient sense. He studies the Arabic on the facing page, and realizes that the infidels—how strange it is that they, the devils, have a voice in the Holy Qur'an—are doubting the resurrection of the body, which the Prophet has been preaching. Ahmad, too, can scarcely picture the reconstitution of his body, after he succeeds in leaving it; instead he sees his spirit, that little thing inside him that keeps saying "I . . . I . . . ," entering the next life immediately, as if pushing through a swinging glass door. In this he is like the unbelievers: *bal kadhdhabū bi 'l-ḥaqqi lammā jā'ahum fa-hum fī amrin marīj. They,* he reads in the facing English, *have treated the truth which hath come to them as falsehood; perplexed therefore is their state.*

But God, speaking in His magnificent third-person plural, brushes their perplexity aside: *Will they not look up to the heavens above them, and consider how We have reared it and decked it forth, and that there are no flaws therein?*

The sky above New Prospect, Ahmad knows, is hazy with exhaust smoke and summer humidity, a sepia blur above the jagged rooftops. But God promises that a better sky, a flawless sky, exists above it, with its blazing patterns of blue stars. "We" goes on, *As to the Earth, We have spread it out, and have thrown the mountains upon it, and have caused an upgrowth in it of all beauteous kinds of plants, for insight and admonition to every servant who loveth to turn to God.*

Yes. Ahmad will be God's servant. Tomorrow. The day which is almost upon him. Inches from his eyes, God is describing His rain, which causeth gardens to spring forth, and the grain of harvest, *and the tall palm-trees with date-bearing branches one above the other for man's nourishment.*

And life give we thereby to a dead country. So also shall be the resurrection. A dead country. That is this country.

As simple and unanswerable as the first creation shall the second be. *Are We wearied out with the first creation? Yet are they in doubt with regard to a new creation?*

We created man: and We know what his soul whispereth to him, and We are closer to him than his neck-vein.

This verse has always borne a special, personal meaning for Ahmad; he closes the Qur'an, its pliant leather cover dyed the uneven red of a rose's streaked petals, certain that Allah is present in this small, strange room, loving him, eavesdropping on the whispers of his soul, its inaudible tumult. He feels his neck-vein beat, and hears the traffic of New Prospect, now murmuring, now roaring (motorcycles, corroded mufflers), circulating some blocks away around the great central lake of rubble, and hears it dwindle after the City Hall clock chimes eleven. He falls asleep waiting for the next quarter-hour, though he expected to stay awake all night in the blanched, hovering tremble of his high, selfless joy.

Monday morning. Sleep slips suddenly from him. There is again that sense of a shout dying away. A lump of soreness in his stomach puzzles him, until within seconds he remembers the day, and his mission. He is still alive. Today is the day of a long journey.

He consults his watch, carefully laid on the table next to the Qur'an. It is twenty to seven. Traffic is already audible, traffic whose unsuspecting flow he will join and disrupt. The entire East, God willing, will be paralyzed. He showers in a stall equipped with a torn plastic curtain. He waits for the water to heat up, but when it does not he forces himself into the cold dribble. He shaves his face, though he knows that debate rages over how God prefers to see men face to face. The Chehabs preferred him to shave, since bearded Muslims, even teen-agers, alarmed the kafir customers. Mohammed Atta had shaved, and most of the eighteen other inspired martyrs. The anniversary of their feat was last Saturday, and the enemy will have relaxed his defenses, like the men of the elephant before the assault of birds. Ahmad has brought his gym bag and from it takes clean underwear and socks and his last fresh-laundered white shirt, pleasantly stiffened by a number of pieces of cardboard.

He prays on the prayer rug, the mock-mihrab in its abstract pattern orienting him toward, in the distracting geography of New Prospect, the sacred black Ka'ba in Mecca. In touching his brow to its woven texture, he notices that same faint human odor present in the blue blanket. He has joined a procession of those who have stayed for whatever hidden purpose here in this room before him, showering in the cold rusty water, smoking their cigarettes as the clock chimed. Ahmad eats, though his appetite has vanished within the tension of his stomach, six segments of the orange, half the plastic cup of yogurt, and a significant portion of the bread of Abbas, though the sweetness of its honey and anise seeds strikes him as less than delicious at this hour, with his mighty deed pressing close upon him and crowding upward into his throat like a battle cry. He places the uneaten portion of the sticky holiday bread in the refrigerator, on the biggest piece of shirt cardboard, with the yogurt cup and half-orange, as if for the next tenant, but without attracting ants and roaches to a feast. His mind works through a haze like that which precedes the event described in the Meccan sura called the Blow, *on the day when man shall become like scattered moths and the mountains like tufts of carded wool.*

At seven-fifteen he closes the door behind him, leaving behind in the safe room the Qur'an and the cleanliness instructions for another *shahīd* but taking his gym bag, packed with his soiled underpants, socks, and white shirt. He passes through a dark hallway and emerges onto an empty side street that was moistened by a small rain sometime in the night. Orienting himself by the steeple of City Hall, Ahmad walks north, toward Reagan Boulevard and Excellency Home Furnishings. He deposits his gym bag in the first corner trash can he sees.

The sky is not crystal-clear but damp and gray, a furry low sky bleeding downward tails of vaporous fuzz. The night that has passed has set a gleam on the asphalt streets, their manholes, their shiny dribbles and patches of tar. Dampness adheres to the still-green leaves of bushes straggling beside front steps and porches, and the overlapped strips of aluminum siding, its color baked in. Most of the close-packed houses he passes are not yet fully stirring, though from weakly lit windows at the back, where the kitchens are, sounds of plates and pots and the *Today* show and *Good Morning America* signal breakfasts being consumed, and a Monday like many another in America beginning.

Five

An unseen dog in a house barks at the shadow-sound of Ahmad passing on the sidewalk. A ginger-colored cat with one blind eye like a crazed white marble is huddling close to the front screen door as it waits to be let in; it arches its back and flashes a golden spark from its narrowed good eye, sensing something uncanny in this tall young stranger passing. The air tingles on Ahmad's face but there is not enough of a drizzle to soak his shirt. The starched cotton feels crisp across his shoulders; his black stovepipe jeans sheathe the long legs that float in the watery space below his belt. His running shoes lick up the distance between himself and his fate; where the sidewalk is smooth, the elaborate relief of their soles leaves moist prints. *Who shall teach thee what the Blow is?* he remembers, with the answer: *A raging fire!* The distance to Excellency is half a mile, six blocks of tenements and small enterprise—a Dunkin' Donuts open and a corner grocery ungrated but a pawn shop and an insurance agency still closed. Reagan Boulevard is already loud with traffic, and the school buses have begun to prowl, their angry red lights blinking in rapid seesawing alternation as they swallow the clusters of children waiting with their bright backpacks. For Ahmad there will be no return to school. Central High now seems, with all its menacing clatter and impious mockery, a toylike miniature castle, a childish place of safety and deferred decision.

He waits for the traffic light to display its walking man before he crosses the boulevard. Its oil-stained concrete is more familiar to him as the surface supporting the tires of his truck than as this silent, enigmatically speckled plane beneath his feet. He turns left and approaches from the east, walking past the funeral home with its wide porch and white awnings—UNGER & SON, a strange unctuous hungry name—

and then the tire store that was once a gasoline station, the pumps uprooted but its island intact. Ahmad halts on the curb of Thirteenth Street, looking over to the Excellency lot. The orange truck is not there. Charlie's Saab is not there. Two unknown cars, one gray and one black, are there, diagonally parked in a heedless, space-consuming way, amid signs of mysterious activity: a litter of Styrofoam coffee cups and clamshell-style take-out containers that have been dropped on the cracked concrete and then flattened, in a coming and going of tires, like road kill.

Overhead, the sun burns through the overcast and throws a weak white light, as of a failing flashlight. Before Ahmad can be seen—though no one appears to be sitting in the strange, arrogantly trespassing cars—he ducks right, up Thirteenth Street, and crosses it only when he is hidden behind the screen of bushes and tall weeds that have grown up behind the rusting Dumpster, on property belonging not to Excellency but to the rear of a long-defunct diner in the shape of an old-fashioned trolley car. This boarded-up relic lies at the corner of a narrow street, Frank Hague Terrace, whose row houses, semi-detached, are quiet during the weekdays, until school lets out.

Ahmad consults his watch: seven twenty-seven. He decides to give Charlie until quarter of eight to show up, though their schedule had called for seven-thirty. But then it bears down upon him more and more strongly as the minutes pass that something has gone wrong; Charlie will not show up. This lot is poisoned. This empty space behind the store used to give him a sensation of being watched from above, but now it is not God watching, nor God's breath he feels. He, Ahmad, is watching, with held breath.

A man in a suit abruptly comes out of the back of the

store, onto the loading platform some of whose thick planks still ooze pine sap, and comes down the steps where Ahmad would often idly sit. Here he and Joryleen exited together that night and then parted forever. The man walks boldly to his car and talks to someone over a kind of radio or cell phone in the front seat. His voice, like a policeman's, doesn't care who hears it, but amid the swish of traffic it carries to Ahmad with no more meaning than birdsong. For a second his white face turns full in Ahmad's direction—a well-fed but not happy face, that of an agent for infidel governments, powers that feel power slipping away—but he doesn't see the Arab boy. There is nothing to see, just the Dumpster rusting in the weeds.

Ahmad's heart beats as it did that night with Joryleen. He regrets now the waste, not using her when she had been paid for. But it would have been evil, exploiting her in her fallen condition, though she saw her condition as not so bad and only temporary. Shaikh Rashid would have disapproved. Last night, the shaikh seemed troubled, something was pressing on him he didn't want to share, a doubt of some kind. Ahmad could always sense his teacher's doubts, since it was important to him that there not be any. Now fear invades Ahmad. His face feels swollen. A curse has been laid on this peaceful place, which had been his favorite spot in the world, a waterless oasis.

He begins walking, down silent Hague Terrace—its children at school, its parents at work—for two blocks and then cuts back to Reagan Boulevard, toward the Arab district, where the white truck is hidden. There has been some mix-up, and Charlie must be meeting him there. Ahmad hurries, breaking into a light sweat under the hazy sun. The businesses along Reagan Boulevard deal in big goods—tires, carpeting, wallpaper and paint, major kitchen appliances. Then there are car agencies, mammoth lots holding new automobiles parked as tight as military formations, cars by the acre, windshields and chrome glittering now that the sun is wearing through, reflecting light as if across a wind-tossed wheat field, striking sparks off of strings of shiny triangles and streamers twisted in spirals that slowly turn. A new style of attention-getter, a creation of recent technology, are these weirdly lifelike segmented plastic tubes that when blown full of air from underneath wave their arms and jerk back and forth in torment, in constant beckoning agitation, begging the passerby to pull in and buy an automobile or, if posed at an IHOP, a stack of pancakes. Ahmad, the only person walking on the sidewalk along this stretch of Reagan Boulevard, meets such a tube-giant twice as high as he, a hysterically gesturing green djinni wearing a fixed, pop-eyed smile. Passing it warily, the lone pedestrian feels on his face and ankles the hot air that makes this importuning, agonized, grinning monster appear to live. *God giveth you life*, Ahmad thinks, *then causeth you to die.*

At the next traffic light he crosses the boulevard. He strides down Sixteenth Street toward West Main, through a mostly black section like the one he walked Joryleen home to that time after hearing her sing in church. The way her mouth opened so wide, the milky pinks of it. That time on the second floor, all those beds packed in side by side, maybe he should have let her blow him like she offered to. Less mess, she said. All girls, not just hookers, learn how to do it now, at school there had always been loose crude talk about it, which girls were willing to do it, and which said they liked to swallow it. *Separate yourselves therefore from women and approach them not, until they be cleansed. But when they are*

Five

*cleansed, go in unto them as God hath ordained for you. Verily
God loveth those who turn to Him, and loveth those who seek to
be clean.*

As Ahmad walks along, swift and scissoring in black and
white, yet with a native trace of the American lope, he sees
shabbiness in the streets, the fast-food trash and broken
plastic toys, the unpainted steps and porches still dark from
the morning's dampness, the windows cracked and not
repaired. The curbs are lined with American cars from the
last century, bigger than they ever needed to be and now
falling apart, cracked taillights and no hubcaps and tires flat
in the gutters. Women's voices rise from back rooms in merciless complaint against children who were born uninvited
and now collect, neglected, around the only friendly voices
in their hearing, those from the television set. The *zanj* from
the Caribbean or Cape Verdeans plant flowers and paint
porches and take hope and energy from being in America,
but those born here for generation after generation embrace
dirt and laziness as a protest, a protest of slaves that now persists as a lust for degradation, defying that injunction of all
religions to keep clean. Ahmad is clean. His cold shower this
morning lives as a glowing second skin beneath his clothes,
a foretaste of the great cleansing he is hurrying toward. His
watch says ten of eight.

He moves swiftly, without running. He must not attract
attention, he must slip through the city unseen. Later would
come the headlines, the CNN reports filling the Middle
East with jubilation, making the tyrants in their opulent
Washington offices tremble. For now the tremble, the mission are still his, his secret, his task. He remembers himself
running, crouching and shaking out his naked arms for
looseness, waiting for the starter's pistol to go off and the

knot of boys to unravel forward with an angry hail of thump-
ing feet on Central High's antiquated cinder track, and until
his body took over and his brain dissolved itself in adrenaline he was more nervous then than he is now, because what
he does now occurs within the palm of God's hand, His vast
encompassing will. Ahmad's best official time for the mile
had been 4:48.6, on a springy composition track, green with
embedded red lane lines, over at a regional high school in
Belleville. He had come in third, and his lungs afterwards
felt scorched in the fire of his finishing kick over the last
hundred yards; he had passed two boys, but two more stayed
out of reach of his legs, mirages ahead that kept receding.

After five blocks Sixteenth Street comes into West Main.
Elderly Muslims stand around like soft statues in their dark
suits and the occasional dirty gallabiya. Ahmad finds the Pep
Boys and the Al-Aqsa True Value storefronts, and then the
alley behind them that he and Charlie had walked along to
what had been Costello's Machine Shop. He makes sure
there is no one watching as he draws near to the small side
door of quilted metal painted a vomitous tan. No Charlie
stands outside. There is no sound within. The sun has
burned through, and Ahmad feels his shoulders and back
sweating; his white shirt is no longer pristine. The Monday
is astir a half-block distant on West Main. There is some
traffic, cars and pedestrians, in the alley. He tries the new
brass knob on the door, but it doesn't turn. He keeps twisting it, in exasperation. How can little unthinking bits of
metal balk the will of *as-Samad*, the Perfect?

Fighting panic, Ahmad tries the big door, the sliding door.
It has a handle down low that when turned makes two rods
release a pair of side latches. The handle turns; the door
shocks him by sliding up with a counterweighted ease that

feels like flight, a curved moment of flight before it settles rattlingly into its rails above, in the gloom near the ceiling.

Ahmad has let light into a cave. Charlie is not inside the grimy space, nor are the two operatives, the technician and his younger support. The workbenches and pegboards are just as Ahmad remembers them. The litter and drifts of discarded parts in the corners seem less than before. The garage has been cleaned up, tidied toward some finality. There is a hush as of a tomb that has been robbed the last time. The traffic in the alley throws into the cave dangerous flickers of reflected light; passersby idly glance in. No one is here but the truck is here, the boxy GMC 3500 unprofessionally hand-lettered WINDOW SHADES SYSTEMS.

Ahmad opens the driver's door gingerly and sees that the military-drab box still sits there between the two seats, duct-taped to the milk crate. The ignition key dangles from the dashboard, inviting an intruder to turn it. Two thick insulated wires still trail from the detonator into the truck body. The access door, no higher than a crouching man, slides open only six inches before the wires threaded through it begin to pull tight. Through the six-inch opening Ahmad smells the mixture of ammonium-nitrate fertilizer and nitromethane racing fuel; he sees the ghostly-pale plastic drums, each as high as his waist and each holding one hundred sixty kilograms of the explosive mixture. The glossy white plastic of the containers glimmers like a species of flesh. Spliced yellow wires loop from the blasting caps, enhanced by aluminum powder and pentrite, which are embedded in the bottom of each drum. The twenty-five containers, he can make out in the shadows, have been arranged in a five-by-five square, neatly roped together with doubled clothesline and secured against sliding by taut attachments to the cleats and side bars within the truck body. The whole constitutes a work of modern art, assiduous and opaque. Ahmad remembers the squat technician, the dainty smooth gestures of his oil-tipped hands, and imagines him smiling, gap-toothed, with a workman's innocent pride. They are all, all in this scheme, parts of a beautiful machine, fitted one against another. The others have vanished but Ahmad remains, to put the final piece into its place.

Gently he slides back the little wooden door, restoring the array of loaded plastic drums to their fragrant darkness. They have been entrusted to him. Like him, they are soldiers. He is surrounded by fellow-soldiers even though they have gone silent, leaving no instruction behind. The door at the back of the truck has been padlocked. The big hasp has been swung over and its slot closed over the thick protruding staple and a heavy combination padlock snapped shut there. Ahmad has not been told the combination. He understands the message: he must have faith in his brothers, just as they have faith in him, in their unexplained absence, to proceed with the plan. He has become the surviving lone instrument of the All-Merciful, the Perfect. He has been provided with a truck the twin of one he habitually drives, to make his path straight and smooth. Tentatively, he sits in the driver's seat. The old imitation black leather feels warm, as if just vacated.

An explosion, he remembers from his physics class at Central High, is simply a solid or liquid being rapidly turned into a gas, expanding in less than a second into hundreds of times its former volume. That is all it is. As if from the rim of such an impassive chemical event he sees himself, small and precise, climb into the unaccustomed truck, start the engine, rev it gently, and back it out into the alley.

Five

One small thing nags. Getting out to lower the rattling garage door behind them—him, the truck, and the invisible company of his collaborators—Ahmad feels the juice of the breakfast orange and a suppressed nervous excitement press upon his bladder. He had best lighten himself for the journey ahead. He parks the truck, with its motor idling, on one side of the alley, raises the garage door again, and finds the machine shop's toilet behind a smirched unmarked door in a corner beside the workbench and the pegboard. There is a string that turns on the naked bulb, and a bright porcelain receptacle with an oval eye of dubious water to be flushed when he is done adding the little stream out of himself. He washes his hands scrupulously, using the dispenser of grease-cutting detergent in readiness on the sink. He returns outside and pulls down the rattling door on its knotted cord and realizes with an inner lurch how foolish and dangerous it had been to abandon the truck, its motor running, even for a minute or two. He is not thinking normally, in this exalted yet thin atmosphere of last things. He must keep his head level by conceiving of himself as God's instrument, cool and hard and definite and thoughtless, as an instrument must be.

He consults his Timex: it says eight-oh-nine. Four more minutes lost. He rolls the truck forward, trying to avoid potholes and sudden starts and stops. He is behind the schedule that he and Charlie set, but by less than twenty minutes. Calmer now that the truck is moving, part of the flow of the daily traffic of the world, he turns right out of the alley and then left on West Main, passing again the Pep Boys, with its disturbing cartoon image of three men, Manny, Moe, and Jack, conjoined in one three-headed dwarf body.

The fully awakened city twinkles and swerves around him. He imagines his truck as an encircled rectangle in a heli-

: 285 :

copter view of a car chase, threading through the streets, stopping at lights. This truck handles differently from Excellency, which had an easy sway to it, as if the driver were sitting on the neck of an elephant. Driving Window Shades Systems, he feels no organic sympathy. The steering wheel doesn't fit his hands. Every irregularity in the road surface jars the whole frame. The front wheels persistently tug to the left, as if some accident left the frame bent. The weight—twice what McVeigh had, greater and denser than any load of furniture—pushes him from behind when he brakes at a red light and holds him back when he pulls out on green.

To avoid the center of the town—the high school, the City Hall, the church, the lake of rubble, the stubby glass skyscrapers supplied as sops by the government—Ahmad turns on Washington Street, called that because, Charlie had once told him, in the other direction it goes by a mansion the great general used as one of his New Jersey headquarters. The jihad and the Revolution waged the same kind of war, Charlie explained—the desperate and vicious war of the underdog, the imperial overdog claiming fouls by the rules he has devised for his own benefit.

Ahmad punches on the dashboard radio; it is tuned in to an obnoxious rap station, spouting unintelligible lewdness. He finds WCBS-AM on the dial and is breathlessly told that traffic on the helix into the Lincoln Tunnel is a logjam as usual, stop-and-go, ho-ho-ho. Rapid chatter from a helicopter and rackety pop music follow. He punches the radio off again. In this devilish society there is nothing fit for a man in his last hour to hear. Silence is better. Silence is God's music. Ahmad must be clean, to meet God. An icy trickle high in his abdomen reaches his bowels at the thought of meeting the other self, as close as a vein in his neck, that he has always felt beside him, a brother, a father, but one he could never turn to confront directly in His perfect radiance. Now he, the fatherless, the brotherless, carries forward God's inexorable will; Ahmad hastens to deliver Hutama, the Crushing Fire. More precisely, Shaikh Rashid once explained, Hutama means *that which breaks to pieces.*

There is only one New Prospect interchange off Route 80. Ahmad steers the truck southeast on Washington until Washington meets Tilden Avenue, which feeds directly into 80 in its thunderous plunge, this time of day, toward New York City. Three blocks north of the interchange, at a broad corner where a Getty service station faces a Mobil that includes a Shop-a-Sec, Ahmad sees a somewhat familiar figure hanging on the curb waving, not waving like a man absurdly hoping for a taxi—which don't range free in New Prospect and must be summoned by phone—but waving directly at *him.* Indeed, he points to Ahmad through the windshield; he holds up his hands as if stopping something physically. It's Mr. Levy, wearing a brown suit coat that doesn't match his gray pants. He's dressed for school on this Monday but instead is standing outdoors a mile south of Central High.

The unexpected sight stymies Ahmad. He fights to clear his racing mind. Perhaps Mr. Levy has a message from Charlie, though he didn't think they knew each other; the guidance counselor had never liked his getting the CDL and driving a truck. Or an urgent message from his mother, who for a while this summer would mention Mr. Levy a little too often, in that tone of voice that meant she was embarrassing herself again. Ahmad will not stop, no more than he would for one of those writhing, importuning monsters, made from plastic tubes and blowing air, that bewitch consumers into turning off a thoroughfare.

However, the light at the corner changes and the traffic slows and the truck has to halt. Mr. Levy, moving faster than Ahmad knew he could, dodges through the lanes of stopped traffic and reaches up and raps commandingly on the passenger's window. Confused, conditioned not to show a teacher disrespect, Ahmad reaches over and pushes the unlock button. Better have him inside next to him, the boy hastily reasons, than outside where he can raise an alarm. Mr. Levy yanks open the passenger door and just as the traffic has to move again hoists himself up and flops into the cracked black seat. He slams the door shut. He is panting. "Thanks," he says. "I was getting afraid I'd missed you."

"How did you know I'd be here?"

"There's only one way to get to 80."

"But this isn't my truck."

"I knew it wouldn't be."

"How?"

"It's a long story. All I have are bits and pieces. Window Shades Systems—that's funny. Let in the light. Who says these guys don't have a sense of humor?" He is still panting. Glancing at his profile, where Charlie used to sit, Ahmad is struck by how old the guidance teacher is, removed from the youthful commotion of the high school. Weariness has accumulated under his eyes. His lips look loose, the lid skin below his eyebrows sags. Ahmad wonders how it feels, to be sliding day by day toward a natural death. He himself will never know. Perhaps after being alive as long as Mr. Levy, you don't feel it. Still short of breath, the man sits up, pleased at having achieved his purpose of getting into

Ahmad's truck. "What's this?" he asks, of the drab metal box taped to the plastic crate in the space between the two seats.

"*Don't touch it!*" The words come out so sharply that Ahmad out of politeness adds, "Sir."

"I won't," Mr. Levy says. "But don't you touch it either." He is silent, inspecting it without touching it. "Foreign manufacture, maybe Czech or Chinese. It sure isn't our old standard-issue LD20 detonator. I was in the Army, you know, though they never sent me to Vietnam. That bothered me. I didn't want to go, but I wanted to prove myself. You can understand that. Wanting to prove yourself."

"No. I don't understand," Ahmad says. This abrupt intrusion has confused him; his thoughts feel like bumblebees, blindly bumping at the walls inside his skull. But he continues to steer smoothly, gliding the GMC 3500 through the curving connector onto Route 80, bumper-to-bumper at this commuting hour. He is getting used to the unforgiving way this truck handles.

"As I understand it, they used to rig up explosives inside the Cong's spider holes and seal them in and detonate them with these. Woodchucking, they used to call it. It wasn't pretty. But, then, there wasn't much pretty about the whole business. Except the women. But I heard you couldn't trust even them. They were Cong, too."

Ahmad, his head buzzing, tries to state his position clearly: "Sir, if you make any move to break the wires or interfere with my driving, I will set off four tons of explosives. The yellow is a safety switch, and I'm turning it off now." He moves it to the right—*snap*—and both men wait to see what will happen. Ahmad thinks, *If something happens we will not know it*. Nothing happens, but the switch is now off. It remains only for him to sink his thumb down into the little well whose bottom is the red detonation button, and to wait the microseconds for the ignition of the blasting powder to ripple up through the enhancing pentrite and racing fuel into the tons of nitrate. He feels the smooth red button at the tip of his thumb, without taking his eyes from the jammed highway. If this flabby Jew moves to deflect him he will brush him aside like a piece of paper, like a tuft of carded wool.

"I have no such intentions," Mr. Levy tells him, in the falsely relaxed voice with which he advises failing students, defiant students, students who have given up on themselves. "I just want to tell you a few things that might interest you."

"What things? Tell me, and I'll let you out when we get closer to my destination."

"Well, I guess the main thing is, Charlie's dead."

"Dead?"

"Beheaded, in fact. Gruesome, huh? He'd been tortured before they did it. The body was found yesterday morning, dumped in the Meadows, by the canal south of Giants Stadium. They wanted it found. There was a note attached to it, in Arabic. Evidently Charlie was CIA undercover and the other side finally figured it out."

There had been a father who vanished before his memory could take a picture of him, and then Charlie had been friendly and shown him the roads, and now this tired Jew in clothes as if he dressed in the dark has taken their place, the empty space beside him. "What did the note say, exactly?"

"Oh, I don't know. Same old same old, to the effect that he who breaks his oath punishes himself. God will not deny him his recompense."

"It sounds like the Qur'an, the forty-eighth sura."

"It sounds like the Torah, too. Whatever you say. There's a lot I don't know. I'm coming in late."

"May I ask, how do you know what you do know?"

"My wife's sister. She works in Washington for Homeland Security. She called me yesterday; my wife had mentioned my interest in you, and they wondered if there was a connection. They couldn't find you. Nobody could. I thought I'd give this a try."

"Why should I believe any of what you say?"

"Don't, then. Believe it only if it fits with what you know. My guess is it does. Where is Charlie now, if I'm lying? His wife says he's vanished. She swears he was just in the furniture business."

"What of the other Chehabs, and the men to whom they supplied money?"

Ahmad is being tailgated by a midnight-blue Mercedes driven by an impatient man too young to have earned a Mercedes, unless it was in stock manipulation at the expense of the less fortunate. Such men live expensively in the so-called bedroom towns of New Jersey and jumped from the towers when God brought them down. Ahmad feels superior to this Mercedes driver, and indifferent to his tooting and swerving back and forth as he seeks to dramatize his wish that the white truck were moving less sedately in the middle lane.

Mr. Levy answers, "Gone underground and scattered, I suppose. They caught two men trying to fly to Paris out of Newark, and Charlie's father is in the hospital with what's supposed to be a stroke."

"He suffers from diabetes, truly."

"Whatever. He says he loves this country, and so did his son, and now his son has died for this country. There's one theory that he's the one who fingered his son. The uncle in Florida, the feds have had an eye on him for some time. These agencies are overwhelmed, and don't communicate with one another, but they don't miss *every* trick. The uncle will talk, or somebody will. It's hard to believe one brother had no idea what the other was up to. These Arabs all pressure each other with Islam: how can you say no to the will of Allah?"

"I don't know. I have been denied," Ahmad says stiffly, "the blessing of a brother."

"Small blessing, to go by what I see at school. In jackals, I read somewhere, the pups fight to the death as soon as they're born."

Less stiffly, remembering with a smile, Ahmad tells Mr. Levy, "Charlie was very eloquent for the jihad."

"That was one of his acts, apparently. I never met the guy. He sounds like a loose cannon. His mistake, my sister-in-law said—and all she does is echo her boss, she worships the bozo—his fatal mistake was to wait too long to spring his trap. He'd seen too many movies."

"He watched a great deal of television. He wanted some day to direct commercials."

"My point is, Ahmad, you don't need to do this. It's all over. Charlie never meant for you to go through with it. He was using you to flush out the others."

Ahmad reviews the unfolding, slithering fabric of what he has heard and concludes, "It would be a glorious victory for Islam."

"Islam? How so?"

"It would slay and inconvenience many unbelievers."

"You've got to be kidding," Mr. Levy says, as Ahmad deftly maneuvers the transition from 80 East to 95 South, seizing the inside lane and not allowing the Mercedes to pass him on the right as the bulk of the traffic continues east toward the George Washington Bridge. On the left, the Overpeck River crinkles in the breeze as it flows toward the Hackensack. The truck is on the New Jersey Turnpike, above swampland being exploited in every scrap that can be drained. The Turnpike branches; the leftward branch leads to the Lincoln Tunnel exit. The plotters saw to it that an E-Z Pass transponder is fixed to the center of the truck's windshield; it will let him roll smoothly through the toll booth, without more than a moment's exposure of the youthful driver to the eyes of a toll-taker or guard.

"Think of your mother." The conversational ease has gone from Mr. Levy's voice; a touch of stridency has entered. "She'll not only lose you but she'll become known as the mother of a monster. A madman."

Ahmad is beginning to take pleasure in not being moved by this intruder's arguments. "I have never been essential to my mother," he explains, "though she did, I admit, stick with her assignment once I was unfortunately born. As to the mother of a monster, in the Middle East the mothers of martyrs are highly esteemed and receive a substantial pension."

Mr. Levy says, "I'm sure she'd rather have you than a pension."

"*How* are you sure, may I ask, sir? How well do you know her?"

Gulls, at first a few in his vision through the windshield, then dozens coming into focus, and the dozens becoming hundreds, wheel above a waste site. Beyond their greedy gathering of wings, beyond the sullen Hudson, stands the stone-colored silhouette, notched like an immense key, of the great city, Satan's heart. Lit from the east, its towers loom in shadow from the west, a dust of haze radiant between them. Mr. Levy's silence foretells a new attack on Ahmad's convictions, but for now driver and passenger share without comment their glimpse of one of the world's wonders, suddenly snatched from view as the traffic hurtles onward and is replaced by relatively empty expanses on either side of 95—marsh grass shot through with blue flashes of sky reflected by the watery channels as they wander in the mud. High in his windshield, a silvery cruciform glint escapes Newark International Airport, carving in the milky blank sky a twin-tipped trail like a highway for others to follow, in the web of patterns the air controllers enforce. Ahmad momentarily feels exhilarated, like a plane lifting free of gravity.

Mr. Levy destroys the moment, saying, "Well, what else can we talk about? Giants Stadium. Did you catch the Jets game yesterday? When that kid Carter fumbled the kickoff, I thought to myself, *Here we go again, just like last season.* But no, they pulled it out, thirty-one to twenty-four, though you couldn't relax until that rookie safety Coleman came up with the interception in the last minute of the Bengals' final drive." This is presumably Jewish comedy, which Ahmad ignores. In a more sincere voice, Levy says, "I can't believe you're seriously intending to kill hundreds of innocent people."

"Who says unbelief is innocent? Unbelievers say that. God says, in the Qur'an, *Be ruthless to unbelievers.* Burn them, crush them, because they have forgotten God. They think to be themselves is sufficient. They love this present life more than the next."

"So kill them now. That seems pretty severe."

"It would to you, of course. You are a lapsed Jew, I believe. You believe nothing. In the third sura of the Qur'an it says that not all the gold in the world can ransom those who once believed and now disbelieve, and that God will never accept their repentance."

Five

Mr. Levy sighs. Ahmad can hear moisture, little droplets of fear, rattle in his breath. "Yeah, well, there's a lot of repulsive and ridiculous stuff in the Torah, too. Plagues, massacres, straight from Yahweh to you. Tribes that weren't lucky enough to be chosen—put them under the ban, show them no mercy. They hadn't quite worked out Hell yet, that came with the Christians. Wise up—the priests try to control people through fear. Conjure up Hell—the oldest scare tactic in the world. Next to torture. Hell *is* torture, basically. You really can buy into all this? God as supreme torturer? God as the King of genocide?"

"As the note attached to Charlie said, He will not deny us our recompense. You mention the Torah, in your own tradition. The Prophet had many good words for Abraham. I am interested: Did you ever believe? How did you fall away?"

"I was born fallen away. My father hated Judaism, and his father before him. They blamed religion for the world's misery—it reconciled people to their problems. Then they subscribed to another religion, Communism. But you don't want to hear this."

"I don't mind. It is good for us to seek agreement. Before Israel, Muslims and Jews were brothers—they belonged to the margins of the Christian world, the comic others in their funny clothes, entertainment for the Christians secure in their wealth, in their paper-white skins. Even with the oil, they despised us, cheating the Saudi princes of their people's birthright."

Mr. Levy heaves another sigh. "That's some 'us' you've worked up, Ahmad."

The traffic, already congested, slows and thickens. Signs say NORTH BERGEN, SECAUCUS, WEEHAWKEN, ROUTE 495, TO THE LINCOLN TUNNEL. Though he has never done this before, with or without Charlie, Ahmad follows the signs easily, even as 495, at a spasmodic crawl, performs a complete loop, bringing the traffic down the Weehawken cliff to the level of the river. He imagines a voice at his side saying, *Easy does it, Madman. This isn't rocket science.*

As the roadway descends, mobs of other vehicles are being funneled in from feeder roads south and west. Ahmad sees above the car roofs their eventual common destination, a long face of tawny stonework and white tiles framing three round archways for two lanes each. A sign says TRUCKS TO RIGHT. Other trucks—brown UPS, yellow Ryder, motley tradesmen's pickups, tractor trailers chuffing and squealing as they tug forward their mammoth loads of fresh produce of the Garden State on its way to the kitchens of Manhattan—press right, working their way a few feet at a time, and braking.

"Now is the time to jump out, Mr. Levy. I can't stop once we're in the tunnel."

The guidance counselor puts his hands on his thighs in their mismatched gray trousers so that Ahmad can see he isn't going to touch the door. "I don't think I'll get out. We're in this together, son." His pose is brave, but his voice is hoarse, weak.

"I'm not your son. If you try to get anyone's attention I'll set off the truck right here, in the traffic jam. It's not ideal but it'll kill plenty."

"I'm betting you won't set it off. You're too good a kid. Your mother used to tell me how you couldn't bear to step on a bug. You'd try to get it onto a piece of paper and throw it out the window."

"My mother and you seem to have had a lot of conversations."

"Consultations. We both want the best for you."

"I didn't like to step on bugs, but I don't like touching them either. I was afraid they'd bite, or defecate on my hand."

Mr. Levy laughs offensively; Ahmad insists, "Insects can defecate—we learned that in biology. They have digestive tracts and anuses and everything, just like we do." His brain is racing, battering at its own limits. Because there seems no time left in which to argue, he accepts Mr. Levy's presence beside him as something immaterial, half real, like the sense he has always had of God being closer to him than a brother, of himself as a double being half unfolded, like a book with its two sets of pages bound together, odd and even, read and unread.

Surprisingly, here at the three mouths (Manny, Moe, and Jack) of the Lincoln Tunnel, there are trees and greenery: above the traffic jam, as its tangled seethe of brake lights and directional lights blink on and off, an earth embankment supports a triangular piece of mown grass. Ahmad thinks, *This is the last piece of earth I will ever see,* this little lawn that no one ever stands on or picnics on or has ever noticed before with eyes about to go blind.

A few men and women in blue-gray uniforms are standing around the edges of the coagulated, forward-inching traffic flow. These police appear to be benign onlookers rather than supervisors, chatting in pairs and basking in the reborn, but still hazy, sunshine. For them this jam occurs every weekday in these hours, as much a part of nature as sunrise or tides or the planet's other mindless recurrences. One of the officers is a sturdy female, her cap allowing her bundled fair hair to show at her neck and ears, her breasts pushing against the shirt pockets of her uniform, with its badge and bandolier strap; she has attracted two uniformed males, one white and one black, their teeth exposed in lustful smiles and their waists heavy with dangling weapons. Ahmad looks at his Timex: eight-fifty-five. Forty-five minutes have passed in the truck. It will be over by nine-fifteen.

He has maneuvered the truck to the right, expertly using his mirrors to exploit the merest hesitation in a vehicle beside him. The jam, which felt for a while impenetrable, has sorted itself out into lanes feeding into the two Manhattan-bound tunnels. Suddenly, Ahmad sees, only a half-dozen vans and autos are between him and the right-hand tunnel entrance. There are a U-Haul ten-foot rented van and then a lunch wagon in quilted aluminum, all buttoned-up and latched against the moment when it unfolds its counter and activates its kitchen to feed unfastidious crowds from the sidewalk, and a number of ordinary autos, including a bronze-colored Volvo station wagon holding a family of *zanj*. With a courteous wave Ahmad bids the driver slip in ahead of him into the line that has formed.

"You won't get by the booth," Mr. Levy warns him. He sounds tense, as if a bully is squeezing his chest from behind. "You look too young to be driving out of state."

But there is nobody in the booth built to hold a toll-taker. Nobody. A green light flashes E-Z PASS PAID and Ahmad and the white truck are admitted to the tunnel.

The light inside is instantly strange: tiles not quite white but a sickly cream form close walls around the double stream of trucks and cars. The noise thus contained generates an echo, an undercurrent that slightly dampens it, as if with a watery distance. Ahmad feels himself already to be under water. He imagines the Hudson's black weight overhead, above the tiled ceiling. The artificial light in the tunnel is ample yet not cleansing; the vehicles move, at the speed of the slowest, through a kind of blanched darkness. There are trucks, some so vast the tops of their trailers seem to scrape the ceiling, but also automobiles that in the metallic scramble at the entrance have mixed themselves in with the trucks.

Through his windshield Ahmad looks down through the back window of the bronze station wagon, a V90. Two children seated backward look up at him, hopeful for entertainment. They are not neglectfully dressed but in the same carefully careless, ironically gaudy clothes that white children would be wearing on a family expedition. This black family was doing well, until Ahmad waved them ahead of him into line.

After an initial spurt, a glide into the space won at last by the untangling of the congestion outside the tunnel, the traffic flow is balked by some unseen obstacle or stickiness ahead. Smooth progress has proved to be an illusion. Drivers brake, brake lights glare. Ahmad finds himself not ungrateful for the slowdown, the stop and go. The downward slant of the road surface, which was unexpectedly rough and bumpy for a surface that never saw the weather, threatened to carry him and his passenger and their load too quickly toward the tunnel's nadir, beyond which lay the theoretical weak point, two-thirds of the way through, where, he was advised, the tunnel will bend and be weakest. There his life will end. A shimmer like a heat mirage has possessed his mind's eye: that triangle of tended yet unused grass hung above the tunnel mouth hangs in his mind. He had felt pity for it, so unvisited.

Clearing his dry throat, he uses his voice. "I do not look young," he explains to Mr. Levy. "Men of our Middle-Eastern blood—we mature quicker than Anglo-Saxons.

Charlie used to say I looked twenty-one and could drive the big rigs without anybody stopping me."

"That Charlie, he said a lot," Mr. Levy replies. His voice sounds tight, a hollow teacher's voice.

"Would you rather I did not talk, as the time draws near? It is possible that, though fallen away, you would like to pray."

One of the children in the back of the Volvo, a girl with her bushy hair up in two curious round balls, like the ears of that cartoon mouse once so famous, is trying to attract Ahmad's attention with smiles; he ignores her.

"No," Levy says, as if even that monosyllable hurts to get out. "Talk away. Ask me something."

"Shaikh Rashid. Did your informant know what has happened to him, in this uncovering?"

"For now, he's vanished. But he won't make it back to Yemen, I can promise you. These pricks can't get away with everything forever."

"He came to visit me last night. There seemed a sadness to him. But, then, there always has been. I think his learning is stronger than his faith."

"And he didn't tell you the jig was up? Charlie was found early yesterday morning."

"No. He assured me Charlie would meet me as planned. He wished me well."

"He left you in sole charge."

Ahmad hears the scornful tone and asserts, "I *am* in charge." He brags, "This morning, there were two strange cars at the Excellency lot. I saw a man who had the loud voice of authority talk on a cell phone. I saw him but he did not see me."

At the girl's instigation, she and her little brother press

their faces against their curved window with pop eyes and contorted mouths, to make Ahmad smile, to achieve recognition.

Mr. Levy is slumping in his seat, feigning insouciance or cowering beneath images in his imagination. He says, "One more screw-up from your Uncle Sam. The fuzz was busy getting cups of coffee, telling dirty jokes to each other over the intercom, who knows? Listen. There's something I need to say to you. I fucked your mother."

The tile walls, Ahmad notices, are glowing a rosy red in the reflection of so many taillights coming on as people repeatedly brake. Cars jerk forward a few feet, and brake again.

"We were sleeping together all summer," Levy goes on when Ahmad does not reply. "She was fantastic. I didn't know I could fall in love with anybody ever again—get all those juices flowing again."

"I think my mother," Ahmad tells him, after consideration, "sleeps with people easily. A nurse's aide is at home with the body, and she sees herself as a liberated modern person."

"So don't get all bent out of shape about it, you're telling me: it was no big deal. But it was to me. She became the world to me. Losing her, it's like I had a big operation. I *hurt*. I'm drinking too much. You can't understand."

"No offense, sir, but do understand," Ahmad says, rather loftily. "I am not thrilled to think of my mother fornicating with a Jew."

Levy laughs—a coarse bark. "Hey, come on, we're all Americans here. That's the idea, didn't they tell you that at Central High? Irish-Americans, African-Americans, Jewish-Americans; there are even Arab-Americans."

"Name one."

Levy is taken aback. "Omar Sharif," he says. He knows he could think of others in a less stressful situation.

"Not American. Try again."

"Uh—what was his name? Lew Alcindor."

"Kareem Abdul-Jabbar," Ahmad corrects.

"Thanks. Way before your time."

"But a hero. He overcame great prejudice."

"I think that was Jackie Robinson, but never mind."

"Are we approaching the low point of the tunnel?"

"How would I know? We're approaching everything, eventually. The tunnel doesn't give you much guidance, once you're in here. There used to be cops stationed along these walkways, but you never see them any more. It was discipline detail, but I guess the cops gave up on discipline when everybody else did."

Forward progress has been halted for some minutes. Cars behind them and in front of them begin to honk; the noise travels along the tiles like breath in a huge musical instrument. As if this halt gives them endless leisure, Ahmad turns and asks Jack Levy, "Have you ever, in your studies, read the Egyptian poet and political philosopher Sayyid Qutub? He came to the United States fifty years ago and was struck by the racial discrimination and the open wantonness between the sexes. He concluded that no people is more distant than the American people from God and piety. But the concept of *jāhiliyya*, meaning the state of ignorance that existed before Mohammed, extends also to worldly Muslims and makes them legitimate targets for assassination."

"Sounds sensible. I'll assign him as optional reading, if I live. I've signed up to teach a course in civics this semester. I'm sick of sitting in that old equipment-closet all day trying to talk surly sociopaths out of dropping out. Let 'em drop out, is my new philosophy."

"Sir, I regret to say you will not live. In a few minutes I am going to see the face of God. My heart overflows with the expectation."

Their lane of traffic nudges forward. The children in the vehicle ahead have grown bored with trying to attract Ahmad's attention. The little boy, who wears a billed red cap and an imitation Yankees shirt with pinstripes, has curled up and dozed off in the relentless stop and go, the squealing and chuffing of truck brakes in this tiled Hell of refined petroleum being turned into carbon monoxide. The girl with bushy pigtails, a thumb in her mouth, leans against her brother and gives Ahmad a glazed stare, no longer courting recognition.

"Go ahead. See the bastard," Jack Levy is telling him, ceasing to slump, sitting up, his sickly color chased from his cheeks by excitement. "Go *see* God's fucking face, for all I care. Why should I care? A woman I was crazy about has ditched me, my job is a drag, I wake up every morning at four and can't get back to sleep. My wife—Jesus, it's too sad. She sees how unhappy I am and blames herself, for having gotten so ridiculously fat, and has gone on this crash diet that might kill her. She's in agony, not eating. I want to tell her, 'Beth, forget it, nothing's going to bring us back, us when we were young.' Not that we were ever anything out of the ordinary. We had a few laughs, we used to make each other laugh and enjoyed the simple things, eating out together once a week, going to a movie when we had the energy, now and then taking a picnic up to the tables by the falls. The one child we had, his name is Mark, lives in Albuquerque and just wants to forget us, and who can blame him?

We were the same with our own parents—get away from 'em, they don't get it, they're em*bar*rassing. That philosopher of yours, what was his name?"

"Sayyid Qutub. Properly, Qutb. He was a great favorite of my former teacher, Shaikh Rashid."

"He sounds good on America. Race, sex—they spook us. Once you run out of steam, America doesn't give you much. It doesn't even let you die, what with the hospitals sucking all the money they can out of Medicare. The drug companies have turned doctors into crooks. Why should I hang around until some disease turns me into a cash cow for a bunch of crooks? Let Beth enjoy the little I can leave her; that's the way I feel. I've become a drag on the world, taking up space. Go ahead, push your fucking button. Like the guy on an airplane on Nine-Eleven said to somebody on the cell phone, it'll be quick." Jack reaches across his body toward the detonator and Ahmad for the second time seizes his hand in his own.

"Please, Mr. Levy," he says. "It is mine to do. The meaning changes from a victory to a defeat, if you do it."

"My God, you should be a lawyer. O.K., stop squeezing my hand. I was just kidding."

The girl in the back of the station wagon has seen the brief struggle, and her interest has woken up her brother. Their four bright black eyes stare. In the side of Ahmad's vision, Mr. Levy is rubbing his fist with the other hand. He tells Ahmad, perhaps to soften him with flattery, "You've gotten strong this summer. After our interview you gave me a handshake so limp it was insulting."

"Yes, I am no longer afraid of Tylenol."

"Tylenol?"

"Another graduate of Central High. A dull-witted bully

who has taken possession of a girl I liked. And who liked me, odd as I must have seemed to her. So not only you have romantic difficulties. It is one of the pagan West's grave errors, according to Islamic theorists, to make an idol of an animal function."

"Tell me about the virgins. The seventy-two virgins who will minister to you on the other side."

"The Holy Qur'an does not specify that number of *ḥūrīyyāt*. It says only that they are numerous, and dark-eyed, and have modest glances, and have never been touched by men or djinn."

"Djinn, yet! Oh, my."

"You mock, without knowing the language." Ahmad feels a hated blush steal over his face as he tells his mocker, "Shaikh Rashid explained the djinn and houris as symbols of God's love for us, which is everywhere and ever renewed and cannot be directly comprehended by ordinary mortals."

"O.K., if that's how you see it. I'm not arguing. You can't argue with an explosion."

"What you call an explosion is to me a pinprick, a little opening that admits God's power into the world."

Though it has seemed the moment might never arrive in the balky flow of the traffic, a subtle flattening and slight upward tilt of the tunnel floor tells Ahmad that the low point has been reached, and the curve of the tiled wall ahead, fitfully visible through the tall procession of truck bodies, marks the weak spot where the fanatically tidy and snugly cinched square of plastic barrels should be detonated. His right hand detaches from the steering wheel and hovers over the military-drab metal box, with its little well where his thumb will fit. When he pushes it, he will join God. God will be less terribly alone. *He will greet you as His son.*

"Do it," Jack Levy urges. "I'm going to just relax. Jesus, I've been tired lately."

"For you there will be no pain."

"No, but there will be for plenty of others," the older man responds, slumping way down. But he cannot stop talking. "This isn't the way I pictured it."

"Pictured what?" The echo comes on its own in Ahmad's cleansed and hollowed state.

"Dying. I always thought I'd die in bed. Maybe that's why I don't like being in it. Bed."

He wants to die, Ahmad thinks. *He taunts me to do the deed for him.* In the fifty-sixth sura, the Prophet speaks of *the moment when the soul of a dying man shall come up into his throat.* That moment is here. The journey, the *miraj.* Buraq is ready, his shining white wings rustling, unfolding. Yet in the same sura, "The Event," God asks, *We created you: will you not credit us? Behold the semen you discharge: did you cre- ate it, or We?* God does not want to destroy: it was He who made the world.

The pattern of the wall tiles and of the exhaust-darkened tiles of the ceiling—countless receding repetitions of squares like giant graph paper rolled into a third dimen- sion—explodes outward in Ahmad's mind's eye in the gigan- tic fiat of Creation, one concentric wave after another, each pushing the other farther and farther out from the initial point of nothingness, God having willed the great transition from non-being to being. This was the will of the Benefi- cent, the Merciful, *ar-Rahmān* and *ar-Rahīm*, the Living, the Patient, the Generous, the Perfect, the Light, the Guide. He does not want us to desecrate His creation by willing death. He wills life.

Ahmad returns his right hand to the steering wheel. The

two children in the vehicle ahead, lovingly dressed and groomed by their parents, bathed and soothed every night, gaze toward him solemnly, having sensed the something erratic in his focus, the something unnatural in the expression of his face, mixed with the glaze of his windshield. Reassuringly he lifts the fingers of his right hand from the steering wheel and waves them, like the legs of a beetle on its back. Recognized at last, the children smile, and Ahmad cannot but smile back. He glances at his watch: nine-eighteen. The moment for maximum damage has slipped by; the bend in the tunnel is slowly being pulled into a widening rectangle of daylight.

"Yeah?" Levy asks, as if he has not quite heard Ahmad's response to his last remark. He sits up from his slouched position.

The black children, similarly sensing rescue, make faces through the back window of the Volvo, pulling down the corners of their eyes with their fingers and wagging their protruding tongues. Ahmad tries to smile again and repeats his friendly gesture of finger-waving but weakly; he feels spent. The tunnel's bright mouth grows to swallow him and his truck and its ghosts; together all emerge into the dull but brightening light of another Monday in Manhattan. Whatever was making the traffic in the tunnel so balky, so maddeningly sticky, has dispersed at last, dissolved on an open paved space among apartment buildings of modest height and billboards and brick row houses and, several blocks distant, fragile-looking glass skyscrapers. It could be a nameless spot in northern New Jersey; only the silhouette, dead ahead, of the Empire State Building, once again the tallest building in New York City, signifies otherwise. The bronze station wagon speeds to the right, south. The children are distracted by metropolitan sights, their heads swivelling this way and that, and they do not give Ahmad a farewell wave. He feels snubbed, after the sacrifice he made for them.

Beside him Mr. Levy says "Man!" in stupid imitation of a high-school student. "I'm drenched. You had me convinced." He senses that he has not assumed the right tone and adds, softer, "Well done, my friend. Welcome to the Big Apple."

Ahmad has slowed and then stopped, not quite in the middle of the great wide space. Cars and trucks pushing into freedom behind the halted white truck swerve and blast their horns; side windows slide down and insulting gestures spit out. Ahmad spots the accelerating midnight-blue Mercedes and smiles to think that for all its angry attempts to pass it had been still behind him, with its presumptuous and unworthy investment thief of a driver.

Jack Levy realizes that he is in charge now. "So," he says. "The question becomes, What do we do now? Let's get this truck back to Jersey. They'll be happy to see it. And happy to see you, I regret to say. But you committed no crime, I'll be the first to point out, except drive a load of hazmat out of state on a Class C CDL. They'll probably lift your license, but that's O.K. Delivering furniture wasn't your future anyway."

Ahmad eases the truck forward, less in the way of traffic, waiting for an instruction. "Straight ahead, and left when you can," he is told. "I don't want to go back into any tunnel with you and this thing, thanks. We'll take the George Washington Bridge. Could we put the safety catch back on, do you think?"

Five

Ahmad reaches down, fearful now of disturbing the carefully rigged mechanism. The little yellow lever says *snap;* the ponderous payload remains quiet. Mr. Levy in his relief at still being alive keeps talking. "Turn left at the light up there, that should be Tenth Avenue, I think. I'm trying to remember if the West Side Highway takes trucks. We may have to get on Riverside Drive, or just work up to Broadway and stay on it all the way up to the bridge."

Ahmad lets himself be guided, taking the left turn. The path is straight. "You're driving like a pro," Mr. Levy tells him. "Feel O.K.?" Ahmad nods. "I know you're in shock. Me, too. But there's really no place to park this crate. Once you get to the bridge we're almost home. It turns into 80. We'll go right to police headquarters, behind City Hall. We won't let the bastards intimidate us. Your turning this truck back in one piece makes them look good, and if they have half a brain they know it. It could have been a disaster. Anybody tries to bully you, remind them you were set up by a CIA operative, in a sting operation of very dubious legality. You're a victim, Ahmad—a fall guy. I can't imagine the Department of Homeland Security wants the details out in the media, or hashed over in some courtroom."

Mr. Levy is silent for a block or two, waiting for Ahmad to say something, then says, "I know this may sound premature, but I wasn't kidding about you making a good lawyer. You're cool under pressure. You talk well. In the years to come, Arab-Americans are going to need plenty of lawyers. *Uh-oh.* I guess we're on Eighth Avenue, I thought I had us on Tenth. Keep going—this'll take us onto Broadway at Columbus Circle. I think they still call it that, though the poor wop isn't p.c. any more. The Port Authority Bus Terminal on your left—I'm sure you've been there once or

: 309 :

twice. Then we're going to cross Forty-second Street. I remember when it was real raunchy, but the Disney Corporation has cleaned it up, I guess."

Ahmad wants to focus, amid the yellow taxis and the traffic lights and the pedestrians clustered at every corner, on this novel world around him, but Mr. Levy keeps having thoughts. He says, "It'll be interesting to me to find out if that damn stuff was really connected, or if our side had managed a double cross and it wasn't. That was my hole card, but I was just as happy not to have it played. Thank God you chickened out." This sounds crass in his own ears. "Or relented, let's say. Saw the light."

All around them, up Eighth Avenue to Broadway, the great city crawls with people, some smartly dressed, many of them shabby, a few beautiful but most not, all reduced by the towering structures around them to the size of insects, but scuttling, hurrying, intent in the milky morning sun upon some plan or scheme or hope they are hugging to themselves, their reason for living another day, each one of them impaled live upon the pin of consciousness, fixed upon self-advancement and self-preservation. That, and only that. *These devils*, Ahmad thinks, *have taken away my God.*